STILL

SHORT FICTION
OF THE
AMERICAN WEST
1950 TO THE PRESENT

WILD

EDITED BY

LARRY
McMURTRY

SIMON & SCHUSTER

NEW YORK   LONDON   TORONTO   SYDNEY   SINGAPORE

SIMON & SCHUSTER
Rockefeller Center
1230 Avenue of the Americas
New York, NY 10020

SIMON & SCHUSTER and colophon are registered trademarks of Simon & Schuster, Inc.

Designed by Karolina Harris

Manufactured in the United States of America

1 3 5 7 9 10 8 6 4 2

Library of Congress Cataloging-in-Publication Data
Still wild : short fiction of the American West, 1950 to the present / edited by Larry Mc-
Murtry.
p.   cm.

1. Short stories, American—West (U.S.) 2. West (U.S.)—Social life and customs—Fiction.
3. American fiction—20th century. 4. Western stories. I. McMurtry, Larry.
PS561.S75   2000
813'.01083278—dc21   99-052848
ISBN 0-684-86882-2

To Diana and Mark

CONTENTS

INTRODUCTION

Still Wild is meant to remind readers of, or introduce them to, short fiction by twenty good writers who, at one point or another in their careers, have taken as their subject life in the American West—but taken it in a special way. Theirs is not so much the West of history or the West of geography as it is the West of the imagination: funny, gritty, isolate, searing, tragic, complex.

Part of my intent as a compiler has been to assemble a coming-of-age anthology, because it seems to me that it has only been in the second half of the twentieth century that the West *has* come of age as a producer—as opposed to an importer—of first-rate writers. From the time of the California gold rush to at least the end of World War I, most of the writers who achieved popularity by writing fiction set in the West—writers whose work aspired to be at least a rung or two above the dime novel or the family anecdote—came from the East. Jack London was a native, but most were not, and the work of Owen Wister, Charles King, Zane Grey, Eugene Manlove Rhodes, and others reads now like dude-ranch fiction, a sort of white-collar pulp. Many of these writers loved the West deeply, and, once they found it, never left it, but, still, they wrote as outsiders: fans, rather than natives; and, as

fans, they were likely to wax romantic about the western life that
they saw, or, perhaps, imagined.

Most of them wrote for the illustrated magazines of the late
nineteenth and early twentieth century, where they were matched
in their romanticism by two generations of equally romantic illustrators: Frederick Remington, Alfred Jacob Miller, Charles
Schreyvogel, Frank Schoonover, Nick Eggenhofer, Edward Bor-
ein, Will James, and others. Most of the stories were quite flimsy;
the writers *needed* the illustrators and perhaps were not aware to
what an extent they were in competition with the artists whose
drawings supported their stories.

Indeed, competition with the image is a factor in the development of western writing that is seldom mentioned, though it was
certainly serious. The grandeur of western landscape drew gifted
painters immediately; gifted writers followed in their wake.
Washington Irving's *Tour of the Prairies* (1835) contained some
fairly vivid word pictures, but not as vivid as the actual paintings
of George Catlin, Karl Bodmer, Alfred Jacob Miller, or Thomas
Moran. Then, before the painters quit, the camera arrived, followed in only a few decades by the motion pictures, which,
throughout the whole of the twentieth century, competed vigor-
ously not just with western literature but with *all* literature,
though it was probably in relation to the West that the challenge
movies raised to literature was most acute. It takes a
genius-level descriptive sentence to compete with the beauty of
horses running, a pure kinetic joy that can be had in even the
trashiest western films.

Image-competition apart, there were other reasons why good
writers, in any sort of critical mass, were slow to appear in the
West, the main one being that until the 1950s much of the West
either wasn't settled enough or hadn't been settled long enough
to produce first-rate writers. The severities of pioneer life yield
up no Prousts. The native peoples of the nineteenth-century
West, whether of the plains, the desert, or the coast, at least had

societies, whereas the whites who fought them and displaced them for a time, and a considerable time, mainly just had families. Writers need schooling, need to have at least some contact with a society that values literary effort, but it was not until almost the midpoint of the twentieth century that literate society and reasonably good schooling could be assumed in the West.

Though it may startle several of them to hear it, the simplest thing one can say about the writers in this anthology is that they are not self-educated. Though only a few of them, notably Wallace Stegner and William H. Gass, made full and prominent careers in the academies, all of them have at least drifted through a college campus and gone to a party or two—by which I mean that all of them write with a developed awareness of literary tradition. Wallace Stegner and Jack Kerouac wrote very different prose; Stegner stayed in the academy, whereas Kerouac left it, but both were men who had studied hard, and the same can be said for most of the writers whose stories I have chosen for this book. The younger among them may have gone to school to Donald Barthelme or Raymond Carver, the older ones to Chekhov, Hemingway, Lawrence, Joyce, or Faulkner, but they are all aware—as earlier generations were not—that there had once been giants in the land and that they must first read them if they hope to extend what they had done.

Perhaps the most famous quote in D. H. Lawrence's *Studies in Classic American Literature*, published in 1924, is this: "Never trust the artist. Trust the tale."

I take that to mean that, having located and arranged these twenty stories, I now have license to leave, so that the process of trusting can begin. I could go through the table of contents, pointing out the obvious: that Wallace Stegner never lost sight of the cruelty within the beauty of the West, that Jack Kerouac, in "The Mexican Girl," wrote a great love letter to L.A., and so on. But to track through these twenty stories and chart, for the reader, their themes and affinities, is not my job. Better to go to

Lawrence again, to the essay called "The Spirit of Place," written in 1924:

> The real American day hasn't come yet. Or at least, not yet sunrise. So far it has been the false dawn. . . .

It is no longer 1924. By the time of Lawrence's death, only six years later, Hemingway and Faulkner had already published their best work. The sun had well risen, and it's up there still. The writers in this book all work in the strong western sunlight of the real American day.

—Larry McMurtry

STILL WILD

BUGLESONG

WALLACE STEGNER

From The Collected Stories of Wallace Stegner,
Random House, New York, 1990

There had been a wind during the night, and all the loneliness of the world had swept up out of the southwest. The boy had heard it wailing through the screens of the sleeping porch where he lay, and he had heard the washtub bang loose from the outside wall and roll down toward the coulee, and the slam of the screen doors, and his mother's padding feet after she rose to fasten things down. Through one half-open eye he had peered up from his pillow to see the moon skimming windily in a luminous sky; in his mind he had seen the prairie outside with its woolly grass and cactus white under the moon, and the wind, whining across that endless oceanic land, sang in the screens, and sang him back to sleep.

Now, after breakfast, when he set out through the west pasture on the morning round of his gopher traps, there was no more wind, but the air smelled somehow recently swept and dusted, as the house in town sometimes smelled after his mother's whirlwind cleaning. The sun was gently warm on the bony shoulder blades of the boy, and he whistled, and whistling turned to see if the Bearpaws were in sight to the south. There they were, a ghostly tenuous outline of white just breaking over the bulge of the world: the Mountains of the Moon, the place of running streams and timber and cool heights that he had never seen—only dreamed of on days when the baked clay of the farmyard cracked in the heat and the sun brought cedar smells from fence posts long since split and dry and odorless, when he lay dreaming on the bed in the sleeping porch with a Sears, Roebuck catalogue open before him, picking out the presents he would buy for his mother and his father and his friends next Christmas, or the Christmas after that. On those days he looked often and long at the snowy mountains to the south, while the dreams rose in him like heat waves, blurring the reality of the unfinished shack that was his summer home.

The Bearpaws were there now, and he watched them a moment, walking, his feet dodging cactus clumps automatically, before he turned his attention again to the traps before him, their locations marked by a zigzag line of stakes. He ran the line at a half-trot, whistling.

At the first stake the chain was stretched tightly into the hole. The pull on its lower end had dug a little channel in the soft earth of the mound. Gently, so as not to break the gopher's leg off, the boy eased the trap out of the burrow, held the chain in his left hand, and loosened the stake with his right. The gopher lunged against the heavy trap, but it did not squeal. They squealed, the boy had noticed, only when at a distance, or when the weasel had them. Otherwise they kept still.

For a moment the boy debated whether to keep this one alive for the weasel or to wait till the last trap so that he wouldn't have to carry the live one around. Deciding to wait, he held the chain out, measured the rodent for a moment, and swung. The knobbed end of the stake crushed the animal's skull, and the eyes popped out of the head, round and blue. A trickle of blood started from nose and ears.

Releasing the gopher, the boy lifted it by the tail and snapped its tail-fur off with a dexterous flip. Then he stowed the trophy carefully in the breast pocket of his overalls. For the last two years he had won the grand prize offered by the province of Saskatchewan to the school child who destroyed the most go-phers. On the mantel in town were two silver loving cups, and in a shoe box under his bed in the farmhouse there were already eight hundred and forty tails, the catch of three weeks. His whole life on the farm was devoted to the destruction of the rodents. In the wheat fields he distributed poison, but in the pasture, where stock might get the tainted grain, he trapped, snared, or shot them. Any method he preferred to poisoning: that offered no ex-citement, and he seldom got the tails because the gophers crawled down their holes to die.

Picking up trap and stake, the boy kicked the dead animal down its burrow and scraped dirt over it with his foot. They stunk up the pasture if they weren't buried, and the bugs got into them. Frequently he had stood to windward of a dead and swollen go-pher, watching the body shift and move with the movements of the beetles and crawling things working through it. If such an in-fested corpse were turned over, the beetles would roar out of it, great orange-colored, hard-shelled, scavenging things that made his blood curdle at the thought of their touching him, and after they were gone and he looked again he would see the little black ones, undisturbed, seething through the rotten flesh. So he al-ways buried his dead, now.

Through the gardens of red and yellow cactus blooms he went whistling, half trotting, setting the traps anew whenever a gopher shot upright, squeaked, and ducked down its burrow at his ap-proach. All but two of the first seventeen traps held gophers, and he came to the eighteenth confidently, expecting to take this one alive. But this gopher had gone into the trap head first, and the boy put back into his pocket the salt sack he had brought along as a game bag. He would have to snare or trap one down by the dam.

On the way back he stopped with bent head while he counted

his day's catch of tails, mentally adding this lot of sixteen to the eight hundred and forty he already had, trying to remember how many he had had at this time last year. As he finished his mathematics his whistle broke out again, and he galloped down through the pasture, running for very abundance of life, until he came to the chicken house just within the plowed fireguard.

Under the eaves of the chicken house, so close that the hens were constantly pecking up to its very door and then almost losing their wits with fright, was the made-over beer case that contained the weasel. Screen had been tacked tightly under the wooden lid, which latched, and in the screen was cut a tiny wire door. In the front, along the bottom, a single board had been removed and replaced with screen.

The boy lifted the hinged top and looked down into the cage.

"Hello," he said. "Hungry?"

The weasel crouched, its long snaky body humped, its head thrust forward and its malevolent eyes staring with lidless savagery into the boy's.

"Tough, ain't you?" said the boy. "Just wait, you bloodthirsty old stinker, you. Wait'll you turn into an ermine. Won't I skin you quick, hah?"

There was no dislike or emotion in his tone. He took the weasel's malignant ferocity with the same indifference he displayed in his gopher killing. Weasels, if you could keep them long enough, were valuable. He would catch a lot, keep them until they turned white, and sell their hides as ermine. Maybe he could breed them and have an ermine farm. He was the best gopher trapper in Saskatchewan. Once he had even caught a badger. Why not weasels? The trap broke their leg, but nothing could really hurt a weasel permanently. This one, though virtually three-legged, was as savage and lively as ever. Every morning he had a live gopher for his breakfast, in spite of the protests of the boy's mother that it was cruel. But nothing, she had said, was cruel to the boy.

When she argued that the gopher had no chance when thrown into the cage, the boy retorted that he didn't have a chance when the weasel came down the hole after him either. If she said that the real job he should devote himself to was exterminating the weasels, he replied that then the gophers would get so thick they would eat the fields down to stubble. At last she gave up, and the weasel continued to have his warm meals.

For some time the boy stood watching his captive, and then he turned and went into the house, where he opened the oat box in the kitchen and took out a chunk of dried beef. From this he cut a thick slice with the butcher knife, and went munching into the sleeping porch where his mother was making beds.

"Where's that little double naught?" he asked.

"That what?"

"That little wee trap. The one I use for catching live ones for the weasel."

"Hanging out by the laundry bench, I think. Are you going out trapping again now?"

"Lucifer hasn't had his breakfast yet."

"How about your reading?"

"I'n take the book along and read while I wait," the boy said. "-I'm just goin' down to the coulee at the edge of the dam."

"I *can*, not 'Ine,' son."

"I can," the boy said. "I am most delighted to comply with your request."

He grinned at his mother. He could always floor her with a quotation from a letter or the Sears, Roebuck catalogue.

With the trap swinging from his hand, and under his arm the book—*Narrative and Lyric Poems*, edited by Somebody-or-other—which his mother kept him reading during the summer "so that next year he could be at the head of his class again," the boy walked out into the growing heat.

From the northwest the coulee angled down through the pasture, a shallow swale dammed just above the house to catch the spring runoff of snow water. In the moist dirt of the dam grew ten-foot willows planted as slips by the boy's father. They were the only things resembling trees in sixty miles. Below the dam, watered by the slow seepage from above, the coulee bottom was a parterre of flowers, buttercups in broad sheets, wild sweet pea, and "stinkweed." On the slopes were evening primroses, pale pink and white and delicately fragrant, and on the flats above the yellow and red burgeoning of the cactuses.

Just under the slope of the coulee a female gopher and three half-grown puppies basked on their warm mound. The boy chased them squeaking down their hole and set the trap carefully, embedding it partially in the soft earth. Then he retired back up the shoulder of the swale, where he lay full length on his stomach, opened the book, shifted so that the glare of the sun across the pages was blocked by the shadow of his head and shoulders, and began to read.

From time to time he stopped reading to roll on his side and stare out across the coulee, across the barren plains pimpled with gopher mounds and bitten with fire and haired with dusty woolly grass. Apparently as flat as a table, the land sloped imperceptibly to the south, so that nothing interfered with his view of the ghostly line of mountains, now more plainly visible as the heat increased. Between the boy's eyes and that smoky outline sixty miles away the heat waves rose writhing like fine wavy hair. He knew that in an hour Pankhurst's farm would lift above the swelling knoll to the west. Many times he had seen that phenomenon—had seen his friend Jason Pankhurst playing in the yard or watering horses when he knew that the whole farm was out of sight. It was the heat waves that did it, his father said.

The gophers below had been thoroughly scared, and for a long time nothing happened. Idly the boy read through his poetry lesson, dreamfully conscious of the hard ground under him, feeling the gouge of a rock under his stomach without making any effort to remove it. The sun was a hot caress between his shoulder blades, and on the bare flesh where his overalls pulled above his sneakers it bit like a burning glass. Still he was comfortable, supremely relaxed and peaceful, lulled into a half-trance by the heat and the steamy flower smells and the mist of yellow in the buttercup coulee below.

And beyond the coulee was the dim profile of the Bearpaws, the Mountains of the Moon.

The boy's eyes, pulled out of focus by his tranced state, fixed on the page before him. Here was a poem he knew . . . but it wasn't a poem, it was a song. His mother sang it often, working at the sewing machine in winter.

It struck him as odd that a poem should also be a song, and because he found it hard to read without bringing in the tune, he lay quietly in the full glare of the sun, singing the page softly to himself. As he sang the trance grew on him again; he lost himself entirely. The bright hard dividing lines between individual senses blurred, and buttercups, smell of primrose, feel of hard gravel under body and elbows, sight of the ghosts of mountains haunting the southern horizon, were one intensely felt experience focused by the song the book had evoked.

And the song was the loveliest thing he had ever known. He felt the words, tasted them, breathed upon them with all the ardor of his captivated senses.

The splendor falls on castle walls
And snowy summits old in story. . . .

The current of his imagination flowed southward over the strong gentle shoulder of the world to the ghostly outline of the Mountains of the Moon, haunting the heat-distorted horizon.

O, hark, O hear! How thin and clear,
And thinner, clearer, farther going!
O, sweet and far, from cliff and scar. . . .

In the enchanted forests of his mind the horns of elfland blew, and his breath was held in the slow-falling cadence of their dying.

The weight of the sun had been lifted from his back. The empty prairie of his home was castled and pillared with the magnificence of his imagining, and the sound of horns died thinly in the direction of the Mountains of the Moon.

From the coulee below came the sudden metallic clash of the trap, and an explosion of frantic squeals smothered almost immediately in the burrow. The boy leaped up, thrusting the book into the wide pocket of his overalls, and ran down to the mound. The chain, stretched down the hole, jerked convulsively, and when the boy took hold of it he felt the terrified life at the end of it strain to escape. Tugging gently, he forced loose the gopher's digging claws, and hauled the squirming captive from the hole.

On the way up to the chicken house the dangling gopher with a tremendous muscular effort convulsed itself upward from the broken and imprisoned leg, and bit with a sharp rasp of teeth on the iron. Its eyes, the boy noticed impersonally, were shining black, like the head of a hatpin. He thought it odd that when they popped out of the head after a blow they were blue.

At the cage by the chicken house he lifted the cover and peered through the screen. The weasel, scenting the blood of the gopher's leg, backed against the far wall of the box, yellow body tense as a spring, teeth showing in a tiny soundless snarl.

Undoing the wire door with his left hand, the boy held the trap over the hole. Then he bore down with all his strength on the spring, releasing the gopher, which dropped on the straw-littered floor and scurried into the corner opposite its enemy.

The weasel's three good feet gathered under it and it circled, very slowly, around the wall, its lips still lifted to expose the soundless snarl. The abject gopher crowded against the boards, turned once and tried to scramble up the side, fell back on its broken leg, and whirled like lightning to face its executioner again. The weasel moved carefully, circling.

Then the gopher screamed, a wild, agonized, despairing squeal that made the watching boy swallow and wet his lips. Another scream, wilder and louder than before, and before the sound had ended the weasel struck. There was a fierce flurry in the straw of the cage before the killer got its hold just back of the gopher's right ear, and its teeth began tearing ravenously at the still-quivering body. In a few minutes, the boy knew, the gopher's carcass would be as limp as an empty skin, with all its blood sucked out and a hole as big as the ends of his two thumbs where the weasel had dined.

Still the boy remained staring through the screen top of the cage, face rapt and body completely lost. And after a few minutes he went into the sleeping porch, stretched out on the bed, opened the Sears, Roebuck catalogue, and dived so deeply into its fascinating pictures and legends that his mother had to shake him to make him hear her call to lunch.

THE
CLOSED SEASON

DAVE HICKEY

From Prior Convictions
Southern Methodist University Press, 1989

That dream I had while Virgil and I were down in Edmunds County wasn't so unusual. Once I dreamed that we were honky-tonking down on Lower Main Street when we ran into Pa. He invited both of us into the Rustic Lounge and bought us a Lone Star beer. Then I dreamed that I found Pa laid up in the Osteopathic Hospital where he was dying of cancer; but I only had that cancer dream once, when I was trying to quit cigarettes. I dreamed all the time that Pa was still alive, though, that he showed up at the house—not the new house, but the old house over in South Fort Worth where we lived before Pa started doing well. I would come into the kitchen and Pa would be leaning against the icebox grinning while Mom cussed him for leaving her alone.

I sat on the steps of the old house at sunup, smoking a cigarette and enjoying the first cool bite of autumn. When Pa had added the second story, he had had to put the steps on the outside, and

those were the steps I sat on, in this dream, under the big chinaberry tree, looking at the new asphalt-shingled houses across the
Santa Fe tracks. Behind those neat, square white houses, the
morning sky spangled like the scrubbed bottom of a brass pan,
and the grass in the yard sparkled like green glass. I had to squint
my eyes against the light; then I saw Pa standing in front of me,
or I thought I saw him, because shafts of light slanted around his
head, over his shoulders and between his legs. I could make out
the shiny toes of his alligator boots against the sparkling green
grass. Yellow chinaberry leaves tilted on the grass. The smell of
cottonseed was on the air.

"Hidey, squirt," Pa said.

"Hi, Pa! Let me tell Mom you're here."

"No need to upset your mother," he said, waving his hand. "-
She's doing just fine without me. I came to see you, squirt."

"But we all thought you were dead, Pa, and Mom had all your
clothes altered to fit Virgil and me—"

Pa laughed. No, he said, he wasn't dead but if Mom came out,
he might as well be. He tousled my hair like he used to when I
was a kid, and said he hadn't come all the way from Amarillo to
argue whether he was dead or not. I felt a fool for mentioning
Pa's clothes since at that very minute I had on his old Levi jacket.

"I wonder if you still have my old .410, Gordon?" Pa said.

I couldn't look at him or close my eyes against the glaring
light, so I stared down at the step. The planks had weathered;
black and gray grains ran through them. Pa asked about the shotgun again; his voice was sharp this time.

"You shot yourself with it, Pa," I said, but he went on to say
that the reason he wanted the shotgun was because he and
George and Flickey—two of his old air force buddies—wanted to
fly up to South Dakota and do some hunting. Pa said he had himself a new airplane, a sweet little Jetstream.

"You shot yourself with it, Pa," I said again. "Mom threw it in
the Trinity."

"Well, you're not much help, squirt," Pa said, sticking his thumbs in his gabardine slacks. "I just thought I'd drop by and see if you still had it. That was a fine piece of machinery, Gordon. It deserved to be taken care of."

He stopped me when I stood up and put his arm around my shoulders. Next to my cheek, I could see the black hair curling on his tanned forearm and the yellow cigarette stains on his manicured fingers. Then I looked up into his face and it was Pa all right; his eyes were blue as petunias. There was the mole he cut when he shaved, right next to his left nostril. I have a mole there too, but I use an electric razor.

"Come on, squirt," Pa said. "Don't walk away from me. Virgil wouldn't." I really did love him, but I ran like a scalded cat into the street. The street might have been running with quicksilver. It didn't make any difference to me, in this dream, where Pa lived. He could live in Amarillo and fly anywhere he wanted to with George and Flickey, but I ran toward the street until Virgil was pulling on my ankle. We were hunting down in South Texas, so Pa couldn't have the shotgun anyway. But what the hell, I thought, I can use one of Virgil's guns. Old Virgil had some nice guns: he is also gettin' some nice tail, I'll bet, off Mildred Ranserhoff. But what the hell, I thought, then I couldn't think what the hell what because Virgil's hand was cold and hard on my ankle. Cold air rushed in under the blanket.

"You're freezing my ass, Virgil," I said.

"Well, you better get your frozen ass out of the sack if you're hunting with me," Virgil said, looming over me in the darkness. He pushed his long, stringy cowlick off his forehead and grinned at me.

"I have to use one of your shotguns, Virgil, I—"

"I know it, dumb-butt," Virgil said, dropping my leg.

Without turning on the light, Virgil stuck his feet in his old combat boots and clumped to the door. Every time his left foot hit the floor, his right shoulder dipped from an old rodeo injury.

In his white longhandles and those combat boots, he looked more comical than usual. Three years ago, he got pitched off a bronc out at Fort Stockton. Instead of going to a doctor like any sane man, Virgil packed his shoulder up in ether and ice and won the day-money the next afternoon. According to Virgil, Absorbine Senior cures any disease of man or beast, but his shoulder never did heal right, though he kept it taped up and rubbed down with Absorbine for nearly a month. He keeps pretty much away from rodeoing now—which is all right with Mom.

"I'll fix some breakfast," he said, going through the door. "Since you probably couldn't if you had to."

When Virgil closed the door, I pulled the blanket back over my shoulder and snuggled down into the little nest of warmth I'd made for myself. It was damn cold for this time of the year. My breath fogged in the air, billowing out across the pillow, and I lay there, half awake, and wondered what Mom would do if she knew I was out hunting with Virgil. I remembered the night she threw Pa's guns off the Forest Park bridge. She stood on the bridge with her hair up in curlers, with the cold wind flapping her blue house-coat around her ankles, and dropped the guns over one by one while I waited in the car. I heard Virgil throw some kindling into the stove, and the heavy thuds as he threw some ash logs in on top of the kindling. It was a comfortable sound, so I closed my eyes and slept a little more, dreaming a crazy dream about Virgil and me riding horses, chasing this other horse. Then the kitchen door slammed and, still holding the blanket to my shoulder, I rolled over toward the window.

The moon was down but there was no sign of the dawn; the sky was black and the air was cold and clear. My breath fogged on the pane so I stuck two fingers out from under the blanket to clear it, my fingers squeaking on the cold glass. The gravel road running down to the creek, the barn beside the road and the limestone bluff beyond the creek glowed white in the darkness, while along the crest of the bluff a few scraggly trees were blacker than the sky full of stars. It was still as death out there—until Virgil came striding across my field of vision, looking a little silly since he had thrown his big sheepskin coat on over his longhandles. His legs looked white and skinny between the big coat and the unlaced combat boots.

Virgil trudged up the rise to the water tower and started fooling around with a knob on the pipe. Finally he walked away from the tower, kicking around in the weeds until he found a two-by-four. He picked up the piece of board and swung it like a baseball bat. There wasn't a sound. I could see Virgil's breath trailing in the clear air; I could see the arc of the board as it hit the pipe, and Virgil's lips moving as he cussed it, all in silence. It made me feel so cut off, so lonesome and alone, that I rolled over and stared at the dark ceiling until Virgil yelled from the kitchen for me to come get it before he threw it out and spit in the skillet. I had to run across that cold room and put on my hat and shirt before I could even light a cigarette. By then I had my blood moving, so I pulled on my Levi's and boots quickly and went clumping down the dark hall. The sound of my boots echoing in the hall made me happy. By the time I grabbed the cold knob of the kitchen door and pulled it open, the lonesome feeling was gone. Virgil turned bacon in the skillet. I could smell the sizzling meat as the light and heat rushed around me. In that bright kitchen with the cabinets trimmed in red, with yellow curtains shutting out the dark morning, all that dreaming seemed pretty silly to me. Virgil turned around with the skillet in his hand and told me to get my ass in there and close the door.

The day before, while Virgil and I were driving down from Fort Worth, the Mexican caretaker had hauled a pickup-load of groceries and whiskey out from Randall Springs, so for breakfast we had eggs sunnyside, Canadian bacon, thick toast and milk with ice in it. Afterward we had black coffee from Neiman-Marcus mugs with the Ranserhoff brand on them, and Virgil started to roll a cigarette. I lit a ready-made and watched Virgil's skinny face wrinkle and relax while he worked the tobacco around in the paper. I thought that if the truth were told, I favored Pa a lot more in the face than Virgil did. But inside, it was probably different.

"Your boss has a nice layout here," I said.

"Mmmmm," Virgil said. He licked the paper and fitted the cigarette together. "Mil Ranserhoff's a damn good woman," he said when he was done.

"You like her, huh?" I said. "You could find people in Fort Worth who don't."

"I could find people in Fort Worth who don't like *you*, squirt," Virgil said.

"Don't call me squirt, huh?" I said.

"Mil's damn good with horses, squirt. She just keeps me around 'cause she has them stashed all over the hot-damn state." He put the cigarette neatly in front of him on the table and walked to the cabinet. "Yeah, I like her fine," he said, "regardless of what Mom says."

Mildred Ranserhoff is a hard, blond-headed old girl of about forty who likes whiskey and horses better than people, with the possible exception of Virgil. And what Mom said was that Mildred was a rich tramp and that it killed her soul to go to a party and see her own son standing around in his rough-out boots drinking sidecars—but it went a little deeper than that.

After Virgil got hurt out at Fort Stockton he went to work for Stanley Bracker training quarter horses. Mom didn't think training quarter horses was a very respectable profession, but Stanley was a friend of the family and training horses beat the hell out of rodeoing. Pa had redesigned two DC-3s for the Bracker oil operation and hunted some with Stanley; then when Pa died, Stanley started taking Mom around to the parties, mostly out of politeness, I guess. So as long as Virgil worked for Stanley, she pretty much let him alone. Then there was the run-in over Stanley's Triple-A Rocket Bar colt.

It happened one afternoon while Stanley and Mom were out at

the stables. Stanley was about half-tight and showing off his
horses, but he made the mistake of running that nice little colt
around for a while and putting him up wet. Virgil flipped. He told
Stanley that if he was gonna be careless with four thousand dollars' worth of horse, there wasn't any reason for him, Virgil, to
stay around there. Virgil cussed him out good and proper while
old Stan hung his head and shuffled his boots in the dust. You'd
have thought they caught him eating his soup with his salad fork.
Stanley ended up apologizing all over the place but Virgil quit
him anyway and went to work for Mildred Ranserhoff. Well, that
tore it with Mom. It was bad enough quitting Stanley, but going
to work for Mildred, who has a rough reputation to say the least,
really ripped the sheet. Of course Virgil, not being a social but-
terfly of any kind, didn't really understand. He was just going
where they treated horses right.

As it turned out, he was going where they treated Virgil all
right, too. Just the week before out at Mildred's stable, he mentioned he'd like to shoot some dove and Mildred walked over to
her desk, opened the drawer and tossed him the keys to the ranch
house. Then she sat down and called the Mexican about food and
whiskey. So last Friday, for some reason, Virgil called me. I answered the phone in the hall on my way to class.

"Hey, squirt," he said. "How'dja like to go dove hunting?"

Mom was in the living room playing bridge with some of her
friends, so I lowered my voice and asked where.

"Edmunds County. Mildred's got a place down there that
hasn't been hunted in five years. Also seems the local law is in
somebody's back pocket."

"Damn right," I said. "Damn right I do."

I told Mom we were going to a horse show.

Virgil scratched a kitchen match under the table and lifted the
yellow-blue flame carefully to his cigarette, his blue eyes crossing

a little as he did. After taking a long drag that turned a half-inch of cigarette into ash, he pulled the cigarette from his lips, balanced the ash for a few seconds, then flicked it into the remains of his yellow eggs.

"You ever heard of an ashtray?" I said.

"I prefer the plate, Miz Vanderbilt," Virgil said. "I'm just a crude country boy, not up on citified ways."

He grinned, showing me the gold tooth nestled in the side of his mouth which he got much the same way he got his shoulder. I asked him how he got off calling me citified since we grew up in the same damn house, and Virgil said that everybody who went to college was a citified bastard unless they went to Texas Tech or Sul Ross. I told him that Mildred Ranserhoff probably went to Vassar, and he said that was an altogether different thing. He pushed the dirty plate away, though, and dragged the ashtray over with one finger.

I had to admit, then, that I liked Virgil for all his faults. His worst fault had been his talent for starting a fight at home when we were kids, and then walking out. It was a real gift. Virgil could get everybody in the house cussing and screaming and slamming doors, then walk out the door, climb in his pickup and go off to drink some beer. Sis always locked herself in her room, so that left me to take the crap that was being dealt out. It was a fine talent, though, and I think Pa envied it as much as I did. In fact, Pa probably preferred Virgil to me on most counts, though he never let on.

When Virgil had finished his cigarette, he slid his chair back and stood up, stretching and scratching his stomach. "You clear the table, Miz Vanderbilt," he said. "I'll fetch the weapons."

While he fiddled with the combination on the window box, I scraped and stacked the dishes and the skillet. I had rinsed the dishes off with icy water and decided they were pretty well washed when Virgil asked me if I knew about the time he ran into Pa in New York City.

"No," I said.

"Well, hell," he said, opening the window box and taking out two shotguns in soft leather cases. "It was my first trip to the big city, and my first and last time riding in the Madison Square Garden. Let me tell you, squirt, I wasn't nowhere *near* those old boys' class, never was. At the time of course I said I was getting beat in the hat, but I was getting beat in the saddle and that's for sure. Man, Jimmy *Shoulders* was in that rodeo. Anyway, the day after the show closed I was stove up and broke and sitting around Rockefeller Center looking at the pretty girls when who should come striding by in a silk suit with a big-titted blond on his arm, but Pa. He taken one look at me, and I taken one look at that blond, and he loaned me fifty bucks. The idea was that every time I thought about that blond, I put a big steak in my mouth."

"That's more than he ever loaned me," I said.

"Well, you never caught him in New York City with a blond," Virgil said with a sly grin. "But you know what I did with that money?"

"I guess, knowing you, that you got pretty well drunked up."

"Hell, I wasn't even that smart." I finished wiping off the table with the dishrag and Virgil laid the guns down. "I caught the first subway down to Green Witch Village and got this artist down there on Bleecker Street to do this chalk portrait of me in my riding clothes, number and all. Then I got my boots polished and tipped the boy two dollars. I finally ended up hitchhiking back to Texas and not eating for three days. Pa was dead when I got back."

"He would have got a kick out of it," I said. "He used to tell me if you were gonna spend money sensibly there wasn't any reason to work for it."

"I still have me a pretty good picture, though, or had a pretty good picture. I gave it to Mildred, for Christmas." He untied the strings and reached into the first gun case. Grabbing the end of the stock with one hand, he slipped the leather cover off a Winchester pump with a carved walnut stock. "When was the last time you were out?" Virgil said. "Three years?" He laid the Winchester down and picked up the other case.

"Closer to four. I'm glad you asked me, Virgil."

"What did you tell Mom?"

"I told her we were going to a horse show."

"You know you shouldn't let yourself get bitched at Mom. She's got a right."

"I know she's got a right," I said. "That's a nice gun."

"You damn right it's a nice gun, honcho," Virgil said, balancing the second gun on his palm. It was a Browning automatic, one of those fancy gas-operated, Belgian-made models. Virgil hiked it up under his arm and walked to the cabinet; he took down six boxes of shells and slapped them down on the table.

"We goin' to war, Virgil?" I said.

"Toss me that rag under the sink, will you?"

Virgil wiped the excess oil off the Browning and laid it on the table and I watched it resting there, dark against the white enamel tabletop. I remembered Pa telling me that a good shotgun was the most beautiful piece of machinery in the world, and it had a strange effect on me, watching that gun resting on the table. I remembered things that had happened so long ago that there were no words for them—things that had happened even before I was born. Watching that beautiful Browning, glowing bluey gray and dull walnut against the white table, I felt older and stronger and a little scared—as if everything that had happened since I had been hunting last hadn't happened, had been a dream. Then I noticed Virgil watching me, so I picked up the automatic. It was lighter than I remembered and finer. I ran my hand along the cool walnut stock, then slapped it into my shoulder. The stock was cut for Virgil but it felt fine. I sighted on a pair of antlers over the sink, then looked over the stock at Virgil, who was wiping the oil from the pump mechanism of the Winchester, his forehead wrinkled in concentration.

"I forgot what a thing I used to have for guns," I said, pulling the stock away from my cheek and dropping it from my shoulder.

"It gets in your blood," Virgil said, not looking up. "Calf-ropin's like that for me. Can't look at a calf without gettin' an itchy rope-hand." Putting down the Winchester on the drain-board, he grabbed his Levi's off the stove, where he'd hung them up to warm. He hopped around on one foot while he stuck the other into the jeans.

"You have trouble with the water this morning?"

"Naw, you just got to bang the rust loose."

"We're not gonna get arrested for this, are we?" I said as I walked to the door to get my big coat.

"This is South Texas, old boy," Virgil said. "Everything's squared away."

"Well, let's get moving."

"We're good as gone."

Virgil slipped what was left of a bottle of Wild Turkey bourbon into one of the pockets of his sheepskin coat; then we stood across the table from one another slipping shells into our pockets. When the boxes were empty, Virgil picked up the Browning au-tomatic.

"Gordy, why don't you use the pump? It's a safer gun and I wouldn't want you to . . ."

"Okay, okay," I said. "Jus' so it shoot."

"It shoot, all right," Virgil said, but I had already grabbed the pump and walked out into the cold, dim morning.

The chill would fade when the sun hit the air but as Virgil guided the jeep down the yellow ruts the cold was quick and dry. The rims of my eyes stung, and my nostrils and the tops of my ears above the collar of the coat. I pulled the collar up higher as we passed the barn and turned down toward the foot of the lime-stone bluff. Above the bluff the sky was gray and overcast, and the bluff itself was the same raw color as the clouds.

Virgil drove with both hands on the wheel.

"Little brother?" he said.

"Yeah, Virgil."

"You can use the automatic if you want to."

"Forget it. I couldn't hit anything with a howitzer."

"Well, I'd just as soon use the Winchester. I know you can shoot, for God's sake. You used to shoot circles around me."

"It's all right. I'll use the pump."

"Well, it don't make no nevermind to me," Virgil said, then added, "if you can say that."

"If you can say what?"

"It don't make no nevermind," Virgil said. "That's not good English, is it?"

"Hell, Virgil, it's as good as anything," I said. "Anyway, two years at TCU doesn't make me any kind of authority."

"Well, use whatever gun you want to."

"I'd just as soon use the pump."

"Suit yourself," Virgil said, looking straight ahead at the road.

A breeze lifted out of the grass and slid along the slope. The breeze was still cold, but there was a taste of warm in it—only a taste. We were driving through the taller grass along the creek bank. A few scrub oak overhung the road, and through their bare branches I saw the clouds begin to move like a herd of dirty sheep. The humps and billows of gray slid down the sky toward the bluff that loomed above us now.

"Say, Gordy," Virgil said, "will you do something for me?"

"Sure, what do you want?"

"Well, acknowledgin' the fact that you aren't any kind of authority, I want you to correct me when I say something stupid like 'don't make no nevermind' and all that crap. Whenever I say something really stupid."

"You talk all right, Virgil."

"Hell I do. Not all the time. Sometimes I say something stupid around Mil, that's Mrs. Ranserhoff, and I feel like a fool."

"Okay," I said. "I'll correct you when it's really bad."

Virgil never once looked at me. Tall grass slapped against the side of the jeep, and looking back over my shoulder I could see the slate-green roof of the barn. The grass we had driven through was darker than the rest of the grass on the slope. Virgil was saying, "What I really ought to do, little brother, is to get some dogs. Good hunting dogs and learn to train 'em. Anybody as good with horses as I am ought to be able to train a hound."

"I read in the barbershop the other day that poodles used to be good hunting dogs before the ladies got hold of them," I said.

"That so?" Virgil said. "You know old George Simmons' wife has a poodle that's dyed pink. We ought to sneak over there some evening and steal the little beggar, teach him how to hunt. You know, we'd wash that goddamn dye out and teach him to hunt birds." Virgil grinned. "I bet that little pink peckerwood would have the time of his life."

"He might that," I said.

"Here's the ford," Virgil said. "This creek is called Indian Creek, don't ask me why." He edged the jeep into the dull brown water. As we moved deeper, a brown swell rolled before us and the floating weeds on the far bank rose and fell. At the deepest part of the creek, Virgil pushed the shift lever down into four-wheel low and gunned the motor. "Hang on!" he yelled. We reared out of the water in a flume of spray and bounced onto the steep road that ran up the bluff. A rabbit broke cover and scampered along in front of us. After about fifteen yards the rabbit veered off into the brush and almost fell over his own feet. We followed the yellow-gray ruts up a narrow arroyo until we were about fifty feet from the top; then Virgil stopped.

Another arroyo came running in from the northeast, and on the delta of high ground between the two arroyos, a barbed-wire fence petered out. The dirt had washed from underneath the last fence post and it hung off the incline at a crazy angle, held up by the tangled wire. Resting his arm on top of the windshield, Virgil pointed upward.

"Fence up there runs a good two mile," he said. "If you take that side and I take this one, there's a chance we won't kill each other if we fire away from the fence."

We didn't speak for a while. I leaned against the spare tire slipping shells into the breech of the Winchester while Virgil sat on the hood and loaded the Browning. Down below, the creek riffled through some high rocks, and above us the wind shushed through the grass on the plateau. The shaggy clouds were sliding faster now.

"Looks as if it's gonna fair off," I said.

"Yeah," Virgil said, sliding off the hood. "You can still use this gun if you want to."

I just waved my hand and waded into the tall grass at the mouth of the little arroyo. In a minute Virgil was out of sight and I was alone. At the head of the arroyo a scrap of morning blue broke through the clouds; it turned gray and then there was some more blue off to the left. I could hear Virgil crashing brush as he moved up the other arroyo. For some reason I had pumped the Winchester twice, and two red shells lay in the damp grass. I reinserted the shells and stood with my feet apart, resting the butt of the stock into my hipbone; then I slapped the stock into my shoulder, sighting on the tops of the windswept scrub oaks along the crest of the bluff. There was sun up there, and a few remaining leaves winked gold and green. This was the way Pa used to shoot when he was showing off at the gun club. Virgil and I would sit on the ground outside the box while Pa stood on the line with the stock into his hip and his black hair flaring in the wind. "Pull!" he'd shout, yanking the gun to his shoulder and firing in the same movement. The pigeon didn't break, it disappeared. Virgil and I would tell Pa what a fine shot he was and Pa would smile and wink. He always did things the hard way, but he was a damn fine shot.

I picked my way through the cenizo and around the occasional patch of prickly pear that grew along the arroyo. My sweat chilled on my forehead and I wished to hell Virgil was walking with me, but it was just like him, leaving me alone. It was a Vernon family trait, leaving people alone, except for Mom and she tended in the other direction, and I was in my same old fix. Pa was four years dead, and nothing had changed. I was in the thick of a family fight, just like always, with Pa yanking on my butt and Mom yanking on my head, and Virgil, that son of a bitch, squatting off in the corner with a silly grin on his face. I was so mad at Virgil for leaving me alone that if he'd walked up, I might have shot him.

Then I tripped over a root and landed with my hand square in a patch of nettle. This revived me proper, so I climbed on up the arroyo, scratching my palm and thinking about Pa. It was funny, I could only remember him doing two things: having dinner in the old house with the chinaberry trees and fooling with guns. Sometimes after dinner he climbed the stairs to my room with an armload of guns. We would clean them together and he would tell me about being a boy in Orange, Texas, and how much he hated cotton farming. That was how he got to flying, as a crop duster in a little Piper after the war. Then he and two of his hard-drinking air force buddies went into the airplane business. They ended up redesigning old multi-engine jobs into posh executive planes, and coining the money. It was about this time we sold the old house with the chinaberry trees, moved to the west side, and Mom started in on us to call him "Dad" instead of "Pa." My little sis changed but Virgil and I never could. So, finally, there seemed to be two men living in the house. One was "Dad" and the other was "Pa." Pa took us hunting or out to the gun club and Dad flew to New York and Washington and down to South America where some of the big honchos down there were his best customers.

When I was a kid, I was never sure that the fellow in the narrow gray suit was Pa. It was, though; they buried him in a narrow gray suit and a South American general, who was in town at the time, came to the funeral in a private limousine. After the service he gave Virgil and me one of his medals and told us that Pa was "muy simpático." I hadn't thought about all these things for a long time. In some ways they were all thought out for me since they didn't explain anything. So I thought about that blond in New York, which didn't explain anything either, and nearly stepped on a blue jay. The jay clattered, burst in an explosion of blue feathers right past my face. My hand jerked on the Winchester so hard that I nearly fell down again, but suddenly I was at the head of the arroyo.

Rolling country spread away from me in the sun which shone through two gray ranks of clouds. The light, falling at a sharp angle, washed the prairie grass on the ridges bright yellow and left the coulees full of shadows. Starting to walk, I spotted the fence about thirty yards to my right. The muzzle of the Winchester watched the tangled sod in front of me, but I kept losing my balance and weaving. The slightest ridge or dip in the sod threw me off balance; stale coffee rose up in my throat, my stomach gathered into a fist, and I sweated like a hog. It took every bit of concentration I had just to put one foot in front of the other. A whole flight of dove could have broken and I would have never known because I was watching the grass at my feet. The grass was brown at the top and darker green down on the body, then yellow and purplish red down next to the sod, like veins. I stopped and looked around but Virgil was no place to be seen and I felt naked and alone under the sky. It had been stupid for us to split up when we could have hunted just as well together, but here I was. So I tried to think about Virgil and Mildred Ranserhoff and Virgil asking me, of all people, to tutor his English, but the thoughts slipped right out of my mind. It was like grabbing minnows in a bucket. All I could think about was that goddamn lonesome prairie, and the effort it took to walk.

There was a lone hackberry about fifty yards to my left and I started moving toward it. The idea of getting under that hackberry really appealed to me. I glanced around from time to time, pretending to myself that I was hunting, but that just reminded me of the Winchester in my hands and the shells in the magazine. When I reached the hackberry I leaned against the rough bark. I just leaned there taking deep breaths while sweat ran down the side of my nose. I was so damn glad to be underneath something. Three little ants crawled out of the bark onto the shoulder of my coat, but I let them be. A scudding cloud covered the sun and the gold drained away from the ridges. I was sweating something terrible now, so I unbuttoned my coat and sat down in the soft damp grass with my back against the tree. With both hands I held Virgil's shotgun upright between my knees. For no reason I tried to hold as still as possible. I tried not to move at all, to blank every little thought out of my mind, but there were thoughts that I couldn't understand and couldn't stop. They swirled just below the surface, like black bass in a dark pond, and I couldn't stop them. I sat there and watched my knuckles whiten on the breech of the Winchester. I hooked one thumb in the trigger guard, but other than moving those three bones in my thumb, I held perfectly still. I even held my eyes still, gazing past the gun at the gray country. The gun seemed to disappear when I focused my eyes on the prairie. The prairie spread as far as I could see into the pale blue horizon, but I dropped my eyes. The butt of the stock slid an inch or two toward the damp heels of my boots. It was the damnedest thing, since I was holding so still, to see that fine carved walnut stock slide smoothly through the grass, and the smooth deep muzzle lower toward my face. Until my thumb had moved, I didn't realize that I had taken the safety off. It was probably an old reflex, but no, I knew exactly what that guy sitting under the hackberry was doing. He was trying to keep as quiet as possible, but the blood kept gushing and pumping through his wrists so it was impossible to keep completely quiet. So he thought about blood: about his blood, and his pa's and his brother's. Then he realized that his blood was thinking.

For a second, when the shot rang out, and for two or three seconds longer, while the noise echoed around me, I didn't know whether I was alive or dead. Then slowly, so slowly that if you had been watching me you probably couldn't tell, I pulled the muzzle of the Winchester away from my forehead. I heard Virgil calling, something about birds, but his voice died and everything was quiet again. Off to my right I saw the birds, two bandtails, skimming over the top of the grass. If I didn't want to take a chance of hitting Virgil, I would have to fire with the birds going away at an angle. I scrambled to my feet, bringing up the gun. The birds, coming fast and staying close together, began to climb. A piece of sun broke under the clouds and their fluttering brown bodies were burned against the light. Giving the first bird a slight lead, I squeezed the trigger. The shot hurt my ears and knocked me back a step, but I didn't fall on my ass.

I hadn't led him quite enough. The second bird, though, was caught full. It was knocked about two feet along the path of the shot, then it fell like a rock. The lead bird bucked in its flight. It lifted its wings two or three more times, and then started to cut a clean arc toward the ground with one wing swinging behind it like a free rudder. Watching those birds fall, I knew I had killed one hell of a lot more than two pigeons. I had killed my pa—not finally, maybe, not forever, I knew, but for that rising moment at least, I had really fucking *done it* and I felt so light I could have flown. Virgil ran toward me, holding the automatic out from his body. He came up smiling and panting with his gold tooth glinting in the sun, and grabbed me around the shoulders.

"You shoot good, old boy," he said, shaking me like a rag doll.

"Shoot well," I said.

"Huh?"

"The right way to say it is 'You shoot well,' " I said.

CHICKENS

DAO STROM

From The Southern Anthology
Southern Prize, *1996*

The relatives were waking up. Hus Madsen could hear them moving around inside the van and the storage shed where they had slept in their sleeping bags. Hus took his cigarettes and headed down the hill to smoke and admire the view. The relatives had arrived just two days ago to visit the Madsens' new home. It was only the second time Hus had met them in the five years he and Tran had been married. Walking down the steep driveway, he kicked up the fresh red dirt with his boots, and stepped onto the concrete foundation they had poured for the house just last week. He stood there and looked out over the valley with his arms folded across his chest. He could see the mid-August sun rising over the mountains and the river winding soundlessly through the bottom of the valley.

Behind him, from the top of the driveway, he heard the dogs' collars jingling and their paws scraping excitedly on the ground as the trailer door banged open against the sharp morning air.

Then, he began to hear the voices of the relatives. They spoke in slow, broken English, or rapidly and loudly in their native tongue which he didn't understand a word of. He had insisted, when he married Tran, that they speak only English in their home. It was more important for the children to speak the language of the country they were growing up in than for them to be clinging to a culture they had left. It was what he had done himself upon coming to America, twenty-two long years ago, and if they were to succeed in this society, it was what they would have to learn as well.

Of the three children, only the youngest girl was his by blood. The other two had come with their mother from Vietnam by boat, just three months before he had met them. While in the refugee camp, Tran had written an article about her and her children's experiences, which had been published in a Sacramento newspaper. Hus was in Sacramento looking into a transfer of air bases when he read the story. He had felt so sorry, because he had heard these stories before, he knew these people could prosper if only someone would give them the chance and the right circumstances. And then it occurred to him. He had no one else. He was forty-two years old, still living alone. He had a cat, a Siamese the lady upstairs had asked him to watch when she went away on vacation, and then had never come back. He was not an unattractive man, rather the opposite. Women had often said things to him, that he looked like he should be on TV. But all these women he had known were flighty and frivolous, and they got on his nerves. He had given up. These women, they knew nothing of struggle, or hardship, or endurance. They would never understand him, the things he had gone through. But here, as he read the story in the paper, here was a woman who had done some fighting in her lifetime. Here was a woman for whom life had not been easy. Here was a woman who had endured, who possessed character. He sat in his tiny two-room apartment, and wrote a letter to the newspaper. He wanted to do something for this woman who was

a fighter. It meant something to him. What could he do, he
wrote.

When they met, his heart went out to her and to himself also,
in a strange way. They were married two weeks later.

The girls were coming down the hill, holding hands with the girl
cousin. He couldn't remember all the cousins' names, and he
couldn't pronounce them all, either. There were seven of them
and the second-oldest was the only girl, named Huong, maybe
seventeen. He knew her because he thought her the most pleasant and considerate of all the cousins. When they ate dinner, the
boys left their plates on the table, and Huong did all the cleaning.
As they came down the hill, he called out to them, "Well, good
morning! Come and look at the view. I'll bet you've never seen a
view like this before." He held his cigarette away from his lips as
he spoke.

His daughters, he noticed, had been dressed up in the flimsy,
strapless dresses the relatives had brought as gifts. They had been
wearing these foolish outfits both days since the relatives had arrived. Even on a woman with a full figure, the dresses would have
looked nothing more than cheap, he thought. The seven-year-
old's dress was glittery and purple, and his four-year-old was
wearing a satiny blue one. They came tottering toward him down
the steep drive in high-heeled shoes that were far too big for
them and only made them look more ridiculous. He hadn't
known what to say without seeming rude, so he had decided,
from the beginning, not to even acknowledge the dresses.

"Hi, Daddy," the girls exclaimed.

"Aunt Mary and I made the girls look very pretty," said
Huong, smiling brightly. She was wearing a tiger-striped bathing
suit and a floppy straw hat.

"Why don't you show your cousins how to take a bath?" Hus
said to the girls.

The girls got excited at this suggestion. "We'll show you the way we take a bath in the country!"

"Good idea," said Hus.

He watched as the girls hobbled over to the rack of gallons and showed their cousin how to feel for the warmest gallons of water. The rack was made of wood and had black sandpaper nailed to it to absorb the sun's heat. They each picked up a gallon and started back up the hill. It was good, he thought, to see his four-year-old daughter lugging the heavy gallon of water as well as her older sister and cousin did. He heard his seven-year-old explaining, "See, the sun heats up the water." He called after them, "Make sure you lather first!"

His wife came out of the trailer. She was a very small-boned woman, wearing cut-off jeans with cowboy boots. She was speaking in Vietnamese with her sister, the one they called Aunt Mary, and the two of them were laughing. The sister's husband, who they called Uncle John, was smoking a cigarette, standing outside the trailer with his shirt unbuttoned to below his chest. His eyes were narrow, his brown skin mottled, and he had a straight, black moustache. He wore a cheap gold necklace and he was a skinny man, at least a head shorter than Hus. Hus had never understood men who wore necklaces. Uncle John saw Hus and waved his hand.

"Come, eat!" he said in his thick accent, and nodded his chin and waved his cigarette in the air.

Hus put a hand on his stomach and shook his head. "No thank you," he said loudly. "I have to go check on the pups." He pointed to the doghouse on the hill. Then, he stepped off the foundation and dropped his cigarette, grinding it into the dirt with the heel of his boot.

Since the doghouse sat on a slope, at night sometimes the puppies rolled down the hill in their sleep and fell into the trench that had been dug for the septic system. The trench was six feet deep and the dirt at the bottom was still fresh and moist. He walked along the length of the trench now, searching it. This was something he usually got the boy out of bed in the mornings to do. That morning, there were two puppies whining and clawing at the bottom of the trench. He felt some irritation that the boy had not been out there first thing in the morning to help the puppies. But the boy was a teenager, fourteen, and what more could one expect? He hopped down into the trench, and picked each puppy up by the scruff of its neck. They kicked their legs and yelped. They were so young, they had not yet opened their eyes. As he held them up and looked at their soft faces, he imagined how, in or out of the trench, the world was still dark for them. He wondered, could they feel him helping them even when they couldn't see him? Later, when their eyes opened and they could see, would they recognize him as the man who had helped them?

He carried the two puppies back up to the doghouse where the mother dog was nursing, and he carefully set them down among the others.

He heard voices and splashing as he headed back up the hill. At the side of the trailer around the stump the girls usually stood on when Tran bathed them, the cousins were loosely gathered, bathing, each with their own gallon of water, and the girls were instructing them, teetering on their high heels and still wearing the dresses. The cousins were in their bathing suits, the boys small and scrawny in their swim trunks. They were giggling and stomping and shaking themselves as they poured water over their heads. They looked like chickens. Hus couldn't believe these people were his relations.

He walked up the road toward them, lighting another cigarette, and he called out to them that it worked best if they poured the water slowly. "Just enough to get you wet first," he said. "Then put the gallon down, and lather up and shampoo. Then, rinse. Out here in the country, we have to conserve water." As they looked at him, he made lathering motions around his body to illustrate what he meant. They were laughing and smiling at him. They put down their gallons while they rubbed shampoo into their hair. Then, one of the boys picked up a gallon and splashed water at his brothers. They began to shriek and laugh and chase each other around. Seeing this, Hus waved his arms. "Hey, hey," he called, "we have to conserve water here. No horsing around now."

This was the plan Hus had designed for their sewage system: a large septic tank buried deep in the ground and twenty feet of pipe running the length of the trench across the hillside, attached at one end to the porthole of the septic tank and the other—when it was ready—to the sewage pipes beneath the house. For the meantime, however, Hus planned to leave one end of the pipe loose, so that it could be dragged up the hill and attached to the waste tank underneath the trailer at least once every week. The boy, wearing thick rubber gloves, would be in charge of this chore. Hus had already shown him the lever to open the trailer's sewer tank, allowing the waste to flow down the long pipe, through the trench, into the septic tank.

The boy had said nothing, had just stared glumly at the coils of pipe as Hus explained all this to him. Hus had tried to make a joke of it, ruffling the boy's hair and joking, "You may hate it now, but one day you'll realize, this was one of the most interesting experiences of your life! Hey, how many kids get a chance to man a septic tank every week anyway?" Of Tran's two children before Hus, only the boy was old enough to realize the changes they had gone through in coming from Vietnam and his mother remarrying. While Tran's daughter had accepted Hus easily, the boy was gloomy and reticent. Hus had tried to teach him things, fishing, distinguishing car brands, model airplanes. The boy had listened unenthusiastically, but in private, Hus discovered, the boy worked intently on the model airplanes or drawing pictures of cars. The boy's reclusiveness was frustrating because Hus took it personally.

The large septic tank sat now at the top of the driveway, a huge, black submarine-shaped hunk of iron and aluminum. Today was the day Hus and the boy would drag the tank down the hill and maneuver it into the hole they had dug for it next to the trench. With two thick coils of braided rope, Hus and the boy fastened a harness around the body of the septic tank. The cousins were playing soccer with a deflated ball on the concrete foundation, the girls running after them barefoot in the ridiculous dresses, and Tran had set up lawn chairs in front of the trailer for Aunt Mary and Uncle John, who were lounging in the morning sun with glasses of iced-tea to watch Hus and the boy. As they were finishing the harness, a black Chevrolet truck appeared at the top of the driveway, and a man got out.

"Howdy!" the man called out.

Hus couldn't recall ever having seen this man before, though he recognized the truck from passing it occasionally on the roads. The man was tall and wiry, in his thirties, dressed in jeans and cowboy boots. His muscles showed like knots through the thin fabric of his t-shirt and his arms were covered with tattoos. His skin was sunburnt in patches high on his cheeks, and he wore an orange baseball cap. He had a thick moustache and walked with his hands dangling loosely.

Hus stopped halfway up the driveway. "Hello. What can I do for you?"

The man slowed down and stood a guarded distance from Hus. He looked at Hus, and then behind him at the relatives and the girls and the boy. He hooked one thumb in his belt loop and rubbed his bristled chin with his other hand.

" 'Scuse me if I'm interruptin' your morning, looks like you're having some sorta party, and it sure is a beautiful morning." His eyes shifted beneath his thick eyebrows. "You see, my dog was shot last night. Now I know my dog wasn't the nicest dog, them pitbulls are damn crazy sometimes, but he was still a damn fine dog, and no one had the right to go and shoot him in the night like that." He paused, studying Hus. "Now I been investigating," the man went on, "and I'm just going around asking questions. I don't mean no harm. I know plenty of folk out here didn't like my dog. But I got my rights, no one shoulda shot my dog. Now I'm just coming by t'ask you, mister, did you see or hear anything unusual last night roundabout 11:30 P.M. or so?"

"No, I'm afraid I did not," replied Hus. "Sorry."

"Well, mister," said the man, tipping back his hat and raising his chin, "can I ask you then, what were you and your folk up to roundabout that time last night?"

"We were asleep," said Hus. He remembered having heard from neighbors down the road about a pitbull sneaking around and killing chickens and chasing kids on bikes. Hus thought, it's probably a good thing that pitbull got shot. A dog's personality was nothing more than a reflection of the man who owned him. "I don't think I can help you anymore. Good luck, however." Hus turned his back to walk away, but the man raised his voice and called out after him.

"Well, mister, I been hearin' maybe otherwise. Some other fella gave me your address, says you're the new people and he's seen your truck driving past my pitbull a number of times."

Hus's eyes swept over the relatives, who had come up the driveway and were standing, staring at him. He turned to face the man again, but the image of the relatives had stuck in his mind and he saw himself as the man must have seen him, with all his brown-skinned, slant-eyed relatives in a scattered line behind him, wearing their cheap secondhand clothing, the scrawny boys in their swim trunks and Huong in her floppy hat and tiger-striped bathing suit. Hus could read the man's disgust at the sight, and felt a shameful anger rise up inside himself because he understood that feeling of repulsion himself. Hus felt a pain in his stomach. His stomach was terrifically sensitive to stress and different foods, and he had developed an ulcer recently. Sometimes when the pain rose in his gut, it made him furious at everything, regardless of his true intentions. Hunger and lack of discipline could do this to dogs, too, he thought. Especially pitbulls who were mean by nature and might turn on you at any moment.

"Now I don't mean to jump to no conclusions," the man said, "but I hear you mighta been out last night, and there ain't no one else around here I figure woulda shot a man's dog."

"As I already said, we were asleep."

"How do I know that for sure?" The man took a step forward and flung one arm in a palm-up gesture toward Hus. His other arm hung at his side, swaying with the natural motion of his body. It occurred to Hus that the man was probably an alcoholic. "You got yourself proof?"

"You can ask anyone here," said Hus, feeling heat rise behind his teeth.

"How do I know you ain't just goddamn lying?" the man said sternly. He put his hands on his hips and leaned forward. "How do I know maybe you weren't all up drinking last night and decided, hey, let's go out and look for a dog to shoot!"

Hus was certain the man must be drunk. "You're an insensible man," he said, "you're wasting my time."

"Hey!" Tran had come to stand a few feet behind Hus, and now both men looked at her, Hus turning halfway around. She was standing with her feet spread and her hands on her hips. In her broken English, she exclaimed, "I his wife! He was asleep with me last night, I know!" She was a small woman, and her eyes were beady behind her thick glasses. Looking at her standing there so defiantly, Hus felt embarrassed at the sight of her.

The man made a hooting noise. "Oh, mama," he chuckled.

He laughed again and shook his moustached face like he was impressed. He looked directly at Tran, and her face began to turn red. She took a step backwards and her gaze shifted. Her mouth opened and closed. The man shrugged, "I ain't said nothing."

"What did I just tell you!" Hus shouted. As he strode forward, in the back of his mind he was vaguely aware of the fact that he had not just told the man anything to justify him shouting out this question. The man stumbled backwards a step, and Hus stopped a foot from him. "Get off my property," Hus said lowly. "I swear to you, you don't know what you're dealing with if you don't get off this property this instant. By God, I swear to you, I mean it." The blood had drained from his face, and he felt cold and somehow violated. He didn't want the girls to see him like this.

The man tugged on the bill of his hat and twitched his moustache. He seemed to be looking for a foothold but wasn't able to find one. Finally, he turned his back with an abrupt, jerking motion, and sauntered back to his truck. He climbed into the cab and turned over the ignition. The truck roared. There was a hissing noise in its grill. The man put his tattooed forearm on the window frame, leaned his head out and shouted, "Now listen, I won't forget this, y'hear me?" Then, he put his truck in gear and backed out of the driveway. The tires spit pebbles up out of the gravel.

Hus turned and walked stiffly back to the septic tank. His wife and the relatives and the children were all looking at him. The boy was standing close to the septic tank, kicking at it with the toe of his sneaker. His wife was still standing with her hands on her hips, her face flushed red. This is how they all stood, Hus thought, all of them looking to him.

"That not a very friendly man," said Aunt Mary, who was standing up now in front of her lawn chair. She looked with concern toward Tran.

Hus spoke up, "She's alright now. She just has to learn that not everybody is friendly." He caught his wife's glance and could see that she was upset with him. He couldn't tell if it was because of

what he had just said or if she was just upset about the whole inci-
dent. What else should he have done? He told himself irritably
that she did not understand. The men in her culture were different than men in America and men where he had come from as
well, and she just didn't understand that. Aunt Mary was saying
something in Vietnamese to his wife. His wife said something
back in a curt voice. He tried to chuckle. "Tell them that's not
how everyone out here in the country is," he said, realizing that
this would be the story the relatives would tell when they went
back to San Diego. They would say to the people they knew, this
is what people in the country are like.

He wished he could prove to them how wrong they would be.

The man returned about an hour later. He was carrying a bottle
of wine in his right hand. Hus and the boy had dragged the septic
tank to the edge of the driveway, and were beginning to ease it
down the slope. The relatives were gathered around watching,
and Hus felt he was educating them by allowing them the chance
to watch this work being done. His girls sat above them all in a
tree with their Barbie dolls. The chickens were pecking and
scratching in the chicken coop on the hill. The dogs began to bark
when they spotted the man coming down the driveway.

The man raised his arms over his head as he approached. "I
came to apologize, is all," he said, and held the bottle of wine out
to Hus. "I was jumping the gun and I just wanted to come say
how sorry I am for making a mess of your morning like I did."

Hus looked at the wine bottle without knowing what to do
with it. He was reminded of his ulcer, which was the reason he no
longer drank alcohol.

"That's fine," said Hus. It wasn't easy for him to say. He didn't
want to accept the wine at all. "Tran," he called to his wife, "why
don't you come take this?"

Tran came over from the trailer and took the bottle, smiling
politely. Hus told himself, she'll have to learn, she shouldn't smile
so sweetly at a man like this one.

The man wiped his hands on his jeans. "My name's William, by the way." He stuck out his hand, and Hus shook it. The man's hand was thin and sticky.

"Hus Madsen," he said. "My wife, Tran."

"Hello, missus." The man tipped his hat. "I do apologize for my rotten behavior this morning."

Tran nodded and smiled, and carried the wine back to the trailer.

The man licked his lips. "Y'know, I went down to that bastard Wes Walker's place," he said. "I was jumping the gun earlier, I realize now, because that Walker could've shot my dog, too." The boy, behind Hus, dropped his end of the rope and knelt to pet the big black mother dog, who had come up to them, tail wagging. Hus wiped his brow and propped one hand on the side of the septic tank. He wanted the man to leave so they could get back to work. "Now what do you say," the man continued, "we go on down to Wes Walker's place, and we pay him a visit? You and your boy, or even just you and me, Hoss. You're a big fella."

"I'm afraid not," Hus said, not bothering to correct the man's pronunciation.

"You know," the man interrupted, his upper body swaying, "when I came by and I told Walker my predicament, y'know what he says? He says he don't give a flying shit about my dog. And that kinda attitude, well I don't trust that." The man leaned forward, eager to convince Hus, "I told him, 'well I don't give a shit about yer wife.' He says to me get off his property or else he's gonna shoot *me*. And I knew right there, I thought of you, Hoss, so sensible and calm—ain't it apparent, I tell myself, that man there was an intelligent man—and it was plain to me then that Wes Walker must be the man I should be talking to." He grinned assuredly. "Now what do you say, huh? I just want some company along."

Hus frowned. "We're too busy here to help you with that."

The man removed his hat and spun it on his fingers. He wiped at his flattened hair. "Wouldn't take more than a minute. We go there, we show 'im, we leave."

"Dad," said the boy, hesitantly, "I still wanna go swimming today."

"You be quiet now," Hus told the boy. The boy was not even looking at him, he was looking down at the dirt with his hand rested on the dog's head.

Hus turned back to the man. "We have work to do here," he said. "I can't help you. It's none of my business. I'm sorry about your dog."

"Well, I understand," said the man, and put his hat back on. "Enjoy the wine." He left them without saying goodbye.

Hus and the boy had gotten the septic tank down the hill and were maneuvering it into position above the hole. They had had to brace themselves against the weight of the tank, Hus in front pulling the rope over his shoulder and leaning so far forward his knees almost dug into the ground, and the boy at the back of the tank, pushing. Hus wondered if the boy was pushing as hard as he could. The girls had climbed down from the tree and were running around, chasing the chickens out of the way of the oncoming tank, waving their Barbie dolls in front of them. Hus was afraid they might fall into the hole or the trench, and they were distracting him. "Get out of the way!" he was shouting at them, when he heard the man's truck again.

The man strode to the edge of the driveway and stood with his feet spread and his fists on his hips. "Hey!" he called down. "I gotta talk to you, Hoss."

Hus wiped his brow and let go of the rope. He walked to the end of the tank and stopped beside the boy. The boy shielded his eyes and looked up the hill at the man. Hus folded his arms across his chest. The two of them were sweating and dusty.

"What's the problem?" Hus called back to the man.

"I got a problem with my dog that got shot last night," yelled the man.

"I thought we discussed this already," said Hus.

"I gotta say, Hoss, I think you been lyin' to me."

Hus took a deep breath and hooked his hands tiredly on his hips. He looked for a moment at his dirty shoes.

"Yeah, I think you been lyin' to me," the man repeated. "Wes Walker ain't the one who done it, and I know that 'cause he proved it to me. And I got some news for you—"

"You get off my goddamn property now," Hus said, raising his voice.

The man paced a few steps back and forth at the edge of the driveway. "No, I'm not done here. I know who shot my dog, lemme tell you—"

"No one here shot your dog," said Hus as calmly as he could.

"Yeah?" The man nodded his chin in the direction of the trailer, where Uncle John was standing. "I know something you oughta know about. I know that maybe your boy told Jungle Jose over there to sneak out in the middle of the night to shoot my dog. What about that?"

Hus stared incredulously at the man. He also saw his wife on the doorstep of the trailer, a distance behind the man. She was looking at the man's back. She had poured herself a glass of wine and was holding it with both hands. The boy shuffled his feet miserably. Hus wondered suddenly, how had he gotten himself into this situation, into this life?

"If you don't get off my property, I'm going to have to call the police," Hus threatened. But he was tired and slightly bewildered.

"Oh no, I'm not leaving yet, y'hear me?" yelled the man, "I'm not leaving until you tell me yes, my people shot your poor dog, and then you give me some money so I can go out and buy myself a new one. Another damn pitbull, that's right." The man paced back and forth, and then strode back to his truck, reached into the bed of it, and came out grunting and dragging something. He heaved it over his shoulder, carried it onto the driveway and threw it down on the rocks. The pitbull's body was limp and pale and the bullet wound was visible in the middle of its rib cage.

Hus could not believe this. He stared at the man, furious.

The man pointed to the dead dog. "Now, listen, I'm going to leave this here for you, alright? It's all yours now."

Hus was on the driveway suddenly. He didn't know how he had gotten there. He shoved the man aside and reached for the dog. He lifted the cold body, felt the weight of it and the coarseness of its short fur against his forearms and chest, and he began to walk with it in his arms up the driveway.

The man shouted "Hey!" behind him.

They all watched him. He continued to walk, not knowing himself what he would do, down the road.

As he walked, it occurred to him what he was at that moment: a forty-six-year-old man carrying a dead dog down a dirt road. He thought how hard he had worked in his life and of the difficult choices he had made. And this man here, this lazy, worthless man who had thrown his dead dog on the ground, this man would never be capable of understanding such things. This man was a worthless, filthy person who had allowed his dog to be shot. As he continued to walk, it slowly dawned on Hus that the man had probably shot his dog himself. Drunk and mad at the dog for harassing the neighbors, the man had gone out and shot his own dog. And then he had looked at the clock. He had remembered that it was 11:30 P.M. By morning, the man had convinced himself that someone else must've come out and shot the dog. This was what Hus believed, the more he thought about it, the farther he walked with the dog in his arms. Hus was sure of it.

The man yelled after him, "You lousy son of a bitch! Where do you think you're taking my goddamn dog!"

Hus stopped in the middle of the dusty road. He looked around himself at the trees and the brilliant blue sky and the sunshine. He gently let the dog's body down in the grass on the side of the road. He turned around slowly, his gaze sweeping over the tangled oak trees and pines descending into thickening clusters down the hill on one side of him. He saw his family and the relatives and his boy all scattered up the road watching him, the man pushing through them and swinging his arms. On the other side of the road, there was a driveway which Hus knew led up to the Nerwinskis' house. In the pastures alongside the driveway, there were sheep grazing.

The man caught up to Hus and stepped over the dead dog in the grass without glancing at it.

"You bastard fucker," said the man. He slammed his fist into his palm, coming toward Hus and stopping just short of touching him. "What do you think you're doing?"

"I think it's time for you to remove your dog and yourself from here. I think you've outstayed your welcome by now, don't you?"

Hus's family and the relatives were trickling down the road toward them. The boy and two of the cousins came and stood a few feet behind the man, glancing from Hus and the man to the dead dog. Hus saw his girls and Huong holding hands at the back of the crowd. His girls were carrying along their Barbie dolls.

"I've got something to say to you, Hoss," the man spoke quickly. "I know things, maybe you wouldn't be so sure of your people's innocence if you knew. I seen your boy out on his motorbike going past my place before. And I been told that just last week there was a boy on a motorbike chasing around my dog with his BB gun. I been told that just today when I was out asking questions of my good neighbors."

Hus believed the man must be lying. "To be honest with you," said Hus, "it's probably best your dog was shot. It was probably a mistreated animal and vicious because of your mistreatment." Hus caught sight of the boy, who was staring open-mouthed at the man. Hus felt the pain in his stomach flare all the way to his ribs suddenly. He straightened his back and tried to stand taller.

He faced the boy. "Is this true?" he asked him.

The boy began to stare at his feet. The man laughed once. "The dog was chasing me," the boy mumbled, "but it was a long time ago. I was on my motorcycle one day and I fell off because he was chasing me and he almost bit me."

Hus was mad at everyone now. "And then you fired at this animal with your BB gun, did you?"

The boy shrugged, not looking up, and shifted his feet in the grass.

"Like the time with the rattlesnake?" One day earlier that summer, there had been a rattlesnake under the old Ping-Pong table behind the trailer, and the boy had stupidly tried to shoot it with his air rifle, with his sisters standing nearby. Hus had come running and shouted at him when he saw this happening, what if a pellet ricocheted off the leg of the table and hit one of his sisters in the eye? What then?

The boy was still looking at his feet. "I didn't hurt his dog. He made me fall off my bike. And it happened a long time ago."

The man stood between Hus and the boy, looking back and forth from one to the other. The man folded his arms and grinned. Maybe, Hus thought, it was best in life to just suspect everyone of having done something wrong.

"And what were you doing just driving around with your BB gun on your motorcycle? Don't you know that is a stupid thing to do? That is a stupid, stupid thing to do!" Hus leaned toward the boy. "Stupid!" He put force behind this word and his voice was fierce and deep. "I would expect you to know better, Ty. Is that what you do? Answer me. Why were you driving around with your BB gun on your motorcycle? Is this something you do regularly?"

The boy shook his head. His shoulders moved up and down, thinly.

"You answer me now," demanded Hus.

"Yeah, you tell him now," added the man, but Hus ignored him.

"You tell me," said Hus to the boy, "do you drive your motorcycle around with your BB gun?"

The boy mumbled, "I wasn't, I didn't have it with me, I came
back and got it." He glared briefly toward Hus and then away.

Hus nodded. "So you came back and got your gun. You meant
to come back and specifically shoot at this dog." He felt grossly
deceived. "That is what they call premeditated, do you understand? How do we know you didn't decide to do this again, last
night? I can't be sure of anything now, can I?"

"No, you can't," the man agreed.

"I fell off my bike, ok? I almost got bit! That dumb dog was
trying to bite me! But I never *shot* him!" The boy's face twisted
and he crossed his arms tightly over his chest and hunched his
shoulders. He began to cry.

There was silence for a moment, just the boy sniffling. Hus
didn't know what to say next. He stood staring at the boy with his
eyes so fiercely focused, they ached. He stepped back in the grass.

"You do a thing that stupid again and you'll be sorry," he said.
But he meant it not as a threat from himself, no, he just wanted
the boy to learn something, something about life, this. He said
sternly, "You don't make dumb moves like that. Let me tell you."

The boy sniffled and wiped at his eyes.

The man began to point his finger. "Now I'm holding you re-
sponsible, Hoss. Maybe I don't know the details, but you got
something amiss here, buddy—"

Hus's wife came forward while the man was talking and put her
arm around the boy. She glared at Hus, and Hus believed they
were all, the relatives and kids, glaring at him in the same hateful
manner. He felt alone. The man was still talking when Tran said,
"You being too hard on Ty. I think you being unreasonable. We
go home now, forget everything." The man's talking faltered.
Tran nudged Ty's shoulders, trying to turn him away with her. Ty
shrugged her off but followed when she started to walk away.

Hus watched them. Tran headed back up the dirt road toward

home, and Aunt Mary and two of the boy cousins started to follow. Uncle John and the other boys were still looking toward Hus
and the man. Hus noticed his youngest daughter was crying, and
Huong knelt beside her. The older little girl was glancing rapidly
between Hus and Tran, and Hus saw the little girl's dark hair
swinging in a light way against her neck. It looked cheerful and
nonchalant.

"You take your dead dog and leave," Hus told the man. He
nodded toward the driveway across the road. "I'm going to go
call the police now. You can decide what you're going to do next."

Hus stepped over the dead dog and walked slowly across the
road. The man didn't stop him. Hus walked up the Nerwinskis'
driveway to their house. The sheep grazing in the pastures raised
their heads briefly as Hus went by. Hus stepped onto the Nerwinskis' porch and rang the doorbell. The Nerwinskis were an old
retired couple. They let him in, nodding pleasantly. The TV
murmured in the living room and Hus could hear the tinkling of
wind chimes from outside an open window.

Hus was sweaty and dusty, and his clothes smelled bad, he was
sure. "There's a man harassing my family," was all he could say. "I
need to call the police."

The old couple directed him to the phone and he strode across
their floor, tracking clumps of dirt with his boots.

As he laid his hand on the phone, he caught sight of the dirt he
had tracked over their clean floor. His stomach turned painfully
and he abruptly moved his hand to it, frowning. The old couple's
faces lit up in alarm. Then, Mr. Nerwinski brought Hus a chair. It
was a simple, sturdy wood chair. Hus sat down, leaning back and
breathing heavily. He was unable to thank them or apologize
right away. Mr. Nerwinski went back to stand beside his wife.
Hus saw them, the old couple, standing in the middle of their living room watching him with wondering, sad eyes. He saw them
amongst their weathered furniture and full bookshelves and the
framed pictures on the walls, pictures of children young and

grown, and a strange melancholy washed over him. He sat in their chair beside their phone on its polished oak stand until the roll of pain in his stomach subsided.

"It's nothing," Hus said then, "I'm very sorry. I'll be just a minute." He tried to chuckle to ease the awkwardness.

Mrs. Nerwinski smiled tenderly and shook her head. "Poor young man," she said.

Hus raised his chin. "No, no, I'm fine," he said and nodded briskly. He sat with his back straight and reached for the phone again. He laid his other hand on his thigh, and tried to keep his face from clouding.

The man and the dog and all of Hus's family were gone when Hus came down the Nerwinskis' driveway. He walked back up the road home by himself. He felt hollow inside, but there was peace in the long grass that grew alongside the road and the sound of the birds in the trees.

When Hus reached the top of his driveway, he saw the trailer and Tran and the others standing about. They stopped talking when they saw him. His daughters ran up to him, exclaiming "Daddy's back!" and he patted their heads and said, "Yep, we're all home now." He picked up his youngest daughter and carried her on his hip down the driveway. When he reached the trailer, he set her down and nodded briefly toward Tran, and went inside. He poured water from the gallon by the sink over his hands. He rubbed his hands together and then wiped them dry on his jeans. He saw the bottle of wine sitting on the counter and thought that they should probably throw it out.

Hus went back outside and saw Tran and the relatives and Ty and the girls, all of them gathered around the front of the trailer. Their eyes gazed at him dark and blank, except for the girls, who were bumping hips in the dirt and paying more attention to their dresses flaring around their legs. And Ty, who was standing with his arms crossed and looking away down the hill. Hus did not know how he would speak to them.

"Everything's alright now," he said, and gave a reassuring chuckle. The quiet of the countryside filled his ears. He wondered if they cared what he thought or not. He half hoped that they did not. "He won't be coming back, that man," he said. Then he added, addressing the girls, "It's time to feed the animals now. There's no reason to forget that." The girls ran to get the dog dishes, and he added, "Make sure you give them fresh water now too."

Hus looked at his wife. She was putting on the galoshes she used to walk in the chicken coop. She didn't like to walk on the chicken droppings in her good boots. Hus waved at her.

"No, no," he said, "I'll do it. I'll feed the chickens today."

Outside the coop, Hus scooped up a cup of poultry feed and entered the chicken pen. As he scattered the feed around his feet in handfuls, the chickens surrounded him. His shadow stretched over them long and broad, and he feared what he might do.

ROMERO'S SHIRT

DAGOBERTO GILB

From The Magic of Blood,
University of New Mexico Press, 1993

Juan Romero, a man not unlike many in this country, has had jobs in factories, shops, and stores. He has painted houses, dug ditches, planted trees, hammered, sawed, bolted, snaked pipes, picked cotton and chile and pecans, each and all for wages. Along the way he has married and raised his children and several years ago he finally arranged it so that his money might pay for the house he and his family live in. He is still more than twenty years away from being the owner. It is a modest house even by El Paso standards. The building, in an adobe style, is made of stone which is painted white, though the paint is gradually chipping off or being absorbed by the rock. It has two bedrooms, a den which is used as another, a small dining area, a living room, a kitchen, one bathroom, and a garage which, someday, he plans to turn into another place to live. Although in a development facing a paved street and in a neighborhood, it has the appearance of being on almost half an acre. At the front is a garden of cactus—nopal, ocotillo, and agave—and there are weeds that grow tall with yellow flowers which seed into thorn-hard burrs. The rest is dirt and rocks of various sizes, some of which have been lined up to form a narrow path out of the graded dirt, a walkway to the front porch—where, under a tile and one-by tongue and groove overhang, are a wooden chair and a love seat, covered by an old bedspread, its legless frame on the red cement slab. Once the porch looked onto oak trees. Two of them are dried-out stumps; the remaining one has a limb or two which still can produce leaves, but with so many amputations, its future is irreversible. Romero seldom runs water through a garden hose, though in the back yard some patchy grass can almost seem suburban, at least to him, when he does. Near the corner of his land, in the front, next to the sidewalk, is a juniper shrub, his only bright green plant, and Romero does not want it to yellow and die, so he makes special efforts on its behalf, washing off dust, keeping its leaves neatly pruned and shaped.

These days Romero calls himself a handyman. He does odd jobs, which is exactly how he advertises—"no job too small"—in the throwaway paper. He hangs wallpaper and doors, he paints, lays carpet, does just about anything someone will call and ask him to do. It doesn't earn him much, and sometimes it's barely enough, but he's his own boss, and he's had so many bad jobs over those other years, ones no more dependable, he's learned that this suits him. At one time Romero did want more, and he'd believed that he could have it simply through work, but no matter what he did his children still had to be born at the county hospital. Even years later it was there that his oldest son went for serious medical treatment because Romero couldn't afford the private hospitals. He tried not to worry about how he earned his money. In Mexico, where his parents were born and he spent much of his youth, so many things weren't available, and any work which allowed for food, clothes, and housing was to be honored—by the standards there, Romero lived well. Except this wasn't Mexico, and even though there were those who did worse even here, there were

many who did better and had more, and a young Romero too often felt ashamed by what he saw as his failure. But time passed,
and he got older. As he saw it, he didn't live in poverty, and *here*,
he finally came to realize, was where he was, where he and his
family were going to stay. Life in El Paso was much like the
land—hard, but one could make do with what was offered. Just as
his parents had, Romero always thought it was a beautiful place
for a home.

Yet people he knew left—to Houston, Dallas, Los Angeles,
San Diego, Denver, Chicago—and came back for holidays with
stories of high wages and acquisition. And more and more people
crossed the river, in rags, taking work, his work, at any price.
Romero constantly had to discipline himself by remembering the
past, how his parents lived; he had to teach himself to appreciate
what he did have. His car, for example, he'd kept up since his
early twenties. He'd had it painted three times in that period and
he worked on it so devotedly that even now it was in as good a
condition as almost any car could be. For his children he tried to
offer more—an assortment of clothes for his daughter, lots of
toys for his sons. He denied his wife nothing, but she was a
woman who asked for little. For himself, it was much less. He
owned some work clothes and T-shirts necessary for his jobs as
well as a set of good enough, he thought, shirts he'd had since before the car. He kept up a nice pair of custom boots, and in a
closet hung a pair of slacks for a wedding or baptism or important
mass. He owned two jackets, a leather one from Mexico and a
warm nylon one for cold work days. And he owned a wool plaid
Pendleton shirt, his favorite piece of clothing, which he'd bought
right after the car and before his marriage because it really was
good-looking besides being functional. He wore it anywhere and
everywhere with confidence that its quality would always be both
in style and appropriate.

***

The border was less than two miles below Romero's home, and he could see, down the dirt street which ran alongside his property, the desert and mountains of Mexico. The street was one of the few in the city which hadn't yet been paved. Romero liked it that way, despite the run-off problems when heavy rains passed by, as they had the day before this day. A night wind had blown hard behind the rains, and the air was so clean he could easily see buildings in Juárez. It was sunny, but a breeze told him to put on his favorite shirt before he pulled the car up alongside the house and dragged over the garden hose to wash it, which was something he still enjoyed doing as much as anything else. He was organized, had a special bucket, a special sponge, and he used warm water from the kitchen sink. When he started soaping the car he worried about getting his shirt sleeves wet, and once he was moving around he decided a T-shirt would keep him warm enough. So he took off the wool shirt and draped it, conspicuously, over the juniper near him, at the corner of his property. He thought that if he couldn't help but see it, he couldn't forget it, and forgetting something outside was losing it. He lived near a school, and teenagers passed by all the time, and also there was regular foot-traffic—many people walked the sidewalk in front of his house, many who had no work.

After the car was washed, Romero went inside and brought out the car wax. Waxing his car was another thing he still liked to do, especially on a weekday like this one when he was by himself, when no one in his family was home. He could work faster, but he took his time, spreading with a damp cloth, waiting, then wiping off the crust with a dry cloth. The exterior done, he went inside the car and waxed the dash, picked up some trash on the floorboard, cleaned out the glove compartment. Then he went for some pliers he kept in a toolbox in the garage, returned and began to wire up the rear license plate which had lost a nut and bolt and was hanging awkwardly. As he did this, he thought of other things he might do when he finished, like prune the juniper. Except his old shears had broken, and he hadn't found another used pair, because he wouldn't buy them new.

An old man walked up to him carrying a garden rake, a hoe, and some shears. He asked Romero if there was some yard work needing to be done. After spring, tall weeds grew in many yards, but it seemed a dumb question this time of year, particularly since there was obviously so little ever to be done in Romero's yard. But Romero listened to the old man. There were still a few weeds over there, and he could rake the dirt so it'd be even and level, he could clip that shrub, and probably there was something in the back if he were to look. Romero was usually brusque with requests such as these, but he found the old man unique and likeable and he listened and finally asked how much he would want for all those tasks. The old man thought as quickly as he spoke and threw out a number. Ten. Romero repeated the number, questioningly, and the old man backed up, saying well, eight, seven. Romero asked if that was for everything. Yes sir, the old man said, excited that he'd seemed to catch a customer. Romero asked if he would cut the juniper for three dollars. The old man kept his eyes on the evergreen, disappointed for a second, then thought better of it. Okay, okay, he said, but, I've been walking all day, you'll give me lunch? The old man rubbed his striped cotton shirt at his stomach.

Romero liked the old man and agreed to it. He told him how he should follow the shape which was already there, to cut it evenly, to take a few inches off all of it just like a haircut. Then Romero went inside, scrambled enough eggs and chile and cheese for both of them and rolled it all in some tortillas. He brought out a beer.

The old man was clearly grateful, but since his gratitude was keeping the work from getting done—he might talk an hour about his little ranch in Mexico, about his little turkeys and his pig—Romero excused himself and went inside. The old man thanked Romero for the food, and, as soon as he was finished with the beer, went after the work sincerely. With dull shears—he sharpened them, so to speak, against a rock wall—the old man snipped garishly, hopping and jumping around the bush, around and around. It gave Romero such great pleasure to watch that this was all he did from his front window.

The work didn't take long, so, as the old man was raking up the clippings, Romero brought out a five-dollar bill. He felt that the old man's dancing around that bush, in those baggy old checkered pants, was more inspiring than religion, and a couple of extra dollars was a cheap price to see old eyes whiten like a boy's.

The old man was so pleased that he invited Romero to that little ranch of his in Mexico where he was sure they could share some aguardiente, or maybe Romero could buy a turkey from him—they were skinny but they could be fattened—but in any case they could enjoy a bottle of tequila together, with some sweet lemons. The happy old man swore he would come back no matter what, for he could do many things for Romero at his beautiful home. He swore he would return, maybe in a week or two, for surely there was work that needed to be done in the back yard.

Romero wasn't used to feeling so virtuous. He so often was disappointed, so often dwelled on the difficulties of life, that he had become hard, guarding against compassion and generosity. So much so that he'd even become spare with his words, even with his family. His wife whispered to the children that this was because he was tired, and, since it wasn't untrue, he accepted it as the explanation too. It spared him that worry, and from having to discuss why he liked working weekends and taking a day off during the week, like this one. But now an old man had made Romero wish his family were there with him so he could give as much, *more*, to them too, so he could watch their spin around dances—he'd missed so many—and Romero swore he would take them all into Juárez that night for dinner. He might even convince them to take a day, maybe two, for a drive to his uncle's house in Chihuahua instead, because he'd promised that so many years ago—so long ago they probably thought about somewhere else by now, like San Diego, or Los Angeles. Then he'd take them there! They'd go for a week, spend whatever it took. No expense could be so great, and if happiness was as easy as some tacos and a five-dollar bill, then how stupid it had been of him not to have offered it all this time.

Romero felt so good, felt such relief, he napped on the couch. When he woke up he immediately remembered his shirt, that it was already gone before the old man had even arrived—he remembered they'd walked around the juniper before it was cut. Nevertheless, the possibility that the old man took it wouldn't leave Romero's mind. Since he'd never believed in letting down, giving into someone like that old man, the whole experience became suspect. Maybe it was part of some ruse which ended with the old man taking his shirt, some food, money. This was how Romero thought. Though he held a hope that he'd left it somewhere else, that it was a lapse of memory on his part—he went outside, inside, looked everywhere twice, then one more time after that—his cynicism had flowered, colorful and bitter.

Understand that it was his favorite shirt, that he'd never thought of replacing it and that its loss was all Romero could keep his mind on, though he knew very well it wasn't a son, or a daughter, or a wife, or a mother or father, not a disaster of any kind. It was a simple shirt, in the true value of things not very much to lose. But understand also that Romero was a good man who tried to do what was right and who would harm no one willfully. Understand that Romero was a man who had taught himself to not care, to not want, to not desire for so long that he'd lost many words, avoided many people, kept to himself, alone, almost always, even when his wife gave him his meals. Understand that it was his favorite shirt and though no more than that, for him it was no less. Then understand how he felt like a fool paying that old man who, he considered, might even have taken it, like a fool for feeling so friendly and generous, happy, when the shirt was already gone, like a fool for having all those and these thoughts for the love of a wool shirt, like a fool for not being able to stop thinking them all, but especially the one reminding him that this was what he had always believed in, that loss was what he was most prepared for. And so then you might understand why he began to stare out the window of his home, waiting for someone to walk by absently with it on, for the thief to pass by, careless. He kept a watch out the window as each of his children came in, then his wife. He told them only what had happened and, as always, they left him alone. He stared out that window onto the dirt street, past the ocotillos and nopales and agaves, the junipers and oaks and mulberries in front of other homes of brick or stone, painted or not, past them to the buildings in Juárez, and he watched the horizon darken and the sky light up with the moon and stars, and the land spread with shimmering lights, so bright in the dark blot of night. He heard dogs barking until another might bark farther away, and then another, back and forth like that, the small rectangles and squares of their fences plotted out distinctly in his mind's eye as his lids closed. Then he heard a gust of wind bend around his house, and then came the train, the metal rhythm getting closer until it was as close as it could be, the steel pounding the earth like a beating heart, until it diminished and then faded away and then left the air to silence, to its quiet and dark, so still it was like death, or rest, sleep, until he could hear a grackle, and then another gust of wind, and then finally a car.

He looked in on his daughter still so young, so beautiful, becoming a woman who would leave that bed for another, his sons still boys when they were asleep, who dreamed like men when they were awake, and his wife, still young in his eyes in the morning shadows of their bed.

Romero went outside. The juniper had been cut just as he'd wanted it. He got cold and came back in and went to the bed and blankets his wife kept so clean, so neatly arranged as she slept under them without him, and he lay down beside her.

GOOD ROCKIN' TONIGHT

WILLIAM HAUPTMAN

From Good Rockin' Tonight,
Bantam Books, New York, 1988

The year Elvis died was a strange year, and I remember it not only because of what happened to my brother, Bubba, but because that was the year we had our first transsexual here in Nortex. Bobby Joe Pitts, who worked for Builders' Supply, told the wife and kids he still loved them, but he couldn't stand it any longer: He'd always felt like a woman in a man's body and wanted to go to Houston for a sex-change operation.

He'd been saving money for years in a secret account and was all ready to go through with it. But the doctor in Houston was cautious. He told Bobby Joe he should try wearing women's clothes for six months before the operation, since there would be no going back. So Bobby Joe came to our church, First Methodist, looking something like Mary Tyler Moore. His family took it hard. The preacher suggested, after the services, that he go to the Unitarian church instead, where they took homosexuals and drug addicts. Bobby Joe stormed out, saying we were hypocrites and had no spirit of Christian love.

The first nice day rolled around, he was out at Skyline Country Club, just like every other year, for his eighteen holes of Saturday morning golf. Harley Otis told me when I walked into the locker room. Said Bobby Joe expected to play in the club tournament, but against the women. Harley was disgusted. "I guess it had to happen here," he said, snorting and throwing his shoes all the way across the room, where they hit the big picture of Arnold Palmer on the locker room wall.

I felt sorry for Bobby Joe and went out to where he was teeing off alone. He said he was no different from that doctor who became a lady tennis pro. "They're just threatened," he said primly. About that time, Harley drove past in his electric cart and shouted out, asking Bobby Joe if he was for the ERA. Bobby Joe shot him the finger.

That night I sat on my patio, drinking Jack Daniel's and looking up at the stars. Through the sliding glass doors, I could see my wife watching her favorite program. Hell, I could see Bobby Joe's point of view. I might like being a woman myself if I looked like Mary Tyler Moore. Trouble was, I wouldn't; and neither would Bobby Joe. I doubted any amount of plastic surgery could do the trick. My wife, alone there in the den, laughed at something on television, and I felt like a ghost. I decided the world was changing so fast nobody could keep up with it.

I'm a doctor myself, obstetrics and gynecology, and I've got a little office across the street from the hospital. Who should come see me the next day but my old high school sweetheart, Nadine MacAfee, whom I'd seen no more than two or three times in all the years since graduation. But my heart still stopped when I saw her there in the reception room.

In my office, she told me she'd like to get off the pill and try some other form of contraception. She dropped hints about her loneliness and talked nostalgically about the days when we'd gone steady; and I soon realized she was looking for romance. I was so nervous I thought I was going to stammer for the first time in years, and resorted to a trick the speech therapist had taught me: flipping my pencil up and catching it, not thinking too much about what I was saying.

"Look, Nadine," I said finally, "if it's all the same, I'd rather not examine you. But I can recommend another doctor."

"That's all right, Ross," she said. "I understand."

She had once been so shy, and this was a pretty bold thing for her to do. But I had never gone all the way with Nadine in high school and I wasn't about to now. I wanted to keep her the way she was in my memory—full of innocence and mystery. So I took out the bottle I keep in my desk drawer, we had a drink, and I got her talking about her kids, my pencil flipping just like old Johnny Carson's.

When I showed her out, my brother, Bubba, who was a big wheel with the Prudential Insurance Company, was sitting in the reception room with a long face on. When I asked him what was wrong, he told me Elvis had died and we had to celebrate his passing away. "The King is gone," he said, "and nobody will ever replace him." I sent the rest of my patients home.

I hadn't known Elvis was so important to my brother, but then I really didn't know Bubba anymore. We played golf now and then, but our wives hated each other, which seems to be the rule, not the exception; so we never saw each other socially, not at all.

We drove out to a bar in the new shopping mall, where neither of us had ever been. Thank God It's Friday's it was called, and I think it was supposed to look like Greenwich Village.

"What the hell has happened here?" my brother said.

"How do you mean, Bubba?"

"What's happened to this town? Why is everyone pretending they're in New York City?"

"I don't know, Bubba; I guess it's television."

To me, the whole shopping mall was a depressing place. Nobody had been able to rest until we got one, just like every other town. There must have been a thousand editorials in the paper about it. On the way in, we'd passed droves of sad-looking teenagers hanging out around the fountain, and I'd thought how much happier we looked out at the Pioneer Drive-In, in our cars. But everyone was proud of the mall as they could be, and who was wrong, them or me?

Harley Otis was there, right in the thick of it, wearing polyester pants, white loafers with gold chains, a leather jacket, and a Dacron shirt with the collar spread out on his shoulders. There was also a little gold chain around his neck.

"Who you tryin' to look like, Harley?" my brother asked. "The Six Million Dollar Man?"

Harley took it as a compliment and started telling us how he'd just gotten back from a Successful Life course in Dallas where he'd learned the importance of a Positive Mental Attitude. "You've got to set goals for yourself," he said.

"What's your goal, Harley?"

"Right now, I'm buckin' for president of Kiwanis. But my immediate goal is to get into Tina Eubank's pants."

I looked over and there was Tina, twice divorced, standing by the jukebox. It didn't look like he'd have too much trouble. "Y'all have a nice day," Harley said, and slid toward her.

Then we drove out the Fort Worth Highway, my brother talking about everything he hated, from women's lib to *People* magazine. I hadn't seen him like this for years. There had been a time, when I was in med school and my brother was driving a truck, when he developed all sorts of theories about why this country was going to pieces. He also claimed to have seen UFOs and talked to them on his CB. I finally diagnosed the problem when I discovered he was taking "L.A. turnarounds"—those biphetamine capsules truckers use on long hauls. Once he started working for the Prudential, he settled down and that side of him disappeared.

But now he was driving too fast and talking crazy, like he used to; looking around at everything and not liking what he saw. Just then, I heard a siren and saw flashing blue lights, and a highway patrol car pulled us over.

It was Floyd Simms, whom I hadn't seen in maybe fifteen years. "Could I see your operator's license?" he asked, all business, holding his metal clipboard.

"It's Bubba Moody, Floyd."

"You were exceeding a posted speed limit of fifty-five miles per hour, and it looks to me like you got alcoholic beverages in the car."

"Floyd, don't you remember? We took shop together."

"Yeah, I remember. But shitfire, Bubba, you were driving like a bat."

"Floyd, Elvis died today."

"I heard."

"My brother and I are drinking to his memory. Don't give me the cold shoulder, Floyd. Have a drink with us and let's remember all the good and bad old days."

"Well, I do get off duty in half an hour," Floyd said, looking across the car at me and grinning. "That really you, Ross?"

Then the three of us went out to the old colored man's place. It was my brother's idea. You could have knocked me over with a stick when I saw it was still there, the little redbrick building with the sign that said HOT PIT COOKED BAR-B-QUE.

The old man himself, who had a big stomach and a pencil mustache (Fats Domino, we had called him), opened the counterweighted lid of the stove. Inside was at least a chine of beef. He cut off slabs and put them on bread. Then he added half a green onion and a wedge of longhorn cheese and wrapped it all in butcher paper.

We carried our sandwiches to a table, and the other customers, all colored (black, I corrected myself), sort of looked at us without looking at us, for Floyd still wore his highway patrol uniform; then got up and left, dropping their trash in the garbage can on the way out.

"See, big brother?" Bubba said. "The past is still here, all around us."

I couldn't take my eyes off my sandwich. It sat there on the tabletop, which was bare except for a Louisiana Hot Sauce bottle full of toothpicks. Grease spotted the butcher paper. I took a bite and it ran down my chin. Lord, it was good.

Bubba returned from the cooler with three bottles of Royal Crown Cola, the old-style bottles with the yellow pyramids on them. "Look at that," he said softly, staring at his bottle. "Would you look at that?" Then he drank it.

"What are you up for, Floyd?" he said.

"My wife's going to be wondering where I am," Floyd said, and when Bubba gave him a sour look, added, "Shitfire, Bubba, there's a good program on tonight. About Vince Lombardi."

I nodded. "My wife's not home. Tonight's her yoga class. Y'all could come over and watch it." What was I saying "y'all" for? I hadn't said "y'all" in years.

"What's so important about Vince Lombardi?" Bubba said. "You never knew him. A night like this comes once in a lifetime, and tonight the three of us are going to the Cotton Bowling Palace."

So we drove on down to the long, low building on Holiday Creek, full of the odor of paste wax and the thunder of balls; and the same people were there who had always been there, roughnecks and refinery workers and railroad brakemen. I was clumsy at first, dropping the ball on the lane with a thud; but Bubba was greasing them in right off. We didn't bother to keep score. None of us could remember how. We just bowled, and I relaxed, for by now the evening was lost, anyway, watching Bubba cut up, bowling like Don Carter, and so forth. He could always impersonate anyone he wanted. Mom said his version of me was deadly. When he came over and dropped down beside me in one of the green plastic chairs, I felt a stab of brotherhood and socked him on the arm, the way I would have in the old days.

"Hey, Bubba," I said. "You old son of a bitch."

"You're not sorry you're not home watching the life of old Vince Lombardi?"

"No, Bubba. I genuinely enjoyed this night."

"Life is a road."

"Yes, Bubba. Life is a road." I waited for him to finish, so drunk the bowling balls sounded like they were rolling through my head.

"Once I thought I knew who I was and where I was going. I could see the road ahead. But I lost my way."

Floyd was out on the lane, yelling. A pin had fallen outside the gate, and when nobody appeared to help, he walked up the lane, slipping and falling down, and got it himself. People were laughing at him.

"There was only one person of our time who never stopped. Who became the person he dreamed of becoming."

"Who's that?"

"Elvis," my brother said.

Do you know what he did then? He stepped up to the booth where you got your shoes and where they called your number when your lane was ready. He grabbed the microphone away from the fat lady who was sitting there and sang "Love Me Tender" to her. It started as a joke, but this was the day Elvis had died, and when he finished, the place was dead quiet. Then everyone applauded and started shouting, "More, more," and I was shouting, too. And he did sound exactly like Elvis, although I never thought he looked like him at all. I thought he looked more like Conway Twitty.

***

One year later to the day, I was riding down Highway 82 in a white Cadillac Eldorado. The oil-well pumping jacks nodded in the fields, the blacktop shimmered in the heat, and in the front seat was my brother Bubba, wearing a white jump suit with silver studs, his hair dyed black. The sign on the side of the car read:

EL TEX AS
BUBBA MOODY KING OF ROCK AND ROLL
NORTEX' OWN ELVIS

Floyd Simms was driving, wearing Las Vegas shades and the Robert Hall suit Bubba had bought him at the Hub Clothing Store.

Bubba had done better than I would have believed, perfecting his act at Kiwanis and Rotary dances. He'd also done benefits for the crippled and retarded children, which people liked, and borrowed enough money to lease this Eldorado just like the one Elvis had. Now we were on our way to the first stop on Bubba's summer tour, which was to end at Six Flags Over Texas. There was to be a convention of Elvis Presley impersonators, and Bubba intended to prove he was the best in the world.

"This is the life, isn't it?" he said, looking back at me and grinning. "Man, sometimes I feel so good I've got to go out and take a walk through K-Mart to bring myself down."

We stopped at the Cow Lot in Nocona, where Bubba bought a pair of ostrich-hide boots and gave the owner an eight-by-ten autographed glossy photo, which he thumbtacked on the wall next to the photos of Willie Nelson, Arthur Godfrey, Howard Hughes, and all the other celebrities who, down through the years, had bought Nocona boots.

When we got back in the car, Bubba said, "Floyd, I think I'm going to ask you to dye your hair red so I can call you Red West." That was Elvis's bodyguard. Bubba really wanted to make the act authentic.

We came to a billboard that said we were eight miles from Decatur, home of Dico Sausage, and showed a pair of rolling dice. "Pull over, Floyd," Bubba said.

He struck a karate pose in front of the billboard and Floyd took his picture with the Polaroid Swinger. I was getting back in the car when I heard a buzz just like an electric alarm clock going off.

"Christ, Bubba, what the hell you doing?" Floyd said. Bubba had picked up a baby rattlesnake out of the ditch and was making like he was going to kiss it, holding it inches away from his lips.

"Get a picture, get a picture," he shouted, laughing like an idiot.

We drove on through more North Texas and finally into Decatur, where a banner across the street proclaimed Bubba's show. "The King is here," my brother said.

Floyd parked and we walked into the high school, across the street from the red-granite courthouse. The band was already setting up. Down in the dressing room, Bubba put on his makeup and I sat on a box of textbooks in the corner and watched. Already you could hear people filling the auditorium upstairs. "Sounds like a good crowd," Bubba said, gluing on his fake sideburns.

Then a local disc jockey appeared with a tape recorder and Miss Billie Tucker, president of Bubba's North Texas fan club. She'd brought along a list she'd compiled of characteristics Bubba and Elvis had in common. The disc jockey held up his microphone and she read it, perspiration on her upper lip.

"Both Elvis and Bubba are Capricorns," she said. "Both were truck drivers, both stationed with the army in Germany, and both were devoted to their mothers. Both are overweight, both like Cadillac Eldorados, and both like to stay up all night. Both have fantastic sex appeal . . ."

Good Lord, I thought. These people are serious.

Upstairs, I found myself in an ordinary high school auditorium. There were flags of the United States and Texas on either side of the stage. The ceiling was high, yellowish globes shedding a dim light. Probably the Pledge of Allegiance had been said here thousands of times. Tonight it was full of more middle-aged women than I'd ever seen in one place, and the clicking of high heels and pocketbooks was a constant roar.

Then the house lights went down and it got dead silent. The curtain rose in the darkness and a spotlight stabbed down and my brother leaped into it. He tore into "Heartbreak Hotel" like a man possessed. My brother, who had been good, had gotten better. Maybe he really was the best. He had all the moves down, and from this distance it made no difference at all that he wasn't a carbon copy of Elvis.

He sang "Blue Suede Shoes" and "Don't Be Cruel" and "Jailhouse Rock" and spoke of the series of miracles that had brought Elvis to the top in so short a time. He said Elvis had loved black music and made a plea for integration and sang "In the Ghetto." All this time, he was throwing scarves into the audience and women were fighting for them. Then he said, "There's been a great loss of faith in this country. Maybe it was Nixon, maybe Vietnam. I voted for Nixon, but he betrayed us. He thought he could get away with fooling us rednecks." He looked around, his face incandescent in the spotlight. "That's right. I'm a redneck. So are you. And so was Elvis. We're the people who kept the faith."

There was more, but I don't really remember all he said; and he didn't write it down, he spoke right from the heart. He asked for a moment of silence for the boys who had died in Vietnam, and sang "How Great Thou Art." Then he ripped right into "Hound Dog" and disappeared without an encore. The lights came up and we were back in that shabby little auditorium with flags on either side of the stage.

The audience went wild, like they'd just woke up, and I ran downstairs to Bubba's dressing room, where you could hear them stomping on the floor overhead.

Then Floyd said, "Here come the autograph hounds," and opened the door and they poured in. Bubba signed his own glossies as fast as they could shove them at him, and pretty soon a woman grabbed his gold chain and tore it right off his neck.

"We'd better get out of here, Bubba," Floyd said, and we shoved through the crowd. But they had our way blocked and we had to detour into the girls' rest room. Bubba was still laughing, but to tell the truth I was scared. We climbed out the window and ran across the parking lot, where someone from the band was waiting in the Eldorado. We all piled in and drove off, a crowd of women following us all the way to the corner.

"They shoulda had cops there," Bubba said after a while. "I told them we'd need cops. Floyd, you'd better start packing a rod. You're gonna need it if there's any more crowd scenes like this."

At Six Flags, Bubba demolished the other Elvis impersonators. What surprised me was how many there were. They came in all shapes and sizes, and one had come from as far away as Nebraska. There was only one who was serious competition: Claude Thibodeaux, from New Iberia, Louisiana, who billed himself as the Cajun Elvis. He had flash, but nobody could beat Bubba for sheer impact.

Right after his performance, Bubba was approached by someone who wanted to manage him. Elvis Presley's manager, as everyone knows, was Colonel Tom Parker. This was Bud Parker, late a colonel in the U.S. Air Force. The coincidence tickled them both. He promised Bubba in one year he'd be playing Caesar's Palace in Las Vegas.

I was packing my suitcase when Bubba came into my room and said, "Big brother, you and me are going to Houston."

"What for?"

"Looka here at this telegram."

The telegram was from Nancy Jo Miller, who'd been Bubba's

high school love. She was married now and lived in Houston. She said she'd read about his act, congratulated him, and hoped they could get together sometime.

Sometimes my brother dumbfounded me. But I couldn't say no, and anyway, he was paying for the tickets. So instead of going home, we flew to Houston on Trans Texas, got a rented car and a room at the Holiday Inn.

Nancy Jo lived in a $200,000 brick colonial on the edge of Houston, with pine trees growing in the front yard. Bubba had this idea he wanted to drop in and surprise her, so we didn't phone ahead. He slipped on his shades and I rang the doorbell. I felt sorry for Bubba: He was as nervous as a kid on his first date.

Just for a moment I saw Nancy Jo as she really was, a little faded around the eyes and mouth. But the years had been good to her. I suppose you could say she resembled Angie Dickinson— which, in a way, was a hell of a lot better than she'd looked in high school.

"Oh, my Lord," she said, when she saw Bubba in his white Elvis jump suit, and gave a short, embarrassed laugh that was cut off as if by a knife. Then she said, "I'll make y'all bloody marys," and disappeared into the kitchen.

"This was a mistake," Bubba said. He was trembling so hard I had to hold him up.

Nancy Jo came back and we sat in the tiny front room with the big picture window, which I knew was almost never used except for guests. What with the baby grand piano and the big sofa and the glass-topped coffee table, there was hardly room for the three of us; but from the first, I don't even think they knew I was there. They were totally absorbed in each other. She poured out the story of all that had happened since they'd seen each other last, and I stared at the celery stalk in my bloody mary and tried not to listen.

Nancy Jo had intended to marry Bubba, but he had to do his army service, and there seemed to be all the time in the world; so she went to Dallas and enrolled in stewardess school. She pictured herself wearing that cute uniform and doing favors for the passengers, bringing them pillows and playing with their kids.

She lived with some other stews on Gaston Avenue, and there were some pretty wild parties; but Nancy Jo locked herself in her room and did crossword puzzles and wrote love letters to Bubba.

It was the airplane that did her in. The other stews hung out in the galley, where you could meet pro football players and rich oilmen. Nancy Jo didn't want a rich oilman: She was going to have Bubba. So she fought it.

But the airplane was the most boring place in the world. The kids were snotty and their parents were cross and didn't appreciate the favors you did for them. There was nothing to do but look out the window, and when you did, what did you see? Clouds.

In the end, she went to the galley, which was like a nickel-plated singles bar, so tiny you couldn't turn around without bumping into some horny guy. There she met Calvin Sloate, a corporate lawyer for Texaco; and they drank Scotch out of tiny bottles while the galley roared like a sea shell, rocking slightly in the rough air 20,000 feet over Indianapolis.

"I'm sorry, Bubba," she said. "But you were going to be in the army for another year and that seemed like forever. I had to get off that airplane." So she had married Calvin, and now seventeen years had flashed by like nothing at all.

"We've got a condo in Vero," she said, "and one in Aspen, and last year we went skiing at Sundance and Lisa had her picture taken with Robert Redford."

"Lisa?" Bubba asked in a flat voice.

"My daughter," she said, showing us another picture. "That's her with her Arabian stallion. She loves horses."

She showed us the rest of the house. We stood for a moment at the door of Calvin's study, like visitors at a museum looking into one of those rooms closed off with a velvet rope. Calvin had a collection of beer cans, one from every country in the world; a pair of expensive shotguns; and a lampshade made of *Playboy* center-folds. I had already noticed his radar-equipped bass boat in the driveway.

In the bedroom, she slid back the closet door and showed us her $500 Italian shoes. Bubba just looked at her and said, "You know you broke my heart, don't you?"

"Oh, Bubba, don't say that. It sounds so horrible. And, anyway, how could I know you cared that much? Look here."

She took from under her costly shoes the old high school year-book; and there, on the same page, were their pictures. Their faces were soft and unformed but shining with a sort of light. Bubba had a flattop with "fenders"—long on the sides and short on the top. Over his face he had written, in blue ballpoint pen: "Had a lot of good times with you and hope to see more of you next year. Bubba."

"Couldn't you have said more than that?" she asked, tears in her eyes. "How was I to know I was so important to you?"

"In those days," Bubba said, "you won the game of love by pretending you didn't care. Yeah, that's all we thought love was, a game. But it turned out to be a more serious game than we thought."

At this point I left the room, phoned a cab, and went back to the Holiday Inn. I don't think they missed me. It rained, and there I spent the rest of the afternoon watching *Return to Earth*, a TV movie about the life of an astronaut, and drinking Jack Daniel's. Later, Bubba came back. "Well, big brother," he said, "-it's all settled. She's leaving her husband and I'm leaving my wife, and everything's going to be like it was." He'd been walking around in the rain and his clothes were soaked.

But I was skeptical that Bubba could so easily turn back the clock. Now that he'd become a star, he thought anything was possible. To me, he was like that astronaut who'd achieved his boyhood dream and went to the moon; but sooner or later, he had to come back down to earth and be an ordinary person like the rest of us. On the plane home, Bubba turned to me and said, "Big brother, I'm going to tell you something. You're the only one who'll understand."

"Yes, Bubba?"

"My whole life, I've felt like I was in the wrong body or something. But when I'm Elvis . . . I got it right. I'm the person I should have been, the person I've always known I could be."

Now it struck me that this was what Bobby Joe Pitts, the would-be transsexual, had said. Like Bubba, he only felt like himself when he was somebody else.

"Do you know what I'm saying?" Bubba whispered, holding my shoulder in an iron grip.

Yes, I knew. At the best moments of my life—when I hit a good golf shot or had a woman I adored—I felt like someone else. A version of me, maybe, but a version that was to Ross Moody what a Cadillac Eldorado was to a Ford Pinto. I doubted you could totally become that perfect version of yourself. Bubba felt that way now, but he could not be El Tex As for the rest of his life.

But that was the happiest I ever saw Bubba. On this flight, we had, instead of a stewardess, a male flight attendant. Ordinarily, Bubba would have made some sarcastic comment; but on that day, he seemed at peace with himself. I slept most of the way, but once I woke up. Bubba, in the hollow roar of the cabin, was looking through the porthole and smiling down at the dark world below.

When he broke the news to his wife, Jan, she knew just how to take it: like Jill Clayburgh in that movie about the New York woman, nodding, her eyes closed, finishing his sentences for him.

"And so," he said, "I am going to—"

"Move out. All right, buster, go ahead. Do yourself a big favor."

They were standing in the den, and she poked through the big glass bowl on top of the television set full of matchbooks from every restaurant they'd ever been to.

"You'd just better get yourself a good lawyer," she told him.

The strange thing, he said, was that she seemed almost glad. Here it was, the crisis predicted so often. Now she would learn to think for herself and be happy (like Rhoda once she got rid of that slob, Joe), maybe even write a book. The possibilities were endless.

"There is one more thing," Bubba said. "Here is a list of our close friends whom I do not want you to sleep with, as they would be laughing at me behind my back."

"Thank you," she said. "I know just what to do with it."

She slept with the first one, Bubba's boss at the Prudential, that very night; and spent the rest of the week working her way down the list.

Nancy Jo also left Calvin Sloate but, on the advice of a girlfriend, went to a therapist, and the first thing he did was tell her not to make any more sudden moves.

She phoned Bubba and said, "I'm living in an apartment complex with plastic ivy on the walls. There's nobody here but kids; and my lawyer says I won't get any kind of settlement, since I moved out. Bubba, I'm having second thoughts."

So Bubba sped down to Houston, even though he was starting another tour in a few days. Nancy Jo wouldn't see him right away: She had to look through her appointment book and set a date. When they finally got together, all she would do was talk for hours. She had a whole new vocabulary and she wouldn't drink bloody marys anymore, just white wine and something called Amaretto, which Bubba said tasted like Log Cabin syrup.

She was changing, slipping away; but Bubba was desperate to prove he could accept her under any conditions. He went to see her therapist himself and even took her to a Woody Allen movie.

* * *

I didn't see Bubba for months. At the end of his tour, he phoned from Abilene and asked if I'd come down. I found him that night at the Cross Plains Motel, a real dump.

His appearance shocked me: He'd gained maybe forty pounds. He said, "Did you bring your little black bag?"

"Yeah. What for?"

"You got any speed in it?"

I was offended and told him to forget it. He said it was hard for him to keep his weight down, being on the road and all and eating nothing but junk food. But I wouldn't be talked into it. Then I went right into the john and flushed all my pills down the toilet.

When I came back out, Bubba was talking to Floyd, who had his hair dyed red. I sat down and noticed my chair had a Rocking R brand on the arm. It was Roy Rogers furniture, probably bought for some kid thirty years ago, and it had ended up here in this terrible motel. For the first time, I glimpsed the sadness singers talk about of being on the road, and thought it was getting to Bubba.

Floyd said he had a girl for Bubba. "Tell her I'll meet her in one hour," Bubba said. "The usual conditions."

The conditions under which Bubba met his fans were these: They had to be between the ages of thirty-five and forty-five, they had to provide their own car, and they had to park on a dirt road on the edge of town. When Bubba appeared in the Eldorado, they flashed their lights if it was safe. Then Bubba parked and came ahead on foot, bringing his own bottle.

I thought this was a foolish, adolescent thing to do, and told him so.

"You know, big brother," he said, "I feel sorry for you. You been fooling around with women's private parts for so long you've forgotten what they're for."

Like everything Bubba said, there was some truth to this. In my years as a gynecologist, I'd examined most of the girls I'd worshipped in high school, and it meant less than nothing to me. It made me wonder about my choice of profession.

"When are you playing Las Vegas?" I asked him.

"Colonel Parker says I'm not ready for Vegas. I need one more thing to put me over the top—plastic surgery, so I'm identical to Elvis. 'Course, there'll be no goin' back—but it's worth it if it gets me to Caesar's Palace."

"No," I said. "No, Bubba. You can't do that."

"Why not?"

I couldn't exactly say, but I was thinking: If he loses his face, he loses himself.

"Bobby Joe Pitts decided not to," I said.

"Bobby Joe Pitts?"

"You know. The plastic surgeon told him he should try living like a woman. Well he joined a women's group, and now he's changed his mind. He says he thought men were boring, but women have the most boring conversations in the world."

This got my brother furious. "Are you comparing me to some miserable little pervert? Christ, Bobby Joe . . . why, he wore a brassiere under his football jersey the whole senior year. And we thought he was joking!"

"Will Nancy Jo love you if you don't have your own face?"

He took a pistol out of the desk drawer, a Colt Python, and spun it around his finger and said, "Nancy Jo doesn't know what she wants. Last time I talked to her, she said she wanted space. I said, 'Hell, you can have all the space you want, once we're married.'" He aimed the pistol at the television screen, where Elvis was singing to Ann-Margret. It was a reshowing of *Viva Las Vegas* on cable TV.

"His voice sorta went to pieces, didn't it?" Bubba said. "Frankly, I think I'm better now than he ever was."

"Bubba, put down that gun."

"Come on," he said. "I'm going to get some nooky."

So Floyd drove us out to the edge of town, where we parked on a dirt road and could see ahead, dimly, the outline of another car.

"She's not flashing her lights," Floyd said. "It must not be safe yet."

I rolled down the window. There was a full moon that night and I thought I could hear the distant yip of coyotes.

When I mentioned it, Floyd said, "Ain't no more coyotes in this county. Farmers wiped them out with traps and poisoned bait."

Still, I thought I could hear them, as I had on so many nights when we'd driven out on Red River Road.

"Do you have to do this, Bubba? What about Nancy Jo?"

"A man's got to get his satisfaction. And if you can't be near the one you love, love the one you're near."

The headlights of the other car flashed.

Bubba opened the door.

"Don't go, Bubba."

"You know, big brother," he said, "you ought to come with me. It would do you good to see how those ladies give me all that good X-rated sex they been holding out on their husbands all these years." He came around and opened my door. "Just stand outside and listen. She won't mind. Thrill to the days of yesteryear, big brother. Come along with me and I'll show you how good that low-rent lovin' can still be."

And, God help me, I did. My heart was pounding, but I stepped out of the car and followed my brother down the road in the moonlight.

"You know, Bubba, you are a devil. You have the damnedest way of getting people to do what you want."

"Don't I know it?"

"You were right about me being a gynecologist and all. Somehow, I lost interest in women. It just slipped away from me like everything else."

"The things closest to you go first," he said. "They slip away so softly you don't notice. You wake up one morning the stranger in a strange land."

"You're right," I said. "But women are . . . everything."

"Yea, verily, good buddy."

"Sex may be the secret of American life. In fact, I see now . . ."

But I don't know what I saw, for what happened next drove everything out of my head. The headlights of the car came on, blinding us, and we heard a male voice say, "Try to screw my wife, will you, you sons of bitches! I'll kill you!" Then a shotgun went off and I heard the shot rip through the air right over our heads. The car was rolling toward us and Bubba and I were running back down the road.

"The fence, big brother," Bubba shouted, "hit for the fence." And I dove under it, the barbed wire tearing the coat right off my back. Then we were stumbling through the prickly pear, the shotgun still going off and one pellet stinging the back of my neck like a yellow jacket.

Bubba grabbed me and threw me down. The car stopped and a spotlight probed around until it found us. Bubba leaped up, his fists balled, a foolhardy, magnificent sight. I thought: This is the end of your life, Ross.

Then we heard Floyd laughing and barking like a dog. "Come out, come out, wherever you are, Elvis."

It was all a big joke.

Bubba picked up a clod and threw it at the car, but Floyd only laughed harder. The band had been in on it—I could hear them laughing, too. My face was scratched and my palms were full of cactus thorns, and I could feel cold air on my back where my jacket had been ripped off.

Bubba climbed over the fence and threw himself at Floyd. They circled in the headlights, Bubba throwing wild punches and Floyd dodging them, shouting, "Shitfire and save matches, Bubba. Can't you take a joke?"

"Joke! We coulda been hurt running around in that god-damned cactus patch."

"Oh, hell, you're just pissed off 'cause we pulled that same trick on you in high school. I never thought you'd be stupid enough to fall for it twice."

That stopped Bubba. "All right," he said. "So I did. But this time it wasn't funny. We're grown men now, not high school kids."

Floyd kept laughing.

"All right, Floyd, you're fired. That's right. I'm giving you notice."

Somebody from the band stepped forward and said he thought Bubba was being too harsh, and Bubba fired him, too. He looked around and said, "Anybody else?"

Then everybody said it was fine with them; they were getting fed up with Bubba, anyway. There were some bitter words. It ended up with us going back to the motel and them going off to a honky-tonk to get drunk.

On the way back, Bubba began wondering where he was going to get another band. His troubles were multiplying and he said, "Maybe I should just shoot myself."

"Don't talk that way, Bubba."

At the motel, the television was still on, nothing showing on the screen now but snow. I went into the bathroom, threw my torn jacket in the trash can, and started putting iodine on the scratches on my face. The shot lifted me right off the floor.

He was sitting on the bed, holding the pistol. The television was exploded, a bullet through the picture tube. "I always wanted to know how he felt when he did that," Bubba said. "Now I know."

Things went downhill fast after that. My brother never found another band. The bookings dried up and Colonel Parker lost interest. The IRS was now investigating Bubba's income taxes, and in the middle of it all he got a Dear John letter from Nancy Jo saying she'd fallen in love with her psychiatrist.

He went down to Houston with the idea of confronting her but, instead, went to Calvin Sloate's house. Calvin himself answered the door and Bubba said, "I'm the son of a bitch who ran off with your wife."

"I know," Calvin said. "You're Bubba Moody. Come on in and let's let it all hang out."

Bubba, feeling numb all over, walked into Lisa's room. She was lying on her bed under a John Travolta poster.

"Your mother doesn't love me anymore," he said.

"I know. I think she's making a big mistake."

"You're the closest thing to her, the way she once was," Bubba said. "You're beautiful."

"Thanks, Bubba. I like your looks, too."

"Will you marry me?"

"Are you serious?"

"Dead serious," he said, and kissed her on her teenage lips.

When he turned around, Calvin was standing in the door.

Bubba phoned from Houston and said he'd been shot in the leg. It was nothing serious—Calvin had used a .22 target pistol. Before I left, I went over to tell Jan, who'd just gotten back from a trip to Las Vegas with Harley Otis. When I got there, she was gluing silver dollars to the top of the coffee table.

"Look here at all the money I won," she said. "Seems like my luck just won't quit."

When she heard about Bubba, she said, "That's his problem. All that's behind me now. I'm starting over."

She disappeared into the kitchen and I was left alone with the television. Tom Snyder was interviewing a judge in California who'd started divorcing fifty people in a group. There were no lawyers required, he just asked everyone if they had irreconcilable differences. When they said they did, he pronounced them divorced and they headed for the door. The men moved slowly, but the women were smiling and hopeful, and I thought how much better women seemed to adjust to modern life. "So would you say this is . . . the coming thing?" Tom Snyder asked, and the judge said it was.

"Notice anything different?" she said, coming back into the room.

"No. Is your hair shorter?"

She told me she'd had silicone injections. "Come on, Ross, you know my breasts always drooped."

"No, Jan. I've never noticed."

She put down her glass of white wine and lay on the floor. "See? They're nice and hard. They're the same standing up or laying down. They're just like doorknobs."

"I honestly can't tell the difference, Jan."

She leaned so close I could feel her breath on my cheek. "Go ahead and put your hand on them. I don't mind. Feel the difference for yourself."

I excused myself and drove home, the whole side of my face burning like I'd stood too close to a hot stove.

So Bubba never got his plastic surgery or a trip to Las Vegas (although his wife did). He ended up driving a truck again, but to me he seemed happier, and I found I enjoyed knowing him more than I had since we were kids. He still, however, had his problems with the IRS, and one night, in the dead of that winter, he tapped on my patio doors. We sat outside, in the darkness, while my wife watched *Family Feud*. (She seemed to draw strength from that program: She never missed it.)

"The government lawyers are coming Monday," Bubba said, "and I'm liable to do a couple of years in prison."

I told him I'd lend him money, but he said after the divorce he couldn't face going to court again.

"Let's take one last ride out Red River Road," he said, "in case I never see it again."

So we took a six-pack and drove out and parked on the edge of town, where the pumping jacks rose and fell in the fields on either side.

"You know," he said, "Elvis himself couldn't make it today. Everything today glorifies the loser, the person who can't help himself. Someone like me doesn't stand a chance. Yeah, it's the decade of the loser; and it's the losers who did me in. Come on, big brother, let's go ride those pumping jacks."

So we did. He could always talk me into anything. He sat on one end and I on the other, hanging on for dear life, and we rose and fell like two kids on a gigantic seesaw.

"Well, if that's the way this country's going to be," he shouted over the roar of the diesel, "they can have it. I want no part of it. I'll go right on, trying to do the impossible. Look, big brother," he said, reaching over his head as the pumping jack rose, "I can touch the moon."

Then he fell off. I thought he was dead. But he groaned and threw up in the weeds, and I cleaned him off as best I could.

"We'd better go home, Bubba," I said.

"He never died," Bubba said. "Not really."

"He did die, Bubba. Of a heart attack. We've all got to get older and die."

"No, big brother. I'll let you in on a secret. You and I are going to be the first people in history who don't."

The men from the IRS came on Monday, but Bubba was gone. Floyd, who was now back with the highway patrol, found his truck parked by the side of the road near Electra. There'd been lots of UFO sightings the night before. A farmer near Bowie found his cows dead, emptied out; nothing left of them but horns, hooves, and hide, and not a drop of blood on the ground, either. The lights of Bubba's truck were still on, and his CB radio, the key turned to SEND. Floyd found one footprint in the sandy soil just the other side of the fence, apparently headed for a strange depression in the ground, where all the grass was dead. It made the front page of the papers, and the sermon that Sunday was "A Close Encounter with Your God."

***

Then things got more or less back to normal here in Nortex. Bobby Joe Pitts started a marriage counseling service. He saw himself as someone who'd known the problem from both sides, a sort of Kissinger in the war between the sexes. Harley Otis got a divorce and married Jan, but it wasn't long before she showed up at Stolen Hours, a new bar for housewives where they could drink all afternoon, watch the soaps, and perhaps have a casual affair. Floyd forgot his grudge against Bubba and we spent several nights talking about all that had happened. "I'll tell you one thing," he said. "Your brother was the most remarkable person ever born around here."

In October, I finally made love to Nadine MacAfee. But we both discovered that what we had looked forward to for so long took only moments to do, and naturally this was a disappointment. We parted friends, but it confirmed my idea that the past is a closed book: You don't tamper with it.

But that night I couldn't sleep, and long after they played the national anthem on television, and showed the airplane and the prayer, I was still pacing the floor and feeling like a ghost. Then the phone rang.

"Hello, big brother."

For a moment I couldn't see or speak. "I just wanted to let you know," Bubba said, "I'm still on the planet Earth. In fact, I'm in Globe, Arizona."

"It's good to hear your voice, Bubba."

"It's good to hear yours. Hey, this is great country out here. Leaving that town was the best thing I ever did." He told me he was working as a disc jockey, but he had big plans. There was an old abandoned drive-in out on the edge of town, and he was going to renovate it and call it Bubba's Fifties Burger.

"You know," he said. "Carhops on roller skates, neon lights, and on the jukebox some of that great old rock and roll."

"Better keep a low profile, Bubba. You're still a wanted man."

"Don't worry about that," he said. "The road's right out my back door. And if I have to split, well, that won't be so bad either. If there's a prettier sight than an American blacktop road goin' nowhere in the moonlight, I don't know what it is."

There was a click, then nothing but echoes along one thousand miles of telephone cable.

Well, goddamn. I took three or four shots of Jack Daniel's and did a sort of dance out there on my patio, hopping around under the stars. Then I got in the car to go tell Floyd the good news: that the King was still with us.

THE
MEXICAN GIRL

JACK KEROUAC

From On the Road
Viking, 1957

I had bought my ticket and was waiting for the L.A. bus when all of a sudden I saw the cutest little Mexican girl in slacks come cutting across my sight. She was in one of the buses that had just pulled in with a big sigh of airbrakes and was discharging passengers for a rest stop. Her breasts stuck out straight; her little thighs looked delicious; her hair was long and lustrous black; and her eyes were great blue windows with timidities inside. I wished I was on her bus. A pain stabbed my heart, as it did every time I saw a girl I loved who was going the opposite direction in this too big world. "Los Angeles coach now loading in door two," says the announcer and I get on. I saw her sitting alone. I dropped right opposite her on the other window and began scheming right off. I was so lonely, so sad, so tired, so quivering, so broken, so beat that I got up my courage, the courage necessary to approach a strange girl, and acted. Even then I had to spend five minutes beating my thighs in the dark as the bus rolled down the road. "You gotta, you gotta or you'll die! Damn fool talk to her! What's wrong with you? Aren't you tired enough of yourself by now?" And before I knew what I was doing I leaned across the aisle to her (she was trying to sleep on the seat). "Miss, would you like to use my raincoat for a pillow?" She looked up with a smile and said, "No, thank you very much." I sat back trembling; I lit a butt. I waited till she looked at me, with a sad little sidelook of love, and I got right up and leaned over her. "May I sit with you, Miss?"

"If you wish."

And this I did. "Where going?"

"L.A." I loved the way she said L.A.; I love the way everybody says L.A. on the Coast; it's their one and only golden town when all is said and done.

"That's where I'm going too!" I cried. "I'm very glad you let me sit with you, I was very lonely and I've been traveling a hell of a long time." And we settled down to telling our stories. Her story was this; she had a husband and child. The husband beat her so she left him, back at Sabinal south of Fresno, and was going to L.A. to live with her sister awhile. She left her little son with her family, who were grape pickers and lived in a shack in the vineyards. She had nothing to do but brood and get mad. I felt like putting my arms around her right away. We talked and talked. She said she loved to talk with me. Pretty soon she was saying she wished she could go to New York too. "Maybe we could!" I laughed. The bus groaned up Grapevine Pass and then we were coming down into the great sprawls of light. Without coming to any particular agreement we began holding hands, and in the same way it was mutely and beautifully and purely decided that when I got my hotel room in L.A. she would be beside me. I ached all over for her; I leaned my face in her beautiful hair. Her little shoulders drove me mad, I hugged her and hugged her. And she loved it.

"I love love," she said closing her eyes. I promised her beautiful love. I gloated over her. Our stories were told, we subsided into silence and sweet anticipatory thoughts. It was as simple as that. You could have all your Peaches and Vi's and Ruth Glenarms and Marylous and Eleanors and Carmens in this world, this was my girl and my kind of girlsoul, and I told her that. She confessed she saw me watching from the bus station bench. "I thought you was a nice college boy."

"Oh I'm a college boy!" I assured her. The bus arrived in Hollywood. In the gray dirty dawn, like the dawn Joel McCrea met Veronica Lake in the diner in the picture *Sullivan's Travels*, she slept in my lap. I looked greedily out the window; stucco houses and palms and drive-ins, the whole mad thing, the ragged promised land, the fantastic end of America. We got off the bus at Main Street which was no different than where you get off a bus in Kansas City or Chicago or Boston, redbrick, dirty, characters drifting by, trolleys grating in the hopeless dawn, the whorey smell of a big city.

And here my mind went haywire, I don't know why. I began getting foolish paranoiac visions that Teresa, or Terry, her name, was a common little hustler who worked the buses for a guy's bucks by making regular appointments like ours in L.A. where she brought the sucker first to a breakfast place, where her boy waited, and then to a certain hotel to which he had access with his gun or his whatever. I never confessed this to her. We ate breakfast and a pimp kept watching us; I fancied Terry was making secret eyes at him. I was tired and felt strange and lost in a faraway, disgusting place. The goof of terror took over my thoughts and made me act petty and cheap. "Do you know that guy?" I said.

"What guy you mean, ho-ney?" I let it drop. She was slow and hung up in everything she did; it took her a long time to eat, she chewed slowly and stared into space, and smoked a cigarette slowly, and kept talking, and I was like a haggard ghost suspicioning every move she made, thinking she was stalling for time. This was all a fit of sickness. I was sweating as we went down the

street hand in hand. Fellows kept turning and looking at us. The
first hotel we hit had a vacant room and before I knew it I was
locking the door behind me and she was sitting on the bed taking
off her shoes. I kissed her meekly. Better she'd never know. To relax our nerves I knew we needed whiskey, especially me. I ran out
and fiddled all over for twelve blocks hurrying till I found a pint
of whiskey for sale at a newsstand. I ran back all energy. Terry was
in the bathroom fixing her face. I poured one big drink in a wa-
terglass and we had slugs. Oh it was sweet and delicious and
worth my whole life and lugubrious voyage. I stood behind her at
the mirror and we danced in the bathroom that way. I began talking about my friends back East. I said, "You oughta meet a great
girl I know called Dorie. She's a sixfoot redhead. If you came to
New York she'd show you where to get work."

"Who is this sixfoot redhead?" she demanded suspiciously.
"Why do you tell me about her?" In her simple soul she couldn't
fathom my kind of glad nervous talk. I let it drop. She began to
get drunk in the bathroom.

"Come on to bed!" I kept saying.

"Sixfoot redhead, hey? And I thought you was a nice college
boy, I saw you in your nice sweater and I said to myself, 'Hmm
ain't he nice'—No! And no! And no! You have to be a goddam
pimp like all of them!"

"What in the hell are you talking about?"

"Don't stand there and tell me that sixfoot redhead ain't a
madam, 'cause I know a madam when I hear about one, and you,
you're just a pimp like all the rest of 'em I meet, everybody's a
pimp."

"Listen, Terry, I am not a pimp. I swear to you on the Bible I
am not a pimp. Why should I be a pimp. My only interest is you."

"All the time I thought I met a nice boy. I was so glad, I hugged
myself and said, 'Hmm a real nice boy instead of a damn pimp!' "

"Terry," I pleaded with all my soul, "please listen to me and
understand. I'm not a pimp, I'm just Sal Paradise, look at my wal-

let." And an hour ago I thought *she* was a hustler. How sad it was. Our minds with their store of madness had diverged. O gruesome life how I moaned and pleaded and then I got mad and realized I was pleading with a dumb little Mexican wench and I told her so; and before I knew it I picked up her red pumps and threw them at the bathroom door and told her to get out. "Go on, beat it!" I'd sleep and forget it; I had my own life; my own sad and ragged life forever. There was a dead silence in the bathroom. I took my clothes off and went to bed. Terry came out with tears of sorriness in her eyes. In her simple and funny little mind had been decided the fact that a pimp does not throw a woman's shoes against the door and does not tell her to get out. In reverent and sweet silence she took her things off and slipped her tiny body into the sheets with me. It was brown as grapes. Her hips were so narrow she couldn't bear a child without getting gashed open; a Caesarian scar crossed her poor belly. Her legs were like little sticks. She was only four-foot-ten. I made love to her in the sweetness of the weary morning. Then, two tired angels of some kind, hung up forlornly in an L.A. shelf, having found the closest and most delicious thing in life together, we fell asleep and slept till late afternoon.

For the next fifteen days we were together for better or worse. We decided to hitchhike to New York together; she was going to be my girl in town. I envisioned wild complexities, a season, a new season. First we had to work and earn enough money for the trip. Terry was all for starting at once with my twenty dollars. I didn't like it. And like a damnfool I considered the problem for two days reading the want ads of wild new L.A. papers I'd never seen before in my life, in cafeterias and bars, until my twenty'd dwindled to twelve. The situation was growing. We were happy as kids in our little hotel room. In the middle of the night I got up because I couldn't sleep, pulled the cover over baby's bare brown shoulder, and examined the L.A. night. What brutal, hot, siren-whining nights they are! Right across the street there was trou-

ble. An old rickety rundown roominghouse was the scene of some
kind of tragedy. The cruiser was pulled up below and the cops
were questioning an old man with gray hair. Sobbings came from
within. I could hear everything, together with the hum of my hotel neon. I never felt sadder in my life. L.A. is the loneliest and
most brutal of American cities; New York gets godawful cold in
the winter but there's a feeling of whacky comradeship somewhere in some streets. L.A. is a jungle.

South Main Street, where Terry and I took strolls with hot-
dogs, was a fantastic carnival of lights and wildness. Booted cops
frisked people on practically every corner. The beatest characters
in the country swarmed on the sidewalks—all of it under those
soft Southern California stars that are lost in the brown halo of
the huge desert encampment L.A. really is. You could smell tea,
weed, I mean marijuana floating in the air, together with the chili
beans and beer. That grand wild sound of bop floated from beer-
parlor jukes, Dizzy and Bird and Bags and early Miles; it mixed
medleys with every kind of cowboy and boogiewoogie in the
American night. Everybody looked like Hunkey. Wild Negroes
with bop caps and goatees came laughing by; then longhaired
brokendown hipsters straight off Route 66 from New York, then
old desert rats carrying packs and heading for a park bench at the
Plaza, then Methodist ministers with raveled sleeves, and an occasional Nature Boy saint in beard and sandals. I wanted to meet
them all, talk to everybody, but Terry hurried along, we were
busy trying to get a buck together, like everybody else.

We went to Hollywood to try to work in the drugstore at Sunset and Vine. The questions that were asked of us in upstairs offices to determine our fitness for the slime of the sodafountain
greaseracks were so sinister that I had to laugh. It turned my gut.
Sunset and Vine!—what a corner! Now there's a corner! Great
families off jalopies from the hinterlands stood around the sidewalk gaping for sight of some movie star and the movie star never
showed up. When a limousine passed they rushed eagerly to the

curb and ducked to look: some character in dark glasses sat inside with a bejeweled blonde. "Don Ameche! Don Ameche!" "No George Murphy! George Murphy!" They milled around looking at one another. Luscious little girls by the thousands rushed around with drive-in trays; they'd come to Hollywood to be movie stars and instead got all involved in everybody's garbage, including Darryl Zanuck's. Handsome queer boys who had come to Hollywood to be cowboys walked around wetting their eyebrows with hincty fingertip. Those beautiful little gone gals cut by in slacks in a continuous unbelievable stream; you thought you were in heaven but it was only Purgatory and everybody was about to be pardoned, paroled, powdered and put down; the girls came to be starlets; they up-ended in drive-ins with pouts and goosepimples on their bare legs. Terry and I tried to find work at the drive-ins. It was no soap anywhere, thank God. Hollywood Boulevard was a great screaming frenzy of cars; there were minor accidents at least once a minute; everybody was rushing off toward the farthest palm . . . and beyond that was the desert and nothingness. So they thought. You don't expect everybody to know that you can find water in a kopash cactus, or sweet taffy in your old mesquite. Hollywood Sams stood in front of swank restaurants arguing exactly, loudly and showoff the same way Broadway Sams argue on Jacobs Beach sidewalks, New York, only here they wore lightweight suits and their talk was even more dreary and unutterably cornier. Tall cadaverous preachers shuddered by. Seventy-year-old World Rosicrucian ladies with tiaras in their hair stood under palms signifying nothing. Fat screaming women ran across the Boulevard to get in line for the quiz shows. I saw Jerry Colonna buying a car at Buick Motors; he was inside the vast plateglass window fingering his mustachio, incredible, real, like seeing the Three Stooges seriously ashen-faced in a real room. Terry and I ate in a cafeteria downtown which was decorated to look like a grotto, with metal tits spurting everywhere and great impersonal stone buttoxes belonging to deities of fish and soapy Neptune. People ate lugubrious meals around the waterfalls, their faces green with marine sorrow. All the cops in L.A. looked like handsome gigolos; obviously, they'd come to L.A. to make the movies. Everybody had come to make the movies, even me. Terry and I were finally reduced to trying to get jobs on South Main Street among the beat countermen and dishgirls who made no bones about their beatness and even there it was no go. We still had twelve dollars.

"Man, I'm going to get my clothes from Sis and we'll hitchhike to New York," said Terry. "Come on man. Let's do it. If you can't boogie I know I'll show you how." That last part was a song of hers she kept singing, after a famous record. We hurried to her sister's house in the sliverous Mexican shacks somewhere beyond Alameda Avenue. I waited in a dark alley behind Mexican kitchens because her sister wasn't supposed to see me and like it. Dogs ran by. There were little lamps illuminating the little rat alleys. I stood there swigging from the bottle of wine and eying the stars and digging the sounds of the neighborhood. I could hear Terry and her sister arguing in the soft warm night. I was ready for anything. Terry came out and led me by the hand to Central Avenue, which is the colored main drag of L.A. And what a wild place it is, with chickenshacks barely big enough to house a jukebox and the jukebox blowing nothing but blues, bop and jump. We went up dirty tenement stairs and came to the room of Terry's friend, Margarina, a colored girl apparently named by her loving mother after the spelling on an oleo wrapper. Margarina, a lovely mulatto, owed Terry a skirt and a pair of shoes; her husband was black as spades and kindly. He went right out and bought a pint of whiskey to host me proper. I tried to pay part of it but he said no. They had two little children. The kids bounced on the bed, it was their play-place. They put their arms around me and looked at me with wonder. The wild humming night of Central Avenue, the night of Hamp's *Central Avenue Breakdown*, howled and boomed along outside. They were singing in the halls, singing from their windows, just hell be damned and lookout. Terry got her clothes and we said goodbye. We went down to a chicken-shack and played records on the jukebox. Yakking with our beer we decided what to do: we decided to hitch to New York with our remaining monies. She had five dollars coming from her sister; we rushed back to the shacks. So before the daily room rent was due again we packed up and took off on a red car to Arcadia, California, where Santa Anita racetrack is located under snowcapped mountains as I well knew from boyhood pastings of horse-race pictures in sad old notebooks showing Azucar winning in 1935 the great $100,000 'Cap and you see dim snows heaped over the backstretch mountains. Route 66. It was night. We were pointed toward that enormity which is the American continent. Holding hands we walked several miles down the dark road to get out of the populated district. It was a Saturday night. We stood under a roadlamp thumbing when suddenly cars full of young kids roared by with streamers flying. "Yaah! yaah! we won! we won!" they all shouted. Then they yoo-hooed us and got great glee out of seeing a guy and a girl on the road. Dozens of them passed in successive jalopies, young faces and "throaty young voices" as the saying goes. I hated every one of them. Who did they think they were yaahing at somebody on the road because they were little high school punks and their parents carved the roast beef on Sunday afternoons. Nor did we get a ride. We had to walk back to town and worst of all we needed coffee and had the misfortune of going into the same gaudy wood-laced place with old soda johns with beerfountain mustaches out front. The same kids were there but we were still minding our own business. Terry and I sipped our coffee and cocoa. We had battered bags and all the world before us . . . all that ground out there, that desert dirt and rat tat tat. We looked like a couple of sullen Indians in a Navajo Springs sodafountain, black bent heads at a table. The schoolkids saw now that Terry was a Mexican, a Pachuco wildcat; and that her boy was worse than that. With her pretty nose in the air she cut out of there and we wandered together in the dark up along the ditches of highways. I carried the bags and wanted to carry more. We made tracks and cut along and were breathing fogs in the cold night air. I didn't want to go on another minute without a warm night's rest in a warm sack together. Morning be damned, let's hide from the world another night. I wanted to fold her up in my system of limbs under no light but stars in the window. We went to a motel court and asked if they had a cabin. Yes. We bought a comfortable little suite for four dollars. I was spending my money anyhow. Shower, bath towels, wall radio and all, just for one more night. We held each other tight. We had long serious talks and took baths and discussed things on the pillow with light on and then with light out. Something was being proved, I was convincing her of something, which she accepted, and we concluded the pact in the dark, breathless. Then pleased, like little lambs.

In the morning we boldly struck out on our new plan. Terry wore her dark glasses with authority. Her pretty little severe face beneath, with the noble nose, almost hawk-like Indian nose, but with upswerved cute hollow cheekbones to make an oval and a prettywoman blush, with red ruby full lips and Aunt Jemima skirt teeth, mud nowhere on her but was imprinted in the pigment of the Mongol skin. We were going to take a bus to Bakersfield with the last eight dollars and work picking grapes. "See instead of going to New York now we're all set to work awhile and get what we need, then we'll go, in a bus, we won't have to hitchhike, you see how no good it is . . . ."

We arrived in Bakersfield in late afternoon, with our plan to hit every fruit wholesaler in town. Terry said we could live in tents on the job. The thought of me lying there in a tent, and picking grapes in the cool California mornings after nights of guitar music and wine with dipped grapes, hit me right. "Don't worry about a thing."

But there were no jobs to be had and much confusion with

everybody giving confused Indian information and innumerable tips ("Go out to County Road you'll find Sacano") and no job materialized. So we went to a Chinese restaurant and had a dollar's worth of chow mein among the sad Saturday afternoon families, digging them, and set out with reinforced bodies. We went across the Southern Pacific tracks to Mexican town. Terry jabbered with her brethren asking for jobs. It was night now, we had a few dollars left, and the little Mextown street was one blazing bulb of lights: movie marquees, fruit stands, penny arcades, Five and Tens and hundreds of rickety trucks and mudspattered jalopies parked all over. Whole Mexican fruitpicking families wandered around eating popcorn. Terry talked to everybody. I was beginning to despair. What I needed, what Terry needed too, was a drink so we bought a quart of California port wine for 35 cents and went to the railyards to drink. We found a place where hoboes had drawn up crates to sit over fires. We sat there and drank the wine. On our left were the freight cars, sad and sooty red beneath the moon; straight ahead the lights and airport pokers of Bakersfield proper; to our right a tremendous aluminum Quonset warehouse. I remembered it later in passing. Ah it was a fine night, a warm night, a wine-drinking night, a moony night, and a night to hug your girl and talk and spit and be heavengoing. This we did. She was a drinking little fool and kept up with me and passed me and went right on talking till midnight. We never moved from those crates. Occasionally bums passed, Mexican mothers passed with children, and the prowl car came by and the cop got out to leak but most of the time we were alone and mixing up our souls more and ever more till it would be terribly hard to say goodbye. At midnight we got up and goofed toward the highway.

Terry had a new idea. We would hitch to Sabinal, her hometown up the San Joaquin Valley, and live in her brother's garage. Anything was all right to me, especially a nice garage. On the road I made Terry sit down on my bag to make her look like a woman in distress and right off a truck stopped and we ran for it all gleegiggles. The man was a good man, his truck was poor. He roared and crawled on up the Valley. We got to Sabinal in the wee hours of the morning not until after that tired sleepy beau' pushed his old rattle rig from Indian Ponce de Leon Springs of down-valley up the screaming cricket fields of grape and lemon four hours, to let us off, with a cheerful "So long pard," and here we were with the wine finished (I, while she slept in the truck). Now I'm stoned. The sky is gray in the east. "Wake, for morning in the bowl of night . . ." There was a quiet leafy square, we walked around it, past sleeping sodafountains and barber shops, looking for some garage. There was no garage. Ghostly white houses. A whistle stop on the S.P. A California town of old gold-bottle times. She couldn't find her brother's garage but now we were going to find her brother's buddy, who would know. Nobody home. It all went on in rickety alleys of little Mextown Sabinal, wrong side of the tracks. As dawn began to break I lay flat on my back in the lawn of the town square, and I'd done that once before when they thought I was drowned in an eastern resort, and I kept saying over and over, "You won't tell what he done up in Weed will you? What'd he do up in Weed? You won't tell will you? What'd he do up in Weed?" This was from the picture *Of Mice and Men* with Burgess Meredith talking to the big foreman of the ranch; I thought we were near Weed. Terry giggled. Anything I did was all right with her. I could lay there and go on saying "What'd he do up in Weed?" till the ladies come out for church and she wouldn't care.

Because her brother was in these parts I figured we'd be all set soon and I took her to an old hotel by the tracks and we went to bed comfortably. Five dollars left. It was all smelling of fresh paint in there, and old mahogany mirrors and creaky. In the bright sunny morning Terry got up early and went to find her brother. I slept till noon; when I looked out the window I suddenly saw an S.P. freight going by with hundreds of hoboes reclining on the flatcars and in gons and rolling merrily along with packs for pillows and funny papers before their noses and some munching on good California grapes picked up by the watertank. "Damn!" I yelled. "Hooee! It *is* the promised land." They were all coming from Frisco; in a week they'd all be going back in the same grand style.

Terry arrived with her brother, his buddy, and her child. Her brother was a wildbuck Mexican hotcat with a hunger for booze, a great good kid. His buddy was a big flabby Mexican who spoke English without much accent and was anxious to please and over-concerned to prove something. I could see he had always had eyes for Terry. Her little boy was Raymond, seven years old, darkeyed and sweet. Well there we were, and another wild day began.

Her brother's name was Freddy. He had a '38 Chevvy. We piled into that and took off to parts unknown. "Where we going?" I asked. The buddy did the explaining, Ponzo, that's what everybody called him. He stank. I found out why. His business was selling manure to farmers, he had a truck. We were going to check on that. Freddy always had three or four dollars in his pocket and was happygolucky about things. He always said "That's right man, there you go—dah you go, dah you go!" And he went. He drove 70 miles an hour in the old heap and we went to Madera beyond Fresno, throwing dust back of our tires, and saw farmers about manure. Their voices drawled to us from the hot sun open. Freddy had a bottle. "Today we drink, tomorrow we work. Dah you go man—take a shot." Terry sat in back with her baby; I looked back at her and saw a flush of homecoming joy on her face. She'd been driving around like this for years. The beautiful green countryside of October in California reeled by madly. I was guts and juice again and ready to go.

"Where do we go now man?"

"We go find a farmer with some manure layin around—to-morrow we drive back in the truck and pick up. Man we'll make a lot of money. Don't worry about nothing."

"We're all in this together!" yelled Ponzo, who wouldn't have got the manure by himself. I saw this was so—everywhere I went everybody was in it together. We raced through the crazy streets of Fresno and on up the Valley to some farmers in certain backroads. Ponzo got out of the car and conducted confused conversations with old Mexicans; nothing of course came of it.

"What we need is a drink!" yelled Freddy and off we went to a crossroads saloon. Americans are always drinking in crossroads saloons on Sunday afternoon; they bring their kids; there are piles of manure outside the screendoor; they gabble and brawl over brews and grow haggly baggly and you hear harsh laughter rising from routs and song, nobody's really having any fun but faces get redder and time flies fading faster. But everything's fine. Come nightfall the kids come crying and the parents are drunk. Around the jukebox they go weaving back to the house. Everywhere in America I've been in crossroads saloons drinking with whole families. The kids eat popcorn and chips and play in back or sneak stale beers for all I know. Freddy and I and Ponzo and Terry sat there drinking and shouting. Vociferous types. The sun got red. Nothing had been accomplished. What was there to accomplish? "Mañana," said Freddy, "mañana, man, we make it; have another beer, man, dah you go, DAH YOU GO!" We staggered out and got in the car; off we went to a highway bar. This one had blue neons and pink lights. Ponzo was a big loud vociferous type who knew everybody in San Joaquin Valley apparently from the way every time we clomped into a joint he'd let out loud Ho-Yo's. Now I had a few bucks left and ruefully counted them. Festooned all over my brain were the ideas of going back home to New York at once with this handful of change, hitching as I'd been doing at Bakersfield that night, leave Terry with her wild brothers and mad Mexican manure piles and mañanas of crazy beer. But I was having a hell of a time. From the highway bar I went with Ponzo alone in the car to find some certain farmer; instead we wound up in Madera Mextown digging the girls and trying to pick up a few for him and Freddy; and then, as purple dusk descended over the grape country, I found myself sitting dumbly in the car as he argued with some old farmer at the kitchen door about the price of a watermelon the old man grew in the backyard. We had a watermelon, ate it on the spot and threw the rinds on the old Mexican's dirt sidewalk. All kinds of pretty little girls were cutting down the darkening street. I said "Where the hell are we?"

"Don't worry man," said big Ponzo, "tomorrow we make a lot of money, tonight we don't worry." We went back and picked up Terry and the others and wailed to Fresno in the highway lights of night. We were all raving hungry. We bounced over the railroad tracks and hit the wild streets of Fresno Mextown. Strange Chinamen hung out of windows digging the Sunday night streets; groups of Mex chicks swaggered around in slacks; mambo blasted from jukeboxes; the lights were festooned around like Halloween. We went into a restaurant and had tacos and mashed pinto beans rolled in tortillas; it was delicious. I whipped out my last shining four dollars and change which stood between me and the Atlantic shore and paid for the lot. Now I had three bucks. Terry and I looked at each other. "Where we going to sleep tonight baby?"

"I don't know." Freddy was drunk; now all he was saying was "Dah you go man—dah you go man" in a tender and tired voice. It had been a long day. None of us knew what was going on, or what the Good Lord appointed. Poor little Raymond fell asleep against my arm. We drove back to Sabinal. On the way we pulled up sharp at a roadhouse on the highway, 99, because Freddy wanted one last beer. In back were trailers and tents and a few rickety motel-style rooms. I inquired about the price and it was two bucks for a cabin. I asked Terry how about that and she said great, because we had the kid on our hands now and had to make him comfortable. So after a few beers in the saloon, where sullen Okies reeled to the music of a cowboy band and sprawled drawling at sticky tables where they'd been swiggling brew since one o'clock in the afternoon and here it was twelve hours later and all the stars out and long sleepy, Terry and I and Raymond went into a cabin and got ready to hit the sack. Ponzo kept hanging around, talking to us in the starry door; he had no place to sleep. Freddy slept at his father's house in the vineyard shack. "Where do you live, Ponzo?" I asked.

"Nowhere, man. I'm supposed to live with Big Rosey but she threw me out last night. I'm goin to get my truck and sleep in it tonight." Guitars tinkled. Terry and I gazed at the stars together from the tiny bathroom window and took a shower and dried each other.

"Mañana," she said, "everything'll be all right tomorrow, don't you think so Sal-honey man?"

"Sure baby, mañana." It was always mañana. For the next week that was all I heard, Mañana, a lovely word and one that probably means heaven. Little Raymond jumped in bed, clothes and all and went to sleep; sand spilled out of his shoes, Madera sand. Terry and I had to get up in the middle of the night and brush it off the sheets. In the morning I got up, washed and took a walk around the place. Sweet dew was making me breathe that human fog. We were five miles out of Sabinal in the cotton fields and grape vineyards along highway 99. I asked the big fat woman who owned the camp if any field tents were vacant. The cheapest one, a dollar a day, was vacant. I fished up that last dollar and moved into it. There was a bed, a stove and a cracked mirror hanging from a pole; it was delightful. I had to stoop to get in, and when I did there was my baby and my baby-boy. We waited for Freddy and Ponzo to arrive with the truck. They arrived with beer and started to get drunk in the tent. "Great tent!"

"How about the manure?"

"Too late today—tomorrow man we make a lot of money, to-day we have a few beers. What do you say, beer?" I didn't have to be prodded. "Dah you go—DAH YOU GO!" yelled Freddy. I began to see that our plans for making money with the manure truck would never materialize. The truck was parked outside the tent. It smelled like Ponzo. That night Terry and I went to sleep in the sweet night air and made sweet old love. I was just getting ready to go to sleep when she said, "You want to love me now?"

I said, "What about Raymond?"

"He don't mind. He's asleep." But Raymond wasn't asleep and he said nothing.

The boys came back the next day with the manure truck and drove off to find whiskey; they came back and had a big time in the tent. Talking about the great old times when they were kids here and when they were kids in Calexico and their eccentric old uncles from Old Mexico and the fabulous characters out of the past I missed. "You tink I'm crazy!" yelled Freddy wildeyed, his hair over his eyes. That night Ponzo said it was too cold and slept on the ground in our tent wrapped in a big tarpaulin smelling of cowflaps. Terry hated him; she said he hung around her brother just to be close to her. He was probably in love with her. I didn't blame him.

Nothing was going to happen except starvation for Terry and me, I had a dime left, so in the morning I walked around the countryside asking for cottonpicking work. Everybody told me to go to a farm across the highway from the camp. I went; the farmer was in the kitchen with his women. He came out, listened to my story, and warned me he was only paying so much per hundred pound of picked cotton. I pictured myself picking at least three hundred pounds a day and took the job. He fished out some old long canvas bags from the barn and told me the picking started at dawn. I rushed back to Terry all glee. On the way a grapetruck went over a bump in the road and threw off great bunches of grape on the hot tar. I picked it up and took it home. Terry was glad. "Raymond and me'll come with you and help."

"Pshaw!" I said. "No such thing!"

"You see, you see, it's very hard picking cotton. If you can't boogie I know I show you how." We ate the grapes and in the evening Freddy showed up with a loaf of bread and a pound of hamburg and we had a picnic. In a larger tent next to ours lived a whole family of Okie cottonpickers; the grandfather sat in a chair all day long, he was too old to work; the son and daughter, and their children, filed every dawn across the highway to my farmer's field and went to work. At dawn the next day I went with them. They said the cotton was heavier at dawn because of the dew and you could make more money than in the afternoon. Nevertheless they worked all day from dawn to sundown. The grandfather had come from Nebraska during the great plague of the thirties, that old selfsame dustcloud, with the entire family in a jalopy truck. They had been in California ever since. They loved to work. In the ten years the old man's son had increased his children to the number of four, some of whom were old enough now to pick cotton. And in that time they had progressed from ragged poverty in Simon Legree fields to a kind of smiling respectability in better tents, and that was all. They were extremely proud of their tent. "Ever going back to Nebraska?"

"Pshaw, there's nothing back there. What we want to do is buy a trailer." We bent down and began picking cotton. It was beautiful. Across the field were the tents, and beyond them the sere brown cottonfields that stretched out of sight, and over that the brown arroyo foothills and then as in a dream the snowcapped Sierras in the blue morning air. This was so much better than washing dishes on South Main Street. But I knew nothing about cottonpicking. I spent too much time disengaging the white ball from its crackly bed; the others did it in one flick. Moreover my fingertips began to bleed; I needed gloves, or more experience. There was an old Negro couple in the field with us. They picked cotton with the same Godblessed patience their grandfathers had practiced in pre-war Alabama: they moved right along their rows, bent and blue, and their bags increased. My back began to ache. But it was beautiful kneeling and hiding in that earth; if I felt like resting I just lay down with my face on the pillow of brown moist earth. Birds sang an accompaniment. I thought I had found my life's work. Terry and Raymond came waving at me across the field in the hot lullal noon and pitched in with me. Damn if he wasn't faster than I was!!—a child. And of course Terry was twice as fast. They worked ahead of me and left me piles of clean cotton to add to my bag, my long lugubrious nightmare bag that dragged after me like some serpent or some bedraggled buttoned dragon in a Kafkean dream and worse. My mouth drops just to think of that deep bag. Terry left workmanlike piles, Raymond little childly piles. I stuck them in with sorrow. What kind of an old man was I that I couldn't support my own can let alone theirs. They spent all afternoon with me; the earth is an Indian thing. When the sun got red we trudged back together. At the end of the field I unloaded my burden on a scale, to my surprise it weighed a pound and a half only, and I got a buck fifty. Then I borrowed one of the Okie boys' bicycles and rode down 99 to a crossroads grocery where I bought cans of spaghetti and meat-balls, bread, butter, coffee and five-cent cakes, and came back with the bag on the handlebars. L.A.-bound traffic zoomed by; Fresno-bound harassed my tail. I swore and swore. I looked up at the dark sky and prayed to God for a better break in life and a better chance to do something for the little people I loved. No-body was paying any attention to me up there. I should have known better. It was Terry who brought my soul back; on the tent stove she warmed up the food and it was one of the greatest meals of my life I was so hungry and tired. Sighing like an old Negro cottonpicker, I reclined on the bed and smoked a cigarette. Dogs barked in the cool night. Freddy and Ponzo had given up calling in the evenings. I was satisfied with that. Terry curled up beside me, Raymond sat on my chest, and they drew pictures of animals in my notebook. The light of our tent burned on the frightful plain. The cowboy music twanged in the roadhouse and carried across the fields all sadness. It was all right with me. I kissed my baby and we put out the lights.

In the morning the dew made the tent sag; I got up with my towel and toothbrush and went to the general motel toilet to wash; then I came back, put on my pants, which were all torn from kneeling in the earth and had been sewed by Terry in the evening; put on my ragged strawhat, which had originally been Raymond's toy hat; and went across the highway with my canvas cottonbag. The cotton was wet and heavy. The sun was red on moist earth.

Every day I earned approximately a dollar and a half. It was just enough to buy groceries in the evening on the bicycle. The days rolled by. I forgot all about the East and the ravings of the bloody road. Raymond and I played all the time: he liked me to throw him up in the air and down on the bed. Terry sat mending clothes. I was a man of the earth precisely as I had dreamed I would be in New York. There was talk that Terry's husband was back in Sabinal and out for me; I was ready for him. One night the Okies went berserk in the roadhouse and tied a man to a tree and beat him with two-by-fours. I was asleep at the time and only heard about it. From then on I carried a big stick with me in the tent in case they got the idea we Mexicans were fouling up their trailer camp. They thought I was a Mexican, of course; and I am.

But now it was getting on in October and getting much colder in the nights. The Okie family had a woodstove and planned to stay for the winter. We had no stove, and besides the rent for the tent was due. Terry and I bitterly decided we'd have to leave and try something else. "Go back to your family," I gnashed. "For God's sake you can't be batting around tents with a baby like Raymond; the poor little tyke is cold." Terry cried because I was criticizing her motherly instincts; I meant no such thing. When Ponzo came in the truck one gray afternoon we decided to see her family about the situation. But I mustn't be seen and would have to hide in the vineyard. "Tell your mother you'll get a job and help with the groceries. Anything's better than this."

"But you're going, I can hear you talk."

"Well I got to go *some*time—"

"What do you mean, sometime. You said we'd stick together and go to New York together. Freddy wants to go to New York too! Now! We'll all go."

"I dunno, Terry, goddamit I dunno—"

We got in the truck and Ponzo started for Sabinal; the truck broke down in some backroad and simultaneously it started to rain wildly. We sat in the old truck cursing. Ponzo got out and toiled in the rain in his torn white shirt. He was a good old guy after all. We promised each other one more big bat. Off we went to a rickety bar in Sabinal Mextown and spent an hour sopping up the cerveza as the rain drove past the door and the jukebox boomed those brokenhearted campo lovesongs from old Mexico, sad, incredibly sad like clouds going over the horizon like dogs on their hind legs, the singer breaking out his wild Ya Ya Henna like the sound of a coyote crying, broken, half laughter, half tears. I was through with my chores in the cottonfield, I could feel it as the beer ran through me like wildfire. We screamed happily our insane conversations. We'd do it, we'd do everything! I could feel the pull of my own whole life calling me back. I needed fifty dollars to get back to New York. While Terry and Ponzo drank I ran in the rain to the post-office and scrawled a penny postcard request for $50 and sent it to my aunt; she'd do it. I was as good as saved; lazy butt was saved again. It was a secret from Terry.

The rain stopped and we drove to Terry's family shack. It was situated on an old road that ran between the vineyards. It was dark when we got there finally. They let me off a quarter-mile up the road and drove to the door. Light poured out of the door; Terry's six other brothers were playing their guitars and singing all together like a professional recording and beautiful. ". . . si tu corazón . . ." The old man was drinking wine. I heard shouts and arguments above the singing. They called her a whore because she'd left her no good husband and gone to L.A. and left Raymond with them. At intervals the brothers stopped singing to re-

group their choruses. The old man was yelling. But the sad fat
brown mother prevailed, as she always does among the great Fel-
laheen peoples of the world, and Terry was allowed to come back
home. The brothers began to sing gay songs, fast. I huddled in
the cold rainy wind and watched everything across the sad vineyards of October in the Valley. My mind was filled with that great
song "Lover Man" as Billie Holiday sings it; I had my own con-
cert in the bushes. "Someday we'll meet, and you'll dry all my
tears, and whisper sweet little words in my ear, hugging and akiss-
ing, Oh what we've been missing, Lover Man Oh where can you
be . . ." It's not the words so much as the great harmonic tune and
the way Billie sings it, like a woman stroking her man's hair in soft
lamplight. The winds howled. I got cold. Terry and Ponzo came
back and we rattled off in the old truck to meet Freddy, who was
now living with Ponzo's woman Big Rosey; we tooted the horn
for him in woodfence alleys. Big Rosey threw him out, we heard
yelling and saw Freddy running out with his head ducking.
Everything was collapsing. Everybody was laughing. That night
Terry held me tight, of course, and told me not to leave. She said
she'd work picking grapes and make enough money for both of
us; meanwhile I could live in Farmer Heffelfinger's barn down
the road from her family. I'd have nothing to do but sit in the
grass all day and eat grapes. "You like that?"

   I rubbed my jaw. In the morning her cousins came to the tent
to get us in the truck. These were also singers. I suddenly realized
thousands of Mexicans all over the countryside knew about Terry
and I and that it must have been a juicy romantic topic for them.
The cousins were very polite and in fact charming. I stood on the
truck platform with them as we rattlebanged into town, hanging
on to the rail and smiling pleasantries, talking about where we
were in the war and what the pitch was. There were five cousins
in all and every one of them was nice. They seemed to belong to
the side of Terry's family that didn't act up like her brother
Freddy. But I loved that wild Freddy. He swore he was coming to

New York and join me. I pictured him in New York putting off everything till mañana. He was drunk in a field someplace today.

I got off the truck at the crossroads and the cousins drove Terry and Raymond home. They gave me the high-sign from the front of the house: the father and mother weren't home. So I had the run of the house for the afternoon, digging it and Terry's three giggling fat sisters and the crazy children sitting in the middle of the road with tortillas in their hands. It was a four-room shack; I couldn't imagine how the whole family managed to live in there, find room. Flies flew over the sink. There were no screens, just like in the song: "The window she is broken and the rain she's coming in . . ." Terry was at home now and puttering around pots. The sisters giggled over True Love magazines in Spanish showing daguerreotype brown covers of lovers in great, somehow darker more passionate throes, with long sideburns and huge worries and burning secret eyes. The little children screamed in the road, roosters ran around. When the sun came out red through the clouds of my last Valley afternoon Terry led me to Farmer Heffelfinger's barn. Farmer Heffelfinger had a prosperous farm up the road. We put crates together, she brought blankets from the house, and I was all set except for a great hairy tarantula that lurked at the pinpoint top of the barnroof. Terry said it wouldn't harm me if I didn't bother it. I lay on my back and stared at it. I went out to the cemetery and climbed a tree. In the tree I sang "Blue Skies." Terry and Raymond sat in the grass; we had grapes. In California you chew the juice out of the grapes and spit the skin and pits away, the gist of the grape is always wine. Nightfall came. Terry went home for supper and came to the barn at nine o'clock with my secret supper of delicious tortillas and mashed beans. I lit a woodfire on the cement floor of the barn to make light. We made love on the crates. Terry got up and cut right back to the shack. Her father was yelling at her, I could hear him from the barn. "Where have you been? What you doing running around at night in the fields?" Words to that effect.

She'd left me a cape to keep warm, some old Spanish garment, I
threw it over my shoulder and skulked through the moonlit vineyard to see what was going on. I crept to the end of a row and
kneeled in the warm dirt. Her five brothers were singing melodi-
ous songs in Spanish. The stars bent over the little roof; smoke
poked from the stovepipe chimney. I smelled mashed beans and
chili. The old man growled. The brothers kept right on singing.
The mother was silent. Raymond and the kids were giggling on
one vast bed in the bedroom. A California home; I hid in the
grapevines digging it all. I felt like a million dollars; I was adven-
turing in the crazy American night. Terry came out slamming the
door behind her. I accosted her on the dark road. "What's the
matter?"

"Oh we fight all the time. He wants me to go to work tomorrow. He says he don't want me fooling around with boys. Sallie-
boy I want to go to New York with you."

"But how?"

"I don't know honey. I'll miss you. I love you."

"But I can't stay here."

"You say what you like, I know what you mean. Yes yes, we lay
down one more time then you leave." We went back to the barn; I
made love to her under the tarantula. What was the tarantula doing? We slept awhile on the crates as the fire died. She went back
at midnight; her father was drunk; I could hear him roaring; then
there was silence as he fell asleep. The stars folded over the sleeping countryside.

In the morning Farmer Heffelfinger stuck his head through
the horse gate and said, "How you doing young fella?"

"Fine. I hope it's all right my staying here."

"Sure. You going with that little Mexican floozie?"

"She's a very nice girl."

"Pretty too. S'got blue eyes. I think the bull jumped the fence
there . . ." We talked about his farm.

Terry brought my breakfast. I had my handbag all packed and

ready to go back East, as soon as I picked up my money in Sabinal. I knew it was waiting there for me. I told Terry I was leaving. She had been thinking about it all night and was resigned to it. Emotionlessly she kissed me in the vineyards and walked off down the row. We turned at a dozen paces, for love is a duel, and looked at each other for the last time. "See you in New York Terry," I said. She was supposed to drive to New York in a month with her brother. But we both knew she wouldn't make it somehow. At a hundred feet I turned to look at her. She just walked on back to the shack, carrying my breakfast plate in one hand. I bowed my head and watched her. Well lackadaddy, I was on the road again. I walked down the highway to Sabinal eating black walnuts from the walnut tree, then on the railroad track balancing on the rail.

TRUE ROMANCE

RON HANSEN

From Nebraska, *The Atlantic Monthly Press, 1989*
First published in Esquire

It was still night out and my husband was shaving at the kitchen sink so he could hear the morning farm report and I was peeling bacon into the skillet. I hardly slept a wink with Gina acting up, and that croupy cough of hers. I must've walked five miles. Half of Ivan's face was hanging in the circle mirror, the razor was scraping the soap from his cheek, and pigs weren't dollaring like they ought to. And that was when the phone rang and it was Annette, my very best friend, giving me the woeful news.

Ivan squeaked his thumb on the glass to spy the temperature—still cold—then wiped his face with a paper towel, staring at me with puzzlement as I made known my shock and surprise. I took the phone away from my ear and said, "Honey? Something's killed one of the cows!"

He rushed over to the phone and got to talking to Annette's husband, Slick. Slick saw it coming from work—Slick's mainly on night shift; the Caterpillar plant. Our section of the county is on a

party line: the snoops were getting their usual earful. I turned out
the fire under the skillet. His appetite would be spoiled. Ivan and
Slick went over the same ground again; I poured coffee and sugar
and stirred a spoon around in a cup, just as blue as I could be, and
when Ivan hung up, I handed the cup to him.

He said, "I could almost understand it if they took the meat,
but Slick says it looks like it was just plain ripped apart."

I walked the telephone back to the living room and switched
on every single light. Ivan wasn't saying anything. I opened my
robe and gave Gina the left nipple, which wasn't so standing-out
and sore, and I sat in the big chair under a shawl. I got the feeling
that eyes were on me.

Ivan stood in the doorway in his underpants and Nebraska
sweatshirt, looking just like he did in high school. I said, "I'm just
sick about the cow."

He said, "You pay your bills, you try and live simple, you pray
to the Lord for guidance, but Satan can still find a loophole, can't
he? He'll trip you up every time."

"Just the idea of it is giving me the willies," I said.

Ivan put his coffee cup on the floor and snapped on his gray
coveralls. He sat against the high chair. "I guess I'll give the sheriff a call and then go look at the damage."

"I want to go with you, okay?"

The man from the rendering plant swerved a winch truck up the
pasture until the swinging chain cradle was over the cow. His tires
skidded green swipes on grass that was otherwise white with
frost. I scrunched up in the pickup with the heater going to beat
the band and Gina asleep on the seat. Ivan slumped in the sheriff's car and swore out a complaint. The man from the rendering
plant threw some hydraulic levers and the engine revved to un-
spool some cable, making the cradle clang against the bumper.

I'd never seen the fields so pretty in March. Every acre was green winter wheat or plowed earth or sandhills the color of camels. The lagoon was as black and sleek as a grand piano.

Gina squinched her face up and then discovered a knuckle to chew as the truck engine raced again; and when the renderer hoisted the cow up, a whole stream of stuff poured out of her and dumped on the ground like boots. I slaughtered one or two in my time. I could tell which organs were missing.

Ivan made his weary way up the hill on grass that was greasy with blood, then squatted to look at footprints that were all walked over by cattle. The man from the plant said something and Ivan said something back, calling him Dale, and then Ivan slammed the pickup door behind him. He wiped the fog from inside the windshield with his softball cap. "You didn't bring coffee, did you?"

I shook my head as he blew on his fingers. He asked, "What good are ya, then?" but he was smiling. He said, "I'm glad our insurance is paid up."

"I'm just sick about it," I said.

Ivan put the truck in gear and drove it past the feeding cattle, giving them a look-over. "I gotta get my sugar beets in."

I thought: the cow's heart, and the female things.

Around noon Annette came over in Slick's Trans Am and we ate pecan rolls hot from the oven as she got the romance magazines out of her grocery bag and began reading me the really good stories. Gina played on the carpet next to my chair. You have to watch the little booger every second because she'll put in her mouth what most people wouldn't step on. Annette was four months pregnant but it hardly showed—just the top snap of her jeans was undone—and I was full of uncertainty about the outcome. Our daytime visits give us the opportunity to speak candidly about things like miscarriages or the ways in which we are ironing out our problems with our husbands, but on this occasion

Annette was giggling about some goofy woman who couldn't figure out why marriage turned good men into monsters, and I got
the ugly feeling that I was being looked at by a Peeping Tom.

Annette put the magazine in her lap and rapidly flipped pages
to get to the part where the story was continued, and I gingerly
picked Gina up and, without saying a peep to Annette, walked
across the carpet and spun around. Annette giggled again and
said, "Do you suppose this actually happened?" and I said yes,
pulling my little girl tight against me. Annette said, "Doesn't she
just crack you *up*?" and I just kept peering out the window. I
couldn't stop myself.

That night I took another stroll around the property and then
poured diet cola into a glass at the kitchen sink, satisfying my thirst.
I could see the light of the sixty-watt bulb in the barn, and the cows
standing up to the fence and rubbing their throats and chins. The
wire gets shaggy with the stuff; looks just like orange doll hair. Ivan
got on the intercom and his voice was puny, like it was trapped in a
paper cup. "Come on out and help me, will you, Riva?"

"Right out," is what I said.

I tucked another blanket around Gina in the baby crib and
clomped outside in Ivan's rubber boots. They jingled as I crossed
the barnyard. The cattle stared at me. One of the steers got up on
a lady and triumphed for a while, but she walked away and he
dropped. My flashlight speared whenever I bumped it.

Ivan was kneeling on straw, shoving his arm in a rubber glove.
An alarm clock was on the sill. His softball cap was off and his
long brown hair was flying wild as he squatted beside the side-
laying cow. Her tail whisked a board, so he tied it to her leg with
twine. She was swollen wide with the calf. My husband reached
up inside her and the cow lifted her head indignantly, then settled
down and chewed her tongue. Ivan said, "P.U., cow! You stink!"
He was in her up to his biceps seemed like.

"You going to cut her?"

He shook his head as he snagged the glove off and plunked it down in a water bucket. "Dang calf's kaput!" He glared at his medicine box and said, "How many is that? Four out of eight? I might as well give it up."

I swayed the flashlight beam along the barn. Window. Apron. Pitchfork. Rope. Lug wrench. Sickle. Baling wire. And another four-paned window that was so streaked with pigeon goop it might as well've been slats. But it was there that the light caught a glint of an eye and my heart stopped. I stepped closer to persuade myself it wasn't just an apparition, and what I saw abruptly disappeared.

Ivan ground the tractor ignition and got the thing going, then raced it backward into the barn, not shutting the engine down but slapping it out of gear and hopping down to the ground. He said, "Swing that flashlight down on this cow's contraption, will ya, Riva?" and there was some messy tugging and wrestling as he yanked the calf's legs out and attached them to the tractor hitch with wire. He jumped up to the spring seat and jerked into granny, creeping forward with his gaze on the cow. She groaned with agony and more leg appeared and then the shut-eyed calf head. My husband crawled the tractor forward more and the calf came out in a surge. I suctioned gunk out of its throat with a bulb syringe and squirted it into the straw but the calf didn't quiver or pant; she was patient as meat and her tongue spilled onto the paint tarp.

Ivan scowled and sank to his knees by the calf. The mother cow struggled up and sniffed the calf and began licking off its nose in the way she'd been taught, but even she gave up in a second or two and hung her head low with grief.

"Do you know what killed it?"

Ivan just gaped and said, "You explain it." He got up and plunged his arms into the water bucket. He smeared water on his face.

I crouched down and saw that the calf was somehow split open and all her insides were pulled out.

After the sheriff and the man from the rendering plant paid their visits, the night was just about shot. Ivan completed his cold-weather chores, upsetting the cattle with his earliness, and I pored over Annette's romance magazines, gaining support from each disappointment.

Ivan and I got some sleep and even Gina cooperated by being good as can be. Ivan arose at noon but he was cranky and under-standably depressed about our calamities, so I switched off *All My Children* and suggested we go over to Slick's place and wake him up and party.

Annette saw I was out of sorts right away, and she generously agreed to make our supper. She could see through me like glass. At two we watched *General Hospital*, which was getting crazier by the week according to Annette—she thought they'd be off in outer space next, but I said they were just keeping up with this wild and woolly world we live in. Once our story was over, we made a pork roast and boiled potatoes with chives and garlic butter, which proved to be a big hit. Our husbands worked through the remain-ing light of day, crawling over Slick's farm machinery, each with wrenches in his pockets and grease on his skin like war paint.

Annette said, "You're doing all right for yourself, aren't you, Riva."

"I could say the same for you, you know."

Here I ought to explain that Annette went steady with Ivan in our sophomore year, and I suspect she's always regretted giving him to me. If I'm any judge of character, her thoughts were on that subject as we stood at the counter and Slick and Ivan came in for supper and cleaned up in the washroom that's off the kitchen. Annette then had the gall to say, "Slick and me are going through what you and Ivan were a couple of months ago."

Oh no you're not! I wanted to say, but I didn't even give her the courtesy of a reply.

"You got everything straightened out, though, didn't you?"

I said, "Our problems were a blessing in disguise."

"I know exactly what you mean," she said.

"Our marriage is as full of love and vitality as any girl could wish for."

Her eyes were even a little misty. "I'm so happy for you, Riva!"

And she was; you could tell she wasn't pretending like she was during some of our rocky spots in the past.

Slick dipped his tongue in a spoon that he lifted from a saucepan and went out of his way to compliment Annette—unlike at least one husband I could mention. Ivan pushed down the spring gizmo on the toaster and got the feeling back in his fingers by working them over the toaster slots. My husband said in that put-down way of his, "Slick was saying it could be UFOs."

"I got an open mind on the subject," said Slick, and Ivan did his snickering thing.

I asked if we could please change the topic of conversation to something a little more pleasant.

Ivan gave me his angry smile. "Such as what? Relationships?"

Slick and Annette were in rare form that night, but Ivan was pretty much of a poop until Slick gave him a number. Ivan bogarted the joint and Slick rolled up another, and by the time Annette and I got the dishes into the sink, the men were swapping a roach on the living-room floor and tooling Gina's playthings around. Annette opened the newspaper to the place that showed which dopey program was on the TV that evening. Slick asked if Ivan planted the marijuana seeds he gave us and Ivan shrugged. Which meant no. Slick commenced tickling Annette. She scooched back against the sofa and fought him off, slapping at his paws and pleading for help. She screamed, "Slick! You're gonna make me pee on myself!"

Ivan clicked through the channels but he was so stoned all he could say was, "What *is* that?"

Annette giggled but got out, *"Creature from the Black Lagoon!"*

I plopped Gina on top of her daddy's stomach and passed around a roach that was pinched with a hairpin. I asked Ivan, "Are you really ripped?" and Ivan shrugged. Which meant yes.

The movie was a real shot in the arm for our crew. My husband rested his pestered head in my lap and I rearranged his long hair. There was a close-up of the creature and I got such a case of the stares from looking at it you'd think I was making a photograph.

Ivan shifted to frown at me. "How come you're not saying anything?"

And I could only reply, "I'm just really ripped."

Days passed without event, and I could persuade myself that the creature had gone off to greener pastures. However, one evening when Ivan was attending a meeting of the parish council, my consternation only grew stronger. Gina and I got home from the grocery store and I parked the pickup close by the feed lot so I could hear if she squalled as I was forking out silage. Hunger was making the cattle ornery. They straggled over and jostled each other, resting their long jaws on each other's shoulders, bawling *mom* in the night. The calves lurched and stared as I closed the gate behind me. I collared my face from the cold and as I was getting into the truck, a cry like you hear at a slaughterhouse flew up from the lagoon.

I thought, I ought to ignore it, or I ought to go to the phone, but I figured what I really ought to do is make certain that I was seeing everything right, that I wasn't making things up.

Famous last words!

I snuggled Gina in the baby crib and went out along the pasture road, looking at the eight-o'clock night that was closing in all around me. I glided down over a hill and a stray calf flung its tail in my headlights as its tiny mind chugged through its options. A yard away its mother was on her side and swollen up big as two hay bales. I got out into the spring cold and inspected the cow even though I knew she was a goner, and then I looked at the woods and the moonlighted lagoon and I could make out just enough of a blacker image to put two and two together and see that it was the creature dragging cow guts through the grass.

The gun rack only carried fishing rods on it, but there was an angel-food-cake knife wedged behind the pickup's toolbox, and that was what I took with me on my quest, my scalp prickling with fright and goosebumps on every inch of me. The chill was mean, like you'd slapped your hand against gravel. The wind seemed to gnaw at the trees. You're making it up, I kept praying, and when I approached the lagoon and saw nothing, I was pleased and full of hope.

The phone rang many times the next day, but I wouldn't get up to answer it. I stayed in the room upstairs, hugging a pillow like a body, aching for the beginning of some other life, like a girl in a Rosemary Rogers book. Once again Annette provided an escape from my doldrums by speeding over in the orange Trans Am—her concern for me and her eternal spunk are always a great boost for my spirits.

I washed up and went outside with Gina, and Annette said, "What on earth is wrong with your phone?"

I only said, "I was hoping you'd come over," and Annette slammed the car door. She hugged me like a girlfriend and the plastic over the porch screens popped. The wind was making mincemeat of the open garbage can. And yet we sat outside on the porch steps with some of Slick's dope rolled in Zig-Zag papers. I zipped Gina into a parka with the wind so blustery. She was trying to walk. She'd throw her arms out and buck ahead a step or two and then plump down hard on her butt. The marijuana wasn't rolled tight enough and the paper was sticking all the time to my lip. I looked at the barn, the silo, the road, seeing nothing of the creature, seeing only my husband urging the tractor up out of a ditch with Slick straddling the gangplow's hookups and hoses. Slick's a master at hydraulics. The plow swung wide and banged as Ivan established his right to the road, then he shifted the throttle up and mud flew from the tires. One gloved hand rested on a fender lamp and he looked past me to our daughter, scowling and acting put out, then they turned into the yard and Annette waved. Ivan lifted his right index finger just a tad, his greeting, then turned the steering wheel hand over hand, bouncing high in the spring seat as Slick clung on for dear life.

Annette said, "My baby isn't Ivan's, you know."

I guess I sighed with the remembering of those painful times.

Annette said, "I'm glad we were able to stay friends."

"Me too," I said, and I scooched out to see my little girl with anangel-food-cake knife in her hands, waddling over to me. "Gina!" I yelled. "You little snot! Where'd you get that?"

She gave it to me and wiped her hands on her coat. "Dut," Gina said, and though my husband would probably have reprimanded her, I knelt down and told her how she mustn't play with knives and what a good girl she was to bring it right to me. She didn't listen for very long, and I put the knife in my sweater pocket for the time being.

Annette was looking peculiar, and I could tell she wanted an explanation, but then there was a commotion in the cattle pen and we looked to where Ivan and Slick were pushing cow rumps aside in order to get close to the trough. They glared at something on the ground out there, and I glanced at the cake knife again, seeing the unmistakable signs of blood.

"I'm going out to the cattle pen," I imparted. "You keep Gina with you."

Annette said, "I hope your stock is okay."

The day was on the wane as I proceeded across the yard and

onto the cow path inside the pen, the cake knife gripped in my
right hand within my sweater pocket. The cattle were rubbing
against the fence and ignorantly surging toward the silage in the
feed trough. Slick was saying, "You oughta get a photograph,
Ivan." My husband kept his eyes on one spot, his gloved hands on
his hips, his left boot experimenting by moving something I
couldn't see.

I got the cattle to part by tilting against them with all my
weight. They were heavy as Cadillacs. And I made my toilsome
way to my husband's side only to be greeted with a look of ill tid-
ings and with an inquiry that was to justify all my grim forebod-
ings. He asked, "Do you know how it happened, Riva?"

I regarded ground that was soggy with blood and saw the
green creature that I'd so fervently prayed was long gone. He was
lying on his scaly back and his yellow eyes were glowering as if
the being were still enraged over the many stabbings into his
heart. Death had been good for his general attractiveness, gloss-
ing over his many physical flaws and giving him a childlike quality that tugged at my sympathy.

Again Ivan nudged the being with his boot, acting like it was
no more than a cow, and asking me with great dismay, "How'd
the dang thing get killed, do ya think?"

And I said, "Love. Love killed it. Love as sharp as a knife."

Slick gazed upon me strangely, and my husband looked at me
with grief as I sank to the earth among the cattle, feeling the
warmth of their breathing. I knew then that the anguish I'd expe-
rienced over those past many months was going to disappear, and
that my life, over which I'd despaired for so long, was going to
keep changing and improving with each minute of the day.

WHITE LINE FEVER

DIANA OSSANA

New Delta Review, *Louisiana State University*, 2000

W hen Tucker had finally gone inside her hot little duplex, the only evidence that Nick Tremayne had
ever lived there was a couple of dirty T-shirts, an old
sports coat and a single sock on the bedroom floor, left behind,
like her, in his haste to be gone. She wondered if this would be
just another binge, or if her husband was gone for good. It was
Friday night; maybe he'd only be away for the weekend. But he'd
never taken his clothes before, had never planned his binges, as
some men might plan a vacation or a fishing trip. The urge just
seized hold of him, as lust seized the tomcats who prowled the
narrow alley behind their two-bedroom duplex in South St.
Louis.

Katie-Michael—Tucker wanted to have a name ready
whichever way matters went—had been kicking with a fury on
the way home from work, but now the child was quiet inside her.
She patted her belly, not wanting the baby to feel her alarm.

Nick, never a morning person, had actually been cheerful at breakfast. "Come on, Harpo," he'd said, coaxing her away from a giant bowl of bananas and milk. Tucker loved it that Nick called her Harpo. Dancing a slow tango to a Neil Young dirge, he nuzzled her neck as they glided back and forth across the kitchen floor, just like the Marx brothers in one of their wacky movies. Probably Nick had already been planning to leave; probably that was why he had been so cheerful.

Staring at the empty drawers and the gaping closet door, Tucker shivered, though the back of her blouse was soaked with sweat. Chills swept over her in waves, like buckets of ice water poured over her head, one after the other.

She barely made it to the bathroom before she threw up.

Early summer heat hung over the city and would for the next four months, unless they were lucky. Tucker was well into her pregnancy now, and always hot, always perspiring. The only relief to be found was standing under the air conditioning vent in front of her tiny desk down at the train yard, or taking a long, cool shower once she got home from work. The landlord had installed a window fan in the front room of their duplex, and it had worked fine for a few weeks in the late spring, though all it managed to do now was pull in the heavy, humid air from outside. She wandered dully back and forth between the stifling rooms, wondering if she would ever lay eyes on her coward of a husband again, wondering how she'd react if he did come back.

Later, still trying to be a dutiful wife, Tucker dragged herself to the laundromat, washed the dirty T-shirts and the one sock along with the rest of her laundry. While she was folding the T-shirts, she began to cry. Washing one sock for a man who had left her felt ridiculous.

When the crying jag ended, she stuffed her clean laundry into a pillowcase, drove to the Clark station to fill the tank on her VW bug, discovered that her Mastercard was missing from her wallet.

When she got home, Tucker phoned the bank, reported it stolen, and learned there was a measly hundred dollars left in their joint savings account. Her husband had withdrawn the other two thousand, which to Tucker meant the end: Nick Tremayne was gone for good.

"This room smells like feet," Blue announced from the bedroom doorway, holding her nose with one hand, a bottle of dish detergent in the other. A joint dangled from the corner of her mouth.

Tucker ignored the remark. Blue Brennan, Tucker's best friend since high school, had lived alone too long, developing standards so exacting that no human being could possibly live up to them, not in Tucker's view. Blue made a beeline for the bathroom, turned both faucets on full blast, used the dish soap for Tucker's bubble bath.

"Men are such dumbfucks," Blue added, though Tucker knew her friend wasn't sorry to have Tucker to herself for a while, until the next dumbfuck came along.

She was dressed in platform sandals and a new shortie rabbit's fur coat. "I know it's a little hot for this, but my mom picked it up yesterday, and I couldn't wait to show it off," Blue said. Then she yanked off the rabbit fur and unbuckled the platforms, flinging them into a corner. "Come on, hon, let's get you cleaned up," she said, half-carrying a clammy, apathetic Tucker into the bathroom. Kneeling down next to the tub, she worked creme rinse into Tucker's snarl of hair.

"Your problem is you've always been a sucker for the 'I love you,' " Blue said, struggling with the sprayer hose, which flailed at her wildly every time she tried to attach it to the bath spigot. "Plus, you could never resist the tall guys—the string beans."

"I guess," Tucker admitted. Of course Blue was right. She loved it that Nick was tall and skinny. And once he told her he loved her, she was a goner.

Blue's bare feet were making squishy noises on the bathmat.

"Like I said, Nicky's a dumbfuck—I mean, what was all that Harpo business about?" Blue was standing up now, still battling with the hose and Tucker's tangle of blond curls.

"It was just a pet name, that's all it was," Tucker said. Her hands were turning into prunes. "Get me out of here before I'm one giant wrinkle."

Nick had been gone three days.

Big Frank Kelly, Tucker's dad—he had named her Tucker because he was determined that his firstborn be a boy and didn't let the mere fact that she wasn't one affect his choice of names—was getting married that afternoon, which meant that Tucker had to put in an appearance, depressed or not. The reception was at the Casa Loma Ballroom, catered by waiters who were dressed like bullfighters. Meg, the unblushing, nasal-voiced bride, announced to Frank's friends and family that she was a former airline stewardess for Ozark Airlines. With her platinum hair and black roots, pushup bra and stiletto heels, she looked to Tucker like a not-so-former stripper—as different from Tucker's mother as a whore from a nun.

When the priest came to the part about love, honor, and obey, Big Frank cleared his throat, and the priest took it for an "I do."

After a few sips of Asti Spumante and before Meg threw her bridal bouquet straight into the punch bowl, Tucker discovered that if she squinted, Meg seemed almost pretty—though in a sad, camouflaged sort of way.

On Sunday, Tucker drove out to look at a Volkswagen van she'd seen advertised on the bulletin board at the laundromat—a like-new 1971, the owner had purred over the phone, and in fact, it was like new: a shiny red number, navy blue curtains with a white daisy pattern covered each of the rear windows. Even the curtains were clean. When she took it for a little test drive, the van cruised fine at 65, handled easily on the interstate, no shimmy in the front end. She gave the owner—a 60's burnout whose velvet phone voice belied his scruffy demeanor—a hundred-dollar deposit check, called Blue from the burnout's greasy kitchen, promised him afterwards that she'd be back the next night with a friend and the title to her VW bug.

"You could move to Arizona," Blue pointed out. Tucker was sprawled on her friend's bedroom floor, studying the Rand McNally.

Tucker didn't know much about Arizona, except that it had lots of sand and cactus, but she was getting excited at the thought of leaving town.

"Why Arizona?" she asked.

"Because I was there once in January, and it was warm enough I could wear my bikini," Blue said.

Loretta Kelly, Tucker's mother, lived alone, except for those few weeks of the year when Willie, Tucker's little brother, was out of jail. There'd been some hope that Willie might straighten up after Loretta divorced Big Frank and moved to a quiet little town off the interstate west of St. Louis. But those hopes were crushed the first week in their new home, when a tornado warning sent them all scurrying into the cellar and Tucker, tripping on a clutter of wires snaking over the lip of the landing, stumbled upon Willie's stash of thirty-two stolen car stereos crammed helter-skelter beneath the stairs.

And even though Loretta and Frank had been divorced for five years, Loretta still wore her wedding band, as if their divorce and Frank's new wife were only figments of someone's warped imagination.

She's getting fat, Tucker thought, as she drove up to her once-slender mother's house and saw Loretta standing there, squinting into the sunlight, one hand on her ample hip, the other guiding a few stray auburn curls back behind her ear.

"I don't think sleeping in one's car is a very practical notion," Loretta said, when Tucker told her she might be moving to Arizona. Otherwise, she had no comment, though she did smooth Tucker's hair as she had when Tucker had been a little girl.

"It'll just be till I can find an apartment, Mama," Tucker said.

The drive back to the interstate was down a two-lane highway, past rolling hills blanketed with wild violets and periwinkles, lonely roads carving narrow paths between one farm and the next. It was monarch season and the orange and black butterflies were everywhere, on rock walls and blooming dogwoods, their patterned wings a sharp contrast to the dense clusters of white flowers. A couple of bird dogs raced across a field, then darted off suddenly, flushing a startled flock of wild turkeys from a blackberry thicket that ran along the edge of the road. The beauty of the midwestern fields was strangely disturbing to Tucker, its perfection almost too idyllic to be real. It was as if the landscape had been painted on a series of huge billboards lining both sides of the road. Tucker was grateful for the clear skies and the sunlight, but it still felt wrong somehow for the landscape to appear so orderly, so symmetrical and pristine, when her own emotions were so scattered.

In fact, she'd never really felt connected to this place, even in the summer; she was always aware that its beauty would be gone in only a few months. She wondered if she would ever feel rooted, serene.

That night, she made up her mind to leave—just leave. She knew she wouldn't be able to stand another dark Missouri winter, the trees melancholy in their nakedness, the air frigid, the light thin and weak. Though autumn lasted only a few weeks, Tucker knew she would miss the change of seasons. The turning of the leaves made her feel happy and sad all at once. A shifting, an urgency, an awareness of time passing. Sort of the way being pregnant made her feel.

When they heard she was leaving for Arizona, Frank and Meg had Tucker over for a good-bye dinner, fried chicken and gravy, the chicken cooked on one side and raw on the other, the gravy so lumpy and thick that at first she'd thought it was mashed potatoes. When Frank asked her why she hadn't touched the chicken, Tucker announced that she'd become a vegetarian—not a total lie. She'd been pondering the notion ever since Blue got food poisoning after wolfing down half a dozen White Castles the night they went back to pick up her new van.

And no time like the present, she decided, studying the bloody puddle on her plate.

After dinner, Tucker showed her father the inside of her new van, demonstrating how the back seat folded down into a bed, a sturdy arrangement she'd constructed herself out of plywood strips and a red Naugahyde remnant she found in a furniture outlet down on Cherokee Street. Frank, never lavish with praise, had to admit he was impressed.

Tucker folded up her bed and went back inside to help clean up the kitchen. She traipsed around the corner balancing a stack of dirty dishes just as her father was about to launch one of his freckled fists into Meg's kisser, her stepmother's two sets of false eyelashes fluttering so fast Tucker thought, for a moment, that she could feel a breeze. A sad, powerful déjà vu swept over her. She dropped the dishes on the counter and grabbed her father's elbow in time to spare Meg from a long night in the emergency room instead of two days in an overpriced motel down at the Lake of the Ozarks, where the newlyweds had decided, during an eye-of-the-hurricane moment over a dessert of half-frozen pound cake, to spend the weekend.

Later, unable to forget the many times Frank had punched her own mother silly for nothing as drastic as undercooking a chicken—for nothing at all, in fact—Tucker started her van in front of her father's overdone house, a coliseum-shaped fountain topped with a water-spitting Madonna on the front lawn, his overdone wife waving frantically and blowing kisses from their lopsided porch, where hundreds of plastic flowers were being guillotined between the wooden trellis and the wrought-iron porch rails.

Tucker felt sorry for her stepmother then, thought she looked like one of those people she had seen in old movies, the ones standing on the deck of a cruise ship, happy and smiling and hopeful, about to leave on what they think is a glorious honeymoon, when what really happens is that the ship sinks somewhere out in the middle of the ocean. No survivors.

Driving back into South St. Louis, while herding the VW bus across four lanes of traffic and expertly negotiating the treacherous Grand Avenue off-ramp, Tucker realized neither of her parents really cared that she was leaving.

Maybe that was what being grown up meant. That your parents didn't care if you left.

"My whole family's here," Tucker said a week later, feeling wan all of a sudden. She sat in Blue's kitchen, everything left from her week-long yard sale stuffed into and on top of the Volkswagen bus. Here she was, almost a thousand dollars richer, ready to pull out of town, headed for a new life, and now she was wavering about leaving.

"But that's the point, Tucker," Blue said. "So you don't raise your kid around your crazy family. So your kids don't turn out like your folks."

"I guess so," Tucker said, still feeling wan.

Later, Blue took her to *her* folks, for a good-bye barbecue.

Fergus Doolan, Blue's stepfather, pale as milk after serving two years in the Jeff City Penitentiary on a felony shoplifting charge, was barbecuing in his backyard, his little wife Dottie glued to his side. Tucker loved Fergus and Dottie. They had been like second parents to her, even though their basement contained a veritable department store of stolen goods—racks jammed with fur coats, shiny Italian suits and silk dresses; tables stacked high with jewelry and small appliances; mattress sets with box springs, even TV sets and stuffed animals, cabbaged from stores all over St. Louis and western Illinois. Fergus loved telling the story of how he'd pinched his beloved Barcalounger from Biederman's right under the nose of the store manager. He loved bragging about what a good little actress Blue had been as a child, able to cry on a dime and hold the attention of the entire sales force while Fergus hefted the big chair onto his back, loaded it into Dottie's pickup, and then rushed back inside, a frantic daddy looking for his lost little girl.

Blue and Tucker watched from the kitchen window as Dottie passed him a joint.

"I wish I felt strong," Tucker said, in the mood for a little sympathy. "I don't know what I'd do if Nick came around and wanted us back." The grill was flaming up, but Dottie and Fergus, making out like teenagers, didn't seem to notice.

"You're a lot stronger than you think, hon." Blue looked outside again and frowned. "Dinner's looking like a crap shoot. We should have stopped by the Soul Queen and picked up a slab of ribs."

Fergus had his hand up Dottie's tube top.

"Look at Romeo. He's so determined to feel Dottie's tit that he hasn't noticed he's grilling his shirttail," Blue said, racing out the back door and grabbing the garden hose. She doused the flaming grill and Fergus's smouldering shirt.

The barbecue tasted like wet charcoal, but they ate it anyway.

When it was time to leave, Tucker stood next to her friend, sobbing like a little girl. They were in front of Blue's tidy little bungalow, admiring the surprise lilies that had come up that morning, their white blooms like giant sighs.

"This good-bye business is getting out of hand," Tucker said, wiping her wet face on her shirtsleeve.

"Don't forget me," Blue said, as Tucker pulled away from the curb.

"Don't forget me," Tucker said, to no one.

Nick's pillow, stained with sleep slobber, lay in the back seat. Tucker hadn't changed the pillowcase because it still held Nick's smell.

One a.m. Saturday night at a Fina all-nighter—Cruel Jack's Food And Gas Wichita Kansas, the primitive sign admonished—and Tucker was so tired she could barely get the nozzle in the gas tank. If she had been a little bit fresher, she would have pumped the gas and been on her way long before the two louts squealed into the gas station, donuting their pickup to a standstill just inches from her van. Heaving obscenities and beer cans out the window, arguing about who would get out and fill the tank, they immediately lost interest in their squabble when they got a good look at Tucker and her blond curls. They both piled out of the driver's side, stumbling over one another in their eagerness.

"I heard that women's hair curls up like that when they're lonesome for lovin'," the stockier of the two said. He had three gold teeth and tiny ears, set too low on the sides of his head. Tucker wondered if his ears had somehow slid down into his fat neck. She looked away, keeping her eyes on the gas pump, knowing that any attempt at small talk would only whet their interest.

The skinny one was so grimy his mother could have been a tire.

"How'd you get your hair to curl up like that, stick your finger in a light socket?" he asked, surveying Tucker from a distance of about a yard.

Tucker didn't answer. She was chanting Hail Mary's over and over to calm herself, a trick learned after the time when Big Frank's rage had accelerated, turned a corner. Tucker and Willie had to stay with their grandmother almost a month that time. Afterwards, she always knew, felt the tension long before the blows started, would lead her baby brother to the bedroom closet. Off to the Holy Mother.

Both men edged closer, cutting the distance to about half a yard.

"I'm too tired for this shit," Tucker said suddenly, yanking the gas nozzle out of the van and drenching them both with low octane Fina leaded. Tired as she was, Tucker hadn't grown up in South St. Louis for nothing.

"You're lucky I don't smoke," she added.

There was a deep laugh from the front of the van. A tall man, with a Marine haircut and caterpillar eyebrows stood there, idly swinging a big key chain.

"I think you boys have met your match. No pun intended," the man said, still laughing.

"That hoosier bitch. She done drenched us with gasoline . . ." the skinny man said, so shocked he could barely talk. The fat one was hastily taking off his shirt.

"You know what, slick? I couldn't care less, long as she pays for it," the tall man with the Marine haircut said. "My suggestion would be for you to get the hell outa here before this young lady gets *really* pissed and sets you both on fire."

"What's a little girl like you doin' out on the road in the middle of the night? Where're your folks?" Jack asked, once they were inside the station. He had invited her into his narrow kitchen, poured her a glass of milk, even made her a chicken sandwich.

"I'm not a little girl," Tucker said, not sure how much she wanted to tell this man. "I'm twenty-five."

"Where's your husband?" he said, noticing her wedding ring.

"Which question you want me to answer first?" Tucker asked, between bites. The chicken was cold and greasy, but she ate the sandwich in about three gulps. She hadn't realized how hungry she was.

"How about the husband one?" Jack said.

Tucker looked at him closely for the first time. Tattoos for skin, all the way down to his fingernails. On the back of his right hand was a crude rendering of a couple holding hands, his fingers their two pair of legs. The tip of his index finger was missing.

"My husband took his problems and went away," she admitted.

"Problems . . . such as?" Jack asked.

Burst blood vessels covered his face like lines on a map. Tucker had no reason to talk to the man. But the fact that the man seemed kind, and that she had never seen him before and would probably never see him again, made her want to trust him.

"He's a drug addict," she said. "Speed, mostly."

Jack reached into his little fridge and grabbed a beer.

"White line fever," he said, after a moment.

Tucker didn't know what he was talking about.

"That's what we called it in Korea. The grunts would take dexedrine, shake lines out on their thumbs. Snort it up like pigs."

"Nick did it that way, too," she said, not wanting to tell him the uglier truth, which was that Nick had long since graduated from snorting. The first time she had watched him soak the yellow tabs of speed until they were transparent, and then saw him shooting up, over and over again, she'd felt sick, violated. As if she had been made to witness a lewd sex act. She didn't want to say the words out loud, didn't want Katie-Michael to hear them. They sounded obscene to her. Pornographic.

Jack's look was a challenge. He knew it without her saying, aimed his cool eyes at Tucker's.

"It's just as well he's gone," Jack said. "And just as well you're gone, too."

Afterwards, they sat down to watch TV in his office just behind the checkout counter. "They don't make movies like they used to," Jack grunted, switching channels until he found *King's Row* on *The Late Late Show*. Tucker had to fight to stay awake through the opening credits. The last thing she remembered was opening her eyes for a moment and seeing Ann Sheridan at the bedside of a crazed Ronald Reagan, who was trying to figure out where his legs had gone.

The terrain widened, flattening out west of Oklahoma City, still green but no longer hummocked as it had been up north. The starter on the van went at a Stuckey's just outside of El Reno. Tucker got a push from a jolly husband-and-wife big rig team fresh out of the DeVry Over-The-Road Driving School in Dubuque, Iowa, popped the clutch in second gear and kept on trucking, figuring she'd get it fixed the next day in Texas.

The Maverick Motel in Amarillo, spare but with solid locks on the doors and $15-a-night rooms, was situated across the street from Bubba's Hilltop Auto Repair. Tucker thought the name was funny, since Amarillo was the flattest place she'd ever seen in her life. She booked two nights for $25 after she assured the clerk she would use the same towels both days and wouldn't be needing maid service. Then she drifted across the old Route 66 and negotiated the van repairs with Bubba, who not only laughed too much but winked after everything he said, as if he and Tucker shared some inside joke.

When she mentioned the hilltop thing to Bubba, he looked shocked.

"Why, this *is* a hill, ma'am. It's the highest point in the whole city. Take a gander," he said, with a sweep of his arm and another wink.

She meandered next door to the Silver Spur Bowling Lanes to pass some time, remembering with an ache how after months of bobbing and weaving, Nick had finally asked her out, taken her bowling on their first real date. She proved to be such a fast learner that Nick was soon using her as a ringer; he even invited all his friends to celebrate the New Year at the big Bowl-A-Rama on Kingshighway. Nick played a couple of games with his buddies first, then made the third game a betting game. His friends all mocked him when he'd announced that Tucker Kelly was his partner. But they shut up after she bowled three strikes in a row. That night was the first time Nick told her he loved her, the first night they made love. That night, Tucker knew she was a goner.

The buck-toothed attendant looked at her funny when she asked to rent bowling shoes, more than likely because she was pregnant, and alone. When she returned the shoes, a rangy Texan who'd been watching her throw strikes one after the other asked her where she learned to bowl like that.

"St. Louis," Tucker said.

"St. Louis?" the attendant chimed in. "Now, that's a far piece. Farthest I've ever been is Oklahoma City. They got that Cowboy Hall of Fame in Oklahoma City."

As Tucker turned to leave, the Texan scribbled something on a matchbook shaped like a cowboy boot. "If you're drivin' through Clovis, this little place has the best chilis rellenos between here and Lordsburg."

She slept a profound, dreamless sleep that night, the murmur of the window unit the only sound in the room.

The Guadalajara Cafe in Clovis, New Mexico, was next door to a veterinarian who was next door to a taxidermist. The front half of a ragged buffalo stared out the taxidermist's display window, glass eyes fixed forever on the train depot across the street.

Tucker ordered the special, chilis rellenos with a side of guacamole, exotic dishes she'd never tasted before. The waiter, a modest young man with a rather formal demeanor, his cap of blond curls a mirror image of Tucker's, was startled to see what appeared to be his twin when she looked up from her menu.

When he brought Tucker's lunch, a trio of diaper-clad little boys trailed after him like baby ducks.

"Pardon me, Señora, but when is your baby to be born?" The waiter's accent belied his blond looks.

Tucker held up three fingers. "Three months. October," she said, watching as the smallest of the little boys jammed a thumb in his mouth and two fingers up his nose. "Enrique, stop that!" The father swatted the child's hand away, but the baby was in a trance. He just stood there in amazement, staring at his father, then at Tucker, cramming his fingers right back up his nose. The father shrugged, then hurried off toward the kitchen, the little boys clinging possum-like to his apron.

The wind was blowing with such force when Tucker stepped outside the cafe that she had to scrape the sand off her teeth once she got inside the van. She shoved *Merle Haggard's Greatest Hits* into the tape player, struggling to keep the van from crossing over the center line as she pulled onto the narrow two-lane highway, dodging bungalow-sized tumbleweeds as she drove.

The plains opened up just outside of Portales, the endless New Mexico sky joined to a horizon so far away Tucker could barely make it out. Sage and yucca dotted the sparse landscape, an occasional tuft of prairie grass bowing low to the constant wind. There was a reassuring quality about such stark, open country. Something permanent, enduring. As if no matter how much time passed, no matter how many times she came this way, it would always be here. Exactly the same, never changing. She was so overwhelmed with a feeling of belonging that her eyes filled with tears. Later, she thought it must have been pregnancy hormones, but it was a powerful emotion that recurred many times, whenever she drove west. She felt her body relax for the first time in weeks. Even her breathing became easier, and she found that she could think about her life with Nick for a little while without feeling so desperate.

They had been far too different from each other, she realized now. How come she'd never seen it? In the beginning, Nick had been impressed by her love of books, even though he himself never cracked anything thicker than the *TV Guide* the entire time they were together. But he quickly came to resent Tucker's appetite for reading. He treated the growing skyscrapers of novels stacked around their bed as an obstacle course between him and his wife. Tucker got so she'd wait until Nick was sound asleep before she'd open a book. But when he started going out after work on the weekends, then during the week, not coming home sometimes for two or three days, books became a wall between sanity and despair.

She knew Nick had been in Vietnam, but she hadn't known about the drugs, didn't find out until she was pregnant, when they'd been married for almost a year. She was too much in love by then, it was too late. It had been like finding out he had a girl-friend, only worse. A whole lot worse.

It had been raining most of the day when Tucker pulled off the freeway in Tucson, the van coughing and sputtering as it lurched down the exit ramp. She jockeyed across the intersection, coast-ing into Valentina's Fina, the lanky attendant second-guessing her predicament and flagging her into one of the repair stalls.

His name was embroidered on his shirt pocket: *Hank*. Just over six feet tall, thin, with hair black as the oil stains on the re-pair bay floor and glasses like Buddy Holly.

"Your battery's dead and gone, lady," he said. "I'll change it out, if you can give me about fifteen minutes." Tucker just stood there, numb. She felt nearly cross-eyed from driving all day in a storm, and more than a little disappointed, since Blue had assured her it rained in Arizona about as often as the sun shone in St. Louis.

The man flashed his open palm at her three times, as if she hadn't understood. "There's pop in the fridge," he added. "Help yourself."

"Pop?" Tucker had never heard the term before.

"You know, pop—soda pop—I'm from Michigan. We call it pop where I'm from."

Tucker looked blank.

"Ma'am, you've got white line fever," the man said, after a mo-ment.

"What?" The man was speaking English. Why couldn't she understand him?

"It's that dazed look folks get when they've been following the lines on the highway for too long." He smiled, amused. "Help yourself to a pop, they're ice cold."

She helped herself to the restroom first, studying her face in the mirror over the sink. Puffy eyes, dark circles, stupefied expression, white line fever—whatever it was, she looked like hell. The bathroom was clean enough that she felt comfortable washing up a bit before she waddled back to the garage.

Hank was writing out the receipt when she returned. He was almost too thin, his stomach concave and his belt loose around his waist. She noticed him looking at her stomach. Then he noticed her noticing, and blushed.

He has sad eyes, she thought.

There was a Best Western next door to the Fina station flashing a VACANCY sign, but it was full, the clerk apologizing for the broken NO on the neon. Tucker stopped at every motel along the strip—no vacancies. The clerk at the Vista Del Sol, an ancient tinderbox next to the railroad tracks, explained that the big gem and mineral show was in town, and there wouldn't be a room anywhere around Tucson for at least a week. Even the KOA north of town was full. The couple who ran the place, Rocco and Michel, two sweet, gossipy middle-aged drag queens who relocated to Tucson from New Orleans after Rocco's rheumatism became intolerable and he could no longer perform his beloved Diana Ross impersonation, made over Tucker like two old grannies when they realized she was going to have a baby. They offered to let her use the showers at the campground for free, until a space opened up.

Later that night, she drove back by the Fina station. The lights were out, and the battered Dodge pickup that had been parked by the restrooms was gone. Hank's truck, she supposed. She pulled the van around back so it couldn't be seen from the street and set up her bed. She slept fitfully, wanting to be out of there at first light, before the attendant returned.

The next two days were spent driving around looking for a place to live. No one in Tucson wanted a tenant who was pregnant and out of work, without a husband. The rents were prohibitive, too, twice what she paid in St. Louis for half the space.

At sunrise on the third day, she awoke to find a paper sack resting on the front bumper. Inside was a package of baby blocks, the wooden kind, with a-b-c's carved into the sides.

Tucker had been in Tucson a week the morning she stepped outside and found Hank leaning against his tailgate, drinking coffee. The restroom marked WOMEN had an OUT OF ORDER sign posted on the door. Time to leave, she figured, but when Hank showed her the restroom—he had scoured it clean, had even installed a papercup dispenser by the sink—she was startled by this unexpected kindness. Startled, and a little wary.

"We'll just leave that OUT OF ORDER sign on the door till you get settled," he said. He held out a key attached to a rawhide string. Tucker didn't take it.

"Don't worry. It's the only key," Hank said. He tossed it to her, forcing her to catch it.

That afternoon, they had takeout from Don's Mexican Deli, carne seca chimichangas enchilada-style, with guacamole and sour cream on the side, a Sonoran delicacy to which Tucker promptly became addicted. She had the same meal at lunch every day for a week.

Hank started bringing her donuts and orange juice in the mornings, tried to put her at ease by making innocent conversation. He'd been born and raised in Ypsilanti, moved to Tucson five years ago after a stint at Fort Huachuca. A few weeks later, when the monsoons came, sitting around Hank's office one evening, he confided to Tucker how three years back he'd fallen in love with a waitress, Shawna, over at the Cabaret Men's Club on Speedway.

"How'd it go?" Tucker asked.

"Went fine, until Shawna got promoted to lap dancer," Hank said. "I told her no wife of mine was gonna be no lap dancer. That's when she left." During dinner at La Fuente, over the din of mariachis, he told her how he'd bought the Fina station cheap after the previous owner's body was found at the foot of "A" Mountain, the victim of an apparent drug deal gone bad. "This town, it's kind of just a big drug store," Hank told her.

As the days turned into weeks, he laid his past out to her, but he never pried, letting Tucker guide the momentum of their friend-ship.

"He doesn't ask any questions, Blue. He's letting me set the pace." Tucker was at her favorite phone booth, next to the lunch counter inside the old Woolworth's downtown. She'd already fed the phone four dollars in quarters, and she and Blue had barely gotten started catching up.

Blue was indignant. "Pace, shmace, he's still just a guy who wants in your pants."

"But he's been so nice . . . maybe he just wants to be friends," Tucker said, wondering why her voice sounded defensive.

"Nice, shmice. Is there something you're not telling me?" Blue demanded. Tucker recognized the tone in her friend's voice: Blue was jealous.

"Give me a break, Blue, I'm gonna have a baby! I don't want to start anything with anybody, no matter how nice they are. Not before Katie-Michael comes."

Or afterwards either, she thought.

"Okay already!" Blue said. But she still sounded jealous.

After Tucker hung up, she sat on one of the stools at the lunch counter and ordered a chicken salad sandwich. While she waited for her food, she twirled around and around on the stool, replay-ing maybe for the hundredth time, what she'd seen and what she'd felt that first day when she walked into her little duplex back in South St. Louis and saw that her husband was gone.

All across the plains, she'd replayed that scene, and replayed it. Sometimes, just remembering the sight of their bedroom—the abandoned drawers on Nick's side of the dresser, the door to the half-empty closet yawning wide, the clothes hamper on its side, the lone sock divorced from its mate, Nick's old moth-eaten sports jacket crumpled on the floor like a corpse—made her feel so shaky and desperate that she would have to pull off the highway until she calmed down. It was as if every object in their bedroom that day had frozen forever in her memory, like an ice sculpture that would never melt.

The shock of that first moment had made her crazy.

Maybe she was still crazy. But if she was, Tucker knew she had to try to get sane again, had to, for the sake of her baby. Nick was still too much with her. Maybe after she had replayed that scene another hundred times, Nick would finally fade away, like a photograph in a newspaper that had been left out in the sun too long.

Surely after Katie-Michael was born, she would feel less vulnerable. Not so brittle.

Hank drove Tucker to the little cafe at the top of Mount Lemmon for Sunday brunch, where she fainted right out of her chair from the altitude. At first, Hank was in a dither, thought she must be having the baby, got real scared. But then she came to, and he practically carried her back to the pickup.

On Labor Day, he took her down to Nogales for Mexican food, but the smell of open sewers and rotting meat made her so sick she spent the entire drive back to Tucson with her head in a paper sack.

"Ain't this fun?" Tucker said, looking up from the paper sack and giving him a wry look. They had just passed the dog track on their way back through South Tucson. "First I faint, then I barf."

Through it all, Hank was sympathetic, patient. He never once complained—picking her up when she passed out, cleaning her up when she puked. No one except Blue had ever been so nice to her before.

No man had ever been so nice to her, not without wanting something in return. It confused Tucker, and made her all the more wary.

In late September, when the mornings turned cool, Hank brought her donuts and hot chocolate, leaning against his pickup truck while she sat in her van with the sliding door open, soaking up the day's first light as it poured over the western rim of the Rincon Mountains.

Hank was as predictable as sun in the desert. And Tucker was restive.

At first, living in the van had been unsettling, and more than a little scary. But she quickly became accustomed to the anonymity and frugality of the homeless: no mail, no phones ringing, no bills to pay. She had plenty of time to read, and all the peace and quiet she wanted. If she needed a change of scenery, all she had to do was drive to another spot. She was tied to Tucson until Katie-Michael was born, but then she and her baby could stay or go, could be off to anywhere they wanted, for as little or as long a time as they chose. She didn't have to answer to anyone.

A week before the baby was due, Hank drove Tucker to Patagonia Lake for a picnic. They rented a little dinghy, Hank blushing crimson when the woman working the boat concession called Tucker his missus, then rowed around the lake while Tucker dragged her fingers in the water, sticking close to shore after she told him she couldn't swim.

"I'm thinking I might move up to Flagstaff after the baby comes," Tucker said. She was sitting on a blanket with her back against a cottonwood tree, the a-b-c blocks that Hank had given her lined up on her stomach like little soldiers. Nick's pillow, having all but lost his smell, was propped under her knees.

Hank sat down beside her. It was the closest they'd ever been to one another physically, except when Tucker was fainting, or else throwing up.

He smelled of aftershave and sweat. A man smell. It took Tucker by surprise.

She felt breathless all of a sudden.

"Please, don't move to Flagstaff." Hank had never been so direct with her before. "I hardly know a thing about you."

"You know I'm from St. Louis," Tucker said. "You know I'm gonna have a baby. You know my husband left me. What else is there?" She was being contrary, she knew—he had been so nice— but she couldn't help it.

"I love you, Tucker."

Katie-Michael did a somersault. The a-b-c blocks went sailing off her stomach.

Tucker avoided the nice man's eyes. She looked past him, toward the low, dark hills of Mexico.

"Aw Hank," Tucker whispered, her voice like a stranger's. "I wish you hadn't said that."

* * *

GLISSANDO

ROBERT BOSWELL

From Living to Be a Hundred,
Knopf, New York, 1994

In the spring of 1970 my father and I lived in a one-bedroom apartment over a laundromat in Lordsburg, New Mexico. He was working as a real-estate agent through the mail, and a short-order cook at a truckstop café during the night. He'd also lifted a master key to the washers downstairs and borrowed coins from the machines as the need arose. To allay suspicion, he took only a handful of change at a time.

On my birthday that May he came home hours early from the S & P Truckstop, bursting through our door with a lemon meringue pie held like a newborn in the crook of his arm. His pockets bulged and jangled with coins. Before he said a word, I knew we were about to move on.

"Fourteen, a golden year," he began, pulling my birthday present, a new deck of playing cards, from his rear pocket and tossing it my way. "Time you learned how to drive an automobile," he said. Then he added, "Good catch," as I snagged the deck before it hit me in the face.

Our only vehicle, a motorcycle—and not a big Harley as he
had once owned, but a little JSA 125—had no headlamp and was
not licensed for street use. He had to take alleys across town and
park behind buildings, locking it up with a chain the way you do a
bicycle. We hadn't owned a car for three years.

"Birds have wings," my father went on, as if explaining himself
to a stranger. "Men got to have automobiles." He set my birthday
pie on the couch that doubled as my bed, then fished through the
stolen coins in his pocket and withdrew a pair of keys looped together by a noose of electrical wire. "Happy fourteenth," he said,
throwing them as he had the cards. "That's your personal set.
Pack your things real quick-like, and let's go for a ride."

An hour later, rumbling out of town in a '64 Chevy Bel Air, he
told me I would no longer go by Jim Wallace, my real name. I
would now answer to Jim Barley.

"Just till you turn eighteen," he said, wiping meringue from his
lips and onto the steering wheel, "then you can call yourself anything you please."

Some of his real-estate deals had not been entirely above
board, and he had decided to go by his half-brother's name, Louis
Barley. Louis had disappeared the year of my birth, but wherever
we moved my father put his photograph on top of the refrigerator. It was Louis who gave me a gap-toothed smile every time I
opened the door for a Coke or an ice cube or to just stand in the
refrigerated air. The new Louis Barley, my father, had gotten a
driver's license using his half-brother's birth certificate.

"What should I call you?" I asked him.

"Father," he said, "same as always. Nothing's changed but the
distance I can put between us and trouble."

A dozen miles out of New Mexico, he pulled the Bel Air onto
the shoulder and killed the engine. "Give your old man a hand,"
he said as he climbed out. In one corner of the car's trunk, among
our clothes and possessions, lay a screwdriver and a set of Arizona
license plates. "The Chevy gets a new identity, too," he ex-

plained. I removed the old plates. He replaced them with the new. My father liked to plan things in detail, and this stop was a calculated part of the trip. Poor timing and bad luck often conspired to ruin his plans, but this evening all went smoothly, which pleased us both.

"One gorgeous night," he said when we had finished and leaned happily against the trunk. The desert rolled around us, dark and seemingly without end. Up above, the sky held an amazing network of stars. He handed me the New Mexico plates, and I sent them whirling over the barren ground. We'd become new people: Louis Barley and his son Jim.

"You got your keys?" he asked me. When I nodded, he pointed to the driver's side.

White specks of gravel embedded in the asphalt sparkled like gems in the Bel Air's headlights. "Hammer that clutch in all the way," he shouted. I obeyed him, then turned the key and the engine came to life. We lurched out onto the dark highway.

He pulled a bottle of rum from beneath the seat, bumping his head against the dashboard as the car jumped forward. "That didn't hurt," he said, rubbing his temple. He began telling a story about his very first drive, how his half-brother Louis had taught him. "Lousy driver himself," my father confided. "Worked the clutch like he was stomping ants."

My heart pounded as we hit fifteen, twenty, thirty miles an hour, the highway all but abandoned—an occasional diesel, a few desert creatures. My father put his hand over mine on the gear shifter, showing me the way down to second, then up and over to third.

"You're getting it." He nodded encouragingly and took another swig of rum. My first time behind the wheel, I took us a distance of one hundred miles.

Alida McGowan was a small and pretty woman whose face would flush red after only a moment in the heat, the pink of her skullcap shining through her thin blond hair, which she cut short like a boy's. She was twenty-two in 1970, ten years younger than my father. Her favorite activity consisted of lying in her underwear on the couch and watching television while sipping iced tea.

She had grown up in Chicago, her father a butcher, but her mother divorced and remarried before Alida turned three. Her second father managed his own grocery, and the third taught high-school French. Alida's mother married her way up the same social scale that Alida, in turn, descended. At seventeen, she ran off with a college boy, leaving him in Los Angeles for an appliance salesman who she abandoned for a ranch hand. His pickup broke down in Arizona where Alida met a diesel mechanic. She was living with him in a Ford van when she encountered Louis Barley.

My father stood five feet, nine inches tall with hair black as a crow's wing. He ironed his shirts and buttoned every button regardless of the weather. He owned a succession of crumpled gray felt hats common to an older generation and wore one all the time, except in bed and in the car. Although he had strong arms, they appeared more swollen than muscular. I wound up with an identical build—something my wife would call wiry when we first met, and scrawny when we broke up.

While Alida looked very much like a modern woman, my father, the brim of his fedora tipped up, looked like a relic. He treated her well, though, and did the same to me. True, he drank, but meanness was not the result. In his whole life he struck me only once. That was later, in Nevada, when things had turned bad between us. To be honest, I'd had it coming.

Our first night out of Lordsburg we slept in the Chevy on a dirt road beside the highway east of Tucson. The following day he managed to drive only a couple of hours. The desert sun reflecting brightly off the hood, combined with his hangover, caused him too much pain. He stopped in Gila Bend, Arizona, pretending it had been our destination all along.

His pretending was something I both recognized and denied. We moved so much, he served not only as my sole parent but as my single enduring friend. I preferred to believe he knew what he was doing, and I did so for a long time, until it was impossible to continue.

Gila Bend was a hot little desert hole, a place to get gas and beer and a second wind for the remainder of whatever long drive you were on. We rented a stucco house painted an aqua color—to look like the ocean, my father claimed. The paint had flaked off in spots, and a gray like bad skies shone beneath it.

He got a job as night clerk at the Space Age Lodge, a concrete-block motel with plastic furniture in the lobby and photos of early space flights on the walls. I joined him behind the registration desk to study. We had left Lordsburg before I finished eighth grade, and he'd decided to compensate by giving me a few lessons of his own. On the evening Alida McGowan stepped into our lives, he had been instructing me in what he called the algebra of blackjack, a complicated system of when to hold and when to ask for a hit.

"No guesswork to it anymore," he told me, shaking his head in awe of such progress as he dealt out five hands. "All mathematical. What you need is a head for numbers, and I think you got one."

At eight that evening Alida appeared at the door. The sun had not set and the temperature outside remained over one hundred degrees. Her face and scalp glowed pink. Her short dress had wide, brightly colored stripes—the sort of thing that would make other people look ugly—and she wore a braided leather strap around one ankle. She lived across the highway with the diesel mechanic but checked in that evening with a truck driver, a big-chested man who wore a John Deere cap.

My father took to her immediately. While the trucker bent over to sign the registration card, my father stared straight into her eyes, smiling and adjusting the brim of his hat. She didn't say a word. If she gave him any kind of signal, I missed it. As she left, she knotted a handful of skirt in her fist as if nervous.

My father lost all interest in the lesson. When I mentioned it, he put his arm around my shoulder and led me outside into the heat. We stood beside the motel's whitewashed walls, and he said softly, "When's the last time you heard of a trucker cashing in before dark?"

He asked as if I'd been with him all those nights at the truck-stop. Then he added, "That any way to leave your vehicle?"

The rig was parked haphazardly in the lot, taking up half the spaces. "Let's give them a call," he said. We went back inside and dialed their room number.

I heard the driver's loud voice coming through the receiver. "Hell, it won't be there more than an hour." The diesel, in fact, pulled out twenty minutes later.

"Jimmy, run over and check on that room." My father watched through the window as the truck rolled over the curb and out into the street. "Stick your ear to the door and see if you hear life."

I ran along the sidewalk that rimmed the Space Age Lodge and leaned up against the green metal door, which was hot to the touch. I couldn't hear anything at first, but I kept listening. It seemed likely the woman had stayed, this being the sort of thing about which my father was invariably right.

In a few seconds she started walking around. Then the television came on. I peered through a gap where the curtains failed to meet and saw Alida McGowan on the bed wearing nothing but panties and a bra, a bottle of dark liquor in her hand.

"Didn't mean for you to pry," my father told me. "Peeking in, that was prying. I only wanted you to listen." He said this seriously but smiling, delighted with the news. "If a customer comes, you say your daddy's fixing an air conditioner and will be right back. Then you call her number."

During the hour he spent with Alida McGowan, no one came to the Space Age Lodge, but I picked up the receiver several times, thinking I would ring them with one phony message or another. Finally, I raced back to her room.

The curtains had been yanked hard so they overlapped. When I pressed my ear against the door this time, I heard the soft and low voice my father got while doing something he enjoyed. I heard her, too, just once, a little laugh that sounded like a wind chime.

Alida moved in with us later that week. My father came home one night with her under his arm, and she never left. Before he even introduced us, she smiled at me and said, "Jimmy always makes me think of jimmying a lock, and Jim makes me think of basketball and the smell of men sweating. You've got a good name. It makes pictures in my head."

I think I fell in love with her right then.

My father got an advance on his paycheck to buy a portable black-and-white Zenith. She lay on the couch half-wrapped in a blanket, drank instant iced tea, and watched whatever came on. We received a clear picture on only two channels, but she never complained—it was not in her nature to object. I often thought she wouldn't even change the channel if I didn't ask to see a certain show.

In all his life, my father had never had anything to do with banks, but as Louis Barley he opened a checking account shortly after Alida moved in. Louis Barley also worked more ambitiously than the man I'd grown up with. Midway through June, the Space Age Lodge promoted him to day clerk. "I'll make manager in another six months," he announced proudly. "Nobody is motivated to stay in Gila Bend but me." He took a second advance to buy an air conditioner for the living room. Before Alida arrived, we'd used just the one in his bedroom and left doors open.

Once he started working days, Alida and I spent a lot of time together in front of the television. I liked to look at her in her underwear, and she didn't seem to mind. As long as my father was at work or asleep she'd lie more or less on top of the blanket, but whenever he sat with us she'd cover herself. She wore white cotton panties, often stained. One pair had a little oval hole just below the elastic waistband. Her bras, white and old-fashioned, revealed less, really, than a bathing top. Later she took to wearing my father's white T-shirts and no bra. She often lay in such a manner that I'd have to leave for a while and go back into my room. When I returned she'd let me know what I missed on television.

Alida told me several stories that summer. The one I remember best had to do with her turning seventeen and her mother throwing a surprise party and inviting the local teenagers, most of whom Alida disliked. They came to her party because of her looks.

"I am pretty, you know," she told me, smiling, her lip curled almost cruelly.

I agreed with her. She described the balloons dangling from the ceiling that had embarrassed her and the stupid gifts—one kid had given her a model car to assemble—and how she had hated all of it. Then a boy handed her a box that jewelry came in, a box made for an expensive ring. Her mother raised her eyebrows and said, "I wonder what that could be." Alida opened it and inside lay a condom. Her mother burst into tears, then shoved the boy in the chest to make him leave.

"I should have been mad at him, too," Alida told me, "but I wasn't."

"Nothing makes you angry," I said.

She shrugged and shook her head as if I had missed the point. "Your mother ever make you miserable?"

"She took off when I was little. We don't know what become of her." I looked at the carpet while I spoke. Talking about my mother embarrassed me. "I only know her from stories I hear."

Alida grunted knowingly. "Your daddy likes to tell stories." She was silent a moment, and then she said, "I could never resist the things my mother hated. My whole life has been an answer to that gift."

I had little idea what she meant, but I smiled and nodded as if it made perfect sense.

A couple of weeks after school began, I got into a fistfight. Clay Lookingpoint, a big kid who was part Indian, said I reminded him of a squat-legged hen. I hit him and broke his nose.

I was accustomed to being new at a school and thought it better to punch someone early on rather than let the abuse build up. I got a swat and was sent home.

I faked the call to my father and walked the short distance to our house. As soon as I stepped inside, I heard a rush of movement. The sliding glass door that led to the backyard opened and closed. "Alida?" I called and walked into the living room. The drapes that covered the door swayed. In the gap between the hem and the floor, an inch of bright sunlight shone on our concrete porch and on a man's big naked feet. As I watched, those feet stepped into pants.

Alida lay on the couch watching TV, the blanket over her as usual. When I started toward the glass door to see who it was dressing on our back stoop, she called my name and patted the couch beside her. As the World Turns flickered on the set and she began filling me in. I might have gone on to the door, but she let the blanket fall. She was not wearing panties. She continued talking about the soap opera, lying on her stomach, her pretty white behind out in the open. She called me again and turned her head to face me. "Jimmy, come over here," she said.

I went to her then. When I reached the couch she unbuttoned my pants, slipped her hand inside my underwear, and took my cock into her mouth. She left it there only a moment, then turned back to the television.

"There'll be more later," she said.

I was immobilized for several moments. Finally, I buttoned my jeans and sat in my regular chair.

In another minute, she got up, without trying to cover herself, and went into the bedroom. When she returned, she was fully clothed.

"You're a part of it now, too," she told me. "So you better keep quiet."

I came home from school the next day during lunch. She took me in her mouth again, just as briefly, then used her hands to finish. I was a boy and it didn't take long.

I found if I ran to and from the house during lunch break, I could get back in time for my next class. Occasionally, that same man was there. Alida locked the front door when he came by, having asked me not to unlock it. Once I hid around back and waited for him to emerge—a big dark man without much hair on his head. Alida told me she used to live with him in a Ford van. She told me then about the other men and her fathers. She trusted me with this because of my dedication to her warm mouth and hands.

"Men fall for me," she said, "but they don't fall in love." She was washing at the kitchen sink. I had trailed her into the room, still buttoning my pants. "If I were a man, I'd find a way to love some-one like me."

"My father loves you," I said. "He says so all the time." Then I added in a whisper, "I love you."

"Your daddy thinks he made me up out of thin air. He thinks whatever he finds must be just what he was looking for." She dried her hands on a dish towel. I waited to see if she had heard my confession. "And you, well . . ." She rolled her eyes. "You just like to get your rocks off."

I laughed with her at this, although we both knew it wasn't the whole truth.

During the last days of the school year, I ran home and she was gone—along with the TV set and all her clothes. I started to call my father, thought better of it, and went back to school instead. I stayed late, sitting in the gym, acting like I was studying, wondering who was next for her, how far down her mother's scale she'd be able to go. Mainly, I kept a textbook in front of my face, hiding my eyes.

When I finally got to the house, my father stood in a corner of the kitchen making hamburger patties. He had a story about Alida that I might have believed if I hadn't already known her better than he did.

"She got a call from her kin in Chicago. Some family trouble," he told me.

I didn't ask for details. I had been angry with him for several days. It gave me an evil pleasure to see him suffering and pretending.

"You just missed her," he continued. "She asked me to give you her love."

"Sure, she did," I said coolly.

He pretended not to hear my tone. Then he added, "I let her have the TV set. Hell, she'd be lost without it, wouldn't she?" He laughed at that.

Later we discovered that she'd taken both air conditioners, which my father thought unfair. For a long time he remained cross with the memory of her.

We lived in Gila Bend another six months. One day at school—I was a sophomore by that time—my father came to the classroom door and whispered with my Civics teacher. Then he gestured for me. The Bel Air, loaded with our belongings and carrying a full tank of gas, waited for us in the parking lot.

"I've got basketball practice tonight," I told him.

"It'll have to wait," he said. We climbed in and drove out of Gila Bend for good.

My father had one story he liked to tell about my mother.

The two of them had drunk whiskey most of a winter night in a honky-tonk in Albuquerque. Somehow there came to be bets

on what songs the piano player would know. My mother wanted
to bet he wouldn't know a song that used all of the keys. She had
gotten it into her head that no such song existed, having heard it
from another piano player way back in her youth—a thing that
had stuck with her for years and she was now, finally, going to use.

My father bet fifty dollars. The man played a familiar song—
sometimes my father would say "Stormy Weather," other times,
"Am I Blue"—and right at the finish, he put his fingers at one end
and ran them all the way down the keys before playing the last
few notes. My father shrugged and reached for his wallet, figuring they'd been had, but Mother became furious, saying you
could do that to any song. "Don't give him the money," she said.

My father knew welshing on a bet was trouble, especially in
the sort of bar they were in. He asked the piano player if there
was sheet music as proof. He couldn't have read the notes of a
scale to save his life, but he studied a few sheets anyway, then returned to the table fifty dollars lighter.

"Called a full glissando, and it was right there in the margins of
the music," he told her. "A trick deal, but he took us fair and
square."

Whenever he related the story to me, he'd say, "Jimmy, that's
why your mother left us. She wanted the kind of life where you
hit every note at least once. We can't begrudge her that."

Before Alida McGowan left us, we took two trips together. The
first was to see the Grand Canyon, a long drive from Gila Bend
even though it's in the same state. My father told me I could invite a
friend to join us. The only person I knew very well, Clay Lookingpoint, agreed to come along. We sat in the back of the Bel Air together. For some reason, Clay had brought a notebook and wrote
me messages. "She your mother?" asked the first one. I shook my
head. Then he wrote, "She rides good in a car." I nodded.

By the time we got to Flagstaff, the sky had grown dark and the

Grand Canyon still remained a good ways off. Our stops to pee and some road construction had thrown off my father's calculations. We ate burgers and fries at a crowded drive-in, then we found a motel nearby, although the original plan had us coming back that same night. Our room, made to look like a log cabin, earned my father's scorn. He spent half an hour pointing out the places where you could tell it was just paneling and not really logs. Alida turned on the television and lay on one of the two beds watching an old movie.

Clay suggested that he and I take a walk. Immediately he led me back to the drive-in where we'd eaten. He claimed to have seen girls living out of a VW camper in the parking lot. "We can go there and screw them," he said. Clay had already turned eighteen. While he couldn't have been called handsome, the little crook I'd given his nose made him seem dangerous in an appealing way. Whether I was handsome didn't matter, I knew, as I was fourteen and looked like a boy.

Clay walked right up to the VW camper parked in a corner of the gravel lot and knocked on the sliding door. When it opened a crack, he said, "We're two Indian men searching for squaws." He smiled grandly and laughed.

The person who opened it—a full-grown woman with lines in her face and wrinkles in her neck—said, "Sally, look at this."

Another woman, younger but with a mean look about her, stuck her head out. "They're searching for squaws," the older one said.

"He don't look Indian." Sally pointed at me.

"Half-breed," Clay told her. "We're Yaqui braves."

"So what is your Indian names?" the older one asked.

Clay pointed at his own chest. "Running Deer with Dick Like Horse." He laughed at this more than anyone else.

"What about you?" Sally lightly put her finger on my nose.

I started to say, "Clay Lookingpoint," the only Indian name I could think of. Instead, I said, "Looking Up Strangers." To which

Clay quickly added "Dresses" and lifted Sally's skirt a few inches.

The older one slapped Clay's hand, saying, "Why don't you chiefs go down to the bowling alley to search for squaws?" Sally shut the sliding door.

"Hey," Clay called out and hammered against the bus with his fist. "Check this one," he said. The cloth curtains parted and both their faces appeared in the door window. They watched as Clay unbuttoned his pants and peed against the side of their van. The women laughed and shook their heads, then the curtains closed.

Clay and I walked back to the motel pretty happy. "They wanted us bad," he said. We laughed and repeated the names we'd made up.

Outside our room we found Alida and my father sitting in the car staring straight ahead, saying nothing. My father lowered his window. "Get in, boys. We're throwing this trip away."

We headed back for Gila Bend, nobody talking for a long time. Clay finally spoke. "Why we going back now?"

He asked my father, but Alida replied. "Louis is a prude," she said.

"That's exactly right," my father said. "And won't any of us say what a certain other in this car is."

Nothing but silence followed. Clay lifted his notebook from the floorboard. He wrote, "Her shirt is backward."

Alida's blouse was not on backward but inside-out. The stitching showed. A little white tag turned up at the back of her neck, saying, "Small." I hadn't noticed her shirt. I was worried that she had told him about us, about me and her. But that hadn't happened.

Years later when I finally asked my father about it, he said only that he'd loved Alida as he'd loved no one since my mother, but Alida didn't have the capacity for love. He didn't want to elaborate, and I didn't press.

That was five years ago, the last time I saw my father alive. He wasn't an old man when he died, his thin hair still black as a crow's wing. A cleaning woman found his body in a dumpster outside a motel in Portales. I borrowed a car from a woman I knew and drove down from Colorado to identify the body. The car, a silver Buick with automatic transmission, had to have a new water pump in Santa Fe. Towing and repair cost me two hundred dollars, which made me think of it as mine, and is why I still drive it.

My father had been sharing a house trailer with a sad-eyed woman not over twenty-five. She had peroxide-blond hair but dark brows and a quivering way of talking that reminded me of a dove cooing. She had no real explanation for his death. We sat in the silver Buick while she drank tequila straight out of the bottle, her head pushed against the seat, weeping. "He treated me like the Queen of Sheba," she told me, "like I was nothing but good." When I pressed for reasons someone might want to knife him, she spoke vaguely of bounced checks, gambling debts, poor timing, bad luck.

The one other trip my father and I made with Alida McGowan came about as the result of a letter from the IRS. Addressed to Louis Barley, the letter requested information about his failure to claim money he'd earned taking the census. That was how my father discovered his half-brother was alive and not paying taxes. The form showed an income of a couple of hundred dollars and an address in Riverside, California. The phone company didn't list any Barleys in Riverside, but the drive was only seven hours. My father decided to take the chance. He guessed he might never get another to see Louis.

We left in the early evening. While he drove, my father told us how his half-brother had disappeared.

"You were all of three months old at the time," he said to me. "Louis decided to go see the Caribbean. He was always big on water. Claimed the Caribbean was clear as the sky. He drove down into Mexico and never come back. I wanted to track him, but your mother didn't want to take you south. Afraid she'd get sick and wouldn't be able to feed you. Other things came up, and I never did find him. Years later I tried. After your mother was gone, too. You remember Mexico?"

I nodded, recalling mainly the long bus rides and the unease my father had felt down there, pretending to understand more than he really did.

"I can speak Spanish," Alida said. She began pointing at clouds, scrub trees, cactus, the lights of approaching cars and re-cited their Spanish names—pretty words that sounded just right, as if those things belonged more to that language than ours.

Near the California line, we left the interstate and headed north on a deserted two-lane that went from Yuma to Blythe. My father pulled off and cut the engine. "I bet you didn't know Jimmy can drive," he said to Alida, then he looked into the back at me. "Got your keys?"

We all three sat in the front, Alida in the middle. I stalled the car on my first attempt to get us moving. "Let her out easy," my father advised. Alida, to soften my embarrassment, confessed that she couldn't drive a stick.

The narrow road had mild curves, and was lit by a bright and persistent moon. I had not driven since my fourteenth birthday, better than a year past, and I had more trouble this time than be-fore, trying as I was to impress Alida.

"Louis and I took a trip like this once," my father began. "Your mother came with us," he told me. To Alida he added, "She had to sit on the hump, too."

"I don't mind," Alida said.

"We'd all been living in Horizon City, Texas, down south of El Paso. A record cold January, snow piling alongside the road. We were heading up to Santa Rosa by way of Las Cruces and Alam-ogordo. Louis had work in Santa Rosa and thought he could get me on. Can't recall what it was because it never panned out."

"How old were you?" I asked him, keeping my eyes on the blacktop.

"Not much older than you are now. Seventeen, I guess. Me and your mother'd been married about a year. Didn't know it, but she was already carrying you."

Alida said, "That means I was just a kid when this went on."

"That'd be right," my father said. "Louis was driving, stomping the clutch every chance he got, as usual. His old Falcon had a powerful heater, and we drank coffee with whiskey from a thermos. Before long we come to White Sands." To Alida, he said, "If you never been there, picture huge mounds of table salt. Damnedest thing you can imagine. Only, this night, it got three leagues stranger. There on top of the white sand was snow." My father shook his head. "White snow on top of white sand in moonlight just like this." He tapped the passenger window. "Louis about got us into a head-on just staring at it."

As he finished the story, the road wound by a rock hill. Suddenly the Colorado River appeared right beside us, moonlight, blue and beautiful, skipping across the water. "Look at that," Alida said. I had to stop the car to keep from driving into the river.

A little after midnight we finally arrived in Riverside. My father, prepared as always, had directions and drove right up to the address, a duplex with a big porch and a gabled roof. Plywood covered the door and window on one side, but the other half was lighted. We gathered before the good door, the three of us, all a little giggly and proud. The trip, already a big success, now presented us with the opportunity to see a ghost.

My father pounded heartily on the door. A man soon opened it. He stared at us only a second before saying, "Son of a bitch." In the harsh electric light, he looked many years older than my father, his skin a shade of gray—like the hide of an elephant. There was a gap between his front teeth.

"Louis," my father said.

We stood in the doorway for a few perfect seconds. Then a

voice called from another room. A thin woman appeared down the hall. She bent forward to look at us, which made me think she had poor vision. As soon as he saw her, my father flinched and quit smiling. He said, "We got the wrong house." He reached in for the knob and pulled the door shut.

On the outskirts of Riverside, we found a seafood restaurant still open. My father ordered lobster for all three of us. He pretended to be in a good mood, although anyone could tell it was an act. "Drove all this way to see a stranger," he said and laughed. He even slapped his knee. Then he called to the waiter for more melted butter, another beer, water, crackers, ice.

I played along with him. I folded a slice of white bread and took a bite from the middle, then peeked through the hole—the sort of thing a six-year-old would do. I wanted desperately to re-capture the happy mood we'd had only an hour earlier.

"You're a pirate," my father said, so eager to be jovial that he confused eyehole with eye patch. "Jimmy's a pirate," he told Alida.

She smiled and nodded. "Shiver my timbers," she said and put her arm around his shoulders.

It was after two by the time we returned to the car. We had all grown quiet. I lay across the backseat and didn't respond when my father called my name.

"I wish I could sleep," he said to Alida.

She turned to him. Her arm appeared along the back of the seat. Her voice was flat and soft. "Who was she?"

"What business is that of yours?" He spoke angrily, in a hushed tone. "She's someone I never knew. Put it that way. I might have thought I did, but I didn't."

I kept picturing the gap-toothed smile, confusing what I saw with what I'd expected. But the thin woman I remembered per-fectly, how she bent over and squinted, as if looking at us from a great distance.

I didn't figure out anything that night, couldn't put two and two together. I understood only that my father was angry and embarrassed, as if those two in the house had conspired to make him play the fool. Up front, he had begun yet another story, the one about the bet with the piano player. Alida glanced into the backseat. She could see I was listening, but she didn't let on.

"Asked the piano man if he had a name for that," my father said. "He called it a full glissando, and I made him write it down. I told her it was right there in the music, but that didn't satisfy her." He shook his head furiously. "Not her. She called me a sap. Truth is, *I* had saved us from a lot of trouble, and *she* had cost us fifty dollars."

Near the Arizona border, he pulled into a rest stop. His stomach was killing him. The lobster, he claimed. "Too rich for my system," he told Alida. As soon as he left, I sat up. I was on my knees with my elbows on the back of the front seat. I watched him cross the dark ground and disappear into the little brick outhouse. The moon had vanished and the night grown dark.

Alida looked at me sadly. She was tired, and bags showed under her eyes. "My parents split when I was two," she told me. "It doesn't have anything to do with your day-in, day-out life."

Her saying this made me angry. It came over me unexpectedly, like a wind that suddenly turns you cold.

"I want you to take care of me," I said, although that didn't convey what I meant. I had unzipped my pants and pulled out my cock. "If you don't, I'll tell him everything."

She clenched her jaw and gave me a long stare. Then she glanced at the door where my father had gone. "Watch for him," she whispered. She bent over the seatback and took me into her mouth. I stayed there no longer than usual. As she pulled away, I felt the hard edge of her teeth. By the time my father returned, I lay on the seat again pretending to sleep.

"Feel better?" Alida asked him.

I didn't want to hear his answer. Something inside me had

turned against him. I covered my ears, making his voice sound far away.

Alida cleared out later that week.

Louis Barley's photograph remained on the refrigerator until I swatted it down myself. I widened the space between his teeth with a kitchen knife and sent the photo spinning over the desert. My father never mentioned its absence and never said a word about Riverside. By this time I had figured it all out. I knew my father was a fool. On several occasions I started to tell him as much, but I kept it to myself a long time.

My father got credit cards in his half-brother's name and ran them up past the limits. When the bills arrived, he came to school and we drove off, heading north to Elkwood, Nevada.

Along the way we stopped at the Grand Canyon. We leaned against a metal railing and looked out over the empty space. The sun, setting through clouds, dappled the canyon with light. On the opposite rim, objects shimmered and moved as if made of water. The view held us a long time.

My father put his arm along my shoulder. He had left his hat in the car. A wind off the canyon ruffled his sleeves and lifted his lank and thinning hair. His collar fluttered against his neck, and I realized that his shirt was a size too large.

"Alida would have liked this," he told me, nodding at the canyon. "It's one of the things I could have given her." He shook his head sadly. "Instead, all she got was a TV and a couple of window units."

He said this as if he owned the place, as if that spectacular distance was his to give instead of the thing we stood helpless before. Despite this, or maybe because of it, I believed he was talking for the both of us. I felt close to him. The anger I'd carried for months abruptly left me. I even thought that it might be gone for good.

It didn't turn out that way. He and I had trouble in Nevada. When I turned seventeen, I took off on my own. But that day at the canyon, anger lifted from my shoulders and my heart opened up. I felt for one last time a boy's unsullied love for his father.

Dusk settled in and turned the air cool. We had stayed a long time. The approaching dark ultimately decided us. We got back in the car and headed north toward hardship and misunderstanding and further betrayal, driving as if we hadn't a care, riding with the windows down, wearing our old names.

DOGS

TOM MCGUANE

From To Skin a Cat
Dutton, 1986, first appeared in Grand Street, *Spring 1986*

No one imagined how it would turn out for Howie Reed. But it all began when he was beaned at the rodeo picnic when the Jacquas, the Hatfields, and the Larrimores all thought that everyone was so sick and tired of having to clean up the fairgrounds that a game would be fun. Howie Reed got beaned in the first inning. It was softball and he didn't even fall down. At fifty-one, he was close to the average age of all the players. It was a stately game with no scores.

Right after that he went on a trip. He was gone for about two weeks, and just before returning, he called his friends to tell them he had walked into a door at the bank and blackened his eyes. When he got home the black eyes were almost gone. But it was clear that he hadn't walked into a glass door. Howie had had his face lifted. It is not possible to really explain the effect on us, his old friends and acquaintances, of his new glossiness: the incisions behind the ears, the Polynesian serenity of his new gaze left many of our circle in Deadrock speechless.

The next time we all got together it was for a trout fry welcoming the new internist to town. In an area of long winters like ours, the entire community grows to hate all its professional people in about five years. A new doctor is taken in with urgent affection. The arrival of Dr. Kellman, fresh from the Indian Health Service at Wolf Point, was no exception. A horseshoe pitch was improvised; an extension cord was found so that a television set could be left running in the yard for guests following serials. Most of us drank and pitched horseshoes or skipped stones on the beautiful river. Howie fainted.

Dr. Kellman examined him and then came over to the carport where some of us had gone to avoid the sun. There, Dr. Kellman assured us that Howie was faking and that we should realize our friend was a mild hysteric; bring him a glass of water, possibly. Even accepting Dr. Kellman's diagnosis, it was awfully touching to see our old friend stretched out with his sleek new face aimed at heaven, the river flowing past him like time itself. In my view, it was either that very time, or the beaning, that explained Howie's face lift and faints. But that didn't lessen my concern for him.

No one noticed exactly when Howie left, but he was gone by the time the party wound down. And if there was any worry over him, it was lost in the uproar of the Kellmans' discovering that the thirteen-year-old corgi the doctor had owned since his medical school days was gone. Sylvan Lundstrom, who was everyone's lawyer and Johnny-on-the-spot, called the police, the sheriff, and the radio station, carefully describing a generic corgi from the Kellmans' American Kennel Club guide to breeds. It would be morning before we could reach the drivers'-training group at the school; they were usually most successful in finding lost dogs. Mrs. Kellman said she wished she knew less about the experimental purposes to which stray dogs were often put.

The dog was not found.

Monday I saw Howie in front of the Bar and Grill at the lunch hour. He was going out, I was going in. Howie is in insurance and busy as all get out, and a good kind of family man. So, the following seemed odd.

"You're on the phone with an old girlfriend," said Howie. "Your wife is at your elbow. Your heart is pounding. Your old girlfriend says, 'Just wanted to call and say I still love ya!' 'You too!' I shout like I'm closing on a huge policy. How much of this the old lady buys, I can't say." Howie shoots off with a little wave. I am not painting Howie as an ugly customer but as a troubled guy who didn't ever talk like this. It used to be you'd bump into him and he'd tell you something homely like the difference between whittling and carving (whittling you're not trying to make something). Now everything seemed sofinal.

Howie's wife went back to South Dakota in September, for good. To show he wasn't upset, Howie had his car painted: JUST MARRIED. He went to a sales conference in Kansas City and forced a landing en route in Bismarck. He had to pay a huge fine for that, which he could certainly afford. But Dr. Kellman assured his new admirers that forcing a landing was a well-known thing disturbed people do. When Howie finally got to Kansas City, his company made him Salesman of the Year.

By October, Howie seemed completely his old self. The face finally seemed to be his own. His wife stayed away. We had another softball game after the fall rodeo. He was still driving the JUST MARRIED car and he was wearing a sweatshirt copy of the Shroud of Turin. He was all over the field and drove in four runs.

Dogs kept disappearing. It was making the paper. Dr. Kellman was not building a practice as rapidly as he wished and he threw a Thanksgiving party, supposedly to introduce Diana, a yellow Labrador he had bought to replace the corgi. He said the corgi had left a hole in his heart that nothing could fill, but he let his pride in the new dog show. We all went to the party, even the other doctors. Howie was so disheveled-looking we asked if he was in disguise. "To be the leading adulterer in a small Montana town," he said mysteriously, "is to spend your life dodging bullets.

It is the beautiful who suffer." His whiskers pressed through the taut skin of his face. For the moment of our nervousness, in the central-heating itch of fall's first frosts, it was as if the house were equipped with self-locking exits. We were quiet in the drifting cigarette smoke for just a moment, then went back to our carefree ways. Right out of the blue Howie added, "What the hell, I forgive you all. Everything I know I learned from Horatio Alger."

The dinner was served buffet style, and we ate with our plates in our laps. The Kellmans' new dog was beautifully trained and took hand signals, retrieving everything from black olives to ladies' pumps with a delicate mouth. When we'd nearly finished eating, Howie said to a young woman, a dental hygienist, in a voice all could hear, "That food was so bad I can't wait for it to become a turd and leave me."

Dr. Kellman diverted our attention by sending Diana on a blind retrieve into the bedroom. When she returned, Howie asked Kellman what he had to "shell out for the mutt." And so on, but it got worse. Spotting a pregnant brunette in her thirties, he said, "I see you've been fucking."

Mrs. Kellman tried to distract Howie by describing the problems she had had keeping the grosbeaks from running every other bird out of the feeder.

"You know what?" said Howie.

"What is that?"

"I wish you were better-looking," he said to Mrs. Kellman.

"Get out now," said the doctor.

"Suits me," said Howie, once the mildest of our chums. "I've monkeyed around here long enough. I prefer white people." So Howie left and the party went on. Actually, the relief of Howie's departure contributed to its being such a terrific party. We all told stories that, for a change, weren't deftly to our own credit. I thought once or twice of making a plea for Howie—we'd been friends the longest—but thought better of it. Dr. Kellman had had to be restrained, once.

When the time came to go, it was discovered that Diana was missing. Mrs. Kellman cried and Dr. Kellman said, "I guess it's pretty clear that crazy son of a bitch has my dog."

In order to keep the police out of it, I agreed to go see Howie. At first I tried to get someone else to do it, but when I saw how anxious some of the others were to call in the authorities, I got a move on. He really had been a friend to all of us. But the pack instinct, whatever that is, was on alert. I think I felt a little of it myself, sort of like "Let's kill Howie."

Anyway, I made the feeling go away and drove up to Howie's house, a cedar-and-stone thing of the kind that went through here a while back. Diana met me at the door. Howie turned and wearily let me follow him inside. Various dogs gathered from the hallways and side room and joined us in the living room. Howie made drinks.

"I'm glad it's you," Howie said, handing me my Scotch. "The bubble had to break. Margie gone. Salesman of the Year. Every breed I ever dreamed of." He gestured sadly at our audience: Diana, a black Lab, an Irish setter of vacant charm, a dachshund, a few mixed-breeds who seemed to have a sheepdog as a common ancestor, all contented. And the old worn-out corgi.

"We didn't know what you were going through," I said. I didn't know who I meant by "we," except that I thought it was in the air when I left the party that we were pulling together over a common cause. "It started I guess when you got beaned." Howie looked at me for a long time.

"That wasn't it. I admit the beaning was what gave me the idea. I fell down to gain time to think. I lay there and thought about how happy I was that my marriage was on the rocks. The time had come to be off my rocker whether I felt like it or not. Margie had a guy but it wasn't enough. Then the company saying the future belonged to me. It was too much. I did the fainting business because I needed a jinx, I was superstitious. One thing led to another and I started grabbing dogs. It sounds crazy, but I felt like

Balboa when he saw the Pacific. I'd never known anything like it. By the way, getting caught is no disgrace."

I took Diana down to the Kellmans, and Dr. Kellman, who is such a young man, made a seemingly prepared speech about how much Diana had cost and how in a practice that was starting slowly, you cannot imagine how slowly, Diana had been a crazy sacrifice both for himself and for Mrs. Kellman. Among the party guests there was the gloom of drama slipping away, of a return to the everyday.

In another two hours, I had restored each dog but one to its rightful owner. The doctor and his wife said they were glad to be shut of the arthritic toothless corgi, hinting it was Howie's punishment to keep it. Howie said it suited him fine.

Anyway, as things go, it just all blew over. And in fact, by spring, when Howie started having some chest pains, probably only from working too hard, he went to Dr. Kellman, joining our new doctor's rapidly growing list of devoted patients.

THE RED CONVERTIBLE

LYMAN LAMARTINE

LOUISE ERDRICH

From Love Medicine,
Henry Holt, New York, 1984

I was the first one to drive a convertible on my reservation. And of course it was red, a red Olds. I owned that car along with my brother Henry Junior. We owned it together until his boots filled with water on a windy night and he bought out my share. Now Henry owns the whole car, and his youngest brother Lyman (that's myself), Lyman walks everywhere he goes.

How did I earn enough money to buy my share in the first place? My own talent was I could always make money. I had a touch for it, unusual in a Chippewa. From the first I was different that way, and everyone recognized it. I was the only kid they let in the American Legion Hall to shine shoes, for example, and one Christmas I sold spiritual bouquets for the mission door to door. The nuns let me keep a percentage. Once I started, it seemed the more money I made the easier the money came. Everyone encouraged it. When I was fifteen I got a job washing dishes at the Joliet Café, and that was where my first big break happened.

It wasn't long before I was promoted to bussing tables, and then the short-order cook quit and I was hired to take her place. No sooner than you know it I was managing the Joliet. The rest is history. I went on managing. I soon became part owner, and of course there was no stopping me then. It wasn't long before the whole thing was mine.

After I'd owned the Joliet for one year, it blew over in the worst tornado ever seen around here. The whole operation was smashed to bits. A total loss. The fryalator was up in a tree, the grill torn in half like it was paper. I was only sixteen. I had it all in my mother's name, and I lost it quick, but before I lost it I had every one of my relatives, and their relatives, to dinner, and I also bought that red Olds I mentioned, along with Henry.

The first time we saw it! I'll tell you when we first saw it. We had gotten a ride up to Winnipeg, and both of us had money. Don't ask me why, because we never mentioned a car or anything, we just had all our money. Mine was cash, a big bankroll from the Joliet's insurance. Henry had two checks—a week's extra pay for being laid off, and his regular check from the Jewel Bearing Plant.

We were walking down Portage anyway, seeing the sights, when we saw it. There it was, parked, large as life. Really as *if* it was alive. I thought of the word *repose*, because the car wasn't simply stopped, parked, or whatever. That car reposed, calm and gleaming, a FOR SALE sign in its left front window. Then, before we had thought it over at all, the car belonged to us and our pockets were empty. We had just enough money for gas back home.

We went places in that car, me and Henry. We took off driving all one whole summer. We started off toward the Little Knife River and Mandaree in Fort Berthold and then we found ourselves down in Wakpala somehow, and then suddenly we were over in Montana on the Rocky Boys, and yet the summer was not even half over. Some people hang on to details when they travel, but we didn't let them bother us and just lived our everyday lives here to there.

I do remember this one place with willows. I remember I laid under those trees and it was comfortable. So comfortable. The branches bent down all around me like a tent or a stable. And quiet, it was quiet, even though there was a powwow close enough so I could see it going on. The air was not too still, not too windy either. When the dust rises up and hangs in the air around the dancers like that, I feel good. Henry was asleep with his arms thrown wide. Later on, he woke up and we started driving again. We were somewhere in Montana, or maybe on the Blood Reserve—it could have been anywhere. Anyway it was where we met the girl.

All her hair was in buns around her ears, that's the first thing I noticed about her. She was posed alongside the road with her arm out, so we stopped. That girl was short, so short her lumber shirt looked comical on her, like a nightgown. She had jeans on and fancy moccasins and she carried a little suitcase.

"Hop on in," says Henry. So she climbs in between us.

"We'll take you home," I says. "Where do you live?"

"Chicken," she says.

"Where the hell's that?" I ask her.

"Alaska."

"Okay," says Henry, and we drive.

We got up there and never wanted to leave. The sun doesn't truly set there in summer, and the night is more a soft dusk. You might doze off, sometimes, but before you know it you're up again, like an animal in nature. You never feel like you have to sleep hard or put away the world. And things would grow up there. One day just dirt or moss, the next day flowers and long grass. The girl's name was Susy. Her family really took to us. They fed us and put us up. We had our own tent to live in by their house, and the kids would be in and out of there all day and night. They couldn't get over me and Henry being brothers, we looked so different. We told them we knew we had the same mother, anyway.

One night Susy came in to visit us. We sat around in the tent talking of this thing and that. The season was changing. It was getting darker by that time, and the cold was even getting just a little mean. I told her it was time for us to go. She stood up on a chair.

"You never seen my hair," Susy said.

That was true. She was standing on a chair, but still, when she unclipped her buns the hair reached all the way to the ground. Our eyes opened. You couldn't tell how much hair she had when it was rolled up so neatly. Then my brother Henry did something funny. He went up to the chair and said, "Jump on my shoulders." So she did that, and her hair reached down past his waist, and he started twirling, this way and that, so her hair was flung out from side to side.

"I always wondered what it was like to have long pretty hair," Henry says. Well we laughed. It was a funny sight, the way he did it. The next morning we got up and took leave of those people.

On to greener pastures, as they say. It was down through Spokane and across Idaho then Montana and very soon we were racing the weather right along under the Canadian border through Columbus, Des Lacs, and then we were in Bottineau County and soon home. We'd made most of the trip, that summer, without putting up the car hood at all. We got home just in time, it turned out, for the army to remember Henry had signed up to join it.

I don't wonder that the army was so glad to get my brother that they turned him into a Marine. He was built like a brick outhouse anyway. We liked to tease him that they really wanted him for his Indian nose. He had a nose big and sharp as a hatchet, like the nose on Red Tomahawk, the Indian who killed Sitting Bull, whose profile is on signs all along the North Dakota highways. Henry went off to training camp, came home once during Christmas, then the next thing you know we got an overseas letter from him. It was 1970, and he said he was stationed up in the northern hill country. Whereabouts I did not know. He wasn't such a hot letter writer, and only got off two before the enemy caught him. I could never keep it straight, which direction those good Vietnam soldiers were from.

I wrote him back several times, even though I didn't know if those letters would get through. I kept him informed all about the car. Most of the time I had it up on blocks in the yard or half taken apart, because that long trip did a hard job on it under the hood.

I always had good luck with numbers, and never worried about the draft myself. I never even had to think about what my number was. But Henry was never lucky in the same way as me. It was at least three years before Henry came home. By then I guess the whole war was solved in the government's mind, but for him it would keep on going. In those years I'd put his car into almost perfect shape. I always thought of it as his car while he was gone, even though when he left he said, "Now it's yours," and threw me his key.

"Thanks for the extra key," I'd say. "I'll put it up in your drawer just in case I need it." He laughed.

When he came home, though, Henry was very different, and I'll say this: the change was no good. You could hardly expect him to change for the better, I know. But he was quiet, so quiet, and never comfortable sitting still anywhere but always up and moving around. I thought back to times we'd sat still for whole afternoons, never moving a muscle, just shifting our weight along the ground, talking to whoever sat with us, watching things. He'd always had a joke, then, too, and now you couldn't get him to laugh, or when he did it was more the sound of a man choking, a sound that stopped up the throats of other people around him. They got to leaving him alone most of the time, and I didn't blame them. It was a fact: Henry was jumpy and mean.

I'd bought a color TV set for my mom and the rest of us while Henry was away. Money still came very easy. I was sorry I'd ever bought it though, because of Henry. I was also sorry I'd bought color, because with black-and-white the pictures seem older and farther away. But what are you going to do? He sat in front of it, watching it, and that was the only time he was completely still. But it was the kind of stillness that you see in a rabbit when it freezes and before it will bolt. He was not easy. He sat in his chair gripping the armrests with all his might, as if the chair itself was moving at a high speed and if he let go at all he would rocket forward and maybe crash right through the set.

Once I was in the room watching TV with Henry and I heard his teeth click at something. I looked over, and he'd bitten through his lip. Blood was going down his chin. I tell you right then I wanted to smash that tube to pieces. I went over to it but Henry must have known what I was up to. He rushed from his chair and shoved me out of the way, against the wall. I told myself he didn't know what he was doing.

My mom came in, turned the set off real quiet, and told us she had made something for supper. So we went and sat down. There was still blood going down Henry's chin, but he didn't notice it and no one said anything, even though every time he took a bit of his bread his blood fell onto it until he was eating his own blood mixed in with the food.

While Henry was not around we talked about what was going to happen to him. There were no Indian doctors on the reservation, and my mom was afraid of trusting Old Man Pillager because he courted her long ago and was jealous of her husbands. He might take revenge through her son. We were afraid that if we brought Henry to a regular hospital they would keep him.

"They don't fix them in those places," Mom said; "they just give them drugs."

"We wouldn't get him there in the first place," I agreed, "so let's just forget about it."

Then I thought about the car.

Henry had not even looked at the car since he'd gotten home, though like I said, it was in tip-top condition and ready to drive. I thought the car might bring the old Henry back somehow. So I bided my time and waited for my chance to interest him in the vehicle.

One night Henry was off somewhere. I took myself a hammer. I went out to that car and I did a number on its underside. Whacked it up. Bent the tail pipe double. Ripped the muffler loose. By the time I was done with the car it looked worse than any typical Indian car that has been driven all its life on reservation roads, which they always say are like government promises—full of holes. It just about hurt me, I'll tell you that! I threw dirt in the carburetor and I ripped all the electric tape off the seats. I made it look just as beat up as I could. Then I sat back and waited for Henry to find it.

Still, it took him over a month. That was all right, because it was just getting warm enough, not melting, but warm enough to work outside.

"Lyman," he says, walking in one day, "that red car looks like shit."

"Well it's old," I says. "You got to expect that."

"No way!" says Henry. "That car's a classic! But you went and ran the piss right out of it, Lyman, and you know it don't deserve that. I kept that car in A-one shape. You don't remember. You're too young. But when I left, that car was running like a watch. Now I don't even know if I can get it to start again, let alone get it anywhere near its old condition."

"Well you try," I said, like I was getting mad, "but I say it's a piece of junk."

Then I walked out before he could realize I knew he'd strung together more than six words at once.

After that I thought he'd freeze himself to death working on that car. He was out there all day, and at night he rigged up a little lamp, ran a cord out the window, and had himself some light to see by while he worked. He was better than he had been before, but that's still not saying much. It was easier for him to do the things the rest of us did. He ate more slowly and didn't jump up and down during the meal to get this or that or look out the window. I put my hand in the back of the TV set, I admit, and fiddled around with it good, so that it was almost impossible now to get a clear picture. He didn't look at it very often anyway. He was always out with that car or going off to get parts for it. By the time it was really melting outside, he had it fixed.

I had been feeling down in the dumps about Henry around this time. We had always been together before. Henry and Lyman. But he was such a loner now that I didn't know how to take it. So I jumped at the chance one day when Henry seemed friendly. It's not that he smiled or anything. He just said, "Let's take that old shitbox for a spin." Just the way he said it made me think he could be coming around.

We went out to the car. It was spring. The sun was shining very bright. My only sister, Bonita, who was just eleven years old, came out and made us stand together for a picture. Henry leaned his elbow on the red car's windshield, and he took his other arm and put it over my shoulder, very carefully, as though it was heavy for him to lift and he didn't want to bring the weight down all at once.

"Smile," Bonita said, and he did.

That picture, I never look at it anymore. A few months ago, I don't know why, I got his picture out and tacked it on the wall. I felt good about Henry at the time, close to him. I felt good having his picture on the wall, until one night when I was looking at television. I was a little drunk and stoned. I looked up at the wall and Henry was staring at me. I don't know what it was, but his smile had changed, or maybe it was gone. All I know is I couldn't stay in the same room with that picture. I was shaking. I got up, closed the door, and went into the kitchen. A little later my friend Ray came over and we both went back into that room. We put the picture in a brown bag, folded the bag over and over tightly, then put it way back in a closet.

I still see that picture now, as if it tugs at me, whenever I pass that closet door. The picture is very clear in my mind. It was so sunny that day Henry had to squint against the glare. Or maybe the camera Bonita held flashed like a mirror, blinding him, before she snapped the picture. My face is right out in the sun, big and round. But he might have drawn back, because the shadows on his face are deep as holes. There are two shadows curved like little hooks around the ends of his smile, as if to frame it and try to keep it there—that one, first smile that looked like it might have hurt his face. He has his field jacket on and the worn-in clothes he'd come back in and kept wearing ever since. After Bonita took the picture, she went into the house and we got into the car. There was a full cooler in the trunk. We started off, east, toward Pembina and the Red River because Henry said he wanted to see the high water.

The trip over there was beautiful. When everything starts changing, drying up, clearing off, you feel like your whole life is starting. Henry felt it, too. The top was down and the car hummed like a top. He'd really put it back in shape, even the tape on the seats was very carefully put down and glued back in layers. It's not that he smiled again or even joked, but his face looked to me as if it was clear, more peaceful. It looked as though he wasn't thinking of anything in particular except the bare fields and windbreaks and houses we were passing.

The river was high and full of winter trash when we got there. The sun was still out, but it was colder by the river. There were still little clumps of dirty snow here and there on the banks. The water hadn't gone over the banks yet, but it would, you could tell. It was just at its limit, hard swollen glossy like an old gray scar. We made ourselves a fire, and we sat down and watched the current go. As I watched it I felt something squeezing inside me and tightening and trying to let go all at the same time. I knew I was not just feeling it myself; I knew I was feeling what Henry was going through at that moment. Except that I couldn't stand it, the closing and opening. I jumped to my feet. I took Henry by the shoulders and I started shaking him. "Wake up," I says, "wake up, wake up, wake up!" I didn't know what had come over me. I sat down beside him again.

His face was totally white and hard. Then it broke, like stones break all of a sudden when water boils up inside them.

"I know it," he says. "I know it. I can't help it. It's no use."

We start talking. He said he knew what I'd done with the car. It was obvious it had been whacked out of shape and not just neglected. He said he wanted to give the car to me for good now, it was no use. He said he'd fixed it just to give it back and I should take it.

"No way," I says, "I don't want it."

"That's okay," he says, "you take it."

"I don't want it, though," I says back to him, and then to emphasize, just to emphasize, you understand, I touch his shoulder. He slaps my hand off.

"Take that car," he says.

"No," I say, "make me," I say, and then he grabs my jacket and rips the arm loose. That jacket is a class act, suede with tags and zippers. I push Henry backwards, off the log. He jumps up and bowls me over. We go down in a clinch and come up swinging hard, for all we're worth, with our fists. He socks my jaw so hard I feel like it swings loose. Then I'm at his ribcage and land a good one under his chin so his head snaps back. He's dazzled. He looks at me and I look at him and then his eyes are full of tears and blood and at first I think he's crying. But no, he's laughing. "Ha! Ha!" he says. "Ha! Ha! Take good care of it."

"Okay," I says, "okay, no problem. Ha! Ha!"

I can't help it, and I start laughing, too. My face feels fat and strange, and after a while I get a beer from the cooler in the trunk, and when I hand it to Henry he takes his shirt and wipes my germs off. "Hoof-and-mouth disease," he says. For some reason this cracks me up, and so we're really laughing for a while, and then we drink all the rest of the beers one by one and throw them in the river and see how far, how fast, the current takes them before they fill up and sink.

"You want to go on back?" I ask after a while. "Maybe we could snag a couple nice Kashpaw girls."

He says nothing. But I can tell his mood is turning again.

"They're all crazy, the girls up here, every damn one of them."

"You're crazy too," I say, to jolly him up. "Crazy Lamartine boys!"

He looks as though he will take this wrong at first. His face twists, then clears, and he jumps up on his feet. "That's right!" he says. "Crazier 'n hell. Crazy Indians!"

I think it's the old Henry again. He throws off his jacket and starts swinging his legs out from the knees like a fancy dancer. He's down doing something between a grouse dance and a bunny hop, no kind of dance I ever saw before, but neither has anyone else on all this green growing earth. He's wild. He wants to pitch whoopee! He's up and at me and all over. All this time I'm laughing so hard, so hard my belly is getting tied up in a knot.

"Got to cool me off!" he shouts all of a sudden. Then he runs over to the river and jumps in.

There's boards and other things in the current. It's so high. No sound comes from the river after the splash he makes, so I run right over. I look around. It's getting dark. I see he's halfway across the water already, and I know he didn't swim there but the current took him. It's far. I hear his voice, though, very clearly across it.

"My boots are filling," he says.

He says this in a normal voice, like he just noticed and he doesn't know what to think of it. Then he's gone. A branch comes by. Another branch. And I go in.

By the time I get out of the river, off the snag I pulled myself onto, the sun is down. I walk back to the car, turn on the high beams, and drive it up the bank. I put it in first gear and then I take my foot off the clutch. I get out, close the door, and watch it plow softly into the water. The headlights reach in as they go down, searching, still lighted even after the water swirls over the back end. I wait. The wires short out. It is all finally dark. And then there is only the water, the sound of it going and running and going and running and running.

GAS STATIONS

MAX APPLE

From The Oranging of America,
Grossman Publishers, New York, 1976

C hances are you've been here too. World's largest, eighty-
three pumps, forty-one urinals, advertised on road signs
as far east as Iowa. Oasis, Wyoming, U.S. 40, hard to
miss as you whiz on by. Even Jack Kerouac on an overnight cross-
country spin used to stop here for soft ice cream. In the golden
days they had their own tables, all those fifties beats, way in the
back by the truckers' shower room. They lumbered in with the
long haulers, left their motors running just like the diesel men,
wore leather too and drank half cups of coffee. The truckers said
"shit" more. Busboys, in retrospect, could tell them apart by the
poems on the napkins.

The counter is fifteen yards long and there must be two hundred
tables. The waitresses wear roller skates except when carrying expensive meals. Everyone chews gum. The girls are all named Ellie.
At their waists, just above the apron, they make change like bus-
drivers out of metal slots. Quarters fly onto tables, dimes trickle
down their legs.

I order hashbrowns and eggs, whole-wheat toast, and coffee. My Chevy is being gassed out front, pump number forty-eight. The place mat tells the incredible story of the man who made all this possible. He dreamed a dream fifty years ago on a cold hillside. He was a Wyoming shepherd boy nuzzled against members of his flock in the biting wind. He dreamed that all his bleating herds became Cashmere goats at five times the price, that Wyoming shriveled up and dove into Texas. He awoke with frostbitten ears, fingers iced into the wool he clutched. While that man awaited the slow-rising sun to warm his limbs and awaken his herds, he vowed a vow.

"This won't be a barren wasteland," he vowed; "men will know that here I froze one night so that after this men shall freeze here no more." He slapped his herd with a long crook. His collies awoke as if it were spring and stretched on their forepaws. The man spit into the icy wind. He named the spot Oasis.

I look up from this saga on the place mat to recall, in the midst of travel, the tiny oasis of my youth, Ted Johnson's Standard. On our own block flew the Texaco star and the Mobil horse, but you couldn't pay us not to fill our Pontiac at Ted Johnson's Standard. He was the magician of the fan belt. With an old rag and one tough weathered hand, he took on radiators foaming and in flame. Where other men displayed girlie calendars, Ted Johnson hung the green cross of safety.

Although he looked like Smokey the Bear, it was engine neglect and rowdy driving that he cautioned against. Whenever a kid short-cut onto Bridge Street across his pumps, Old Ted raised the finger of warning. "Stay to the right, Sonny," he would yell, shaking his gray head over the lapse in safety. He had spotless pumps, his rest rooms glowed in the dark, he bleached the windshield sponges, but it was safety that drew us all to Ted. He wouldn't take your money until he had checked your spare. And it must have worked. He never lost a regular customer to a traffic fatality. He kept the number of deathless days posted above his cash register. At night, after he counted his receipts, Ted read the obituaries and added another safety day. I remember at least 7300. Twenty years of Ted's customers rolling down the road with their spare tires at the ready. They didn't need their suction-cup saints, Ted passed out his own stick-on mottos for the dashboard.

DON'T SWITCH LANES

ALWAYS SIGNAL FIRST

USE THE REARVIEW MIRROR

Yes, Ted Johnson's Standard, here in the middle of the world's biggest rest area, I long for you. They don't clean my windshield and my hood is tinkered with less than a fat girl's skirt. At night, Ted, they won't even make change and in the best of times you have to beg for the rest-room key.

You treated our cars, Ted, like princes from afar. The way Abraham must have washed the feet of angels, so you sponged windshields fore and aft. And those glass-headed pumps of yours looked like the Statue of Liberty lowering her torch to us, cozying up to our rear end.

My waitress rolls up. Her name is Ellie. "We're out of eggs," she says, "how about oatmeal? Twice the protein and none of that troublesome cholesterol. A man your age can't be too careful."

"I'm only thirty," I tell her.

"Not so young. In Korea, in the middle of veins, they found cholesterol at nineteen. The oatmeal's on special today. Think about it." I think about oatmeal while I continue the place-mat saga of Oasis, Wyoming. In 1930 there wasn't a road within a hundred miles. The shepherd boy was twenty-eight then and rode the freight to Grand Forks, South Dakota. With his stick and his collie and his dream, he rode east and almost succumbed, once in Kansas City and again in Chicago, to a fortune in the stockyards. By 1940 he had made a million in suet and owned a mansion on Lake Shore Drive. Big stock men from all over came by to sample his roast beef and pork chops and talk business.

Swift and Armour sent him Christmas gifts. The dog was his only memento of Wyoming.

Still, the millionaire was restless. His vow came back to trouble him. The autumn of 1941 was the worst freeze Chicago ever knew. By October the leaves in all their splendor froze upon the limbs. Thanksgiving was twenty-two below zero, the average for November. People coughed chilled blood into the streets. The stockyards closed. On December 7 the Japanese attacked Pearl Harbor and the millionaire suet man knew who the Jonah was. "I hustled ass back to Wyoming," he said, "before the enemy could make it his own."

First he leveled the land and built towers of fluorescent lamps. There was still no road within fifty miles, but now the man thought of nothing but his vow. "The road will come," he said, and he invested his million in a pinball arcade, a small wax museum, and the earliest version of the restaurant. The gas pumps were an afterthought.

Ellie brings me oatmeal.

"No charge if you don't like it," she says. "They've got twenty pounds of it in the kitchen. It'll be lumpy by noon anyway." She looks over my shoulder while I taste. Her long hair touches the milk in the spoon, the steam rises to both our nostrils.

"It's good," I say.

"It has to be," Ellie answers; "the big boss eats it himself." She nods toward a bald man about twelve tables east of me. He wears a baggy thin-lapeled suit and is daydreaming through his smoky windows. When I finish breakfast I walk over to shake the hand of the man whose history has filled my place mat. He attempts to smile for me but can't quite do it.

"Troubles," I ask, "when you have eighty-three pumps and are a place-mat legend?" He collapses over the table. He buries his head in his hands.

"Personal problems?" I ask. "Health? marital? emotional?"

He picks up his head. "Psychiatrist?" he inquires.

"Only a traveler," I respond, "heading west." He sits up and looks around to make sure that nobody is listening to us. He pulls me close to his shrunken lips. "Arabs," he moans into my ear. "When they couldn't buy the Alamo they started putting the pressure on Oasis. They want Coney Island too and Disneyland. Our government is worrying about U.S. Steel and Armour beef, they don't know the desires of desert folk. I do. My people come from Lebanon, also a land of milk and honey."

To cheer the man I tell him about Ted Johnson's Standard, the example that has strengthened me through breakfast. "A white tile building," I tell him, "round as a mosque. Inside, it was like a solarium. Cut flowers bloomed from the carcasses of dried-out batteries. The Lions Club glass and the March of Dimes cup twinkled in their fullness. Only one grade of motor oil there, the very best, and six-ply treads, mufflers with welded reinforcements, belts and hoses of the finest Indian rubber . . ."

"Enough," says the Oasis man, "you're just a piss-call romantic mooning over the good old days of Rockefeller. Wake up. Ted's Standard belongs to OPEC now. It flies the sign of the Crescent. Turbaned attendants laugh at the idea of a comfort station. They mix foreign coinage in your change."

"What about your help?" I motion toward my Chevy, where a swarthy man peeks beneath the hood. He wipes the oil stick clean with his lips and spits into the radiator.

"Just Mormons in make-up," the Oasis man says. "You can't find a real Arab out here, but I do my best. I want to get the country ready for what's coming. I give out free headdresses all through the holy month of Ramadan. For a nickel I'll sell you an 'Allah Lives' bumper sticker. We closed down on the day Faisal was assassinated. You can't buck the future."

"And what about the Ted Johnsons," I ask, "the men in uniform who made our stations great?"

"Underground," he says, "with the hat blockers and egg candlers, praying for the resurrection of the downtown."

"I don't believe it's so bleak," I say.

"Bleak for you and me," the Oasis man answers, "not so bleak along the Nile and the Euphrates. Every thousand years or so Mesopotamia gets a shot in the arm. It's just history. You can't buck it. You go along."

"I don't see it that way, Mr. Big, no sir, I don't."

Ellie rolls up with another ladle of oatmeal for the boss. "Beware," he says, "watch out for price fixing in radial tires and don't believe what the company tells you about STP." He rouses himself for a moment from his melancholy. "We serve three thousand meals a day here. Where are you headed, California?"

"Righto," I say, not even surprised that he has guessed it.

"Your own station or a dealer owned?"

"Franchise direct from J. Paul Getty, option to buy in five years." The Oasis man can tell that I'm proud of myself.

"Dummy," he says, "in five years you'll be a slave in Tunis." Ellie pulls up a chair and joins us.

"No," I say, "in five years I'll be like Ted Johnson. I'll be fixing flats and tuning engines in the happy hills outside San Francisco. I'll have an '81 Chevy, loaded, and watch the Golden Gate Bridge hanging in the fog."

"More oatmeal for you two?" Ellie asks. "It'll all be lumps by noon." Her perfect legs in their black hose roll toward the kitchen. Sparks fly from her wheels.

"Young man," he tells me, looking away now through the window at what is visible from this angle of his eighty-three pumps, "take it from the King of Octane, there's not a fart's chance for you out there. Go back to school. Learn dentistry. The Third World will need attention to its teeth."

Ellie is back with oatmeal and hot coffee. She sits with us, makes a thin bridge out of her fingers, rests her chin on it as she stares at my oatmeal.

"You've had your day, Mr. Oasis," I tell him. "If the place mat is to be trusted, you've been hot and cold, rich and poor. Now

you can sit at your window and watch the cash roll in. Ted Johnson never looked up except when he had a car on the rack. He
called his place a service station. Your name was your credit over
there."

The millionaire's mouth finally makes it into a huge smile.
"How many pumps will you have?" he asks.

"Three," I tell him loudly. "One each, regular, premium, and
no lead and no locks on the rest room." He breaks into giggles.
People at other tables are looking but I don't care.

"That's right," I continue, "and rubber machines and ten-cent
cokes if I can get them." He is almost rolling in the aisle now.
Tears of happiness leak from the corners of his eyes. "Firecrack-
ers and recaps," I continue, "wheels balanced by hand, and even
mufflers and pipes."

"Stop," he yelps amid his giggles. "I can't take any more." But I
want to go on. "I'll lend out tools too and give a dollar's worth to
anyone who's broke."

Ellie looks into my heart. "Take me with you," she says. "I'll
check crankcase oil and clean windshields. I don't want to be a
harem girl." Her look is as grim as mine. We leave him howling
at the table. I pay my bill and buy her a pair of magnetic dogs. Beside my Chevy, Ellie removes her roller skates. Her black hose
hooked around my antenna rise in the wind. Through the
rearview mirror I see in pursuit the disguised Mormons. Awkwardly they mount their camels and raise curved swords to the
east. My electric starter drowns their desert shrieks. Three hundred and forty cubic inches rumble. I buckle up, Ellie moves
close. Careful on the curves, amid kisses and hopes I give her the
gas.

CUL-DE-SACS

MARK JUDE POIRIER

From Naked Pueblo: Stories
Harmony Books/Random House, New York, 1999

Taking everyone to the Pima Air Museum was a mean idea, I admit. The only other people I remember seeing there that afternoon were four German tourists in fluorescent, synthetic sweatsuits and a few gossiping senior-citizen volunteers hiding from the white sun under a fiberglass ramada. The museum sits in a corner of The Boneyard, a vast dumping ground for spent military aircraft: miles of expired planes, helicopters, and jets, baking and disintegrating in the sun. The actual museum, an echoy old Air Force hangar filled with the thick smell of corn-dogs and popcorn from the snack bar, is home to hundreds of boring seventies exhibits like *Blacks in Uniform* and *Historic Propellers*. But I didn't want to sit around the house all day while Ann and Clarissa went to the mall like they had every Saturday so far that summer; that's why I insisted we all get in the car and drive out to the dead planes.

We spent most of our time on the rock-lined walkways that

wound through a group of fifty or so rotting, fading aircraft in the dirt outside the hangar. We had prepared for the sun with hats and UV-blocking sunglasses, and we were smeared with waxy SPF 45 sunscreen. We smelled tropical. Out there in the aircraft graveyard, our anti-sun measures didn't seem to help, though. I could feel the rays pressing down, sizzling through it all. We stopped at each plane and sat in the shade of one of its wings, if it still had its wings. I'd examine the rivets, peek into the cockpit if possible, and exaggerate my interest in the aerodynamics. Under one, I read aloud from the brochure: "The Convair B-58 Hustler was the first supersonic bomber in history capable of delivering nuclear bombs . . ." Ann pretended to listen to what I was reading. Clarissa sighed loudly and lifted her hair off the back of her neck. My son, Martin, didn't do anything because at that point he was asleep in his stroller, hiding under his ball cap.

Some of the jets were amazingly massive, bigger than strip malls, with windows and engines still intact. Most looked too big to fly, like it was wrong that things that big ever flew. The wheels on the landing gear of some were taller than me with Martin on my shoulders.

"It scares me to think that maybe only one guy was controlling this thing as it hurtled through the sky," I said, gazing up into the greasy shocks and axles of a carrier, one of the last we looked at.

"Can we leave?" Clarissa said. "I'm thirsty."

"This is torture," Ann finally said, pinching her temples like the heat had given her a migraine.

I was keeping Ann and Clarissa in the blasting sun, draining energy from them, making them too tired and grumpy to go off together later on.

"Uncle Ed, that place sucked," Clarissa told me on the way home. "And aim one of those vents over here." She was in the back seat, out of the air conditioner's range. Sweat trailed down her neck and dragged some of her makeup with it. I adjusted the vent on the right, directing it towards her, knowing that the cooled air would never reach her.

"I'll think of something better for next time," I told her. That following weekend, I tried to come up with somewhere as hot and as boring to visit, but not too obviously so. I couldn't. They went off to the mall.

Clarissa had come to stay with us for the summer. She's my older brother's daughter, and that spring she hadn't been able to get along with him. She was eighteen then, headed to Carleton College in Minnesota that fall. Smart, lazy as hell, and, with her honey-colored hair and showgirl legs, attractive in an obvious way. It was her job to take care of Martin and clean the house while Ann and I worked, but all she did was stick Martin in his playpen, lounge around, and watch talk shows. When I'd get home from work, she'd be draped on the couch, asleep, her hair spilled all over the cushions—the TV blaring and snack-food wrappers and crumbs scattered on the floor in front of her. Martin would also be asleep because he'd stayed up late, making Ann and me tired. The thing that really got me was that Ann didn't care that Clarissa was a slacker milking us for five dollars an hour plus free room and board. She liked Clarissa—probably because she didn't get along with any of her coworkers at the bank: "They huddle around *Days of Our Lives* in the lounge from twelve to one every day, and then when they come back out front, all they ever want to talk about is that damn show. And they all wear too much perfume."

Towards the end of June, I'd sneak up to sleeping Clarissa if I returned home before Ann and slam my briefcase down on the coffee table, or I'd pant primitively in her ear. She'd wake up and cuss at me, and complain to Ann about it when Ann got home.

Once, when Clarissa left a half-eaten hot dog on the arm of the couch, I plucked it from its ketchupy bun and slipped it into her hand. I watched as she squeezed the meaty insides out of the casing and onto herself. Then I woke her up by grunting loudly.

"What the hell?" she moaned.

"Interesting dream you were having," I told her.

"What?" she said, sitting up, looking at the mess in her hand. She was confused only for a second.

"You had quite a grip on that wiener."

"You're vile," she said, throwing the hot dog at me.

Then Ann got home, and the two of them went out as usual, leaving me with Martin, who had almost mastered escaping from his playpen. Despite what the pediatrician said about his slower-than-normal, eleventh-percentile verbal development—which shot up to the fifty-second percentile the fall after Clarissa left— Martin was a great two-year-old. Not fussy, not gassy, not wild, and ninety percent toilet-trained. I think he hated Clarissa, too— at least I fantasized that he hated her. We bonded in this hate.

Each night after Ann and Clarissa left and I calmed down, Martin and I went about our routines. I'd slip on my running shoes and strap Martin in his stroller, and off we'd go. I got to know our neighbors that summer. I learned everybody's business. There were only three houses in our cul-de-sac—including ours.

We all lived in model houses for a development that had flopped, gone bankrupt. These homes were priced to move, and because Ann and I thought back then that we'd like to have a few more kids, we couldn't refuse. Four bedrooms and a two-car garage. The homes were big, and all three looked exactly alike: sand-colored stucco, red, Mexican-tile roofs, natural desert xeriscaping in the front, and backyards with peanut-shaped pools enclosed by black wrought-iron fences. I could've walked into the neighbors' house across the street and known right where to find their bathrooms and linen closets.

I wouldn't have done that. The man across the street was a dentist who looked exactly like Rex Morgan, M.D., from the comics page: stiff ink-black hair and pronounced handsome-guy cheekbones. His wife wore baggy, loose clothes and big ceramic beads and spoke with what I always thought was a bogus British accent. She claimed she had worked with Jane Goodall and had a Ph.D. in primate zoology, but I doubted it. They had a pet chimp that she couldn't control. "He's not a pet," she'd say each time she came over to our place to fetch him. "He's been socialized with humans and thinks he's our child. We treat him as such."

Every month when Ann got her period, the chimp would be pounding on our back door, scratching his nails on the screen, showing his yellow fangs, and twisting his pink crayon dick—and screaming and shrieking. He was big, bigger than you'd think a chimp was, with thick linebacker shoulders and feet he could fist-up and punch with. When he was all sexed up, he was not the least bit cute. I'd go upstairs, lean out the bathroom window, and dump pans of cold water on him, refilling from the bathtub faucet. But he wouldn't retreat until his owners came over and calmed him down with a green liquid they'd spray from a perfume atomizer.

They were allowed to keep him because our neighborhood was outside the Tucson city limits. I only knew their last name: Rombough. I called them Chimp People. Their chimp I called Romboner.

To the west of us was a hardy Mormon family of nine giant girls and their giant parents. All the girls had blonde, braided hair and wore frilly dresses and knee-high socks. Swiss Misses of the Sonora Desert. You couldn't tell them apart from one another. Martin called them all Nan because Nan was the one who first baby-sat him—plus Nan was the only thing he could say anyway. His bottle he called Nan, me he called Nan, Ann he called Nan. The Mormon girls had all been good baby sitters: they held Martin and always cleaned the house before we got home. I still don't know why we kept Clarissa on. I should have sent her home to my brother after the first week and had the Swiss Misses baby-sit all summer.

The Swiss Misses never fought, and when they swam, they wore those old-lady-type skirted swimsuits and rubber flower-covered bathing caps. They'd wave to Martin and me from their pool through the twists of wrought iron. We'd wave back and stroll on.

The Chimp People were a little more interesting. Each night, the woman, clad in rudely colored spandex, would do step aerobics or Jazzercise in the living room, and Romboner would sit in the window and clap his long, wrinkled hands. When the dentist got home, he'd kiss the chimp first, then his sweaty wife. Martin and I frequently witnessed this through their ten-by-fourteen picture window. We had that same window at home.

Because the housing development never developed, desolate paved streets with low hills sprawled for miles into the desert. Some teenagers from town would cruise them and leave their crunched beer cans and condom wrappers, but otherwise no one ever went out there. The city planners didn't bother naming any of the streets, not even ours. According to the U.S. Postal Service, we lived on Route 67G, but there were no street signs. That made it difficult to give people directions to our house. If anyone got lost out on those streets, it might've been hours before they got back to civilization. It was a labyrinth of identically barren cul-de-sacs and confusing, curving roads. The development was going to be called Blue Canyons. There were no blue canyons out there. No canyons of any color.

I never got lost pushing Martin in his stroller. We stuck to the same four streets—a three-mile loop with two turn-offs. We'd see mangy coyotes loping through the scrub, nervous jack rabbits, and once in a while a gila monster. Snakes, even rattlers, would lie in the streets in the early evening, warming their bellies on the asphalt. Along the way, I'd pull the orange-vinyl surveyor flags from bushes and stakes and tie them to the stroller. The supply of flags was endless because the developers had planned on building hundreds of homes out there. The surveyors must've spent months placing those flags. Some nights we'd have so many tied to the stroller we'd look like a big Chinese dragon flapping down the street.

I'd push Martin up one big hill and we'd gaze at the sunset behind the city. Some nights, pinks and oranges smudged and flared all over the sky, but other nights the sky was clogged with the filthy grays and browns that the L.A. transplants had dragged to our desert.

Ann was the first person I met when I moved to Tucson from Manhattan, and she didn't really let me meet anyone else. She certainly didn't have a vast circle of friends. She happened to be the associate at the bank who set up my checking and savings accounts the second day I was in town, and she called me that night, saying, "I know you're new here, and I thought you could use a home-cooked meal." She gave me the whole business, and the more I learned about her—she hated her job, couldn't afford to go back to college, mother died when she was ten, apartment complex smelled like pesticide, car in a constant state of disrepair—the more I got sucked in.

It wasn't just pity. She was different then, enthusiastically showing me Tucson, like she had been waiting her whole life for someone new to show it to. "Just wait until August when the monsoons come and lightning lights the sky . . . They whitewash the big A every year for U of A's homecoming . . . The Pima County Fair . . . blah, blah, blah . . ."

We hiked in the Santa Catalinas, drove down to Nogales and bought blankets and got drunk on tequila, looked through the telescopes at the planetarium, went to all the museums, ate at all the little Mexican places on South Sixth Avenue. She was still showing me the city when we got married, still planning weekend outings after Martin was born. I think we finally exhausted the city a few weeks after we moved into the model home.

* * *

I stayed up and waited for Ann and Clarissa each time they went out. Wednesday nights nothing was on TV, especially out there where we couldn't get cable, so I'd do the housework that Clarissa had neglected all week and try to forget the envy and hostility churning in my stomach.

One of those Wednesday nights, I was folding laundry when the two of them returned home. I had it neatly stacked up on the couch to make them feel guilty. They were ruddy from laughing as they walked in.

"Where'd you guys go tonight?" I asked them. I refolded a pair of black panties that had been on the top of the stack. Clarissa and Ann stopped laughing.

"We're not *guys*," Clarissa said, and she snatched the panties out of my hands like I had been sniffing them or something.

"Is Martin asleep?" Ann asked.

"Yes," I said.

That's how most nights were. I pictured them out on the town, stuffing dollar bills in the G-string of some greased-up, rippled male stripper, or line-dancing with cubicle cowboys at the Cactus Moon Cantina.

Another night, before the two of them went out, Ann and I were sitting on the couch in front of the TV, only the TV wasn't on. I had my arm around her, was kissing her ear, hiding under her hair, making her smile. We had talked about her job, how she was beginning to like it better since her boss got transferred. It was the best ten minutes I had spent alone with her that entire summer. Then Clarissa popped in from the kitchen and ruined it.

"Do you want to go back to B.H.T. tonight?" she asked Ann—loudly, rudely.

"I don't know if I can handle two nights in a row," Ann said. She stood up and conspiratorially ushered Clarissa back towards the kitchen.

"You-know-who might be there," Clarissa said. "And those boots!"

They laughed and disappeared into the kitchen, leaving me in front of the blank TV, wondering.

The benches were breaking that summer. We made them where I worked. I went to four years of college and two years of architecture school to draw cement benches. The design offices were attached to the plant, so everything in my work area stunk of cement dust. At the end of each day, my teeth were gritty and my hair was like a powdered wig.

In the center of each bench, there was a stress point that hadn't been accounted for by Quality Control. We'd get calls from customers whose benches had broken, and Lou, the manager, would hook his dimpled fingers over the top of my cubicle, peer at me, and say, "Another one of your benches broke, guy," like it was all my fault. It wasn't. If they had used the cement mix I had suggested when I originally designed the benches, instead of the cheapo aerated mix, there wouldn't have been any problems.

For all of June, I had pretended to be hard at work designing a cement trash can. I could have done it in three days if I had really tried, but it was difficult to get enthusiastic about a trash can—especially a cement one—so I wrote fake memos to the material scientists, flipped through OSHA manuals, played Tetris on my computer.

The only person I liked in the whole company was Lou's secretary, Franny, a trendy woman who behaved like an eighth grader. Every other weekend she drove seven hours to the outlet stores near Palm Springs. It was an Armani summer for her, a summer of muted linen pants and clunky, industrial-looking black boots.

"These shoes would have cost me three hundred dollars in L.A., and I got them for ninety," she said, pointing her toe, rolling her leg from side to side.

"Good deal," I said. "Just don't kick me."

She'd cut me through and let me listen when Lou made his calls for male escorts on Friday afternoons. Lou's first question to the call boy was always, "Do you do fats?" Then it was, "What do you look like? Buff?" And we'd hear the poor guy list his stats, trying to sell himself to blubber-ass Lou.

On the week of the Fourth of July, Lou was gone for an extra three days, which meant Franny could snoop around in his office.

"Ed, I found something juicy," she told me that Wednesday after lunch. "Right there in the bottom drawer, under a bunch of old inventory folders, behind the first-aid kit." Her hands were trembling, she was dancing.

She had discovered a leather-bound scrapbook filled with clippings of Scott Baio. They were mostly from old *Tiger Beat* or *Teen Dream* magazines, back when Scott was on TV all the time as Chachi in *Happy Days*, or Charles in *Charles in Charge*. Towards the end of the book was a meticulously handwritten log of all the different episodes, plus the other times Lou had seen Scott Baio, like on *Circus of the Stars* or as Johnny Carson's guest. There were a few *TV Guide* ads for the more recent shows Scott had been doing, but these were just paper-clipped in a clump to the last page, like Lou hadn't had time to start a second volume. The book was alive: Orderly Obsession, Absolute Devotion, True Love! I imagined faithful Lou combing the magazines in Safeway, watching videotaped episodes of *Happy Days*, writing letters to Scott. Maybe it was somewhat reciprocal, maybe Scott's publicist had sent him form letters and glossy photos showing Scott in a different pose each year. Whatever the case, Lou had it bad: he had the Love Drive.

"I'm leaving," I told Franny. I closed the book and wiped my hands on my pants. It was only two in the afternoon, but I was anxious, taken aback by this discovery. Plus, I just wanted to leave, and Lou wasn't there to tell me I couldn't.

"You can't," she said. She grabbed my wrist and stroked the hair on my arm with her thumb. "I might find something better."

"You might, but I really gotta go."

"Party pooper," she said, defeated. She picked up the scrapbook, shoved it back in the bottom drawer, and kicked the drawer shut with her meaty boot.

I started on my way home, past the airport expressway and past the dusty fairgrounds, before I decided to turn around and away. Clarissa would have just been slouched on the couch watching *Oprah* anyway. I would have walked in and asked her if she had done anything all day, and she would have told me to get a life of my own—and she would have been sort of right.

The Bay Horse Tavern was where I first stopped. Maybe it was the bold orange sign with the stupid-looking, googly-eyed cartoon stallion that snagged me. Maybe it was because the Bay Horse was right next to Dime Vid, a place where you could play outdated video games for a dime. Ann never let me play video games at home. She never let me drink beer, either. "You want to get fat?" she'd say. "Beer makes men fat. Fat men have breasts."

I ordered a dollar bottle of Bud and looked at the Polaroids of the regulars pinned up behind the bar. In each of the pictures, the people pressed their faces together cheek-to-cheek, smiled, and held up whatever they were drinking. When I saw the one of Ann and Clarissa, I gulped my beer and changed stools so I could get a better look. Both of their faces were flashed white, their eyes red as devils, but it was definitely them. A third woman, whose face was also somewhat washed away, was squished between them, and a mustachioed man in a satin Wildcats jacket looked as if he had popped himself in the camera's view at the last second. All smiles, all holding beers.

"See that picture there," I said to the bartender, pointing with my beer bottle.

She was bending over at the other end of the bar, wiping down the inside of a refrigerator. She sighed and trudged across the rubber mats behind the bar, her soiled tennis shoes making squeaking, rubber-on-rubber noises. "Which?" she said.

"That one," I said, standing, pointing with my bottle.

"Ann, Jenny, Clarissa, and that guy from the dart tournament," she said matter-of-factly, like I had challenged her to name them all. She flipped her feathered red hair over her shoulder.

"Clarissa's only eighteen," I said. "Shouldn't be allowed in here. Can I have another?" I held up my bottle.

She popped open another beer for me and said, "How do you know?"

"She's my niece, and Ann's my wife."

The bartender's lip curled up on one side and she spit out a laugh. "You're Ed," she said. "I've heard about you."

"Oh?"

"Yes." She resumed her cleaning of the fridge.

I ordered three more beers and pounded them, still looking at the photos of the regulars. "Tell Ann and Clarissa I said hello when they come in tonight," I said to the bartender as I was leaving, pushing the door into the white burst of sun.

"They only come on Tuesdays and Thursdays," she said.

I was buzzed and bloated as I waddled over to Dime Vid in the blazing afternoon heat.

The woman working at Dime Vid smiled broadly at me when I walked in. I was the only one in there besides her. She was old, maybe seventy, but she wore bright, plastic little-girl barrettes in her long gray hair. "You've just been drinking next door," she said.

"Yes," I said. I handed her a buck. "Dimes, please."

She counted me the dimes from her change belt and disappeared. I put three in Asteroids.

I didn't do very well at Asteroids. In my first game, I lost all three ships before she returned with two beers. My score was around 2,000. You need 10,000 for a free ship.

She handed me an icy Coors, already popped open. If I had

known the Dime Vid lady was giving out free beers, I would have gone there first and skipped the Bay Horse. "Thanks," I said.

"You're playing all wrong," she said. "Save one asteroid on the screen and wait for the flying saucers to come out."

She swigged her beer and shifted her dentures with a clicking sound. Her electric-pink gums and her white teeth were too perfect. They looked wrong in the middle of her weathered, roasted face. "Let me guess," she said. "You're a doctor and you came to relieve some stress."

"I design cement benches," I said. "Now I design cement trash cans." I ran my fingers through my hair to show her the cement dust. She didn't notice.

"Out early for the holiday weekend?"

"A book of Scott Baio pictures scared me." I took my last swig of beer. It was still cold enough to hurt my teeth. I lost my second ship then. It exploded with a dry poof at around 8,000.

"Chachi?"

I tried to explain Lou's Love Drive, how it frightened me a little, and I forgot about the strategy that she had suggested. I blithely blasted away at all the floating asteroids on the screen. Only one saucer came out. I missed it.

"You know," she said, "you can love all different people and things, but when you dig through it all—save that last asteroid—when you dig through it all, the love is the same."

"Only sometimes it's illegal," I said.

It was a little tough behind the wheel for me. I made it to the Taco Bell drive-through window all right, ate three burritos in the parking lot with the engine running and the air conditioning on full blast. From there, I drove a few blocks to the liquor store to buy a six-pack. As I pulled into the parking lot, I scraped the side of my car on a bus-stop sign. The noise it made, that high-pitched grinding squeal, was funny at the time. I lost my side mirror. I was going to get beer, and bring it home, and drink it there, and maybe get fat and grow big-ass tits—all in front of Ann.

I decided that I was bound for jail if I got pulled over, so I cracked open a beer in the car and held it between my thighs.

Ann had probably been home from work for a few hours, I imagined, and she and Clarissa would have to keep sitting around, waiting for me, before they could go out.

I drove east, away from the eye-level sun, to the dead planes near the Air Museum. I skidded into the dirt next to a tall chain-link fence topped with evil twists of prison-quality barbed wire. Every fifty feet or so along the fence there was a red sign: AB-SOLUTELY NO TRESPASSING. GUARD DOGS ON DUTY. PROPERTY OF THE U.S. ARMED FORCES. Bullshit, I thought, looking at all the junked planes. Where would the dogs be? They'd die in the heat. I wanted in The Boneyard. I wanted to climb around on a Con-vair B-58—not that I remembered exactly what one looked like. I wanted to sit in the cockpit and drink my five and a half beers.

I didn't do it.

That sharp, flesh-ripping barbed wire scared me—so did the nonexistent dogs—and I chickened out. Still, I had my beer, and I cracked another as I headed home.

They were all primped and ready to leave when I walked in. Ann was wearing way too much makeup, and her hair was sprayed tall in the front like a bug shield. Clarissa had the same hair going. Proudly, I held the four remaining beers in front of me.

"You're late," Ann said. "And drunk?"

"These are my beers," I said. "And I'm your fat, beer-drinking husband."

"Ed, you're not fat," Ann said. Her eyebrows looked thin. Plucked away.

"I wanna be," I said.

"No beer," she said. "What's with you?"

I walked up to them, and Clarissa retreated to the kitchen. I looked at Ann's eyes: lined in black. They told me she wasn't happy to see me. She hadn't been nervously waiting for me to get home, calling the office, checking up on me. She wasn't relieved that I hadn't died in a car wreck.

I realized then that I wouldn't have kept a scrapbook of Ann pictures. I wouldn't have logged all of her appearances if she had been on TV. I wouldn't have spent that much time thinking about her, and I never would. I staggered to the bathroom.

I was thinking as I stood there in front of the toilet that I should be back in the Convair B-58 Hustler, casually finishing my beer, fiddling with the busted controls, staring up at the swarm of stars beginning to shine in the sky. But I was a wuss, so instead I was back at home, taking a piss, watching the bowl bubble up.

"Where's Martin?" I asked when I returned to the family room.

"Asleep," Ann said. "Clarissa and I are going out now. Are you OK here?" She gathered her purse and keys from the couch, not waiting for me to answer. "Get rid of that beer."

"Have fun," I said. Then I pushed open the kitchen door and also told Clarissa to have fun. She responded by telling me that a girl in her high school was killed by a drunk driver, and then she sneered at me more dramatically than she ever had, lifting her lip and arching her painted-on brows.

"Your hair looks really pretty," I told her.

Martin didn't wake up when I strapped him in his stroller. I brought a beer on our walk. I had put the other three in the refrigerator, shoving Ann's yogurt way in the back, next to the gallon jug of generic barbecue sauce we never used. It was dark outside, and I knew that this would have to be a short walk.

I pushed Martin around our cul-de-sac. The Mormons didn't have any lights on. I imagined they were probably asleep, the girls in beds lined up like in a hospital ward, wearing long flannel nightgowns and sleeping caps pulled down over their scrubbed foreheads.

The Romboughs' home was lit up. Through the big window, I could see them sitting around the dining-room table, wearing party hats. There was a cake, and shiny Mylar balloons were everywhere. One of the balloons had a purple 8 on it. It was Romboner's birthday. Romboner was clapping and smiling and shrieking. They were fussing over him good: adjusting his bib, kissing him on his crinkly monkey lips, singing to him. I bet they had a great scrapbook of Romboner. From the start, they must have taken lots of photos of him.

Martin stirred in his stroller and yawned. He sleepily pointed to the Romboughs and said, "Nan."

"No," I said. "Those are the Romboughs." I pushed the stroller up their driveway with one hand while I drank the last bit of beer. I tossed the can into an oleander, and held Martin up so he could press their glowing doorbell.

Lady Rombough opened the door. The dentist and the chimp were looking on from their places at the birthday table. "May I help you, Ed?"

"No," I said, and I put Martin back in his stroller. The chimp showed me his big teeth—not in the threatening I-want-to-monkey-fuck-your-wife way, but in a playful way.

"What do you need?" she asked.

I looked back at the dentist and Romboner. "Honestly," I said, "I'm not too sure."

MAHATMA JOE

RICK BASS

From Platte River,
Houghton Mifflin/Seymour Lawrence
Boston, New York, 1994

In February, after the chinook blew through, thawing people's faces into smiles and making the women look happy again, and making the men look like men again, rather than pouting little boys—in February, the preacher for the Grass Valley, Mahatma Joe Krag, began a rampage not unlike those of other springs.

It had been a hard winter in northern Montana, so hard that ravens sometimes fell from the sky in midflight, their insides just snapping, it seemed, and like great ragged clumps of black cloth they'd fall into the woods, or into a pasture, landing a few weeks shy of spring.

The stave-ribbed horses—those that the coyotes and wolves had not gotten—would go over and pick the crows up with their teeth and begin eating them, chewing the shiny black feathers.

There was nothing else.

People were so short-tempered that even the saloon closed

down. In past winters they'd gone in to gather, socialize, drink, and complain collectively, but now people got into fights, pistol-pulling duels out in the snow, duels which never killed anyone, not at thirty yards with the .22 pistols the saloon kept on the counter for that purpose. The snow was usually swirling and blowing, which further lessened the risk, though often one of the duelists would injure the other, hitting him in the thigh or the shoulder, and even once, in the case of One-Ball Boyd, in the groin.

It was a bad winter, even for Grass Valley. The valley was long and narrow, and ran northwest-southeast along an old mountain range, the Whiteflesh Mountains, the first inland range off the Pacific. Storms came hauling off of the Siberian Peninsula and crossed the Bering Strait, kicking up eighty- and hundred-foot waves; they crashed into Alaska and then Washington, worked their way over the northwest passes, too strong to be stopped, and hurried over three hundred miles of prairie in eastern Washington, building up speed.

The Grass Valley was the first thing they hit. The valley was shaped like a bottleneck, slightly curved in the middle, and the storms slammed into it and rounded the curve, accelerating.

But it worked the other way during chinooks. Winds from the south raced up the same funnel, blowing hot air through the valley even in winter, melting all the snow in a matter of days, and launching new hatches of insects, buds in the fruit trees, and the smiles of women. Once February came around, the chinook could happen at any time. It became a race between south winds and north winds to see what got to the bottleneck valley first. The temperature could change almost a hundred degrees in twenty-four hours, going from twenty below to sixty or seventy above.

The chinook would last only a week at most, but it was a sign that there would be just one more month of hard freezes left. A long time ago, the town had had a celebration called Naked Days, where no one wore clothes at any time, not even when they went in for groceries, not even when they went into the saloon. People fed their horses naked, slept naked for the first time in six months, and checked their mailboxes naked. There was hardly anyone around, and everyone knew everyone else. It was hard to describe the sense of freedom chinooks brought, after the entrapment of winter.

It had been great fun, that one week each year, the week of warm washes of wind against the bare chest and across the back, warm winds passing between bare thighs. The women all shaved their legs for the first time since the fall and lay out in the melting patches of snow down by the thawing river and got suntans. The men sat at picnic tables in the meadow behind the mercantile, also down by the river, and drank beer, wore dark sunglasses, and told stories. And there were no more duels—but that had all gone on in the old days, before Mahatma Joe Krag came into the valley, down from Alaska, angry and ambitious at not having converted anyone up there to Christianity, not even an Indian, in over six weeks. And now he hadn't scored big in Grass Valley in over twenty years: not since the day he left Alaska. He'd run out of souls up there. Little did he know that those six weeks would be the beginning of a rest-of-his-life drought.

Mahatma Joe put an end to Naked Days almost single-handedly, and it took him only a short time to do it.

He was mortified, during his first chinook, when he went into town and saw naked men and women walking down the streets, naked children playing catch, and was greeted by a naked storekeeper when he went in for his groceries. He was horrified but challenged, and sometimes, at night, delighted: he had found a valley more wicked than any of the mining camps in Alaska, and it was in the continental United States.

Mahatma Joe began to write articles about Naked Days for various evangelical magazines, inviting his fellow preachers to come to the valley the following February, during the next chinook, and witness "an entire valley of naked unsaved savages, and right inside our own country!"

The response was significant. The evangelists would watch the weather fervently in January, sometimes arriving early, anticipating the chinook's passage, calling it correctly even before the weather forecasters did. The evangelists prayed to the sky for the chinook to arrive, so that their business could begin.

The tradition faded. With all the visiting strangers, people in the Grass Valley began to keep their clothes on—around town, anyway.

Mahatma Joe pressed on to other, lesser matters.

He wanted the town to have rules, ever more rules. He wanted to stop the winter fights. He wanted to have a town church, a town Bible study, and a town vegetable garden in the rich meadowland along the Grass River. In summer he wanted the fruits and vegetables all picked and canned and bottled and sent to distant, savage lands. Joe believed that vegetables could calm angry souls, that meat—flesh!—was a temptation of Satan's creation.

Moose grazed in the fertile river meadow during the summer, and ducks floated on the slow blue waters. Elk, with their antlers in velvet, slept in people's yards in the high heat of the afternoon, and tried to get into the hay barns at night. The animals were unafraid of people in the hot windy months, and they would roll in the river's shallows like dogs, trying to escape the biting flies. Small children would walk out and touch the elk's antlers and feed them sugar cubes during those warm spells when rules dissolved.

Men and women would gather back in the saloon shortly before dusk to watch the sunset and discuss the day, telling of what they had seen. Ospreys. Nuthatches. Western flickers. Varied grosbeaks. Pine siskins. They knew all the names, though often would argue about which bird it was that had the crossed bill for cracking seeds. They loved seeing the western canaries, which were a bright yellow but had no song, made no noise.

There was hemlock, too, along the river in places, hemlock that would kill a man in half an hour. It looked like watercress, which some people used in salads. Every now and then someone would mistake hemlock for watercress, and it'd be the end. Everyone knew there were dangers still left to living up in Grass Valley. There were mountain lions, wolverines, bears, and wolves; it was one of the only places like that left.

Besides wanting to turn the entire river meadow into a town farm, a working, thriving plantation for the export of sweetness, Mahatma Joe wanted to get rid of the hemlock.

He spent the silent white winters huddled in the little office behind his cabin, writing venomous letters to editors of the many sinful newspapers across the country, and writing and rewriting various tracts on religion, sex, and education. He drafted and redrafted proposed ordinances. Joe had always imagined the little valley, ringed by snow and glaciers even in summer, as a new place to build something, a new place to get it right. But he needed help. He was sixty-eight by the time he had his final vision.

Sometimes people would move into the valley: young couples who filled in the places of the old-timers who had not made it through the winter. Occasionally they were young singles, a man or a woman running from some piece of extraordinarily bad luck, or a whole life of such luck; or sometimes they were young men and women who had just looked at a map, had seen that there were no paved roads leading into the valley and no towns within forty miles. They had seen how close it was to Canada, and they had wondered if, finally, this might be a place to rest.

They brought guns, traps, saws, books. They always brought a dog, and sometimes two or three, especially the single ones, and always the single women: hardy young women from Illinois and California, Texas and Arkansas, who had seen the name Grass on a map in some city or town library, on a day late in the fall, with end-of-day September light fading and flickering through the windows, with the library closing in half an hour and nowhere to go, no boyfriends, and life over too soon—everything over too soon, and somehow, too, everything just beginning. These women showed up every year, two or three of them, and asked around, found out who had died—who had fallen through the ice, who had been thrown from a horse, who had just disappeared—and they moved in, learning the old ways of the valley, quickly and hungrily, and staying, changing, learning.

One such woman moved to the valley in the fall of Joe's sixty-eighth year, his twentieth year in the valley. Her name was Leena. She had no money, and she came unaware, came in from the South, and put an ad on the bulletin board outside the mercantile asking for a place to stay in exchange for labor—clothes washing, gardening, fence building, horse feeding, whatever. There were no vacancies, no empty cabins when Leena came. She lived in a tent down in the field behind the mercantile for three weeks, frying bacon and washing her hair in the nearby river at night, babysitting children in their homes and running the cash register in the mercantile.

Across the road from the mercantile, at the Red Dog saloon, the patrons played a game called Shake-a-Day: you rolled five weighted dice at once, and if you had three of a kind, you won a free drink. If you rolled four of a kind, you got a free six-pack, and if all five were the same number, you won half of the pot, which was all of the quarters that had been paid in since the last pot was won. The pot usually built up to six or seven hundred dollars before someone finally won it.

Leena would walk into the bar with her dog Sam, buy one drink and sip it slowly, enjoying the talk and learning things about the valley: the names of birds, the names of plants. Everyone sat on a stool with their dog beside them, and watched the dogs.

Leena would finish her drink, find a quarter, pay for her roll of the dice—you could roll only once a day—and lose, always. She never won a drink to take with her across the street and down to the river—a free drink that she could sip by herself while sitting on a boulder over the river, where she could watch the spry bats racing across the top of the current snapping at bugs, and the big trout beginning to leap, and night coming in, her new life in this bowl of a valley. She never won.

She bathed in the river at night. The water was frigid, with blocks of ice bobbing downstream like dirty heads of lettuce, floating past her as she scrubbed her body hard with the washcloth, fighting for breath, the cold taking the air from her lungs and turning her numb. The stars above her when she was in the river, gasping, seemed brighter than when she was not in the river. She had left the most selfish man in the world back in California. Each day of being away from him was a day of happiness, of getting stronger—feelings she never thought she'd have again. Leena would take a deep breath, dunk her head under the water, disappear from the moonlight, like one of the great trout that rose and then splashed back down. She would rinse her hair, scrub under her arms, open her eyes under water, look up at the wavering bright moon, and imagine that she was going to live all her life under the cold river, looking up. The gravel beneath her feet felt good.

She would shake violently then, it was so cold, and burst from the water and run for shore with numb legs, numb arms, sometimes tripping and falling, unable to run properly, with nothing working right at all. But she was clean, cleaner than she had ever been. She'd rub herself dry with a rough towel and crawl into her sleeping bag shivering and pull the bag's drawstring tight around her. Sam slept at her feet. Leena fell asleep with her face and hands still tingling from the river, her feet still numb, but the warmth inside her beginning to glow once more, like something that could never again be chilled. She was poor and her luck was bad, but she was clean.

Sam had been with Leena through three men, three men in six

years. Things had fallen apart, lost their glue, like toys sub-
merged in water, parts drifting away, shy parts, plastic parts that
were never meant to last. They always wanted her to be a certain
way, never wanted her to be able to change her mind or change
anything. Leena fell asleep tingling, sinking, warm and safe,
Sam's breath steady in her ear, with all the stars above her moving, rotating, sliding from view and back down behind the tall
mountains as the earth spun. She would never have another man,
not ever. They were like fish, they were wet, and they were all the
same. There was no connection, no beauty. They just bit at the
hook and were pulled in, and then they did nothing but lie there,
gasping, their eyes turning slowly blue. Leena tumbled through
her dreams, unimperiled by her lack of luck. She had never been
so happy. She had never lived in so clean a place. Sometimes she
thought she could sleep forever. It was good to be in a wild place
where men didn't try to rule you.

Despite the deep good sleeps, Leena was up each morning at
seven, frying bacon as the sun, a late riser, was only beginning to
show over the tops of the tall mountains. Leena had a Frisbee,
and she would go to the meadow with Sam and play, first thing
every morning, right after breakfast.

Sam was daring, acrobatic, even heroic, chasing the Frisbee
wherever it went, even diving into the river after it. He would
race at full speed, tumbling over the little bluff and down into the
water, never looking down to notice where the land ended and
the river began. Surfacing immediately, he'd watch the Frisbee as
it hovered in the air, just beyond his struggles, always a little too
far away.

Leena would cry out whenever he did make a great catch, or
even a great effort. She would clap her hands and pretend that she
was a football coach, as her father had been, back in California.
"Sammy my boy, that's what I like to see. That's the way to do it,
Sammy boy!" she'd shout, laughing and clapping, delighted at
Sam's excitement, his reaction to the praise.

Her laughter carried all the way up and down the narrow valley, trapped in the thin air, living forever in the thin air. Anyone
could hear her. There were no secrets there. Everyone knew who
Sammy was by the end of the first week.

A hawk's summer cry, drifting down over the ragged jumble of
mountains, spread into the foothills and the valley's green, flat
river bottom, which was no wider in some places than a freeway.
Blue water cut through its middle. At noon, back in the woods,
the loggers shut off their saws, sat down and opened their lunchboxes. Five or six miles away, on a still day, you could hear their
laughter down in the valley, sometimes even hear their voices
from up in the mountains, as if angels were speaking.

The valley was a park, green and forever, in the summer.

Leena thought how she wanted a horse with which to explore the
mountains. She wanted a parrot, too, to talk to her, to ride around
on her shoulder. Her life was a river across which she would build
a bridge.

There would be one side, and then the other. Ray, owner of
the mercantile, had told her that he had an old hay barn farther
down the valley, and that he might sell it to her when winter
came, if she still had not found a place to stay. There were holes
in the roof, it was caving in, and the barn was full of years-ago,
dry, no-good hay, but it would be better than the tent, and Leena
began to apply her savings toward that, picturing it. She imagined
the snow coming down as she sat at a table next to a lantern, writing letters, perhaps a letter to her parents, with the parrot on her
shoulder and the horse in its stall, eating hay. Sam would be
asleep at her feet. She would get a cat, too, to catch the mice.

No more men. She saved her wages, twelve dollars a day, for
the winter. It was understood that whatever she had saved, no
matter how much or how little, would be the actual purchase
price of the barn. Leena knew that Ray was counting how much

he paid her, counting how much she spent. She knew that he was watching. That was how men were: watchers, rule makers. But it was all right. After she bought the barn, it would be hers. This valley would be different. This valley still had wild promise.

The barn she was saving for was also along the river, farther upstream where the valley narrowed and the snows fell deeper. Whenever she moved in, Leena knew she would have to walk down to the frozen river with an ax and chop ice to get to the water for the horse to drink, and to get water for cooking. She would have to tie a rope around her waist to keep from getting lost in the heavy snows, and with that same rope around her, she would slip down through the hole into the cold water to bathe quickly. And she would fish through a hole in the ice, farther out, over the center of the river: she would build a fire to stay warm, a fire whose light would attract the dull, cold fish, and through the small hole she would catch them all, as many as she wanted, all night, and she would dry them, smoke them, hang them from the rafters to cure in the cold dry air, and her cabin would smell good, like fresh fish and smoke.

Leena thought about this as spring settled in around them, and she saved her money, knowing these things—for once knowing how something was going to be, and for once in control.

She kept bathing in the river at night, her skin dark when there was no moon. When she rolled over on her back and let the cold water carry her downstream, bits of moss and trout minnows brushed against her legs. Breasts, shoulders, everything became shiny, luminous, when the moon was out. Drifting into a fast current, she would look up at the stars, the moon, and remember only then that she might have gone too far. Breaking out of her trance, she would swim hard upstream, moving like a fish back to where she had started from, and clean.

What Mahatma Joe thought about in the spring-going-to-summer, sitting alone in his tiny office with its woodstove, listening to the sounds of dripping water and the great cakes of ice sliding off his roof, melting and losing their winter grip, was how he was nearing the end, and how he was soon going to be accountable not for the things he had done, but for the things he had not done.

Not enough. He had done a lot, but not enough. He had failed to *change* things, really. He had sent some canned goods, jams and jellies mostly, to Africa from his own modest garden each year. He buried people in the valley when they died, and said words over them. He had put down the Naked Days rebellion almost twenty years ago. But he'd wasted time, too, wasted perhaps a whole life, on other things: on long slow walks through the woods, especially in the fall when the light was gold and strange. He'd wasted time on sinful daydreams. Sometimes, moving through that particular fall light, Mahatma Joe pretended that he had already died and was in an afterlife. The light was so still, so different, and the woods so silent, that some days he believed it, that heaven was here and now, and not in need of alteration or correction.

Sinful!

Winters were spent in the office studying, making notes for imaginary sermons or for services to his wife and servant, Lily. Over the years, she'd heard it all, knew the answers better than he did, and corrected him in lilting, broken Eskimo-English when he faltered, or when he lost his thoughts to his age, forgetting even what it was that he was supposed to be studying. Lily had been his housekeeper in Alaska, and gradually over the years he had just stopped paying her. He had performed the wedding ceremony himself, though he wasn't sure if his license for such things had been current at the time.

"I haven't done anything," he'd tell Lily when he came back to the house late each afternoon. Thousands of pages of sermons, stuffed all around his office. The house would be warm, warmer than it had been in his drafty office, and supper would be cooking, vegetables and meat warming on the woodstove. Mahatma

Joe shot moose and deer when they invaded his garden; bears and elk, too, anything that came slinking around looking for the Lord's produce. He hung the animals in the garage for Lily to skin and butcher. There was always meat.

When Joe came in sad and complaining, Lily would think of what she could say to cheer him up. "God loves you" was her favorite. That was usually the best one, the one he could not argue with when he came in sulky and self-abusing. Mahatma Joe had been a hero among some of the Inuit up in Alaska. He'd converted them to Christianity left and right, packing the church every Sunday, curing people in both their minds and their bodies, chasing fever from their blisters and wounds, and fever from their twisted, ecstatic, free souls, unsaved souls that didn't know the Word from the caw of a raven or the howl of wolves. Joe would shout at the heavens, shaking his fists and looking at his flock with wild eyes that frightened them, and made them want to change. It was as if he had come upon them in the woods and saved them, had fired a shot and killed or wounded some dark beast back in the woods just behind them. The Inuit had treated him like a king, and Lily believed that she'd been lucky enough to go with him when he left: proud to be such a strong man's wife, though sometimes she missed the pay she'd had when she was just a housekeeper.

That six-week slow stretch, when Joe had become disgruntled, and thought he was being called elsewhere—should they have stayed? Lily wondered. Would it have been evil for him to stay in Alaska and just be a regular man, instead of a saint? She understood the drama and attraction of saving souls—changing and controlling the course of a life, or lives—but Lily wondered often what it would have been like if, after running out of souls, Joe had just stayed there and been a regular preacher, just living a regular life instead of moving on and looking for fresh souls, like new meat, like a hunter.

That had been a long time ago. Things had gotten so different once Joe and Lily were across the border, in the Grass Valley. Despite its wildness, its lack of electricity or phones or a single radio station, the people were frightened of nothing, they were wild like animals, and happy—and Lily felt lost. She was shocked at the way they laughed at her husband—laughed at him openly— though she did as Mahatma Joe had instructed her, and prayed for them anyway.

"I have to *do* something," he told her more and more, as the days, and then the seasons, went sliding past, surely moving faster than they had ever moved for anyone else. Joe had been a middle-aged man when he and Lily came to the valley, strong and with a whole new place before him. But now it was no different than how it had ever been. In all of his sixty-eight years he had done nothing.

Joe never received thank-you notes from any of the agencies to whom he sent the jars of tomatoes, the preserved squash, the strawberry jam. He used not to mind it, but as he grew older, it only added to the panic.

Except for Lily, he did not exist. It could already *be* the afterlife, and it was not that much different from the first life, because nothing was happening: nothing major, nothing dangerous, not that he was aware of.

Lily cooked for him. They read magazines together, talked about the garden, reminisced about Alaska, and then compared their lives with those found in the Bible, how what they had done or thought about during the day reminded them of something someone had done in a parable. Then they would go to bed.

They would undress and get under the covers together, still wearing their socks. Another day would slide past as night drew up over them, while outside, in a hard cold that dropped birds from midair, the stars glittered and flashed through the trees, and all through the valley coyotes howled and screamed.

Mahatma Joe would listen to the coyotes and think that he was a sinner for doing *nothing*, and would be startled to realize that he was breathing hard, almost panting.

"*Ssshh,*" Lily would tell him, pulling him closer, patting his back, his shoulders, and his head, lowering it to her breasts. "*Sssh, it be all right, ssshh,*" she said, believing it was the coyotes that were alarming him, coyotes racing across the frozen snow, laughing and yapping, howling, running. "*Sssh, it be all right,*" she would keep saying, and finally, falling into sleep, he would believe her, and would be grateful for it, as if she had come upon him in the forest with a gun and had killed a dangerous thing stalking behind him, and saved his life.

And then, after Joe was asleep, down in her breasts and warm like a child, Lily would put a pillow beneath his head. She would get out of bed, go into the kitchen, dress warmly, and put on the ice skates they had hanging on the wall, which they kept for when children sometimes came by, wanting to skate on the little pond below their garden. Lily kept the ice swept and scraped in winter for just that purpose. It was always ready, and on the rare occasions when children did come to the door asking if they could skate, Mahatma Joe was delighted. He would hurry down to the frozen pond with them, sit on a snowbank with his Bible, and read to them as they skated around and around the tiny hard pond, the sound of steel cutting through frozen water, steel scraping and flashing. The children, ignoring the Scripture, would have their fun as Mahatma Joe read on, tears coming into his old eyes, so much pleasure it brought him to be reading to an audience, to be touching young lives, the most important ones, and the tears would fall from his cheeks, freezing, like small bits of glass.

Lily would now take the skates out below that field of stars, the crunch of frozen snow, with the coyotes singing and howling, their cries echoing all around the narrow valley as if going in circles, start to finish and back to start again. She'd walk down to the pond and put the skates on, and with her hands behind her back and her chin tucked down, she would skate the way she and Joe had seen men and women do at a park in Seattle, so many years ago. It was a small pond, but she would skate as fast as she could anyway, using only her legs, slicing them back and forth like strong scissors, with the cold air racing past her face, and two moons to give her light: the real one cold as stone in the sky above her, and then the one frozen in the ice, reflected, the one that was just ahead of her and then beneath her, passing under her skates as she raced across it, an illusion, behind her, gone.

Lily would skate for hours, her long black hair flowing from beneath her cap. Her eyes watered with pleasure at the speed, and at the feel of it, and at the chance to be doing something that meant absolutely nothing at all, something other than gardening or cooking or cleaning—and she would skate until her legs were trembling, until she could no longer even stand.

She would lie down on the ice and rest, spread-eagled in the center of the pond. She would watch the moon, panting, her face bright as bone, and would imagine that it was watching her.

There were things to think about as she rested. It would be close to daylight now, colder than ever. The coyotes would be silent, resting too. There would be no sound at all. Lily would think about the other life, the one she had left.

Lily would remember Alaska, remember her friends, remember certain colors, certain days, like scraps of cloth. She would close her eyes, still spread-eagled on the ice, and think about her life with Mahatma Joe, and try to feel all of the water beneath her, an entire pond of water beneath the ice.

Sometimes she thought that she could feel it, that she could sense there was something beneath all that ice. But she would grow quickly cold, lying still like that, and would have to get up and go back to the house, where she would hang the skates back up, build the fire again, slip out of her clothes and into bed with Mahatma Joe, who slept so soundly and who looked, each night (especially in winter), as if he were never going to wake up again. His brow would be furrowed, and Lily would smooth it with her thumb, and say again, "*Sssh, ssshhh*, it be all right."

***

The chinooks came, and people behaved fairly well. Mahatma Joe walked down the roads looking for violators, but he rarely saw anyone, clothed or unclothed; the town had changed, especially in the last five years. There was talk of properly paving the road, which was studded with gravel and blue flecks of galena. The town was aging; growing softer, less wild.

The soil began to warm. The snow blanket shrank, spotted itself away, new ovals of earth and dry grass appearing larger each day, opening so suddenly that it surprised people, even though they saw it happen every year.

But it was never the same. Each year was a surprise. Each year winter fooled them, and they forgot all over again that earth and grass lay beneath the snow, that the world was not made of snow and ice, that the real world would reappear quickly when the grace of the chinooks arrived.

Mahatma Joe prowled the river bottom, explored the fecundity of the valley along the river near where Leena had her tent. He jabbed his walking cane into the rich mire. The cane made a sucking sound as he pulled it out. Joe wanted the soil badly. He took handfuls of it home in his coat pockets and sprinkled it over his own poor garden. It occurred to him, and not for the first time, that these were his last days, but somehow he felt more free than he had in the past, felt cleaner, stronger.

It was like walking through the mountains for days and days—for years, even, without seeing anything—and then coming over a pass and looking out and seeing a small town below, glittering in the distance.

He knew, suddenly, that he was almost there, that he did not have far to go. He no longer had to conserve himself. His steps quickened.

Joe became extraordinarily protective of his home garden. Before, he had let the Arctic hares—their white pelage falling away,

shedding to mottled summer brown—sit and warm themselves in
the March light of his garden for a few minutes each day, nibbling
on carrot tops like hungry sinners, before he sent Lily out to
chase them away. Black bears, thin from the winter, sometimes
moved in, digging in the garden for roots, and Joe would shoot
them, and the elk and deer too, for the meat, but he knew this
time that he would not need the meat, and he felt uneasy for the
first time about killing, about taking lives too soon, too early.

Instead, Joe ran the moose and bears out of his garden with his
chain saw. He kept it on the porch, and would crank it up and run
out with it, revving it wildly whenever he saw anything near his
vegetables, even the timid rabbits. Joe shot one black bear, a year-
ling, and hung it on a pole in the garden like a scarecrow, put a
baseball cap on it and let it stand in the sun. Like a dark warm
shadow, the black fur glistened at first but then fell away, as the
winds carried most of the smell farther down the valley and up
the river. Ravens flew in from the woods and rested on the bear's
shoulders, leaning forward and picking at his fur as if leaning in
to tell him a secret.

In April, Mahatma Joe's soil was no longer good enough for him.
He had already managed to raise some beans and a few hardy
tomatoes by covering them with blankets at night and by building
small warming fires up and down the garden. And by midsum-
mer, as ever, he'd probably be able to eke out enough produce to
make his modest shipments to Africa again; but by the end of
April, Joe was discouraged. What had been good enough for him
in the past was no longer adequate, not since his visions of the
larger, better gardens along the river. Joe cut the bear down from
his pole, tilled up his garden in a rage, and burned the remains.
There would be other good gardens in that very spot, but they
would not be his, he knew.

Joe and Lily ordered more seeds from the catalogue and

waited for the full moon. They bought another pair of skates at the thrift store for Mahatma Joe. Lily took him to the pond at night, under a moonless sky with stars glittering above like a throw-net cast over them, and on the thinning shield of ice she taught him to skate, for no other reason than that it was something he had never done before. She also taught him her tribe's songs, which he had once known but had long forgotten.

A full moon appeared. Joe and Lily prepared as if they were going to war, strapping shovels and spades across their backs like rifles, and though the center of the river had thawed and was running fast and cold down the middle, the shorelines were still frozen and packed hard. They laced up their skates, stepped out on the ice, and pushed off, began to glide.

The racing water beside them drowned out the sound of their blades. Lily skated ahead of Joe, being younger and faster, and she leaped small logs that had fallen into the river and were frozen in the ice, leaping like the skaters they had seen in Seattle. Joe tried hard to keep up with her, to stay close to her, and he felt young, felt as quick as the dark river. He watched the moon on her back. He could not wait to get to the valley and sink the first bite of hoe into the centuries-old soil. He wanted to sprinkle the seeds on the dark upturned earth and let the moon's light touch them with its magic before he covered them up. He wanted to sing the songs of a sinner, in order to do good work. To do anything—any kind of work. To keep from disappearing.

She watched them from her tent. Sam's whines had awakened her the first night they came. Leena had thought they were bears until she heard their voices, almost like children's voices, over the strong night rush of the river.

Leena peered at their dark shapes moving along the river, the man and the woman discussing something, then separating, and beginning to swing scythes. The valley bottom was washed in moonlight, a light so bright it seemed brighter than daylight, though the slopes of the mountains and the trees were still in shadow, darker than ever.

But out by the river, in the tall spring grass, everything was silver, and she watched, a little frightened, as they moved through the grass with their scythes, cutting great sweeps of it down.

Renewed with every swing, Joe felt as if he were getting back at something, or as if he were earning something—felling sinners for the Lord, each blade of grass a dirty heathen. He was greedy with the scythe, and went at the grass as if it were an enemy or a threat. He delighted in the smooth ease with which it fell. Perhaps he was even saving souls.

Lily was enthusiastic as well. Forty-five years she had lived, and she'd never been in the midst of such tall, green, *growing* grass. She'd never used a scythe, never walked through waist-high grass, and the smell it made as it was ripped by the scythe almost brought water to her eyes. Her sweeps were smooth, wide, and rhythmic. Lily wanted to take her clothes off and lie down with old Joe in the deep grass under all that light, but knew they were on a mission, that there was only a certain amount of time left, and so she only thought about it, as she cut the grass, and it made her swings easier, gave them a better motion, until after a while she could almost believe that that was what she was doing, lying under the moon in the sea of grass with old Joe, rolling across the pasture in sweeping motions, and it made Lily's swings come easier still. She hummed to herself as she mowed the grass down.

Leena was frightened to see them in what she had come to think of as her field, and was frightened by the speed and force with which the moon-washed grass was disappearing. The man and the woman were working their way up the slope from the river, coming toward her tent, so that it almost looked as if they were searching for her, hunting for her in the tall grass—that that was the reason they were cutting it all down, bushwhacking it.

But she had Sam with her, for protection, and she wanted to get closer, wanted to hear what they were saying to each other, and wanted to hear more closely the tune the woman was humming.

Leena thought that she might even want to help: it looked like it would feel good to cut that grass.

As she watched them, she was suddenly reminded of all the things she had been trying not to think about—California, and the last man, or the one before that. She had wanted to think only of herself. But in watching the grass fall, she was reminded of something else.

Leena crept out of the tent, one hand on Sam's collar, and began to crawl down through the grass toward the voices. She stopped when she had gotten close enough to make out their words and she lay flat, whispering to Sam to lie down beside her.

There was the sound of the river and of a breeze moving through the trees and the grass. The woman was sometimes humming, sometimes singing, using words that Leena had never heard before—such a song as might be used to put a child to sleep, or to keep a child from waking up; it was the kind of song that would mix in with the child's dreams, get tangled up in them. It made Leena want to sleep.

The man was calling out the names of vegetables as he worked. He was swinging hard, swinging the way Leena knew she would swing, though she admired more the grace of the woman's swings.

"Beans! Tomatoes! Kumquats!" snapped the old man, swinging as if his life were riding on it. "Beans! Tomatoes! Kumquats!" He kept repeating his chant as he moved up the hill, until he'd mown down an area sufficient to plant the crops he'd listed. Then he moved over and started a new section, imagining, Leena thought, what lay before him only a little ways into the future. He called out the crops with a strange sort of doubt, as if trying to force them into existence through sheer bravado.

"Corn! Okra! Taters!" he sang, swinging hard with the big

scythe, but Leena could tell that he was getting winded, and that his fury, or fear, was doing him no good.

"Corn! Okra! Taters!" he wheezed in a hoarse voice as he drew closer. Leena had to lie down as flat as she could, clutching Sam to her side. They lay there as the scythe ripped the grass all around them, passing right over their heads, so close that she could have reached out and untied the old man's shoelaces. And then he was moving farther up the hill. He was silent now, but the sound of softly falling grass, like feathers, was all around them, and Leena shivered, delighted with her luck at not being discovered. She lay there like that until daylight, when Mahatma Joe and Lily stopped working and put their skates over their shoulders and walked out to the road toward home.

Leena watched them go and then stood up to shake the grass from her robe and out of her hair. It was a cold morning. The sun was not yet up over the mountains. No one in town was stirring. Leena walked down to the river, pulled her robe and boots off, left them on a rock, then dived into the center of the current, ripping the cold water with her body.

She floated down the river on her back, as she always did, reveling in the sting of the cold water, the way it assured her she was still alive, very alive, even if no one knew it. She thought about how what Mahatma Joe and Lily were doing seemed right, seemed good in a way that she could not define.

When the sun's crescent showed over the treetops, a gold corona promising the day to come, Leena pulled out of the current, turned over on her stomach, and swam back upstream to the rock, got out and dressed, her blood chilled to the center, but feeling strong, and she walked up the hill to her tent.

Fresh grass cuttings gathered on her boots and around her ankles as she walked. The morning smelled good. She wondered if men in this valley were different. She wondered if the women were different. She knew that everything else was—the weather, the seasons, the land. Perhaps other things were different as well.

***

The mercantile had a tall, steep roof, with old high windows
through which dusty sunlight spilled, thin and dry, sunlight tasting of summer, even though it was only April and the river had
still not completely broken up. Some days Leena might sell only
an apple, or a tank of gas. There was a bell over the door that tinkled when it opened, but most days were silent. The loggers who
lived throughout the valley couldn't get into the woods because
of the frost breakup and the muddy roads; it would be another
month before the logging trucks moved in and out of the valley,
and with them the stumpy, bearded men with their heavy boots,
their dirty hands, the orange suspenders holding up thick wool
pants. The men wore hard metal hats. They left flecks of sawdust
everywhere they went, so that Leena would have to sweep up after them whenever they came into the store to buy a candy bar, a
piece of cheese and crackers, a soda pop.

Leena sat on the bench on the porch and worked at making a
crude scythe out of scrap metal she had found, lashing it with
wire to a sturdy green branch she'd broken off a tree. After her
shift was up, she'd go into the woods looking for antlers. She
wanted deer and elk antlers to use as a rake and pitchfork, and
moose antlers to use as a shovel. Mahatma Joe and Lily had been
coming every night, skating down the river along the rim of ice
that grew smaller every day. They were planting now in the rich
black river-bottom earth.

Some nights, as the moon grew darker, Leena would approach
the edge of where they were working and sit, not afraid if they
saw her or not, and half hoping they would, so that perhaps they
would invite her to help. She had found some good elk antlers,
and had made a strong rake.

But Joe and Lily never saw her in the tall night-waving grass.
Mahatma Joe would walk down the furrowed rows, dropping the
seeds in, still chanting each time a scatter of seeds fell—"Pumpkin!

Pumpkin! Pumpkin!"—until Leena felt nearly crazy with the same-
ness of all of it. Lily would crawl behind Joe on her hands and
knees, smoothing and patting the soil down tightly over the seeds
in a careful, promising way that made Leena want to get to know
Lily and be her friend.

Leena was delighted at the control that Lily and Joe had over
the field: how they had cleared and planted it, and were now going to bring it to life and nurture it, controlling when things happened, when things were harvested. It seemed wonderful and
simple, and she sat back in the darkness with her tools and waited
to be asked to join them.

They were there every night, despite the waning moon. They
napped during the day and let their house chores go to pot—dust
accumulating, and weeds growing up around the cabin. Mahatma
Joe had all but abandoned his Bible studies. He had been annoyed
anyway at how he kept forgetting parts of it, parts he used to
know well. They would wake up around four in the afternoon,
when the shadows were beginning to grow longer, and with the
light growing softer, shorter. They would open a can of soup or a
tin of potted meat and eat it cold. They'd each drink a can of beer,
because they felt it helped them skate better. The lane of ice running alongside the river was getting narrower each day, and they
weren't sure what they were going to do when it all melted.
There was only a thin strip left in places. Even in the shade of
deep fir forests, bends in the river that never saw sunlight, there
were young ovals of dark water beginning to appear in the middle
of the ice sheet, dark patches of water that they skated around,
ovals that were growing larger every night. The nights were
growing darker, too, as the moon waned, and Joe and Lily had
begun skating with flashlights, scanning the ice ahead of them for
those deep holes, but still skating fast, skating hard.

Mahatma Joe didn't know what they'd do when all the ice was

gone. He didn't own a horse. He did have an old birch-bark canoe, but he thought that would be too heavy to carry up the road
each morning—four miles, and uphill. He considered Christ's
uphill walk with the crucifix, and he wondered if maybe he could
heft that canoe, if it was for a good cause—the garden—and was
the last chance he had at, if not immortality, then at least salva-
tion. Joe thought that he could, especially with Lily's help. Christ,
after all, had had to carry his load all by himself; but he, Mahatma
Joe, was luckier. Mahatma Joe had Lily to help him.

Joe would drink two beers, sometimes three, getting ready for
the skating, and as the ice lane grew thinner and smaller, Joe began to believe more and more in the canoe.

After the third beer, Mahatma Joe didn't feel frail or old; he
felt young, strong, the way he had felt twenty years ago, when he
had first come into the valley looking for souls. He would let the
current carry him and Lily down into Grass Valley where they
would do their work in the garden, and then he would shoulder
the canoe, balance it over his head and shoulders like a young
man, a young man after souls, and start up the road. He had done
it in Alaska, and he would do it farther south, in the Grass Valley.
Grass Valley was no different. Joe was no different.

The garden grew. The bean plants were up first, ankle-high in the
good soil. On their way down each night, Mahatma Joe and Lily
now spent as much time jumping the black holes of river water as
they did skating. They were in the air, it seemed, every fourth leg-
stroke—skate, skate, skate, and then leap, up over a log or over a
wide patch of water, and then skate, skate, skate, and then it was
time to leap again. It was exhausting, but the beer, and the darkness of night, the black holes appearing right in front of them at
the last second, made it exciting.

As the garden grew, Joe and Lily could not wait to get to it, and
skated toward it eagerly each night, as if toward their children, to

see what changes each day had brought. They felt light-headed, invincible, and it was not from the beers but from the thought of the garden, the strength of its growth, and the sureness that it was only going to get larger and larger.

"Beets! Carrots! Spinach!" Mahatma Joe would sing, preparing for each jump, calling out a vegetable for each stroke of the skates. He was becoming quite good at it, and was less afraid to jump than Lily, who was heavier than he was and who sometimes made the ice splinter when she landed.

It didn't seem right, Lily thought, that she should be carrying so many of the tools when she was heavier than Joe to begin with. It made Lily nervous, so she did not sing anymore, but concentrated, scanning with her flashlight as she tried to skate around the black holes when she could. But sometimes there was no choice, it was too late, and Lily had to leap. She would bite her lips and pretend she was like the people they'd seen in Seattle so long ago, the ones dressed up in glitter and sequins, skating under bright, swirling spotlights, leaping with abandon every time they got the chance. Everyone had applauded, including Joe and Lily.

It had reminded Lily of a dance they had done in her village when she was young, back before the old people had stopped dancing. She didn't remember much about it, didn't know why they did it, knew only that like all the dances, it was done to change something—either to force something to go away, or to force another thing into existence.

All the men in the village would put on feather costumes, wearing any kind of feathers they could; and all the women would form a circle around them and beat drums while the men hopped and danced and pretended to fly around.

It had been a long time ago. Lily knew that the men and women had worn beautiful ceremonial dresses, soft caribou hide, and necklaces made of caribou teeth that rattled when they danced. But she had been gone so long that her memory was beginning to erode. She was taking on an imaginary memory, one such as Joe might remember, where none of the women wore anything, and the men wore only their feathers and loincloths. In Lily's new, confused memory, that was how it was—the dancers had been stripped of all protection, all security, even all humanity, and were returning to the wild and to freedom. Lily remembered that it had been some sort of fertility rite, but whether for crops, or people, or fertility in general, she couldn't remember.

The dance had been held in a great wide pasture in the spring, she remembered, because the snow was leaving, and the nights were warm. She remembered being in the circle of women, watching the strange half-man, half-bird dance, the firelight flickering over them. She remembered being excited at the sound of the drumbeats and chants carrying off into the night, as if trying to change something, or perhaps trying to preserve something. She had never told Joe about it, because she knew he would disapprove of the dancing; and it was not something her village did anymore, anyway.

Lily thought about the children she'd never had. She thought about the life she had never lived, back in her old village. She thought about how it would have been different—neither better nor worse, but different—had she stayed. For a long time it had been enough just to share Joe's vision, just to be near it, but now Lily sometimes woke in the night convinced that she could not breathe. She believed what Joe told her about the next life, but there had been so little in this one that she felt almost ashamed of herself. Skating hard, Lily imagined that she could hear drumbeats that echoed her thinking. She imagined that she was wearing feathers; believed that Joe was *chasing* her, not just following her. For the first time in her life she wanted to get away from him, and she began to skate harder.

Lily turned her flashlight off to confuse him, and began skating all-out, as hard as she could. The river flowed north, into the Fishhead; Lily imagined that the Fishhead might still be frozen too, and that she could skate upriver on it, up through Canada and back into Alaska. She felt as if Joe had taken something of hers, had hidden it, and that she had no power, no manner of getting it back.

Lily could hear Joe's faint, surprised cries behind her. The slush and snow and sheet of floating ice cracked and splintered as she leaned forward and dug in, her dark eyes growing quickly accustomed to the night. She could hear the terror in old Joe's voice, the terror of being abandoned that all men and women knew. Smiling suddenly, Lily knew what the dance back in her village had been about: the men wanted to leave, but the women did not want them to. Those who could fly would be allowed to leave. But Lily did not remember seeing any of them take flight. She thought how Joe would look at the dance, how he would think it was mostly pathetic little half hops and jumps. She laughed, then, at what Joe would surely think was a silly backwoods idea, that any of them could control anything, whether it was the weather, or a crop, or even each other.

Almost surely, such a thought was nonsense.

Mahatma Joe was skating hard, gaining on her, and he heard her laughter, but that was all. If there had been a splash, it had not been distinguishable from the sounds of the river as it hurtled past, carrying cakes and rafts of melting ice along with it, tiny icebergs, pieces of winter, the last to change.

Joe coasted to a stop, turned his flashlight off, and sat down on the ice and cried. He cried as he stretched himself out over the ice. He cried with guilt. He felt the ice crack beneath him, felt the water racing just beneath it, water running in the wrong direction, to the north, against the flow of nature.

After he was through crying—and it did not take that long—he crawled carefully to the shore and took his skates off, hiked out to the road, and walked the rest of the way to the garden, listening to sounds in the night: birds, and the wind.

He walked hurriedly, hoping, in a sort of delirium of sadness, that he might find her in the garden when he got there, a kind of a miracle, her hoeing, having started without him. Had her laughter really been so quickly cut off?

Joe stopped on the rise above town and looked at his dark garden, at the still cabins that were spaced along the river, each with smoke rising from its chimney, and at the river itself, running through the little valley. Even from the ridge he could hear the sound of the rapids.

Joe watched the river, the light brighter over the valley than it had been back in the woods, and when he saw the pale, naked body come floating through the rapids, clearly alive, swimming upstream, and climbing out on the rock by the garden, Joe grew so excited that he fainted. But he was soon up and running across the field, arms outstretched, tripping but not quite falling, saved by love.

Joe ran down the hill with such speed that he imagined he could lift off and fly if he wanted to, though he did not make the attempt. Just knowing that he could, if he wanted to, was enough.

Sam rushed out barking, hackles raised, when Joe drew near the river. Leena, who was standing on the rock drying herself, did not know who it was at first, but then saw the skates hanging over his shoulder, and recognized the shape of his shoulders, his old head. Leena told Sam to stop barking, then asked the man where the other one was, the one who sang while she worked.

"She is gone," said Mahatma Joe. "I thought you were her. She is gone, and she took all her tools with her."

They worked until daylight, shoveling with the moose antlers, weeding with the hoe Leena had made out of the jaw of a moose. The elk antlers scratched good, deep furrows in the earth, like fingernails down her lover's back, Leena remembered, and then she remembered the way Lily had moved through the tall grass with the scythe, sweeping smoothly, sweeping hard, and Leena tried to do the same with her furrowing, her weeding.

The garden was knee-high in places. Joe had not asked her to put her shorts and shirt back on, and Leena had not wanted to; there seemed no need. The plants rubbed against her as she walked through them.

Once the sun's first rim of blaze came over the tallest line of mountains, she went to the river and bathed, and then got out and dressed.

They walked home quickly, Sam running in front of them. Leena carried her tent and clothes in her backpack. They left the antler tools hidden in the garden.

"We will bring a bucket next time," Joe said. "We need to water the plants."

"I don't know how to skate," said Leena.

"That's okay," said Mahatma Joe.

Leena sat in the bow, and Sam in the middle. Mahatma Joe sat in the stern, watching them, and leaned back and trailed his hands in the cold ice-melt river. They had a lantern mounted on the bow, and as they pitched and slid over the little waves, curling up and over, sometimes splashing through the little haystack standing waves, the spray drenched Leena, blew back on Sam, and some of it even misted against old Joe; and the canoe's crazy slides and bounces pitched the lantern's light all over the woods, illuminating one side of the river and then the other, but it rarely showed them what lay directly ahead. Sometimes they would bounce into rocks, hitting them square on, throwing Joe and Leena out of their seats and making Leena drop her paddle. The boat would spin around, sliding down the little tongue of rapids backwards, and without a paddle, Leena would panic and begin to shout, clutching the sides of the boat, trying to will it to turn back around and point in the right direction—but they never capsized, they stayed low in the boat, and eventually they slid through the rapids, through the pitching waves and cool spray, and finally came back out into calmer water.

They would catch up with the paddle Leena had dropped; sometimes she would dive overboard and swim out to get it, in the still waters, and Sam, not wanting to be left alone in the boat with Mahatma Joe, would join her.

The ice along the shoreline was only the thinnest, most intricate paper crust; it was like lace, and Leena wondered how they could have stayed up on it. The nights were getting ever warmer, but the river was still as cold as it had been in winter. Leena had never felt water so cold, and swimming in it excited her.

It took her breath away and tried to numb her muscles and pin her arms at her sides; it tried to make her legs stop kicking and sink, unable to respond to her wishes; but Leena would hold her breath and fight against the cold, would keep swimming. The colder it was, the better she liked it. It was more of a challenge. It was more like being alive.

She would climb back into the canoe when she had the paddle, sliding over the gunwales like some river creature shining in the moonlight. Her teeth would be chattering as she sat back up in the bow. Leena would wring water from her hair to dry in the thin mountain air, slip on her dress, and rub her toes with her hands while Joe took the paddle and navigated, using the flat blade of the paddle as a rudder, looking around the shivering Leena and up ahead, trying to judge where the rocks were, trying to see beyond the lantern's dim glow.

Mayflies followed them down the river; moths swarmed around the lantern. Great brown trout leapt from the water, passing through the air in front of them, gulping moths attracted to the lantern light. The fish followed the canoe downriver, making Sam bark and lunge at them the whole way, almost upsetting the boat.

***

The moon had come back, and was full again. Leena would climb out of the canoe first, and then pull it farther up on shore so that Mahatma Joe could get out. Then she would begin carrying buckets of water up from the river. Each bucket held eight gallons; each full bucket weighed sixty-four pounds. Leena wore leather gloves but still developed red stinging blisters that made her want to cry, want to stop, but she knew that she couldn't, that Joe was not strong enough to carry the water, a big sloshing plastic bucket in each hand, and that if she did not do it, it would not get done.

Her arms felt strained, elongated even, as she hauled the full buckets up to the garden. By the time she got there, the cords in her neck felt stretched out as well. She had to walk pigeon-toed going up the small hill to get the power she needed, but the sound the soil made, drinking up the good water as she poured it, cold and loud, into the furrows, made the trips worth it, always worth it, no matter how much her neck and shoulders ached, no matter how red and tender the palms of her hands were becoming. Her hands would develop calluses soon enough, she knew.

Sam trotted along behind her on each trip to and from the river. The moon shone down on them. Elk and deer tried to approach during the night and nibble at the fresh growth. Mahatma Joe would move toward them through the waist-high beans like a predator, crouched down with one of the antler rakes. He would stalk the deer, then try to run up and attack them with the rake, though they always saw or smelled him coming, and with snorts and whistles they would bound away, white tails flagging, disappearing into the darkness. Joe would settle back down into the beans and wait for the next ambush as Leena emptied the river bucket by bucket, bringing what the garden needed, bringing the very water that perhaps had helped to drown Lily, that had filled, and then left, her lungs.

"Zucchini," Mahatma Joe would mutter to himself, crouched down in the garden. "Asparagus."

He thought of Africa, of dying dust babies, stomachs swollen from malnutrition, reaching their hands out for yams. He would get to heaven yet. He was doing a great thing.

Sometimes Joe would lie down on his side and nap, while all through the night Leena carried water, pouring it into the furrows, not ever having any idea what the garden was for, or why she was doing it—only that it was green and growing. She knew that it was responding to her touch, and she liked that. It made her feel a way that she had forgotten.

Leena vaguely realized that she was working for Joe, and that she was doing his work too, and for free, but she could not help it. She was amazed at the change. What once was meadow was now a cultivated garden, ordered and perfect. She'd quit working in the mercantile, had abandoned her hopes of buying the barn. There was room in Joe's cabin.

The soil splashed to mud as she poured the water; it splashed up around her ankles and got on her shorts, her shirt. Her hair was damp and scraggly from her exhaustion, and each time she went down to the river she wanted to set the buckets down and dive in, clean off, and float down the rapids. But each time, with the water so close, she could not resist making one more trip with the buckets instead, and one more after that, on into morning, until it was too late to swim, until the townspeople were up and moving around, starting the day. People had seen the garden, of course, but had no idea who the gardeners were; but now Joe and Leena were discovered. It did not matter; it was Joe's all-or-nothing garden, his gamble, and nothing mattered.

No one would bother his garden. He had created it, he had worked for it, and it was his. They would respect that.

Joe lay under the broad shade of a giant sunflower plant in the daytime and dozed. The days were dry and warm, the high mountain air thin. Leena would work on until midmorning, until she could carry no more water, and then, not caring whether anyone was looking, she would go over to her rock, strip, and dive in, feeling the dried mud and dust leave her body almost instantly as she plunged deep, her hair flowing around her, diving deep to the bottom, where there was moss and weeds that leaned downstream in the current and tickled her as she swam through it. At the bottom, she would grasp a handful of the weeds and hold on while the cold river pushed against her, cleaning her. She'd hold the air in her lungs and turn colder and colder until she could barely hold her breath any longer—the sun a bright glow above her, seeming closer than it ever seemed—and she'd release her grip then and swim for the top, up toward the brightness, and would break through the surface, gasping, the warm air a shock on her face, and she'd float on farther down with the current.

The men in the Red Dog saloon, loggers mostly, some of them having coffee, were still waiting for spring breakup. Some of them would be drinking beer already, at nine in the morning. They'd taken to sitting out on the porch to watch Leena, immensely grateful for her performance. Each time she went down, the loggers would make bets on how long she would stay under. She became a valley celebrity as she stood on the rock and toweled off, dry and clean again, and put her clothes back on. April turned into May.

She reminded the men of other times, long-ago times, of Naked Days, and of how their valley used to be clean, unchanged. The men who had been thirty-five and forty back then were almost sixty now, and everything had gone by, nothing would ever be the same, and yet nothing had happened.

There was nothing to do but wait for spring breakup, for the warm south winds to melt all the snow in the woods and to dry the roads. Then the men would go out into those woods and erase them, cut as many trees as they could, going back in time— they'd kill the old trees, and plant seedlings that would take ninety, a hundred, sometimes a hundred and fifty years to mature.

They watched Joe and Leena shoulder the birch-bark canoe

and start up the road, carrying it like a crucifix. Once Joe and Leena had carried the canoe up around the bend in the road and were out of sight of the other men, Joe would set his end down, saying that his leg was hurting him, and Leena had to carry it herself the rest of the way.

Her back grew wide like a man's, and her arms grew large and tight. Leena would do what he told her to. She did not know why, only that she did.

They napped in the daytime in separate rooms: Leena on the couch, curled up with Sam, and Mahatma Joe in his room, clutching the pillow as if it were Lily. When dusk fell, they would take the canoe back to the river and begin their journey all over again. They liked working at night because it was not as hot, and they floated down the river toward their garden, dragging a net in the water behind them, lanterns mounted on both ends of the canoe. The net would be full of trout by the time they got there, and it was Leena's job to pull the heavy net up onto shore. Sam would bark and rush in, snapping at the net, alarmed by this writhing, gill-flapping pile. Joe had Leena carry the fish in buckets up to the garden—and he made her bury them alive, for fertilizer.

Leena moved as if in a trance. Her shoulders were now larger than a man's; her legs were thick and sturdy from carrying the canoe up the road every day. Her neck had nearly doubled in size. The night was hers. She no longer felt the need to bathe, and with her added muscle, found it harder to stay afloat anyway. The plants in the garden were chest-high, bearing fruit, and greedily, old Joe went from bush to bush, picking okra, lima beans, snap beans, and tomatoes, filling the plastic buckets with them and taking them to the canoe for Leena to carry home, where he would put them in jars and send them to other countries, remnants of his land, another country, different, but changing—souvenirs from a valley of men.

The loggers went back into the woods in late May. The last of the ice that had trapped Lily melted in June. Passing over that spot one night in the canoe, Joe and Leena looked down and saw her, perfectly preserved in the frigid waters, lying on the bottom, looking the same as she ever had, looking up at them through twelve feet of water as if nothing had ever happened, as if no days had ever gone by.

INDIANS

JON BILLMAN

From When We Were Wolves
Random House, 1999

L ike all prolonged natural disasters, the Dakota dust bowl
bred superstition. Real estate changed hands by the
bushel. The government and railroad boosters had told
dirt-poor eastern farmers that if they moved into the Great
American Desert and plowed, the rains would come. But unlike
the chinch bugs, rain had not followed the plow here. After the
buffalo were gone, the cattle ate the buffalo grass down to nothing. Then came the barbed-wire fences that only wind and soil
and grasshoppers could pass through. After a few good wet years
the droughts came. Then more mice and rabbits and winds.
Without asking, folks in the Dakotas got parts of Texas and Oklahoma, and Canada landed good Dakota bottomland for a whistle.
Townships, counties, entire states began to hold collective days of
prayer to try to coax God into ending the suffering. It was a form
of spiritual cloud-seeding as well as a one-ring circus. Preachers
wrung their hands, looked at their shoes, then at the sky. People's

new hope was that beating the socks off an Indian ball team might change the medicine.

We spent most of the Depression as barnstormers, living like the hoboes who packed the boxcars thick as blackbirds and playing other Indian League reservation teams, civic all-stars, semi-pro teams, barnstorming colored squads, CCC teams, Rotarians, and prison teams for whatever beans, chickens, Grain Belt beer, and gasoline we could get.

We drove around the Dakotas with the windows open, our mouths shut against the dirt that would settle on our teeth. Sometimes the dust would be so bad we had to keep wet handkerchiefs over our faces to breathe. When we were playing well and did have the money, we weren't allowed in most hotels or motor lodges. We stayed in the colored motels, but those were rare in the plains. Usually we stopped the car and slept with fleas and chiggers on wool blankets under the stars. Never rained anyway.

Our pitcher, Job Looks Twice, could tell the weather in his sleeve. "Hot today," he'd say in the relative cool of the morning when we set out in the old Model T for another town. Waves of heat would rise from the hood of the car. Dust rolled in the open windows and stuck to our faces. "Very hot." It was in the last of the wet years that Job, drunk as nine Indians, had fallen asleep on the tracks in downtown Sioux City, giving his right arm to a loaded eastbound grain train.

They could not reattach his arm because they never found it. For a time, just after the accident, Job cursed God and prayed that he might die. But the stump healed without infection, and unlike the rest of the country, Job's personal depression was short-lived. He cropped his hair, bought a new black traveling suit and straw fedora, and—good thing he pitched from the port side—went on to keep us well above .500. This in 1931, when it wouldn't rain any real amount on the plains for another ten years. Ever since the accident, Job could forecast the weather in his sleeve, from some feeling, or nonfeeling, where his arm used to be. We knew it wouldn't rain, for Job's barometric arm told us so. Dust was a part of our lives.

Job was a second generation product of the missionaries and, after the accident, became obsessed with repentance. The loss of the limb had thrown the big lefty off-balance just enough to make his curve ball dance and his slider tail slick and hard. With the stump, which began just above where his elbow had been before Sioux City, he cradled his left-handed, three-fingered glove against his chest. He released the ball, followed through with his good arm, and capped the glove onto his good hand before the pitch reached the strike zone.

Job could field bunts as well as shots rifled at the mound, but he didn't need to have much range as a fielder: the other Indians—Asa Red Owl, Carp Whitehorse, Baptist Thundergrass, Walter and Jacob Elk, Jeremiah "Big Chief" Montgomery, Otis Downwind, and myself—covered the field like a trade blanket. At the plate Job learned to bunt one-handed and usually beat the throw to first.

In those days farmers and bankers would search the dawn sky for signs of rain, but the only clouds were clouds of dust, the only storms the soil-and-wind rollers that blew out of the south and west. "We cannot expect to understand the mysteries of God's weather," Job would say. He believed everything happened for a reason, God's reason. And unlike the rest of the team, Job never tried to question the logic behind it.

Besides his beloved spitball, Job was partial to another illegal gem he called his needleball. At any general store you could buy 78-rpm phonograph needles fifty for a dime. Job kept a few of the needles stuck in the seams of his trousers and a dozen or so more behind the mound under his rosin bag. With a motion that looked like he was simply wiping his only hand, he would unquiver a needle and finger it into the threads of the ball. The weight of the needle put rising zip onto his fastball and a ten-inch break in his nickel curve. Umpires would examine the ball but never find anything because the impact with the mitt or bat knocked the needle from the seams and into the dirt.

Before his accident Job's needleball had nearly killed a white man over to Woonsocket. The guy had used his spikes on Baptist Thundergrass at second base in the first inning, and Job had been brushing him back all afternoon with a salvo of knockdowns at the chest. Job would get the batter nervous and deep in the box, then paint the outside corner for strikes. A fastball in the eighth got away and he caught the batter in the temple. The man appeared dead, but as it turned out, Job only blinded him.

The Woonsocket players, too stunned to charge the mound, hovered around their downed comrade, fanning dust away from his nostrils. A minister climbed out of the stands and stood over the body, saying a prayer for his soul. Big Chief Montgomery walked out of a dirt devil in right field and started the car while the newly blind man held everyone's attention. The Indians lit out of town under cover of a dust storm. Blind man couldn't do more than snap beans for a living. Ever after the Indians steered clear of Woonsocket.

When Job lost his arm to the grain train he had thought it was retribution for the blinding. Arm for an eye. Job believed that if he lived a good life his de-railed arm would be waiting for him when he died.

"Sometimes," he said, "I'll reach for something with the arm that's not there. A tin cup. A baseball. I can feel the thing but can't pick it up. Then I'm aware that it will not be raining anytime soon." Job was sure weather came from heaven. "If my good outweighs the not-good and I make it there, I'll get my arm back. And the blind man from Woonsocket will get his eyes."

As boys, we had an old horsehide ball my father, a missionary from Sioux Falls, had given us. Though I was white and Presbyterian as hell, I had hair black as a crow. I wore it long and braided. I tanned like a buffalo hide under the sun. My father's life work was to save the heathen from the fires of damnation. When the Indians took to barnstorming, I chose baseball over Jesus, packed my Sunday suit in a canvas satchel, and set out for the open prairie with the Everywhere Spirit.

We had all grown up together in Porcupine, playing prairie ball on a sand-and-rock field in the cool of early evening. As kids, when the Cubs and White Sox games were on and the weather allowed for good reception, we would sit cross-legged in the mercantile owned by Asa's mother and listen through the static on a storage-battery neutrodyne set to the Chicago teams on WLS. The nine of us, shiny black hair, no shirts, dirty bare feet, stared at the radio among the canned goods. The radio put the idea of professional baseball into our heads. We would play ball, passing around our one and only glove, taking turns spitting Red Man chaw into the sweet spot and working it in with our fists. We learned to field bad hops bare-handed, bad hops being the rule.

Job stayed out past dark every night, throwing at a red strike zone painted on an outhouse behind the store. Throw, walk, pick up the ball, back to the makeshift mound, throw again at the target he could no longer see. Job's pitching made a slow, metered thump against the weathered wood, like the beating of a drum at sunset.

I began to stay behind with him to catch, where the whistling sound of his pitches became so familiar that soon I could catch Job in the dark. Though I was small and skinny, I grew to realize that my purpose in life would be to wear the secondhand tools of ignorance in the dirt behind home plate.

"How's the arm tonight?" I'd yell to Job as I squatted to catch a fastball, knowing he wouldn't answer. His mind was too busy listening to the electric hum of his pitches.

We got the red-and-gray wool-flannel uniforms, patched and stained, but free, from a women's relief circle over in Mud Butte. The uniforms were at least ten years old, having belonged to a team of white ranch hands. The team name came easy—the felt letters across the chest already scripted: MUD BUTTE INDIANS.

The Indians' play had much in common with the colored teams of the time. We were hustlers. We liked to bunt. We loved to steal third and home. We utilized the squeeze play and the hit-and-run. We knew about sacrificing.

Sometimes our aggressiveness cost us runs. But often, against the better teams—colored teams and semi-pro squads out of Aberdeen or Jamestown or Dickinson or Mobridge or Chadron or Stillwater—we made up the difference between losing and winning through hustle alone. This with only an hour or two of bad sleep in the car and just nine players—no one on the pine. Job Looks Twice had to pitch the entire game, and even double-headers some Sundays. The winning was so easy we sometimes put one of the Elk brothers on the mound and rested Job's arm. Some days we played our hearts out and won. Other days a different luck would pick up a bat and knock us into the next county.

Close calls always went to the other team. Called strikes were unheard-of. Job never argued with umpires, because he knew it was fruitless. The umps had the support of the fans, who sometimes resembled angry mobs. The other teams had to either go down swinging or hit the ball into play so we could glove it.

Our vested interest in winning games went well beyond pride. When we didn't win we didn't get paid. We were in high demand. Our name was hoodoo. Many people believed that beating the Indians would bring a break from the dust. As well as being the catcher, I also arranged the Indians' schedule, which usually meant wiping the layers of dust from my face, tucking my braid down the back of my collar and hustling into town while the rest of the Indians scrounged up supper by the river. Except for Job. We'd find the local watering hole and speak with the mayor, the sheriff, barkeeps, the undertaker, the men who planned the games. They ran ads in the local newspapers, cartoons of feathered savages with big teeth and tomahawks running bases. Word of our winning preceded us, and opposing teams shot beanballs at our heads in the early innings. Sometimes it was a hard sell to get the men interested in playing us at all. "Beat us and maybe it will rain," I told them, their eyes on Job and the arm that wasn't there. *Hell*, their faces would say, *if we can't beat a one-armed Indian baseball team, we don't deserve rain.*

"You shouldn't sell us on rain," Job said to me once on the way back to the river camp. "It will come back to hurt us."

"Sometimes it's the only way I can sell us," I said. The more I sold the Indians as rainmakers, the less Job accompanied me to town, until finally he stopped altogether.

Just before the Indians lost Job to the weather for good, we'd played an honest-to-God rainmaking in Custer and won under a hot, cloudless sky. The pinewoods around Custer were terribly dry and infected with beetles, and fire threatened to flatten the entire town. Heavy woodsmoke from the lumber kilns hung in the brown trees like a premonition. The mill boss let his employees off on a Wednesday afternoon for the game and townsfolk took a desperation holiday. Custer also had gotten word that beating the Indians would bring rain. The Indians beat the Colonels 7 to 0. We were glad for the victory and downright thankful to make it out of town with our hides. They were too mad that we took away their rain to bother paying us. These white towns took their water rights seriously. It was a long time thereafter before Custer got rain.

We kept winning games and it kept not raining. Sometimes we got paid, but most often not. Job began believing in the pattern of winning and no rain, no matter how hard we tried to talk him out of it.

"Maybe it is true," Job said to me after the Custer win. "You say it when you go to town."

"I only say it so they'll want to play us. It's business," I tried to reason.

"We won the game and I know the weather," he said, gripping his empty sleeve. "There is no rain."

"Times are hard," Otis Downwind said. "Back in Winner I saw a porcupine behind the roadhouse eating on a onion."

"So what?"

Otis looked at Job and paused. "Times are hard when a porcupine's gotta eat a onion."

After a few more nonpaying, no-rain wins, when things were looking especially hungry for the Indians, I managed to set up a rainmaking game in Faith, with a couple of other games along the way. We spent the next few days in the car, heading into the setting sun, to Faith, at a bone-jarring thirty miles per hour.

The car wasn't a thing to rely on. The best Model T's lasted about thirty-five thousand miles. Ours had over fifty thousand miles when Asa bought it from an old man in Mitchell. The car handled the rutted dirt roads like a cattle car. The wind and dirt had sandblasted the paint off and the body was rusted nearly through. Now and then it would backfire—Kaboom!—loud as a field gun. For relief from the heat we hung canvas water bags from the door hinges. Condensation formed and made the air blowing over the bags less hot. When the radiator boiled over— which happened every fifty or so miles with the load of us—the bags came in handy. Some days the T started. Other days it didn't.

Tumbleweeds collected along the fencerows and dirt drifted against the tumbleweeds until it almost covered the fences. What grass was left burned. Smoke filled the sky and we never truly did see it blue. Some days, through the haze, a dirt roller would birth out of the horizon. It looked like a thunderstorm, but blacker, angrier. Sometimes it would strike while the Indians would be on a ball field, sometimes we'd be in the middle of nowhere in the Ford. The sun would disappear altogether and there'd be midnight at noon.

On the way to Faith we stopped to wash our uniforms and feet with rocks and powdered soap in a shallow, muddy slew of the Bad River. Job loved to fish for catfish. He would bait his hook with a grasshopper at the end of a braided line on an old cane pole he carried strapped to the car like an antenna. Some folks who had already lost everything lived along the rivers in Hoover camps. They fished for food and when the carp and catfish weren't biting there was no dinner. Out of canned hams and beets, our guys hadn't eaten since early the day before, when we caught a few bluegills and Job beaned a rain crow with a fastball. We roasted the pigeon-tasting bird over the campfire and ate it with coffee.

The next day Job landed a channel cat that must have gone fifteen pounds. He picked up the fish by the lip and walked to a little camp of tents that met with the river and the highway. He gave the cat to a family of sharecroppers with eight or ten young kids.

"What in hell," said Carp Whitehorse. "You gave them our dinner for nothing?"

"Not for nothing," Job said, shaking his stump at the third baseman. "Nothing is for nothing."

Our uniforms dried flapping in the wind on the long drive to Faith.

The Indians blew into town from the east. I slowed the car and idled down Main Street to the ball field at the west end of town, near the sun-bleached Lutheran church. Folks on the square pointed and stared. A brass band warmed up with scales in a weathered gazebo.

The outfield in Faith was dirt, cracked and hard, just like the infield. Barbed wire separated center from the scrabbled wheat field, where brown-and-yellow shoots of Russian wheat gasped for water and fought to stay upright. This wheat held hope. As Job threw me some lifeless pitches and the rest of the Indians played pepper and stretched, the bleachers slowly filled with baseball fans, the convicted, and the simply curious.

"How's the arm tonight?" I yelled to Job.

"Which one?" Job said.

There was at the time a white barnstorming team from a religious settlement up in Michigan called the House of David. They let their hair and beards grow long and God-like and kept Bibles with them in the dugout. We had met the Whiskers on the road before, at chautauquas and county fairs, and respected them because, yes, they preached humbly to the fans before the games, but after the first pitch their spirits were real. Their fervor for God turned into a fervor for baseball and winning. They cursed like Philistines in their blue-and-gray uniforms and threw at batters' heads. A Whisker—pitcher named Benson—eventually made it to the Bigs. The games were as intense as firefights. It was like facing Jesus at every position.

This game would be our first-ever night game. Crude portable lights were trucked in along with generators. The steel stanchions were short and the lights yellow and not very bright, creating shadows behind everything. It made possible an incandescent noon at midnight. To folks in those parts, and even to us, a night baseball game was a miracle.

Farmers and the CCC crews were all off from work and gathered in town at dinnertime to eat and talk about baseball and the possibility of weather. Horses and mules pulled wagonloads of children. A Methodist church had set up an old army tent and a

choir practiced and sipped iced tea. Faith had the feel of the chau-
tauqua.

Drunk on a dram of humidity that some of the old-timers
sensed, the crowd watched us take infield practice. Hope and desperation played on their faces—babies crying, mothers crying, fathers cursing and praying in the same breaths. They cheered our
mistakes while grasshoppers danced in the dusky light that fil-
tered through the dust. Ministers and deacons in dark suits and
straw hats passed walnut collection plates.

From the tin lean-to visitors' dugout, we watched the Whiskers
take infield. "I have felt weather in my arm all day," Job said while
fishing the June bugs from the water bucket with the drinking
gourd. "Tonight there will be weather." The air was heavy with
humidity. Heat lightning flashed to the west. "We will be re-
warded with God's prosperity."

In the hazy twilight both teams racked up errors involving lack
of sight. As it got darker we played blind to the balls that were hit
over the lights, which were many. Line drives hid in the lights and
the outfielders had to react to directions from their infielders. We
communicated with whistles, growls, and shrieks only the Indians
understood. Even Job's breaking balls were hard to pick up in the
shadows, and I had to track them by sound through the batter's
grunts of frustration.

The Indians hit the ball hard and put runners on base all
evening. Except for Job, who seemed to have lost a step in beating
the throw to first. But we did score runs, even driving two long
balls into the wheat, one with two aboard.

The umpiring had been stacked against the Indians from the
very beginning. The umps were Faith Rotarians who didn't see
any benefit in another Indian coup. Job couldn't get a called
strike, and most of his pitches lacked snap and heat and the
Whiskers spent the evening whacking breadbasket strikes into

the outfield and sometimes beyond. I knew Job was convinced that throwing the game would be an offering of something more important than the purse money we would never see, a tithe of weather that would bring the Indians something more. Losing would mean rain, a final truce. Job believed he could control the hellish dry spell and its curse on all the land. He was now willing to lose on purpose, a personal sacrifice that he believed with all his soul would bring a saving rain. The other eight of us weren't convinced and wanted to beat the Whiskers like a drum.

Job kept shaking off the pitches I called, hurling instead easy fastballs, sliders that didn't slide, and change-ups that weren't much of a change. In the fourth I started to the mound to talk some sense into him, but how do you avoid a sermon at a time like that? Our eyes met. He pointed at the storm cell that was building over the Black Hills to the west. I realized I had nothing to say to him that would matter and walked back to my crouch behind the plate. More slow fastballs.

But the Indians battled hard at the plate as well. A pitching duel this wasn't. Both teams batted around two innings in a row.

Indians were up one at the bottom of the ninth, 13 to 12, Whiskers on first and second, two out. From his one-armed stretch Job checked the runners. Then again. He shook off my signs until we agreed on a fastball. His eyes were yellow and sorry, like the chiefs on old tobacco cans. He hadn't licked his fingers or gone to the rosin bag or the seam of his pants for a phonograph needle all game.

Then Job put a dull fastball into the wheelhouse of Joe Garner, the Whiskers' cleanup man. Garner stepped into the bucket, swung through, and massacred the easy mushball. A rainmaker. Otis Downwind in left ran underneath it just to say goodbye. The stitched horsehide that Job had always said possessed the spirit of the horse was still traveling skyward into the humidity when the wind came fast and quiet, ambushing the ball, pulling it down into the surprised glove of Otis Downwind, and ending the game.

From my knees in the dirt—the knees I can feel the big storms with now—I could hear the wall of wind coming toward the diamond like a night train.

Loud claps of thunder boomed just west of center field. Lightning struck the prairie with a dozen electric arrows. "Smell the rain!" the crowd yelled. "The miracle! Do you smell the rain! At last, thank God, the rain!"

The crowd stood, noses skyward, mouths open, like baby birds. For a moment, the Indians, too, were transfixed by the rush of wheat under the black umbrella of clouds. Then, silently, eight of us ran off the field to the car, Otis desperately throwing himself into the crank, trying to turn the engine over.

"Job, come on!" I yelled over the wind, but he didn't move, didn't even turn to look at us. By now, everyone but Otis and me were piled in the car.

The crowd reached to touch the weather, and Job, still on the mound, face to the sky, waved his gloved hand and stump in the air in exaltation. Thunder cracked as the engine fired up and the crowd yelled louder. The car sputtered slowly away from the field, picking up speed toward the dirt highway, as Otis and I ran beside it, still calling for Job.

The storm rolled eastward across the prairie, onto Faith, with the sound of a thousand horses racing to the river, and the wheat was beaten with hailstones the size of baseballs.

ROCK SPRINGS

RICHARD FORD

From Rock Springs,
The Atlantic Monthly Press, New York, 1987

E dna and I had started down from Kalispell, heading for
Tampa–St. Pete where I still had some friends from the
old glory days who wouldn't turn me in to the police. I
had managed to scrape with the law in Kalispell over several bad
checks—which is a prison crime in Montana. And I knew Edna
was already looking at her cards and thinking about a move, since
it wasn't the first time I'd been in law scrapes in my life. She herself had already had her own troubles, losing her kids and keeping
her ex-husband, Danny, from breaking in her house and stealing
her things while she was at work, which was really why I had
moved in in the first place, that and needing to give my little
daughter, Cheryl, a better shake in things.

I don't know what was between Edna and me, just beached by
the same tides when you got down to it. Though love has been
built on frailer ground than that, as I well know. And when I came
in the house that afternoon, I just asked her if she wanted to go to

Florida with me, leave things where they sat, and she said, "Why not? My datebook's not that full."

Edna and I had been a pair eight months, more or less man and wife, some of which time I had been out of work, and some when I'd worked at the dog track as a lead-out and could help with the rent and talk sense to Danny when he came around. Danny was afraid of me because Edna had told him I'd been in prison in Florida for killing a man, though that wasn't true. I had once been in jail in Tallahassee for stealing tires and had gotten into a fight on the county farm where a man had lost his eye. But I hadn't done the hurting, and Edna just wanted the story worse than it was so Danny wouldn't act crazy and make her have to take her kids back, since she had made a good adjustment to not having them, and I already had Cheryl with me. I'm not a violent person and would never put a man's eye out, much less kill someone. My former wife, Helen, would come all the way from Waikiki Beach to testify to that. We never had violence, and I believe in crossing the street to stay out of trouble's way. Though Danny didn't know that.

But we were half down through Wyoming, going toward I-80 and feeling good about things, when the oil light flashed on in the car I'd stolen, a sign I knew to be a bad one.

I'd gotten us a good car, a cranberry Mercedes I'd stolen out of an ophthalmologist's lot in Whitefish, Montana. I stole it because I thought it would be comfortable over a long haul, because I thought it got good mileage, which it didn't, and because I'd never had a good car in my life, just old Chevy junkers and used trucks back from when I was a kid swamping citrus with Cubans.

The car made us all high that day. I ran the windows up and down, and Edna told us some jokes and made faces. She could be lively. Her features would light up like a beacon and you could see her beauty, which wasn't ordinary. It all made me giddy, and I drove clear down to Bozeman, then straight on through the park to Jackson Hole. I rented us the bridal suite in the Quality Court in Jackson and left Cheryl and her little dog, Duke, sleeping while Edna and I drove to a rib barn and drank beer and laughed till after midnight.

It felt like a whole new beginning for us, bad memories left behind and a new horizon to build on. I got so worked up, I had a tattoo done on my arm that said FAMOUS TIMES, and Edna bought a Bailey hat with an Indian feather band and a little turquoise-and-silver bracelet for Cheryl, and we made love on the seat of the car in the Quality Court parking lot just as the sun was burning up on the Snake River, and everything seemed then like the end of the rainbow.

It was that very enthusiasm, in fact, that made me keep the car one day longer instead of driving it into the river and stealing another one, like I should've done and *had* done before.

Where the car went bad there wasn't a town in sight or even a house, just some low mountains maybe fifty miles away or maybe a hundred, a barbed-wire fence in both directions, hardpan prairie, and some hawks riding the evening air seizing insects.

I got out to look at the motor, and Edna got out with Cheryl and the dog to let them have a pee by the car. I checked the water and checked the oil stick, and both of them said perfect.

"What's that light mean, Earl?" Edna said. She had come and stood by the car with her hat on. She was just sizing things up for herself.

"We shouldn't run it," I said. "Something's not right in the oil."

She looked around at Cheryl and Little Duke, who were peeing on the hardtop side-by-side like two little dolls, then out at the mountains, which were becoming black and lost in the distance. "What're we doing?" she said. She wasn't worried yet, but she wanted to know what I was thinking about.

"Let me try it again."

"That's a good idea," she said, and we all got back in the car.

When I turned the motor over, it started right away and the

red light stayed off and there weren't any noises to make you think something was wrong. I let it idle a minute, then pushed the accelerator down and watched the red bulb. But there wasn't any light on, and I started wondering if maybe I hadn't dreamed I saw it, or that it had been the sun catching an angle off the window chrome, or maybe I was scared of something and didn't know it.

"What's the matter with it, Daddy?" Cheryl said from the backseat. I looked back at her, and she had on her turquoise bracelet and Edna's hat set back on the back of her head and that little black-and-white Heinz dog on her lap. She looked like a little cowgirl in the movies.

"Nothing, honey, everything's fine now," I said.

"Little Duke tinkled where I tinkled," Cheryl said, and laughed.

"You're two of a kind," Edna said, not looking back. Edna was usually good with Cheryl, but I knew she was tired now. We hadn't had much sleep, and she had a tendency to get cranky when she didn't sleep. "We oughta ditch this damn car first chance we get," she said.

"What's the first chance we got?" I asked, because I knew she'd been at the map.

"Rock Springs, Wyoming," Edna said with conviction. "Thirty miles down this road." She pointed out ahead.

I had wanted all along to drive the car into Florida like a big success story. But I knew Edna was right about it, that we shouldn't take crazy chances. I had kept thinking of it as my car and not the ophthalmologist's, and that was how you got caught in these things.

"Then my belief is we ought to go to Rock Springs and negotiate ourselves a new car," I said. I wanted to stay upbeat, like everything was panning out right.

"That's a great idea," Edna said, and she leaned over and kissed me hard on the mouth.

"That's a great idea," Cheryl said. "Let's pull on out of here right now."

The sunset that day I remember as being the prettiest I'd ever seen. Just as it touched the rim of the horizon, it all at once fired the air into jewels and red sequins the precise likes of which I had never seen before and haven't seen since. The West has it all over everywhere for sunsets, even Florida, where it's supposedly flat but where half the time trees block your view.

"It's cocktail hour," Edna said after we'd driven awhile. "We ought to have a drink and celebrate something." She felt better thinking we were going to get rid of the car. It certainly had dark troubles and was something you'd want to put behind you.

Edna had out a whiskey bottle and some plastic cups and was measuring levels on the glove-box lid. She liked drinking, and she liked drinking in the car, which was something you got used to in Montana, where it wasn't against the law, but where, strangely enough, a bad check would land you in Deer Lodge Prison for a year.

"Did I ever tell you I once had a monkey?" Edna said, setting my drink on the dashboard where I could reach it when I was ready. Her spirits were already picked up. She was like that, up one minute and down the next.

"I don't think you ever did tell me that," I said. "Where were you then?"

"Missoula," she said. She put her bare feet on the dash and rested the cup on her breasts. "I was waitressing at the AmVets. This was before I met you. Some guy came in one day with a monkey. A spider monkey. And I said, just to be joking, 'I'll roll you for that monkey.' And the guy said, 'Just one roll?' And I said, 'Sure.' He put the monkey down on the bar, picked up the cup, and rolled out boxcars. I picked it up and rolled out three fives. And I just stood there looking at the guy. He was just some guy passing through, I guess a vet. He got a strange look on his face—I'm sure not as strange as the one I had—but he looked kind of sad and surprised and satisfied all at once. I said, 'We can roll again.' But he said, 'No, I never roll twice for anything.' And he sat and drank a beer and talked about one thing and another for a while, about nuclear war and building a stronghold somewhere up in the Bitterroot, whatever it was, while I just watched the monkey, wondering what I was going to do with it when the guy left. And pretty soon he got up and said, 'Well, good-bye, Chipper'—that was this monkey's name, of course. And then he left before I could say anything. And the monkey just sat on the bar all that night. I don't know what made me think of that, Earl. Just something weird. I'm letting my mind wander."

"That's perfectly fine," I said. I took a drink of my drink. "I'd never own a monkey," I said after a minute. "They're too nasty. I'm sure Cheryl would like a monkey, though, wouldn't you, honey?" Cheryl was down on the seat playing with Little Duke. She used to talk about monkeys all the time then. "What'd you ever do with that monkey?" I said, watching the speedometer. We were having to go slower now because the red light kept fluttering on. And all I could do to keep it off was go slower. We were going maybe thirty-five and it was an hour before dark, and I was hoping Rock Springs wasn't far away.

"You really want to know?" Edna said. She gave me a quick glance, then looked back at the empty desert as if she was brooding over it.

"Sure," I said. I was still upbeat. I figured I could worry about breaking down and let other people be happy for a change.

"I kept it a week." And she seemed gloomy all of a sudden, as if she saw some aspect of the story she had never seen before. "I took it home and back and forth to the AmVets on my shifts. And it didn't cause any trouble. I fixed a chair up for it to sit on, back of the bar, and people liked it. It made a nice little clicking noise. We changed its name to Mary because the bartender figured out it was a girl. Though I was never really comfortable with it at home. I felt like it watched me too much. Then one day a guy came in, some guy who'd been in Vietnam, still wore a fatigue coat. And he said to me, 'Don't you know that a monkey'll kill you? It's got more strength in its fingers than you got in your whole body.' He said people had been killed in Vietnam by monkeys, bunches of them marauding while you were asleep, killing you and covering you with leaves. I didn't believe a word of it, except that when I got home and got undressed I started looking over across the room at Mary on her chair in the dark watching me. And I got the creeps. And after a while I got up and went out to the car, got a length of clothesline wire, and came back in and wired her to the doorknob through her little silver collar, then went back and tried to sleep. And I guess I must've slept the sleep of the dead—though I don't remember it—because when I got up I found Mary had tipped off her chair-back and hanged herself on the wire line. I'd made it too short."

Edna seemed badly affected by that story and slid low in the seat so she couldn't see out over the dash. "Isn't that a shameful story, Earl, what happened to that poor little monkey?"

"I see a town! I see a town!" Cheryl started yelling from the backseat, and right up Little Duke started yapping and the whole car fell into a racket. And sure enough she had seen something I hadn't, which was Rock Springs, Wyoming, at the bottom of a long hill, a little glowing jewel in the desert with I-80 running on the north side and the black desert spread out behind.

"That's it, honey," I said. "That's where we're going. You saw it first."

"We're hungry," Cheryl said. "Little Duke wants some fish, and I want spaghetti." She put her arms around my neck and hugged me.

"Then you'll just get it," I said. "You can have anything you want. And so can Edna and so can Little Duke." I looked over at Edna, smiling, but she was staring at me with eyes that were fierce with anger. "What's wrong?" I said.

"Don't you care anything about that awful thing that happened to me?" Her mouth was drawn tight, and her eyes kept cutting back at Cheryl and Little Duke, as if they had been tormenting her.

"Of course I do," I said. "I thought that was an awful thing." I didn't want her to be unhappy. We were almost there, and pretty soon we could sit down and have a real meal without thinking somebody might be hurting us.

"You want to know what I did with that monkey?" Edna said.

"Sure I do," I said.

"I put her in a green garbage bag, put it in the trunk of my car, drove to the dump, and threw her in the trash." She was staring at me darkly, as if the story meant something to her that was real important but that only she could see and that the rest of the world was a fool for.

"Well, that's horrible," I said. "But I don't see what else you could do. You didn't mean to kill it. You'd have done it differently if you had. And then you had to get rid of it, and I don't know what else you could have done. Throwing it away might seem unsympathetic to somebody, probably, but not to me. Sometimes that's all you can do, and you can't worry about what somebody else thinks." I tried to smile at her, but the red light was staying on if I pushed the accelerator at all, and I was trying to gauge if we could coast to Rock Springs before the car gave out completely. I looked at Edna again. "What else can I say?" I said.

"Nothing," she said, and stared back at the dark highway. "I should've known that's what you'd think. You've got a character that leaves something out, Earl. I've known that a long time."

"And yet here you are," I said. "And you're not doing so bad. Things could be a lot worse. At least we're all together here."

"Things could always be worse," Edna said. "You could go to the electric chair tomorrow."

"That's right," I said. "And somewhere somebody probably will. Only it won't be you."

"I'm hungry," said Cheryl. "When're we gonna eat? Let's find a motel. I'm tired of this. Little Duke's tired of it too."

Where the car stopped rolling was some distance from the town, though you could see the clear outline of the interstate in the dark with Rock Springs lighting up the sky behind. You could hear the big tractors hitting the spacers in the overpass, revving up for the climb to the mountains.

I shut off the lights.

"What're we going to do now?" Edna said irritably, giving me a bitter look.

"I'm figuring it," I said. "It won't be hard, whatever it is. You won't have to do anything."

"I'd hope not," she said and looked the other way.

Across the road and across a dry wash a hundred yards was what looked like a huge mobile-home town, with a factory or a refinery of some kind lit up behind it and in full swing. There were lights on in a lot of the mobile homes, and there were cars moving along an access road that ended near the freeway overpass a mile the other way. The lights in the mobile homes seemed friendly to me, and I knew right then what I should do.

"Get out," I said, opening my door.

"Are we walking?" Edna said.

"We're pushing."

"I'm not pushing." Edna reached up and locked her door.

"All right," I said. "Then you just steer."

"You're pushing us to Rock Springs, are you, Earl? It doesn't look like it's more than about three miles."

"I'll push," Cheryl said from the back.

"No, hon. Daddy'll push. You just get out with Little Duke and move out of the way."

Edna gave me a threatening look, just as if I'd tried to hit her. But when I got out she slid into my seat and took the wheel, staring angrily ahead straight into the cottonwood scrub.

"Edna can't drive that car," Cheryl said from out in the dark. "She'll run it in the ditch."

"Yes, she can, hon. Edna can drive it as good as I can. Probably better."

"No she can't," Cheryl said. "No she can't either." And I thought she was about to cry, but she didn't.

I told Edna to keep the ignition on so it wouldn't lock up and to steer into the cottonwoods with the parking lights on so she could see. And when I started, she steered it straight off into the trees, and I kept pushing until we were twenty yards into the cover and the tires sank in the soft sand and nothing at all could be seen from the road.

"Now where are we?" she said, sitting at the wheel. Her voice was tired and hard, and I knew she could have put a good meal to use. She had a sweet nature, and I recognized that this wasn't her fault but mine. Only I wished she could be more hopeful.

"You stay right here, and I'll go over to that trailer park and call us a cab," I said.

"What cab?" Edna said, her mouth wrinkled as if she'd never heard anything like that in her life.

"There'll be cabs," I said, and tried to smile at her. "There's cabs everywhere."

"What're you going to tell him when he gets here? Our stolen car broke down and we need a ride to where we can steal another one? That'll be a big hit, Earl."

"I'll talk," I said. "You just listen to the radio for ten minutes and then walk on out to the shoulder like nothing was suspicious. And you and Cheryl act nice. She doesn't need to know about this car."

"Like we're not suspicious enough already, right?" Edna looked up at me out of the lighted car. "You don't think right, did you know that, Earl? You think the world's stupid and you're smart. But that's not how it is. I feel sorry for you. You might've *been* something, but things just went crazy someplace."

I had a thought about poor Danny. He was a vet and crazy as a shit-house mouse, and I was glad he wasn't in for all this. "Just get the baby in the car," I said, trying to be patient. "I'm hungry like you are."

"I'm tired of this," Edna said. "I wish I'd stayed in Montana."

"Then you can go back in the morning," I said. "I'll buy the ticket and put you on the bus. But not till then."

"Just get on with it, Earl." She slumped down in the seat, turning off the parking lights with one foot and the radio on with the other.

The mobile-home community was as big as any I'd ever seen. It was attached in some way to the plant that was lighted up behind it, because I could see a car once in a while leave one of the trailer streets, turn in the direction of the plant, then go slowly into it. Everything in the plant was white, and you could see that all the trailers were painted white and looked exactly alike. A deep hum came out of the plant, and I thought as I got closer that it wouldn't be a location I'd ever want to work in.

I went right to the first trailer where there was a light, and knocked on the metal door. Kids' toys were lying in the gravel around the little wood steps, and I could hear talking on TV that suddenly went off. I heard a woman's voice talking, and then the door opened wide.

A large Negro woman with a wide, friendly face stood in the doorway. She smiled at me and moved forward as if she was going to come out, but she stopped at the top step. There was a little Negro boy behind her peeping out from behind her legs, watching me with his eyes half closed. The trailer had that feeling that no one else was inside, which was a feeling I knew something about.

"I'm sorry to intrude," I said. "But I've run up on a little bad luck tonight. My name's Earl Middleton."

The woman looked at me, then out into the night toward the freeway as if what I had said was something she was going to be able to see. "What kind of bad luck?" she said, looking down at me again.

"My car broke down out on the highway," I said. "I can't fix it myself, and I wondered if I could use your phone to call for help."

The woman smiled down at me knowingly. "We can't live without cars, can we?"

"That's the honest truth," I said.

"They're like our hearts," she said, her face shining in the little bulb light that burned beside the door. "Where's your car situated?"

I turned and looked over into the dark, but I couldn't see anything because of where we'd put it. "It's over there," I said. "You can't see it in the dark."

"Who all's with you now?" the woman said. "Have you got your wife with you?"

"She's with my little girl and our dog in the car," I said. "My daughter's asleep or I would have brought them."

"They shouldn't be left in the dark by themselves," the woman said and frowned. "There's too much unsavoriness out there."

"The best I can do is hurry back." I tried to look sincere, since everything except Cheryl being asleep and Edna being my wife was the truth. The truth is meant to serve you if you'll let it, and I wanted it to serve me. "I'll pay for the phone call," I said. "If you'll bring the phone to the door I'll call from right here."

The woman looked at me again as if she was searching for a truth of her own, then back out into the night. She was maybe in her sixties, but I couldn't say for sure. "You're not going to rob me, are you, Mr. Middleton?" She smiled like it was a joke between us.

"Not tonight," I said, and smiled a genuine smile. "I'm not up to it tonight. Maybe another time."

"Then I guess Terrel and I can let you use our phone with Daddy not here, can't we, Terrel? This is my grandson, Terrel Junior, Mr. Middleton." She put her hand on the boy's head and looked down at him. "Terrel won't talk. Though if he did he'd tell you to use our phone. He's a sweet boy." She opened the screen for me to come in.

The trailer was a big one with a new rug and a new couch and a living room that expanded to give the space of a real house. Something good and sweet was cooking in the kitchen, and the trailer felt like it was somebody's comfortable new home instead of just temporary. I've lived in trailers, but they were just snailbacks with one room and no toilet, and they always felt cramped and unhappy—though I've thought maybe it might've been me that was unhappy in them.

There was a big Sony TV and a lot of kids' toys scattered on the floor. I recognized a Greyhound bus I'd gotten for Cheryl. The phone was beside a new leather recliner, and the Negro woman pointed for me to sit down and call and gave me the phone book. Terrel began fingering his toys and the woman sat on the couch while I called, watching me and smiling.

There were three listings for cab companies, all with one number different. I called the numbers in order and didn't get an answer until the last one, which answered with the name of the second company. I said I was on the highway beyond the interstate and that my wife and family needed to be taken to town and I would arrange for a tow later. While I was giving the location, I looked up the name of a tow service to tell the driver in case he asked.

When I hung up, the Negro woman was sitting looking at me with the same look she had been staring with into the dark, a look that seemed to want truth. She was smiling, though. Something pleased her and I reminded her of it.

"This is a very nice home," I said, resting in the recliner, which felt like the driver's seat of the Mercedes, and where I'd have been happy to stay.

"This isn't *our* house, Mr. Middleton," the Negro woman said.

"The company owns these. They give them to us for nothing. We have our own home in Rockford, Illinois."

"That's wonderful," I said.

"It's never wonderful when you have to be away from home, Mr. Middleton, though we're only here three months, and it'll be easier when Terrel Junior begins his special school. You see, our son was killed in the war, and his wife ran off without Terrel Junior. Though you shouldn't worry. He can't understand us. His little feelings can't be hurt." The woman folded her hands in her lap and smiled in a satisfied way. She was an attractive woman, and had on a blue-and-pink floral dress that made her seem bigger than she could've been, just the right woman to sit on the couch she was sitting on. She was good nature's picture, and I was glad she could be, with her little brain-damaged boy, living in a place where no one in his right mind would want to live a minute. "Where do *you* live, Mr. Middleton?" she said politely, smiling in the same sympathetic way.

"My family and I are in transit," I said. "I'm an ophthalmologist, and we're moving back to Florida, where I'm from. I'm setting up practice in some little town where it's warm year-round. I haven't decided where."

"Florida's a wonderful place," the woman said. "I think Terrel would like it there."

"Could I ask you something?" I said.

"You certainly may," the woman said. Terrel had begun pushing his Greyhound across the front of the TV screen, making a scratch that no one watching the set could miss. "Stop that, Terrel Junior," the woman said quietly. But Terrel kept pushing his bus on the glass, and she smiled at me again as if we both understood something sad. Except I knew Cheryl would never damage a television set. She had respect for nice things, and I was sorry for the lady that Terrel didn't. "What did you want to ask?" the woman said.

"What goes on in that plant or whatever it is back there beyond these trailers, where all the lights are on?"

"Gold," the woman said and smiled.

"It's what?" I said.

"Gold," the Negro woman said, smiling as she had for almost all the time I'd been there. "It's a gold mine."

"They're mining gold back there?" I said, pointing.

"Every night and every day." She smiled in a pleased way.

"Does your husband work there?" I said.

"He's the assayer," she said. "He controls the quality. He works three months a year, and we live the rest of the time at home in Rockford. We've waited a long time for this. We've been happy to have our grandson, but I won't say I'll be sorry to have him go. We're ready to start our lives over." She smiled broadly at me and then at Terrel, who was giving her a spiteful look from the floor. "You said you had a daughter," the Negro woman said. "And what's her name?"

"Irma Cheryl," I said. "She's named for my mother."

"That's nice. And she's healthy, too. I can see it in your face." She looked at Terrel Junior with pity.

"I guess I'm lucky," I said.

"So far you are. But children bring you grief, the same way they bring you joy. We were unhappy for a long time before my husband got his job in the gold mine. Now, when Terrel starts to school, we'll be kids again." She stood up. "You might miss your cab, Mr. Middleton," she said, walking toward the door, though not to be forcing me out. She was too polite. "If *we* can't see your car, the cab surely won't be able to."

"That's true." I got up off the recliner, where I'd been so comfortable. "None of us have eaten yet, and your food makes me know how hungry we probably all are."

"There are fine restaurants in town, and you'll find them," the Negro woman said. "I'm sorry you didn't meet my husband. He's a wonderful man. He's everything to me."

"Tell him I appreciate the phone," I said. "You saved me."

"You weren't hard to save," the woman said. "Saving people is what we were all put on earth to do. I just passed you on to whatever's coming to you."

"Let's hope it's good," I said, stepping back into the dark.

"I'll be hoping, Mr. Middleton. Terrel and I will both be hoping."

I waved to her as I walked out into the darkness toward the car where it was hidden in the night.

The cab had already arrived when I got there. I could see its little red-and-green roof lights all the way across the dry wash, and it made me worry that Edna was already saying something to get us in trouble, something about the car or where we'd come from, something that would cast suspicion on us. I thought, then, how I never planned things well enough. There was always a gap between my plan and what happened, and I only responded to things as they came along and hoped I wouldn't get in trouble. I was an offender in the law's eyes. But I always *thought* differently, as if I weren't an offender and had no intention of being one, which was the truth. But as I read on a napkin once, between the idea and the act a whole kingdom lies. And I had a hard time with my acts, which were oftentimes offender's acts, and my ideas, which were as good as the gold they mined there where the bright lights were blazing.

"We're waiting for you, Daddy," Cheryl said when I crossed the road. "The taxicab's already here."

"I see, hon," I said, and gave Cheryl a big hug. The cabdriver was sitting in the driver's seat having a smoke with the lights on inside. Edna was leaning against the back of the cab between the taillights, wearing her Bailey hat. "What'd you tell him?" I said when I got close.

"Nothing," she said. "What's there to tell?"

"Did he see the car?"

She glanced over in the direction of the trees where we had hid the Mercedes. Nothing was visible in the darkness, though I could hear Little Duke combing around in the underbrush tracking something, his little collar tinkling. "Where're we going?" she said. "I'm so hungry I could pass out."

"Edna's in a terrible mood," Cheryl said. "She already snapped at me."

"We're tired, honey," I said. "So try to be nicer."

"She's never nice," Cheryl said.

"Run go get Little Duke," I said. "And hurry back."

"I guess *my* questions come last here, right?" Edna said.

I put my arm around her. "That's not true."

"Did you find somebody over there in the trailers you'd rather stay with? You were gone long enough."

"That's not a thing to say," I said. "I was just trying to make things look right, so we don't get put in jail."

"So *you* don't, you mean." Edna laughed a little laugh I didn't like hearing.

"That's right. So I don't," I said. "I'd be the one in Dutch." I stared out at the big, lighted assemblage of white buildings and white lights beyond the trailer community, plumes of white smoke escaping up into the heartless Wyoming sky, the whole company of buildings looking like some unbelievable castle, humming away in a distorted dream. "You know what all those buildings are there?" I said to Edna, who hadn't moved and who didn't really seem to care if she ever moved anymore ever.

"No. But I can't say it matters, because it isn't a motel and it isn't a restaurant."

"It's a gold mine," I said, staring at the gold mine, which, I knew now, was a greater distance from us than it seemed, though it seemed huge and near, up against the cold sky. I thought there should've been a wall around it with guards instead of just the lights and no fence. It seemed as if anyone could go in and take what they wanted, just the way I had gone up to that woman's trailer and used the telephone, though that obviously wasn't true.

Edna began to laugh then. Not the mean laugh I didn't like, but a laugh that had something caring behind it, a full laugh that

enjoyed a joke, a laugh she was laughing the first time I laid eyes
on her, in Missoula in the East Gate Bar in 1979, a laugh we used
to laugh together when Cheryl was still with her mother and I
was working steady at the track and not stealing cars or passing
bogus checks to merchants. A better time all around. And for
some reason it made me laugh just hearing her, and we both
stood there behind the cab in the dark, laughing at the gold mine
in the desert, me with my arm around her and Cheryl out rustling
up Little Duke and the cabdriver smoking in the cab and our
stolen Mercedes-Benz, which I'd had such hopes for in Florida,
stuck up to its axle in sand, where I'd never get to see it again.

"I always wondered what a gold mine would look like when I
saw it," Edna said, still laughing, wiping a tear from her eye.

"Me too," I said. "I was always curious about it."

"We're a couple of fools, aren't we, Earl?" she said, unable to
quit laughing completely. "We're two of a kind."

"It might be a good sign, though," I said.

"How could it be? It's not our gold mine. There aren't any
drive-up windows." She was still laughing.

"We've seen it," I said, pointing. "That's it right there. It may
mean we're getting closer. Some people never see it at all."

"In a pig's eye, Earl," she said. "You and me see it in a pig's
eye."

And she turned and got in the cab to go.

The cabdriver didn't ask anything about our car or where it was,
to mean he'd noticed something queer. All of which made me feel
like we had made a clean break from the car and couldn't be connected with it until it was too late, if ever. The driver told us a lot
about Rock Springs while he drove, that because of the gold mine
a lot of people had moved there in just six months, people from
all over, including New York, and that most of them lived out in
the trailers. Prostitutes from New York City, who he called "B-

girls," had come into town, he said, on the prosperity tide, and Cadillacs with New York plates cruised the little streets every night, full of Negroes with big hats who ran the women. He told us that everybody who got in his cab now wanted to know where the women were, and when he got our call he almost didn't come because some of the trailers were brothels operated by the mine for engineers and computer people away from home. He said he got tired of running back and forth out there just for vile business. He said that *60 Minutes* had even done a program about Rock Springs and that a blow-up had resulted in Cheyenne, though nothing could be done unless the boom left town. "It's prosperity's fruit," the driver said. "I'd rather be poor, which is lucky for me."

He said all the motels were sky-high, but since we were a family he could show us a nice one that was affordable. But I told him we wanted a first-rate place where they took animals, and the money didn't matter because we had had a hard day and wanted to finish on a high note. I also knew that it was in the little nowhere places that the police look for you and find you. People I'd known were always being arrested in cheap hotels and tourist courts with names you'd never heard of before. Never in Holiday Inns or TraveLodges.

I asked him to drive us to the middle of town and back out again so Cheryl could see the train station, and while we were there I saw a pink Cadillac with New York plates and a TV aerial being driven slowly by a Negro in a big hat down a narrow street where there were just bars and a Chinese restaurant. It was an odd sight, nothing you could ever expect.

"There's your pure criminal element," the cabdriver said and seemed sad. "I'm sorry for people like you to see a thing like that. We've got a nice town here, but there're some that want to ruin it for everybody. There used to be a way to deal with trash and criminals, but those days are gone forever."

"You said it," Edna said.

"You shouldn't let it get *you* down," I said to him. "There's more of you than them. And there always will be. You're the best advertisement this town has. I know Cheryl will remember you and not *that* man, won't you, honey?" But Cheryl was asleep by then, holding Little Duke in her arms on the taxi seat.

The driver took us to the Ramada Inn on the interstate, not far from where we'd broken down. I had a small pain of regret as we drove under the Ramada awning that we hadn't driven up in a cranberry-colored Mercedes but instead in a beat-up old Chrysler taxi driven by an old man full of complaints. Though I knew it was for the best. We were better off without that car; better, really, in any other car but that one, where the signs had turned bad.

I registered under another name and paid for the room in cash so there wouldn't be any questions. On the line where it said "Representing" I wrote "Ophthalmologist" and put "M.D." after the name. It had a nice look to it, even though it wasn't my name.

When we got to the room, which was in the back where I'd asked for it, I put Cheryl on one of the beds and Little Duke beside her so they'd sleep. She'd missed dinner, but it only meant she'd be hungry in the morning, when she could have anything she wanted. A few missed meals don't make a kid bad. I'd missed a lot of them myself and haven't turned out completely bad.

"Let's have some fried chicken," I said to Edna when she came out of the bathroom. "They have good fried chicken at Ramadas, and I noticed the buffet was still up. Cheryl can stay right here, where it's safe, till we're back."

"I guess I'm not hungry anymore," Edna said. She stood at the window staring out into the dark. I could see out the window past her some yellowish foggy glow in the sky. For a moment I thought it was the gold mine out in the distance lighting the night, though it was only the interstate.

"We could order up," I said. "Whatever you want. There's a menu on the phone book. You could just have a salad."

"You go ahead," she said. "I've lost my hungry spirit." She sat

on the bed beside Cheryl and Little Duke and looked at them in a
sweet way and put her hand on Cheryl's cheek just as if she'd had
a fever. "Sweet little girl," she said. "Everybody loves you."

"What do you want to do?" I said. "I'd like to eat. Maybe *I'll*
order up some chicken."

"Why don't you do that?" she said. "It's your favorite." And
she smiled at me from the bed.

I sat on the other bed and dialed room service. I asked for
chicken, garden salad, potato and a roll, plus a piece of hot apple
pie and iced tea. I realized I hadn't eaten all day. When I put
down the phone I saw that Edna was watching me, not in a hateful way or a loving way, just in a way that seemed to say she didn't
understand something and was going to ask me about it.

"When did watching me get so entertaining?" I said and
smiled at her. I was trying to be friendly. I knew how tired she
must be. It was after nine o'clock.

"I was just thinking how much I hated being in a motel without a car that was mine to drive. Isn't that funny? I started feeling
like that last night when that purple car wasn't mine. That purple
car just gave me the willies, I guess, Earl."

"One of those cars *outside* is yours," I said. "Just stand right
there and pick it out."

"I know," she said. "But that's different, isn't it?" She reached
and got her blue Bailey hat, put it on her head, and set it way back
like Dale Evans. She looked sweet. "I used to like to go to motels,
you know," she said. "There's something secret about them and
free—I was never paying, of course. But you felt safe from everything and free to do what you wanted because you'd made the de-
cision to be there and paid that price, and all the rest was the good
part. Fucking and everything, you know." She smiled at me in a
good-natured way.

"Isn't that the way this is?" I was sitting on the bed, watching
her, not knowing what to expect her to say next.

"I don't guess it is, Earl," she said and stared out the window.

"I'm thirty-two and I'm going to have to give up on motels. I can't keep that fantasy going anymore."

"Don't you like this place?" I said and looked around at the room. I appreciated the modern paintings and the lowboy bureau and the big TV. It seemed like a plenty nice enough place to me, considering where we'd been.

"No, I don't," Edna said with real conviction. "There's no use in my getting mad at you about it. It isn't your fault. You do the best you can for everybody. But every trip teaches you something. And I've learned I need to give up on motels before some bad thing happens to me. I'm sorry."

"What does that mean?" I said, because I really didn't know what she had in mind to do, though I should've guessed.

"I guess I'll take that ticket you mentioned," she said, and got up and faced the window. "Tomorrow's soon enough. We haven't got a car to take me anyhow."

"Well, that's a fine thing," I said, sitting on the bed, feeling like I was in shock. I wanted to say something to her, to argue with her, but I couldn't think what to say that seemed right. I didn't want to be mad at her, but it made me mad.

"You've got a right to be mad at me, Earl," she said, "but I don't think you can really blame me." She turned around and faced me and sat on the windowsill, her hands on her knees. Someone knocked on the door, and I just yelled for them to set the tray down and put it on the bill.

"I guess I *do* blame you," I said, and I was angry. I thought about how I could've disappeared into that trailer community and hadn't, had come back to keep things going, had tried to take control of things for everybody when they looked bad.

"Don't. I wish you wouldn't," Edna said and smiled at me like she wanted me to hug her. "Anybody ought to have their choice in things if they can. Don't you believe that, Earl? Here I am out here in the desert where I don't know anything, in a stolen car, in a motel room under an assumed name, with no money of my own, a kid that's not mine, and the law after me. And I have a choice to get out of all of it by getting on a bus. What would you do? I know exactly what you'd do."

"You think you do," I said. But I didn't want to get into an argument about it and tell her all I could've done and didn't do. Because it wouldn't have done any good. When you get to the point of arguing, you're past the point of changing anybody's mind, even though it's supposed to be the other way, and maybe for some classes of people it is, just never mine.

Edna smiled at me and came across the room and put her arms around me where I was sitting on the bed. Cheryl rolled over and looked at us and smiled, then closed her eyes, and the room was quiet. I was beginning to think of Rock Springs in a way I knew I would always think of it, a lowdown city full of crimes and whores and disappointments, a place where a woman left me, instead of a place where I got things on the straight track once and for all, a place I saw a gold mine.

"Eat your chicken, Earl," Edna said. "Then we can go to bed. I'm tired, but I'd like to make love to you anyway. None of this is a matter of not loving you, you know that."

Sometime late in the night, after Edna was asleep, I got up and walked outside into the parking lot. It could've been anytime because there was still the light from the interstate frosting the low sky and the big red Ramada sign humming motionlessly in the night and no light at all in the east to indicate it might be morning. The lot was full of cars all nosed in, a couple of them with suitcases strapped to their roofs and their trunks weighed down with belongings the people were taking someplace, to a new home or a vacation resort in the mountains. I had laid in bed a long time after Edna was asleep, watching the Atlanta Braves on television, trying to get my mind off how I'd feel when I saw that bus pull away the next day, and how I'd feel when I turned around and there stood Cheryl and Little Duke and no one to see about them but me alone, and that the first thing I had to do was get hold of some automobile and get the plates switched, then get them some breakfast and get us all on the road to Florida, all in the space of probably two hours, since that Mercedes would certainly look less hid in the daytime than the night, and word travels fast. I've always taken care of Cheryl myself as long as I've had her with me. None of the women ever did. Most of them didn't even seem to like her, though they took care of me in a way so that I could take care of her. And I knew that once Edna left, all that was going to get harder. Though what I wanted most to do was not think about it just for a little while, try to let my mind go limp so it could be strong for the rest of what there was. I thought that the difference between a successful life and an unsuccessful one, between me at that moment and all the people who owned the cars that were nosed into their proper places in the lot, maybe between me and that woman out in the trailers by the gold mine, was how well you were able to put things like this out of your mind and not be bothered by them, and maybe, too, by how many troubles like this one you had to face in a lifetime. Through luck or design they had all faced fewer troubles, and by their own characters, they forgot them faster. And that's what I wanted for me. Fewer troubles, fewer memories of trouble.

I walked over to a car, a Pontiac with Ohio tags, one of the ones with bundles and suitcases strapped to the top and a lot more in the trunk, by the way it was riding. I looked inside the driver's window. There were maps and paperback books and sunglasses and the little plastic holders for cans that hang on the window wells. And in the back there were kids' toys and some pillows and a cat box with a cat sitting in it staring up at me like I was the face of the moon. It all looked familiar to me, the very same things I would have in my car if I had a car. Nothing seemed surprising, nothing different. Though I had a funny sensation at that moment and turned and looked up at the windows along the back of the motel. All were dark except two. Mine and another one. And I wondered, because it seemed funny, what would you think a man was doing if you saw him in the middle of the night looking in the windows of cars in the parking lot of the Ramada Inn? Would you think he was trying to get his head cleared? Would you think he was trying to get ready for a day when trouble would come down on him? Would you think his girlfriend was leaving him? Would you think he had a daughter? Would you think he was anybody like you?

THE
THIRD THING
THAT KILLED
MY FATHER OFF

RAYMOND CARVER

From Where I'm Calling From,
Atlantic Monthly Press, New York, 1988

I'll tell you what did my father in. The third thing was Dummy, that Dummy died. The first thing was Pearl Harbor. And the second thing was moving to my grandfather's farm near Wenatchee. That's where my father finished out his days, except they were probably finished before that.

My father blamed Dummy's death on Dummy's wife. Then he blamed it on the fish. And finally he blamed himself—because he was the one that showed Dummy the ad in the back of *Field and Stream* for live black bass shipped anywhere in the U.S.

It was after he got the fish that Dummy started acting peculiar. The fish changed Dummy's whole personality. That's what my father said.

I never knew Dummy's real name. If anyone did, I never heard it. Dummy it was then, and it's Dummy I remember him by now. He was a little wrinkled man, bald-headed, short but very powerful in the arms and legs. If he grinned, which was seldom, his lips folded back over brown, broken teeth. It gave him a crafty expression. His watery eyes stayed fastened on your mouth when you were talking—and if you weren't, they'd go to someplace queer on your body.

I don't think he was really deaf. At least not as deaf as he made out. But he sure couldn't talk. That was for certain.

Deaf or no, Dummy'd been on as a common laborer out at the sawmill since the 1920s. This was the Cascade Lumber Company in Yakima, Washington. The years I knew him, Dummy was working as a cleanup man. And all those years I never saw him with anything different on. Meaning a felt hat, a khaki workshirt, a denim jacket over a pair of coveralls. In his top pockets he carried rolls of toilet paper, as one of his jobs was to clean and supply the toilets. It kept him busy, seeing as how the men on nights used to walk off after their shifts with a roll or two in their lunchboxes.

Dummy carried a flashlight, even though he worked days. He also carried wrenches, pliers, screwdrivers, friction tape, all the same things the millwrights carried. Well, it made them kid Dummy, the way he was, always carrying everything. Carl Lowe, Ted Slade, Johnny Wait, they were the worst kidders of the ones that kidded Dummy. But Dummy took it all in stride. I think he'd gotten used to it.

My father never kidded Dummy. Not to my knowledge, anyway. Dad was a big, heavy-shouldered man with a crew-haircut, double chin, and a belly of real size. Dummy was always staring at that belly. He'd come to the filing room where my father worked, and he'd sit on a stool and watch my dad's belly while he used the big emery wheels on the saws.

Dummy had a house as good as anyone's.

It was a tarpaper-covered affair near the river, five or six miles from town. Half a mile behind the house, at the end of a pasture, there lay a big gravel pit that the state had dug when they were paving the roads around there. Three good-sized holes had been scooped out, and over the years they'd filled with water. By and by, the three ponds came together to make one.

It was deep. It had a darkish look to it.

Dummy had a wife as well as a house. She was a woman years younger and said to go around with Mexicans. Father said it was busybodies that said that, men like Lowe and Wait and Slade.

She was a small stout woman with glittery little eyes. The first time I saw her, I saw those eyes. It was when I was with Pete Jensen and we were on our bicycles and we stopped at Dummy's to get a glass of water.

When she opened the door, I told her I was Del Fraser's son. I said, "He works with—" And then I realized. "You know, your husband. We were on our bicycles and thought we could get a drink."

"Wait here," she said.

She came back with a little tin cup of water in each hand. I downed mine in a single gulp.

But she didn't offer us more. She watched us without saying anything. When we started to get on our bicycles, she came over to the edge of the porch.

"You little fellas had a car now, I might catch a ride with you."

She grinned. Her teeth looked too big for her mouth.

"Let's go," Pete said, and we went.

There weren't many places you could fish for bass in our part of the state. There was rainbow mostly, a few brook and Dolly Varden in some of the high mountain streams, and silvers in Blue Lake and Lake Rimrock. That was mostly it, except for the runs of steelhead and salmon in some of the freshwater rivers in late fall. But if you were a fisherman, it was enough to keep you busy.

No one fished for bass. A lot of people I knew had never seen a bass except for pictures. But my father had seen plenty of them when he was growing up in Arkansas and Georgia, and he had high hopes to do with Dummy's bass, Dummy being a friend.

The day the fish arrived, I'd gone swimming at the city pool. I remember coming home and going out again to get them since Dad was going to give Dummy a hand—three tanks Parcel Post from Baton Rouge, Louisiana.

We went in Dummy's pickup, Dad and Dummy and me.

These tanks turned out to be barrels, really, the three of them crated in pine lath. They were standing in the shade out back of the train depot, and it took my dad and Dummy both to lift each crate into the truck.

Dummy drove very carefully through town and just as carefully all the way to his house. He went right through his yard without stopping. He went on down to within feet of the pond. By that time it was nearly dark, so he kept his headlights on and took out a hammer and a tire iron from under the seat, and then the two of them lugged the crates up close to the water and started tearing open the first one.

The barrel inside was wrapped in burlap, and there were these nickel-sized holes in the lid. They raised it off and Dummy aimed his flashlight in.

It looked like a million bass fingerlings were finning inside. It was the strangest sight, all those live things busy in there, like a little ocean that had come on the train.

Dummy scooted the barrel to the edge of the water and poured it out. He took his flashlight and shined it into the pond. But there was nothing to be seen anymore. You could hear the frogs going, but you could hear them going anytime it newly got dark.

"Let me get the other crates," my father said, and he reached over as if to take the hammer from Dummy's coveralls. But Dummy pulled back and shook his head.

He undid the other two crates himself, leaving dark drops of blood on the lath where he ripped his hand doing it.

From that night on, Dummy was different.

Dummy wouldn't let anyone come around now anymore. He put up fencing all around the pasture, and then he fenced off the pond with electrical barbed wire. They said it cost him all his savings for that fence.

Of course, my father wouldn't have anything to do with Dummy after that. Not since Dummy ran him off. Not from fishing, mind you, because the bass were just babies still. But even from trying to get a look.

One evening two years after, when Dad was working late and I took him his food and a jar of iced tea, I found him standing talking with Syd Glover, the millwright. Just as I came in, I heard Dad saying, "You'd reckon the fool was married to them fish, the way he acts."

"From what I hear," Syd said, "he'd do better to put that fence round his house."

My father saw me then, and I saw him signal Syd Glover with his eyes.

But a month later my dad finally made Dummy do it. What he did was, he told Dummy how you had to thin out the weak ones on account of keeping things fit for the rest of them. Dummy stood there pulling at his ear and staring at the floor. Dad said, Yeah, he'd be down to do it tomorrow because it had to be done. Dummy never said yes, actually. He just never said no, is all. All he did was pull on his ear some more.

When Dad got home that day, I was ready and waiting. I had his old bass plugs out and was testing the treble hooks with my finger.

"You set?" he called to me, jumping out of the car. "I'll go to the toilet, you put the stuff in. You can drive us out there if you want."

I'd stowed everything in the back seat and was trying out the wheel when he came back out wearing his fishing hat and eating a wedge of cake with both hands.

Mother was standing in the door watching. She was a fair-skinned woman, her blonde hair pulled back in a tight bun and fastened down with a rhinestone clip. I wonder if she ever went around back in those happy days, or what she ever really did.

I let out the handbrake. Mother watched until I'd shifted gears, and then, still unsmiling, she went back inside.

It was a fine afternoon. We had all the windows down to let the air in. We crossed the Moxee Bridge and swung west onto Slater Road. Alfalfa fields stood off to either side, and farther on it was cornfields.

Dad had his hand out the window. He was letting the wind carry it back. He was restless, I could see.

It wasn't long before we pulled up at Dummy's. He came out of the house wearing his hat. His wife was looking out the window.

"You got your frying pan ready?" Dad hollered out to Dummy, but Dummy just stood there eyeing the car. "Hey, Dummy!" Dad yelled. "Hey, Dummy, where's your pole, Dummy?"

Dummy jerked his head back and forth. He moved his weight from one leg to the other and looked at the ground and then at us. His tongue rested on his lower lip, and he began working his foot into the dirt.

I shouldered the creel. I handed Dad his pole and picked up my own.

"We set to go?" Dad said. "Hey, Dummy, we set to go?"

Dummy took off his hat and, with the same hand, he wiped his wrist over his head. He turned abruptly, and we followed him across the spongy pasture. Every twenty feet or so a snipe sprang up from the clumps of grass at the edge of the old furrows.

At the end of the pasture, the ground sloped gently and became dry and rocky, nettle bushes and scrub oaks scattered here and there. We cut to the right, following an old set of car tracks, going through a field of milkweed that came up to our waists, the dry pods at the tops of the stalks rattling angrily as we pushed through. Presently, I saw the sheen of water over Dummy's shoulder, and I heard Dad shout, "Oh, Lord, look at that!"

But Dummy slowed down and kept bringing his hand up and moving his hat back and forth over his head, and then he just stopped flat.

Dad said, "Well, what do you think, Dummy? One place good as another? Where do you say we should come onto it?"

Dummy wet his lower lip.

"What's the matter with you, Dummy?" Dad said. "This your pond, ain't it?"

Dummy looked down and picked an ant off his coveralls.

"Well, hell," Dad said, letting out his breath. He took out his watch. "If it's still all right with you, we'll get to it before it gets too dark."

Dummy stuck his hands in his pockets and turned back to the pond. He started walking again. We trailed along behind. We could see the whole pond now, the water dimpled with rising fish. Every so often a bass would leap clear and come down in a splash.

"Great God," I heard my father say.

We came up to the pond at an open place, a gravel beach kind of.

Dad motioned to me and dropped into a crouch. I dropped too. He was peering into the water in front of us, and when I looked, I saw what had taken him so.

"Honest to God," he whispered.

A school of bass was cruising, twenty, thirty, not one of them under two pounds. They veered off, and then they shifted and came back, so densely spaced they looked like they were bumping up against each other. I could see their big, heavy-lidded eyes watching us as they went by. They flashed away again, and again they came back.

They were asking for it. It didn't make any difference if we stayed squatted or stood up. The fish just didn't think a thing about us. I tell you, it was a sight to behold.

We sat there for quite a while, watching that school of bass go so innocently about their business, Dummy the whole time pulling at his fingers and looking around as if he expected someone to show up. All over the pond the bass were coming up to nuzzle the water, or jumping clear and falling back, or coming up to the surface to swim along with their dorsals sticking out.

Dad signaled, and we got up to cast. I tell you, I was shaky with excitement. I could hardly get the plug loose from the cork handle of my pole. It was while I was trying to get the hooks out that I felt Dummy seize my shoulder with his big fingers. I looked, and in answer Dummy worked his chin in Dad's direction. What he wanted was clear enough, no more than one pole.

Dad took off his hat and then put it back on and then he moved over to where I stood.

"You go on, Jack," he said. "That's all right, son—you do it now."

I looked at Dummy just before I laid out my cast. His face had gone rigid, and there was a thin line of drool on his chin.

"Come back stout on the sucker when he strikes," Dad said. "Sons of bitches got mouths hard as doorknobs."

I flipped off the drag lever and threw back my arm. I sent her out a good forty feet. The water was boiling even before I had time to take up the slack.

"Hit him!" Dad yelled. "Hit the son of a bitch! Hit him good!"

I came back hard, twice. I had him, all right. The rod bowed over and jerked back and forth. Dad kept yelling what to do.

"Let him go, let him go! Let him run! Give him more line! Now wind in! Wind in! No, let him run! Woo-ee! Will you look at that!"

The bass danced around the pond. Every time it came up out of the water, it shook its head so hard you could hear the plug rattle. And then he'd take off again. But by and by I wore him out and had him in up close. He looked enormous, six or seven pounds maybe. He lay on his side, whipped, mouth open, gills working. My knees felt so weak I could hardly stand. But I held the rod up, the line tight.

Dad waded out over his shoes. But when he reached for the fish, Dummy started sputtering, shaking his head, waving his arms.

"Now what the hell's the matter with you, Dummy? The boy's got hold of the biggest bass I ever seen, and he ain't going to throw him back, by God!"

Dummy kept carrying on and gesturing toward the pond.

"I ain't about to let this boy's fish go. You hear me, Dummy? You got another think coming if you think I'm going to do that."

Dummy reached for my line. Meanwhile, the bass had gained some strength back. He turned himself over and started swimming again. I yelled and then I lost my head and slammed down the brake on the reel and started winding. The bass made a last, furious run.

That was that. The line broke. I almost fell over on my back.

"Come on, Jack," Dad said, and I saw him grabbing up his pole. "Come on, goddamn the fool, before I knock the man down."

That February the river flooded.

It had snowed pretty heavy the first weeks of December, and turned real cold before Christmas. The ground froze. The snow stayed where it was. But toward the end of January, the Chinook wind struck. I woke up one morning to hear the house getting buffeted and the steady drizzle of water running off the roof.

It blew for five days, and on the third day the river began to rise.

"She's up to fifteen feet," my father said one evening, looking over his newspaper. "Which is three feet over what you need to flood. Old Dummy going to lose his darlings."

I wanted to go down to the Moxee Bridge to see how high the water was running. But my dad wouldn't let me. He said a flood was nothing to see.

Two days later the river crested, and after that the water began to subside.

Orin Marshall and Danny Owens and I bicycled out to Dummy's one morning a week after. We parked our bicycles and walked across the pasture that bordered Dummy's property.

It was a wet, blustery day, the clouds dark and broken, moving fast across the sky. The ground was soppy wet and we kept coming to puddles in the thick grass. Danny was just learning how to cuss, and he filled the air with the best he had every time he stepped in over his shoes. We could see the swollen river at the end of the pasture. The water was still high and out of its channel, surging around the trunks of trees and eating away at the edge of the land. Out toward the middle, the current moved heavy and swift, and now and then a bush floated by, or a tree with its branches sticking up.

We came to Dummy's fence and found a cow wedged in up against the wire. She was bloated and her skin was shiny-looking and gray. It was the first dead thing of any size I'd ever seen. I remember Orin took a stick and touched the open eyes.

We moved on down the fence, toward the river. We were afraid to go near the wire because we thought it might still have electricity in it. But at the edge of what looked like a deep canal, the fence came to an end. The ground had simply dropped into the water here, and the fence along with it.

We crossed over and followed the new channel that cut directly into Dummy's land and headed straight for his pond, going into it lengthwise and forcing an outlet for itself at the other end, then twisting off until it joined up with the river farther on.

You didn't doubt that most of Dummy's fish had been carried off. But those that hadn't been were free to come and go.

Then I caught sight of Dummy. It scared me, seeing him. I motioned to the other fellows, and we all got down.

Dummy was standing at the far side of the pond near where the water was rushing out. He was just standing there, the saddest man I ever saw.

"I sure do feel sorry for old Dummy, though," my father said at supper a few weeks after. "Mind, the poor devil brought it on himself. But you can't help but be troubled for him."

Dad went on to say George Laycock saw Dummy's wife sitting in the Sportsman's Club with a big Mexican fellow.

"And that ain't the half of it—"

Mother looked up at him sharply and then at me. But I just went on eating like I hadn't heard a thing.

Dad said, "Damn it to hell, Bea, the boy's old enough!"

He'd changed a lot, Dummy had. He was never around any of the men anymore, not if he could help it. No one felt like joking with him either, not since he'd chased Carl Lowe with a two-by-four stud after Carl tipped Dummy's hat off. But the worst of it was that Dummy was missing from work a day or two a week on the average now, and there was some talk of his being laid off.

"The man's going off the deep end," Dad said. "Clear crazy if he don't watch out."

Then on a Sunday afternoon just before my birthday, Dad and I were cleaning the garage. It was a warm, drifty day. You could see the dust hanging in the air. Mother came to the back door and said, "Del, it's for you. I think it's Vern."

I followed Dad in to wash up. When he was through talking, he put the phone down and turned to us.

"It's Dummy," he said. "Did in his wife with a hammer and drowned himself. Vern just heard it in town."

***

When we got out there, cars were parked all around. The gate to the pasture stood open, and I could see tire marks that led on to the pond.

The screen door was propped ajar with a box, and there was this lean, pock-faced man in slacks and sports shirt and wearing a shoulder holster. He watched Dad and me get out of the car.

"I was his friend," Dad said to the man.

The man shook his head. "Don't care who you are. Clear off unless you got business here."

"Did they find him?" Dad said.

"They're dragging," the man said, and adjusted the fit of his gun.

"All right if we walk down? I knew him pretty well."

The man said, "Take your chances. They chase you off, don't say you wasn't warned."

We went on across the pasture, taking pretty much the same route we had the day we tried fishing. There were motorboats going on the pond, dirty fluffs of exhaust hanging over it. You could see where the high water had cut away the ground and carried off trees and rocks. The two boats had uniformed men in them, and they were going back and forth, one man steering and the other man handling the rope and hooks.

An ambulance waited on the gravel beach where we'd set ourselves to cast for Dummy's bass. Two men in white lounged against the back, smoking cigarettes.

One of the motorboats cut off. We all looked up. The man in back stood up and started heaving on his rope. After a time, an arm came out of the water. It looked like the hooks had gotten Dummy in the side. The arm went back down and then it came out again, along with a bundle of something.

It's not him, I thought. It's something else that has been in there for years.

The man in the front of the boat moved to the back, and together the two men hauled the dripping thing over the side.

I looked at Dad. His face was funny the way it was set.

"Women," he said. He said, "That's what the wrong kind of woman can do to you, Jack."

But I don't think Dad really believed it. I think he just didn't know who to blame or what to say.

It seemed to me everything took a bad turn for my father after that. Just like Dummy, he wasn't the same man anymore. That arm coming up and going back down in the water, it was like so long to good times and hello to bad. Because it was nothing but that all the years after Dummy drowned himself in that dark water.

Is that what happens when a friend dies? Bad luck for the pals he left behind?

But as I said, Pearl Harbor and having to move back to his dad's place didn't do my dad one bit of good, either.

BROKEBACK MOUNTAIN

ANNIE PROULX

From Close Range: Wyoming Stories,
Scribner, New York, 1999
First published in *The New Yorker, 1997*

T hey were raised on small, poor ranches in opposite corners of the state, Jack Twist in Lightning Flat, up on the
Montana border, Ennis del Mar from around Sage, near
the Utah line, both high school dropout country boys with no
prospects, brought up to hard work and privation, both rough-
mannered, rough-spoken, inured to the stoic life. Ennis, reared by
his older brother and sister after their parents drove off the only
curve on Dead Horse Road, leaving them twenty-four dollars in
cash and a two-mortgage ranch, applied at age fourteen for a
hardship license that let him make the hour-long trip from the
ranch to the high school. The pickup was old, no heater, one
windshield wiper, and bad tires; when the transmission went,
there was no money to fix it. He had wanted to be a sophomore,
felt the word carried a kind of distinction, but the truck broke
down short of it, pitching him directly into ranch work.

In 1963, when he met Jack Twist, Ennis was engaged to Alma

Beers. Both Jack and Ennis claimed to be saving money for a
small spread; in Ennis's case that meant a tobacco can with two
five-dollar bills inside. That spring, hungry for any job, each had
signed up with Farm and Ranch Employment—they came together on paper as herder and camp tender for the same sheep
operation north of Signal. The summer range lay above the tree
line on Forest Service land on Brokeback Mountain. It would be
Jack Twist's second summer on the mountain, Ennis's first. Neither of them was twenty.

They shook hands in the choky little trailer office in front of a
table littered with scribbled papers, a Bakelite ashtray brimming
with stubs. The venetian blinds hung askew and admitted a trian-
gle of white light, the shadow of the foreman's hand moving into
it. Joe Aguirre, wavy hair the color of cigarette ash and parted
down the middle, gave them his point of view.

"Forest Service got designated campsites on the allotments.
Them camps can be a couple a miles from where we pasture the
sheep. Bad predator loss, nobody near lookin after em at night.
What I want—camp tender in the main camp where the Forest
Service says, but the *herder*"—pointing at Jack with a chop of his
hand—"pitch a pup tent on the Q.T. with the sheep, out a sight,
and he's goin a *sleep* there. Eat supper, breakfast in camp, but *sleep
with the sheep*, hundred percent, *no fire*, don't leave *no sign*. Roll up
that tent every mornin case Forest Service snoops around. Got
the dogs, your .30-.30, sleep there. Last summer had goddamn
near twenty-five percent loss. I don't want that again. *You*," he
said to Ennis, taking in the ragged hair, the big nicked hands, the
jeans torn, button-gaping shirt, "Fridays twelve noon be down at
the bridge with your next-week list and mules. Somebody with
supplies'll be there in a pickup." He didn't ask if Ennis had a
watch but took a cheap round ticker on a braided cord from a box
on a high shelf, wound and set it, tossed it to him as if he weren't
worth the reach. "*Tomorrow mornin* we'll truck you up the jump-
off." Pair of deuces going nowhere.

They found a bar and drank beer through the afternoon, Jack telling Ennis about a lightning storm on the mountain the year before that killed forty-two sheep, the peculiar stink of them and the way they bloated, the need for plenty of whiskey up there. At first glance Jack seemed fair enough, with his curly hair and quick laugh, but for a small man he carried some weight in the haunch and his smile disclosed buckteeth, not pronounced enough to let him eat popcorn out of the neck of a jug, but noticeable. He was infatuated with the rodeo life and fastened his belt with a minor bull-riding buckle, but his boots were worn to the quick, holed beyond repair, and he was crazy to be somewhere, anywhere, else than Lightning Flat.

Ennis, high-arched nose and narrow face, was scruffy and a little cave-chested, balanced a small torso on long, caliper legs, and possessed a muscular and supple body made for the horse and for fighting. His reflexes were uncommonly quick, and he was far-sighted enough to dislike reading anything except Hamley's saddle catalog.

The sheep trucks and horse trailers unloaded at the trailhead, and a bandy-legged Basque showed Ennis how to pack the mules—two packs and a riding load on each animal, ring-lashed with double diamonds and secured with half hitches—telling him, "Don't never order soup. Them boxes a soup are real bad to pack." Three puppies belonging to one of the blue heelers went in a pack basket, the runt inside Jack's coat, for he loved a little dog. Ennis picked out a big chestnut called Cigar Butt to ride, Jack a bay mare that turned out to have a low startle point. The string of spare horses included a mouse-colored grullo whose looks Ennis liked. Ennis and Jack, the dogs, the horses and mules, a thousand ewes and their lambs flowed up the trail like dirty water through the timber and out above the tree line into the great flowery meadows and the coursing, endless wind.

They got the big tent up on the Forest Service's platform, the kitchen and grub boxes secured. Both slept in camp that first night, Jack already bitching about Joe Aguirre's sleep-with-the-sheep-and-no-fire order, though he saddled the bay mare in the dark morning without saying much. Dawn came glassy-orange, stained from below by a gelatinous band of pale green. The sooty bulk of the mountain paled slowly until it was the same color as the smoke from Ennis's breakfast fire. The cold air sweetened, banded pebbles and crumbs of soil cast sudden pencil-long shadows, and the rearing lodgepole pines below them massed in slabs of somber malachite.

During the day Ennis looked across a great gulf and sometimes saw Jack, a small dot moving across a high meadow, as an insect moves across a tablecloth; Jack, in his dark camp, saw Ennis as night fire, a red spark on the huge black mass of mountain.

Jack came lagging in late one afternoon, drank his two bottles of beer cooled in a wet sack on the shady side of the tent, ate two bowls of stew, four of Ennis's stone biscuits, a can of peaches, rolled a smoke, watched the sun drop.

"I'm commutin four hours a day," he said morosely. "Come in for breakfast, go back to the sheep, evenin get em bedded down, come in for supper, go back to the sheep, spend half the night jumpin up and checkin for coyotes. By rights I should be spendin the night here. Aguirre got no right a make me do this."

"You want a switch?" said Ennis. "I wouldn't mind herdin. I wouldn't mind sleepin out there."

"That ain't the point. Point is, we both should be in this camp. And that goddam pup tent smells like cat piss or worse."

"Wouldn't mind bein out there."

"Tell you what, you got a get up a dozen times in the night out there over them coyotes. Happy to switch but give you warnin I can't cook worth a shit. Pretty good with a can opener."

"Can't be no worse than me, then. Sure, I wouldn't mind a do it."

They fended off the night for an hour with the yellow

kerosene lamp, and around ten Ennis rode Cigar Butt, a good night horse, through the glimmering frost back to the sheep, carrying leftover biscuits, a jar of jam, and a jar of coffee with him for the next day, saying he'd save a trip, stay out until supper.

"Shot a coyote just first light," he told Jack the next evening, sloshing his face with hot water, lathering up soap, and hoping his razor had some cut left in it, while Jack peeled potatoes. "Big son of a bitch. Balls on him size a apples. I bet he'd took a few lambs. Looked like he could a eat a camel. You want some a this hot water? There's plenty."

"It's all yours."

"Well, I'm goin a warsh everthing I can reach," he said, pulling off his boots and jeans (no drawers, no socks, Jack noticed), slopping the green washcloth around until the fire spat.

They had a high-time supper by the fire, a can of beans each, fried potatoes, and a quart of whiskey on shares, sat with their backs against a log, boot soles and copper jeans rivets hot, swapping the bottle while the lavender sky emptied of color and the chill air drained down, drinking, smoking cigarettes, getting up every now and then to piss, firelight throwing a sparkle in the arched stream, tossing sticks on the fire to keep the talk going, talking horses and rodeo, roughstock events, wrecks and injuries sustained, the submarine *Thresher* lost two months earlier with all hands and how it must have been in the last doomed minutes, dogs each had owned and known, the military service, Jack's home ranch, where his father and mother held on, Ennis's family place, folded years ago after his folks died, the older brother in Signal and a married sister in Casper. Jack said his father had been a pretty well-known bull rider years back but kept his secrets to himself, never gave Jack a word of advice, never came once to see Jack ride, though he had put him on the woollies when he was a little kid. Ennis said the kind of riding that interested him lasted longer than eight seconds and had some point to it. Money's a good point, said Jack, and Ennis had to agree. They were respectful of each other's opinions, each glad to have a companion where none had been expected. Ennis, riding against the wind back to the sheep in the treacherous, drunken light, thought he'd never had such a good time, felt he could paw the white out of the moon.

The summer went on and they moved the herd to new pasture, shifted the camp; the distance between the sheep and the new camp was greater and the night ride longer. Ennis rode easy, sleeping with his eyes open, but the hours he was away from the sheep stretched out and out. Jack pulled a squalling burr out of the harmonica, flattened a little from a fall off the skittish bay mare, and Ennis had a good raspy voice; a few nights they mangled their way through some songs. Ennis knew the salty words to "Strawberry Roan." Jack tried a Carl Perkins song, bawling "What I say-ay-ay," but he favored a sad hymn, "Water-Walking Jesus," learned from his mother, who believed in the Pentecost, and that he sang at dirge slowness, setting off distant coyote yips.

"Too late to go out to them damn sheep," said Ennis, dizzy drunk on all fours one cold hour when the moon had notched past two. The meadow stones glowed white-green and a flinty wind worked over the meadow, scraped the fire low, then ruffled it into yellow silk sashes. "Got you a extra blanket I'll roll up out here and grab forty winks, ride out at first light."

"Freeze your ass off when that fire dies down. Better off sleepin in the tent."

"Doubt I'll feel nothin." But he staggered under canvas, pulled his boots off, snored on the ground cloth for a while, woke Jack with the clacking of his jaw.

"Jesus Christ, quit hammerin and get over here. Bedroll's big enough," said Jack in an irritable sleep-clogged voice. It was big enough, warm enough, and in a little while they deepened their intimacy considerably. Ennis ran full throttle on all roads whether fence mending or money spending, and he wanted none of it when Jack seized his left hand and brought it to his erect cock. Ennis jerked his hand away as though he'd touched fire, got to his knees, unbuckled his belt, shoved his pants down, hauled Jack onto all fours, and, with the help of the clear slick and a little spit, entered him, nothing he'd done before but no instruction manual needed. They went at it in silence except for a few sharp intakes of breath and Jack's choked "Gun's goin *off*," then out, down, and asleep.

Ennis woke in red dawn with his pants around his knees, a top-grade headache, and Jack butted against him; without saying anything about it, both knew how it would go for the rest of the summer, sheep be damned.

As it did go. They never talked about the sex, let it happen, at first only in the tent at night, then in the full daylight with the hot sun striking down, and at evening in the fire glow, quick, rough, laughing and snorting, no lack of noises, but saying not a goddam word except once Ennis said, "I'm not no queer," and Jack jumped in with "Me neither. A one-shot thing. Nobody's business but ours." There were only the two of them on the mountain, flying in the euphoric, bitter air, looking down on the hawk's back and the crawling lights of vehicles on the plain below, suspended above ordinary affairs and distant from tame ranch dogs barking in the dark hours. They believed themselves invisible, not knowing Joe Aguirre had watched them through his 10x42 binoculars for ten minutes one day, waiting until they'd buttoned up their jeans, waiting until Ennis rode back to the sheep, before bringing up the message that Jack's people had sent word that his uncle Harold was in the hospital with pneumonia and expected not to make it. Though he did, and Aguirre came up again to say so, fixing Jack with his bold stare, not bothering to dismount.

In August Ennis spent the whole night with Jack in the main camp, and in a blowy hailstorm the sheep took off west and got among a herd in another allotment. There was a damn miserable time for five days, Ennis and a Chilean herder with no English trying to sort them out, the task almost impossible as the paint brands were worn and faint at this late season. Even when the numbers were right Ennis knew the sheep were mixed. In a disquieting way everything seemed mixed.

The first snow came early, on August 13th, piling up a foot, but was followed by a quick melt. The next week Joe Aguirre sent word to bring them down, another, bigger storm was moving in from the Pacific, and they packed in the game and moved off the mountain with the sheep, stones rolling at their heels, purple cloud crowding in from the west and the metal smell of coming snow pressing them on. The mountain boiled with demonic energy, glazed with flickering broken-cloud light; the wind combed the grass and drew from the damaged krummholz and slit rock a bestial drone. As they descended the slope Ennis felt he was in a slow-motion, but headlong, irreversible fall.

Joe Aguirre paid them, said little. He had looked at the milling sheep with a sour expression, said, "Some a these never went up there with you." The count was not what he'd hoped for, either. Ranch stiffs never did much of a job.

"You goin a do this next summer?" said Jack to Ennis in the street, one leg already up in his green pickup. The wind was gusting hard and cold.

"Maybe not." A dust plume rose and hazed the air with fine grit and he squinted against it. "Like I said, Alma and me's gettin married in December. Try to get somethin on a ranch. You?" He looked away from Jack's jaw, bruised blue from the hard punch Ennis had thrown him on the last day.

"If nothin better comes along. Thought some about going back up to my daddy's place, give him a hand over the winter, then maybe head out for Texas in the spring. If the draft don't get me."

"Well, see you around, I guess." The wind tumbled an empty feed bag down the street until it fetched up under the truck.

"Right," said Jack, and they shook hands, hit each other on the shoulder; then there was forty feet of distance between them and nothing to do but drive away in opposite directions. Within a mile Ennis felt like someone was pulling his guts out hand over hand a yard at a time. He stopped at the side of the road and, in the whirling new snow, tried to puke but nothing came up. He felt about as bad as he ever had and it took a long time for the feeling to wear off.

In December Ennis married Alma Beers and had her pregnant by mid-January. He picked up a few short-lived ranch jobs, then settled in as a wrangler on the old Elwood Hi-Top place, north of Lost Cabin, in Washakie County. He was still working there in September when Alma Jr., as he called his daughter, was born and their bedroom was full of the smell of old blood and milk and baby shit, and the sounds were of squalling and sucking and Alma's sleepy groans, all reassuring of fecundity and life's continuance to one who worked with livestock.

When the Hi-Top folded they moved to a small apartment in Riverton, up over a laundry. Ennis got on the highway crew, tolerating it but working weekends at the Rafter B in exchange for keeping his horses out there. A second girl was born and Alma wanted to stay in town near the clinic because the child had an asthmatic wheeze.

"Ennis, please, no more damn lonesome ranches for us," she said, sitting on his lap, wrapping her thin, freckled arms around him. "Let's get a place here in town."

"I guess," said Ennis, slipping his hand up her blouse sleeve and stirring the silky armpit hair, fingers moving down her ribs to the jelly breast, the round belly and knee and up into the wet gap all the way to the north pole or the equator depending which way you thought you were sailing, working at it until she shuddered and bucked against his hand and he rolled her over, did quickly

what she hated. They stayed in the little apartment, which he favored because it could be left at any time.

The fourth summer since Brokeback Mountain came on and in
June Ennis had a general-delivery letter from Jack Twist, the first
sign of life in all that time.

> Friend this letter is a long time over due. Hope you get it.
> Heard you was in Riverton. Im coming thru on the 24th,
> thought Id stop and buy you a beer. Drop me a line if you can,
> say if your there.

The return address was Childress, Texas. Ennis wrote back, "You
bet," gave the Riverton address.

The day was hot and clear in the morning, but by noon the
clouds had pushed up out of the west rolling a little sultry air before them. Ennis, wearing his best shirt, white with wide black
stripes, didn't know what time Jack would get there and so had
taken the day off, paced back and forth, looking down into a
street pale with dust. Alma was saying something about taking his
friend to the Knife & Fork for supper instead of cooking it was so
hot, if they could get a babysitter, but Ennis said more likely he'd
just go out with Jack and get drunk. Jack was not a restaurant
type, he said, thinking of the dirty spoons sticking out of the cans
of cold beans balanced on the log.

Late in the afternoon, thunder growling, that same old green
pickup rolled in and he saw Jack get out of the truck, beat-up Re-
sistol tilted back. A hot jolt scalded Ennis and he was out on the
landing pulling the door closed behind him. Jack took the stairs
two and two. They seized each other by the shoulders, hugged
mightily, squeezing the breath out of each other, saying son of a
bitch, son of a bitch; then, and as easily as the right key turns the
lock tumblers, their mouths came together, and hard, Jack's big

teeth bringing blood, his hat falling to the floor, stubble rasping, wet saliva welling, and the door opening and Alma looking out for a few seconds at Ennis's straining shoulders and shutting the door again and still they clinched, pressing chest and groin and thigh and leg together, treading on each other's toes until they pulled apart to breathe and Ennis, not big on endearments, said what he said to his horses and daughters, "Little darlin."

The door opened again a few inches and Alma stood in the narrow light.

What could he say? "Alma, this is Jack Twist. Jack, my wife, Alma." His chest was heaving. He could smell Jack—the intensely familiar odor of cigarettes, musky sweat, and a faint sweetness like grass, and with it the rushing cold of the mountain. "Alma," he said, "Jack and me ain't seen each other in four years." As if it were a reason. He was glad the light was dim on the landing but did not turn away from her.

"Sure enough," said Alma in a low voice. She had seen what she had seen. Behind her in the room, lightning lit the window like a white sheet waving and the baby cried.

"You got a kid?" said Jack. His shaking hand grazed Ennis's hand, electrical current snapped between them.

"Two little girls," Ennis said. "Alma Jr. and Francine. Love them to pieces." Alma's mouth twitched.

"I got a boy," said Jack. "Eight months old. Tell you what, I married a cute little old Texas girl down in Childress—Lureen." From the vibration of the floorboard on which they both stood Ennis could feel how hard Jack was shaking.

"Alma," he said. "Jack and me is goin out and get a drink. Might not get back tonight, we get drinkin and talkin."

"Sure enough," Alma said, taking a dollar bill from her pocket. Ennis guessed she was going to ask him to get her a pack of cigarettes, bring him back sooner.

"Please to meet you," said Jack, trembling like a run-out horse.

"Ennis—" said Alma in her misery voice, but that didn't slow

him down on the stairs and he called back, "Alma, you want
smokes there's some in the pocket a my blue shirt in the bedroom."

They went off in Jack's truck, bought a bottle of whiskey, and
within twenty minutes were in the Motel Siesta jouncing a bed. A
few handfuls of hail rattled against the window, followed by rain
and a slippery wind banging the unsecured door of the next room
then and through the night.

The room stank of semen and smoke and sweat and whiskey, of
old carpet and sour hay, saddle leather, shit and cheap soap. Ennis
lay spread-eagled, spent and wet, breathing deep, still half tumes-
cent; Jack blew forceful cigarette clouds like whale spouts, and
said, "Christ, it got to be all that time a yours a-horseback makes
it so goddam good. We got to talk about this. Swear to God I
didn't know we was goin a get into this again—yeah, I did. Why
I'm here. I fuckin knew it. Red-lined all the way, couldn't get here
fast enough."

"I didn't know where in the *hell* you was," said Ennis. "Four
years. I about give up on you. I figured you was sore about that
punch."

"Friend," said Jack, "I was in Texas rodeoin. How I met
Lureen. Look over on that chair."

On the back of a soiled orange chair he saw the shine of a
buckle. "Bull ridin?"

"Yeah. I made three fuckin thousand dollars that year. Fuckin
starved. Had to borrow everthing but a toothbrush from other
guys. Drove grooves across Texas. Half the time under that cunt
truck fixin it. Anyway, I didn't never think about losin. Lureen?
There's some serious money there. Her old man's got it. Got this
farm-machinery business. Course he don't let her have none a the
money, and he hates my fuckin guts, so it's a hard go now but one
a these days—"

"Well, you're goin a go where you look. Army didn't get you?" The thunder sounded far to the east, moving from them in its red wreaths of light.

"They can't get no use out a me. Got some crushed vertebrates. And a stress fracture, the arm bone here, you know how bull ridin you're always leverin it off your thigh?—she gives a little ever time you do it. Even if you tape it good you break it a little goddam bit at a time. Tell you what, hurts like a bitch afterward. Had a busted leg. Busted in three places. Come off the bull and it was a big bull with a lot a drop, he got rid a me in about three flat and he come after me and he was sure faster. Lucky enough. Friend a mine got his oil checked with a horn dipstick and that was all she wrote. Bunch a other things, fuckin busted ribs, sprains and pains, torn ligaments. See, it ain't like it was in my daddy's time. It's guys with money go to college, trained athaletes. You got to have some money to rodeo now. Lureen's old man wouldn't give me a dime if I dropped it, except one way. And I know enough about the game now so I see that I ain't never goin a be on the bubble. Other reasons. I'm gettin out while I still can walk."

Ennis pulled Jack's hand to his mouth, took a hit from the cigarette, exhaled. "Sure as hell seem in one piece to me. You know, I was sittin up here all that time tryin to figure out if I was—? I know I ain't. I mean, here we both got wives and kids, right? I like doin it with women, yeah, but Jesus H., ain't nothin like this. I never had no thoughts a doin it with another guy except I sure wrang it out a hunderd times thinkin about you. You do it with other guys, Jack?"

"Shit no," said Jack, who had been riding more than bulls, not rolling his own. "You know that. Old Brokeback got us good and it sure ain't over. We got to work out what the fuck we're goin a do now."

"That summer," said Ennis. "When we split up after we got paid out I had gut cramps so bad I pulled over and tried to puke, thought I ate somethin bad at that place in Dubois. Took me about a year to figure out it was that I shouldn't a let you out a my sights. Too late then by a long, long while."

"Friend," said Jack. "We got us a fuckin situation here. Got a figure out what to do."

"I doubt there's nothin now we can do," said Ennis. "What I'm sayin, Jack, I built a life up in them years. Love my little girls. Alma? It ain't her fault. You got your baby and wife, that place in Texas. You and me can't hardly be decent together if what happened back there"—he jerked his head in the direction of the apartment—"grabs on us like that. We do that in the wrong place we'll be dead. There's no reins on this one. It scares the piss out a me."

"Got to tell you, friend, maybe somebody seen us that summer. I was back there the next June, thinkin about goin back—I didn't, lit out for Texas instead—and Joe Aguirre's in the office and he says to me, he says, 'You boys found a way to make the time pass up there, didn't you,' and I gave him a look but when I went out I seen he had a big-ass pair a binoculars hangin off his rearview." He neglected to add that the foreman had leaned back in his squeaky wooden tilt chair and said, "Twist, you guys wasn't gettin paid to leave the dogs baby-sit the sheep while you stemmed the rose," and declined to rehire him. Jack went on, "Yeah, that little punch a yours surprised me. I never figured you to throw a dirty punch."

"I come up under my brother K.E., three years older'n me, slugged me silly ever day. Dad got tired a me come bawlin in the house and when I was about six he set me down and says, Ennis, you got a problem and you got a fix it or it's goin a be with you until you're ninety and K.E.'s ninety-three. Well, I says, he's bigger'n me. Dad says, You got a take him unawares, don't say nothin to him, make him feel some pain, get out fast and keep doin it until he takes the message. Nothin like hurtin somebody to make him hear good. So I did. I got him in the outhouse, jumped him on the stairs, come over to his pillow in the night while he was sleepin and pasted him damn good. Took about two days. Never had trouble with K.E. since. The lesson was, Don't say nothin and get it over with quick." A telephone rang in the next room, rang on and on, stopped abruptly in mid-peal.

"You won't catch me again," said Jack. "Listen. I'm thinkin, tell you what, if you and me had a little ranch together, little cow-and-calf operation, your horses, it'd be some sweet life. Like I said, I'm gettin out a rodeo. I ain't no broke-dick rider but I don't got the bucks a ride out this slump I'm in and I don't got the bones a keep gettin wrecked. I got it figured, got this plan Ennis, how we can do it, you and me. Lureen's old man, you bet he'd give me a bunch if I'd get lost. Already more or less said it—"

"Whoa, whoa, whoa. It ain't goin a be that way. We can't. I'm stuck with what I got, caught in my own loop. Can't get out of it. Jack, I don't want a be like them guys you see around sometimes. And I don't want a be dead. There was these two old guys ranched together down home, Earl and Rich—Dad would pass a remark when he seen them. They was a joke even though they was pretty tough old birds. I was what, nine years old, and they found Earl dead in a irrigation ditch. They'd took a tire iron to him, spurred him up, drug him around by his dick until it pulled off, just bloody pulp. What the tire iron done looked like pieces a burned tomatoes all over him, nose tore down from skiddin on gravel."

"You seen that?"

"Dad made sure I seen it. Took me to see it. Me and K.E. Dad laughed about it. Hell, for all I know he done the job. If he was alive and was to put his head in that door right now you bet he'd go get his tire iron. Two guys livin together? No. All I can see is we get together once in a while way the hell out in the back a nowhere—"

"How much is once in a while?" said Jack. "Once in a while ever four fuckin years?"

"No," said Ennis, forbearing to ask whose fault that was. "I goddam hate it that you're goin a drive away in the mornin and I'm goin back to work. But if you can't fix it you got a stand it," he said. "Shit. I been lookin at people on the street. This happen a other people? What the hell do they do?"

"It don't happen in Wyomin and if it does I don't know what they do, maybe go to Denver," said Jack, sitting up, turning away from him, "and I don't give a flyin fuck. Son of a bitch, Ennis, take a couple days off. Right now. Get us out a here. Throw your stuff in the back a my truck and let's get up in the mountains. Couple a days. Call Alma up and tell her you're goin. Come on, Ennis, you just shot my airplane out a the sky—give me somethin a go on. This ain't no little thing that's happenin here."

The hollow ringing began again in the next room, and as if he were answering it Ennis picked up the phone on the bedside table, dialed his own number.

A slow corrosion worked between Ennis and Alma, no real trouble, just widening water. She was working at a grocery-store clerk job, saw she'd always have to work to keep ahead of the bills on what Ennis made. Alma asked Ennis to use rubbers because she dreaded another pregnancy. He said no to that, said he would be happy to leave her alone if she didn't want any more of his kids. Under her breath she said, "I'd have em if you'd support em." And under that thought, Anyway, what you like to do don't make too many babies.

Her resentment opened out a little every year: the embrace she had glimpsed, Ennis's fishing trips once or twice a year with Jack Twist and never a vacation with her and the girls, his disinclination to step out and have any fun, his yearning for low-paid, long-houred ranch work, his propensity to roll to the wall and sleep as soon as he hit the bed, his failure to look for a decent permanent job with the county or the power company put her in a long, slow dive, and when Alma Jr. was nine and Francine seven she said, What am I doin, hangin around with him, divorced Ennis, and married the Riverton grocer.

Ennis went back to ranch work, hired on here and there, not getting much ahead but glad enough to be around stock again, free to drop things, quit if he had to, and go into the mountains at short notice. He had no serious hard feelings, just a vague sense of getting short-changed, and showed it was all right by taking Thanksgiving dinner with Alma and her grocer and the kids, sitting between his girls and talking horses to them, telling jokes, trying not to be a sad daddy. After the pie Alma got him off in the kitchen, scraped the plates and said she worried about him and he ought to get married again. He saw she was pregnant, about four, five months, he guessed.

"Once burned," he said, leaning against the counter, feeling too big for the room.

"You still go fishin with that Jack Twist?"

"Some." He thought she'd take the pattern off the plate with the scraping.

"You know," she said, and from her tone he knew something was coming, "I used to wonder how come you never brought any trouts home. Always said you caught plenty. So one time I got your creel case open the night before you went on one a your little trips—price tag still on it after five years—and I tied a note on the end of the line. It said, 'Hello, Ennis, bring some fish home, love, Alma.' And then you come back and said you'd caught a bunch a browns and ate them up. Remember? I looked in the case when I got a chance and there was my note still tied there and that line hadn't touched water in its life." As though the word "water" had called out its domestic cousin, she twisted the faucet, sluiced the plates.

"That don't mean nothin."

"Don't lie, don't try to fool me, Ennis. I know what it means. Jack Twist? Jack Nasty. You and him—"

She'd overstepped his line. He seized her wrist and twisted; tears sprang and rolled, a dish clattered.

"Shut up," he said. "Mind your own business. You don't know nothin about it."

"I'm goin a yell for Bill."

"You fuckin go right ahead. Go on and fuckin yell. I'll make him eat the fuckin floor and you too." He gave another wrench that left her with a burning bracelet, shoved his hat on backward and slammed out. He went to the Black and Blue Eagle bar that night, got drunk, had a short dirty fight, and left. He didn't try to see his girls for a long time, figuring they would look him up when they got the sense and years to move out from Alma.

They were no longer young men with all of it before them. Jack had filled out through the shoulders and hams; Ennis stayed as lean as a clothespole, stepped around in worn boots, jeans, and shirts summer and winter, added a canvas coat in cold weather. A benign growth appeared on his eyelid and gave it a drooping appearance; a broken nose healed crooked.

Years on years they worked their way through the high meadows and mountain drainages, horse-packing into the Big Horns, the Medicine Bows, the south end of the Gallatins, the Absarokas, the Granites, the Owl Creeks, the Bridger-Teton Range, the Freezeouts and the Shirleys, the Ferrises and the Rattlesnakes, the Salt River range, into the Wind Rivers over and again, the Sierra Madres, the Gros Ventres, the Washakies, the Laramies, but never returning to Brokeback.

Down in Texas Jack's father-in-law died and Lureen, who inherited the farm-equipment business, showed a skill for management and hard deals. Jack found himself with a vague managerial title, traveling to stock and agricultural-machinery shows. He had some money now and found ways to spend it on his buying trips. A little Texas accent flavored his sentences, "cow" twisted into "kyow" and "wife" coming out as "waf." He'd had his front teeth filed down, set with steel plugs, and capped, said he'd felt no pain, wore Texas suits and a tall white hat.

In May of 1983 they spent a few cold days at a series of little ice-bound, no-name high lakes, then worked across into the Hail Strew River drainage.

Going up, the day was fine, but the trail deep-drifted and slopping wet at the margins. They left it to wind through a slashy cut, leading the horses through brittle branch wood, Jack lifting his head in the heated noon to take the air scented with resinous lodgepole, the dry needle duff and hot rock, bitter juniper crushed beneath the horses' hooves. Ennis, weather-eyed, looked west for the heated cumulus that might come up on such a day, but the boneless blue was so deep, said Jack, that he might drown looking up.

Around three they swung through a narrow pass to a southeast slope where the strong spring sun had had a chance to work, dropped down to the trail again, which lay snowless below them. They could hear the river muttering and making a distant train sound a long way off. Twenty minutes on they surprised a black bear on the bank above them rolling a log over for grubs, and Jack's horse shied and reared, Jack saying "Wo! Wo!" and Ennis's bay dancing and snorting but holding. Jack reached for the .30–.06 but there was no need; the startled bear galloped into the trees with the lumpish gait that made it seem it was falling apart.

The tea-colored river ran fast with snowmelt, a scarf of bubbles at every high rock, pools and setbacks streaming. The ochre-branched willows swayed stiffly, pollened catkins like yellow thumb-prints. The horses drank and Jack dismounted, scooped icy water up in his hand, crystalline drops falling from his fingers, his mouth and chin glistening with wet.

"Get beaver fever doin that," said Ennis, then, "Good enough place," looking at the level bench above the river, two or three fire rings from old hunting camps. A sloping meadow rose behind the bench, protected by a stand of lodgepole. There was plenty of dry wood. They set up camp without saying much, picketed the horses in the meadow. Jack broke the seal on a bottle of whiskey, took a long, hot swallow, exhaled forcefully, said, "That's one a the two things I need right now," capped it and tossed it to Ennis.

On the third morning there were the clouds Ennis had expected, a gray racer out of the West, a bar of darkness driving wind before it and small flakes. It faded after an hour into tender spring snow that heaped wet and heavy. By nightfall it had turned colder. Jack and Ennis passed a joint back and forth, the fire burning late, Jack restless and bitching about the cold, poking the flames with a stick, twisting the dial of the transistor radio until the batteries died.

Ennis said he'd been putting the blocks to a woman who worked part-time at the Wolf Ears bar in Signal where he was working now for Car Scrope's cow-and-calf outfit, but it wasn't going anywhere and she had some problems he didn't want. Jack said he'd had a thing going with the wife of a rancher down the road in Childress and for the last few months he'd slank around expecting to get shot by Lureen or the husband, one. Ennis laughed a little and said he probably deserved it. Jack said he was doing all right but he missed Ennis bad enough sometimes to make him whip babies.

The horses nickered in the darkness beyond the fire's circle of light. Ennis put his arm around Jack, pulled him close, said he saw his girls about once a month, Alma Jr. a shy seventeen-year-old with his beanpole length, Francine a little live wire. Jack slid his cold hand between Ennis's legs, said he was worried about his boy who was, no doubt about it, dyslexic or something, couldn't get anything right, fifteen years old and couldn't hardly read, *he* could see it though goddamn Lureen wouldn't admit to it and pretended the kid was O.K., refused to get any bitchin kind a help about it. He didn't know what the fuck the answer was. Lureen had the money and called the shots.

"I used a want a boy for a kid," said Ennis, undoing buttons, "but just got little girls."

"I didn't want none a either kind," said Jack. "But fuck-all has worked the way I wanted. Nothin never come to my hand the right way." Without getting up he threw deadwood on the fire, the sparks flying up with their truths and lies, a few hot points of fire landing on their hands and faces, not for the first time, and they rolled down into the dirt. One thing never changed: the brilliant charge of their infrequent couplings was darkened by the sense of time flying, never enough time, never enough.

A day or two later in the trailhead parking lot, horses loaded into the trailer, Ennis was ready to head back to Signal, Jack up to Lightning Flat to see the old man. Ennis leaned into Jack's window, said what he'd been putting off the whole week, that likely he couldn't get away again until November, after they'd shipped stock and before winter feeding started.

"November. What in hell happened a August? Tell you what, we said August, nine, ten days. Christ, Ennis! Whyn't you tell me this before? You had a fuckin week to say some little word about it. And why's it we're always in the friggin cold weather? We ought a do somethin. We ought a go South. We ought a go to Mexico one day."

"Mexico? Jack, you know me. All the travellin I ever done is goin around the coffeepot lookin for the handle. And I'll be runnin the baler all August, that's what's the matter with August. Lighten up, Jack. We can hunt in November, kill a nice elk. Try if I can get Don Wroe's cabin again. We had a good time that year."

"You know, friend, this is a goddam bitch of a unsatisfactory situation. You used a come away easy. It's like seein the Pope now."

"Jack, I got a work. Them earlier days I used a quit the jobs. You got a wife with money, a good job. You forget how it is bein broke all the time. You ever hear a child support? I been payin out for years and got more to go. Let me tell you, I can't quit this one. And I can't get the time off. It was tough gettin this time—some a them late heifers is still calvin. You don't leave then. You don't. Scrope is a hell-raiser and he raised hell about me takin the week. I don't blame him. He probly ain't got a night's sleep since I left. The trade-off was August. You got a better idea?"

"I did once." The tone was bitter and accusatory.

Ennis said nothing, straightened up slowly, rubbed at his forehead; a horse stamped inside the trailer. He walked to his truck, put his hand on the trailer, said something that only the horses could hear, turned and walked back at a deliberate pace.

"You been a Mexico, Jack?" Mexico was the place. He'd heard. He was cutting fence now, trespassing in the shoot-em zone.

"Hell yes, I been. Where's the fuckin problem?" Braced for it all these years and here it came, late and unexpected.

"I got a say this to you one time, Jack, and I ain't foolin. What I don't know," said Ennis, "all them things I don't know could get you killed if I should come to know them."

"Try this one," said Jack, "and I'll say it just one time. Tell you what, we could a had a good life together, a fuckin real good life. You wouldn't do it, Ennis, so what we got now is Brokeback Mountain. Everthing built on that. It's all we got, boy, fuckin all, so I hope you know that if you don't never know the rest. Count the damn few times we been together in twenty years. Measure the fuckin short leash you keep me on, then ask me about Mexico and then tell me you'll kill me for needin it and not hardly never gettin it. You got no fuckin idea how bad it gets. I'm not you. I can't make it on a couple a high-altitude fucks once or twice a year. You're too much for me, Ennis, you son of a whoreson bitch. I wish I knew how to quit you."

Like vast clouds of steam from thermal springs in winter the years of things unsaid and now unsayable—admissions, declarations, shames, guilts, fears—rose around them. Ennis stood as if heart-shot, face gray and deep-lined, grimacing, eyes screwed shut, fists clenched, legs caving, hit the ground on his knees.

"Jesus," said Jack. "Ennis?" But before he was out of the truck, trying to guess if it was a heart attack or the overflow of an incendiary rage, Ennis was back on his feet, and somehow, as a coat hanger is straightened to open a locked car and then bent again to its original shape, they torqued things almost to where they had been, for what they'd said was no news. Nothing ended, nothing begun, nothing resolved.

What Jack remembered and craved in a way he could neither help nor understand was the time that distant summer on Brokeback when Ennis had come up behind him and pulled him close, the silent embrace satisfying some shared and sexless hunger.

They had stood that way for a long time in front of the fire, its burning tossing ruddy chunks of light, the shadow of their bodies a single column against the rock. The minutes ticked by from the round watch in Ennis's pocket, from the sticks in the fire settling into coals. Stars bit through the wavy heat layers above the fire. Ennis's breath came slow and quiet, he hummed, rocked a little in the sparklight, and Jack leaned against the steady heartbeat, the vibrations of the humming like faint electricity and, standing, he fell into sleep that was not sleep but something else drowsy and tranced until Ennis, dredging up a rusty but still usable phrase from the childhood time before his mother died, said, "Time to hit the hay, cowboy. I got a go. Come on, you're sleepin on your feet like a horse," and gave Jack a shake, a push, and went off in the darkness. Jack heard his spurs tremble as he mounted, the words "See you tomorrow," and the horse's shuddering snort, grind of hoof on stone.

Later, that dozy embrace solidified in his memory as the single moment of artless, charmed happiness in their separate and difficult lives. Nothing marred it, even the knowledge that Ennis would not then embrace him face to face because he did not want to see or feel that it was Jack he held. And maybe, he thought, they'd never got much farther than that. Let be, let be.

Ennis didn't know about the accident for months until his postcard to Jack saying that November still looked like the first chance came back stamped "DECEASED." He called Jack's number in Childress, something he had done only once before, when Alma divorced him, and Jack had misunderstood the reason for the call, had driven twelve hundred miles north for nothing. This would be all right; Jack would answer, had to answer. But he did not. It was Lureen and she said who? who is this? and when he told her again she said in a level voice yes, Jack was pumping up a flat on the truck out on a back road when the tire blew up. The bead was damaged somehow and the force of the explosion slammed the rim into his face, broke his nose and jaw and knocked him unconscious on his back. By the time someone came along he had drowned in his own blood.

No, he thought, they got him with the tire iron.

"Jack used to mention you," she said. "You're the fishing buddy or the hunting buddy, I know that. Would have let you know," she said, "but I wasn't sure about your name and address. Jack kept most a his friends' addresses in his head. It was a terrible thing. He was only thirty-nine years old."

The huge sadness of the Northern plains rolled down on him. He didn't know which way it was, the tire iron or a real accident, blood choking down Jack's throat and nobody to turn him over. Under the wind drone he heard steel slamming off bone, the hollow chatter of a settling tire rim.

"He buried down there?" He wanted to curse her for letting Jack die on the dirt road.

The little Texas voice came slip-sliding down the wire, "We put a stone up. He use to say he wanted to be cremated, ashes scattered on Brokeback Mountain. I didn't know where that was. So he was cremated, like he wanted, and, like I say, half his ashes was interred here, and the rest I sent up to his folks. I thought Brokeback Mountain was around where he grew up. But knowing Jack, it might be some pretend place where the bluebirds sing and there's a whiskey spring."

"We herded sheep on Brokeback one summer," said Ennis. He could hardly speak.

"Well, he said it was his place. I thought he meant to get drunk. Drink whiskey up there. He drank a lot."

"His folks still up in Lightnin Flat?"

"Oh yeah. They'll be there until they die. I never met them. They didn't come down for the funeral. You get in touch with them. I suppose they'd appreciate it if his wishes was carried out."

No doubt about it, she was polite but the little voice was as cold as snow.

The road to Lightning Flat went through desolate country past a dozen abandoned ranches distributed over the plain at eight- and ten-mile intervals, houses sitting blank-eyed in the weeds, corral fences down. The mailbox read JOHN C. TWIST. The ranch was a meagre little place, leafy spurge taking over. The stock was too far distant for him to see their condition, only that they were black baldies. A porch stretched across the front of the tiny brown stucco house, four rooms, two down, two up.

Ennis sat at the kitchen table with Jack's father. Jack's mother, stout and careful in her movements as though recovering from an operation, said, "Want some coffee, don't you? Piece a cherry cake?"

"Thank you, ma'am, I'll take a cup a coffee but I can't eat no cake just now."

The old man sat silent, his hands folded on the plastic table-cloth, staring at Ennis with an angry, knowing expression. Ennis recognized in him a not uncommon type with the hard need to be the stud duck in the pond. He couldn't see much of Jack in either one of them, took a breath.

"I feel awful bad about Jack. Can't begin to say how bad I feel. I knew him a long time. I come by to tell you that if you want me to take his ashes up there on Brokeback like his wife says he wanted I'd be proud to."

There was a silence. Ennis cleared his throat but said nothing more.

The old man said, "Tell you what, I know where Brokeback Mountain is. He thought he was too goddamn special to be buried in the family plot."

Jack's mother ignored this, said, "He used a come home every year, even after he was married and down in Texas, and help his daddy on the ranch for a week, fix the gates and mow and all. I kept his room like it was when he was a boy and I think he appreciated that. You are welcome to go up in his room if you want."

The old man spoke angrily. "I can't get no help out here. Jack used a say, 'Ennis del Mar,' he used a say, 'I'm goin a bring him up here one a these days and we'll lick this damn ranch into shape.' He had some half-baked idea the two a you was goin a move up here, build a log cabin, and help me run this ranch and bring it up. Then this spring he's got another one's goin a come up here with him and build a place and help run the ranch, some ranch neighbor a his from down in Texas. He's goin a split up with his wife and come back here. So he says. But like most a Jack's ideas it never come to pass."

So now he knew it had been the tire iron. He stood up, said you bet he'd like to see Jack's room, recalled one of Jack's stories about this old man. Jack was dick-clipped and the old man was not; it bothered the son, who had discovered the anatomical disconformity during a hard scene. He had been about three or four, he said, always late getting to the toilet, struggling with buttons, the seat, the height of the thing, and often as not left the surroundings sprinkled down. The old man blew up about it and this one time worked into a crazy rage. "Christ, he licked the stuffin out a me, knocked me down on the bathroom floor, whipped me with his belt. I thought he was killin me. Then he says, 'You want a know what it's like with piss all over the place? I'll learn you,' and he pulls it out and lets go all over me, soaked me, then he throws a towel at me and makes me mop up the floor, take my clothes off and warsh them in the bathtub, warsh out the towel, I'm bawlin and blubberin. But while he was hosin me down I seen he had some extra material that I was missin. I seen they'd cut me different like you'd crop a ear or scorch a brand. No way to get it right with him after that."

The bedroom, at the top of a steep stair that had its own climbing rhythm, was tiny and hot, afternoon sun pounding through the west window, hitting the narrow boy's bed against the wall, an ink-stained desk and wooden chair, a B.B. gun in a hand-whittled rack over the bed. The window looked down on the gravel road stretching south and it occurred to him that for Jack's growing-up years that was the only road he knew. An ancient magazine photograph of some dark-haired movie star was taped to the wall beside the bed, the skin tone gone magenta. He could hear Jack's mother downstairs running water, filling the kettle and setting it back on the stove, asking the old man a muffled question.

The closet was a shallow cavity with a wooden rod braced across, a faded cretonne curtain on a string closing it off from the rest of the room. In the closet hung two pairs of jeans crease-ironed and folded neatly over wire hangers, on the floor a pair of worn packer boots he thought he remembered. At the north end of the closet a tiny jog in the wall made a slight hiding place and here, stiff with long suspension from a nail, hung a shirt. He lifted it off the nail. Jack's old shirt from Brokeback days. The dried blood on the sleeve was his own blood, a gushing nosebleed on the last afternoon on the mountain when Jack, in their contortionistic grappling and wrestling, had slammed Ennis's nose hard with his knee. He had stanched the blood, which was everywhere, all over both of them, with his shirtsleeve, but the stanching hadn't held, because Ennis had suddenly swung from the deck and laid the ministering angel out in the wild columbine, wings folded.

The shirt seemed heavy until he saw there was another shirt inside it, the sleeves carefully worked down inside Jack's sleeves. It was his own plaid shirt, lost, he'd thought, long ago in some damn laundry, his dirty shirt, the pocket ripped, buttons missing, stolen by Jack and hidden here inside Jack's own shirt, the pair like two skins, one inside the other, two in one. He pressed his face into the fabric and breathed in slowly through his mouth and nose, hoping for the faintest smoke and mountain sage and salty sweet stink of Jack, but there was no real scent, only the memory of it, the imagined power of Brokeback Mountain of which nothing was left but what he held in his hands.

In the end the stud duck refused to let Jack's ashes go. "Tell you what, we got a family plot and he's goin in it." Jack's mother stood at the table coring apples with a sharp, serrated instrument. "You come again," she said.

Bumping down the washboard road Ennis passed the country cemetery fenced with sagging sheep wire, a tiny fenced square on the welling prairie, a few graves bright with plastic flowers, and didn't want to know Jack was going in there, to be buried on the grieving plain.

A few weeks later, on the Saturday, he threw all the Coffeepot's dirty horse blankets into the back of his pickup and took them down to the Quik Stop Car Wash to turn the high-pressure spray on them. When the wet clean blankets were stowed in the truck bed he stepped into Higgins' gift shop and busied himself with the postcard rack.

"Ennis, what are you lookin for, rootin through them postcards?" said Linda Higgins, throwing a sopping brown coffee filter into the garbage can.

"Scene a Brokeback Mountain."

"Over in Fremont County?"

"No, north a here."

"I didn't order none a them. Let me get the order list. They got it I can get you a hunderd. I got a order some more cards anyway."

"One's enough," said Ennis.

When it came—thirty cents—he pinned it up in his trailer, brass-headed tack in each corner. Below it he drove a nail and on the nail he hung a wire hanger and the two old shirts suspended from it. He stepped back and looked at the ensemble through a few stinging tears.

"Jack, I swear—" he said, though Jack had never asked him to swear anything and was himself not the swearing kind.

Around that time Jack began to appear in his dreams, Jack as he had first seen him, curly-headed and smiling and buck-toothed, talking about getting up off his pockets and into the control zone, but the can of beans with the spoon handle jutting out and balanced on the log was there as well, in a cartoon shape and lurid colors that gave the dreams a flavor of comic obscenity. The spoon handle was the kind that could be used as a tire iron. And he would wake sometimes in grief, sometimes with the old sense of joy and release; the pillow sometimes wet, sometimes the sheets.

There was some open space between what he knew and what he tried to believe, but nothing could be done about it, and if you can't fix it you've got to stand it.

LULLABY

LESLIE MARMON SILKO

From Storyteller,
Arcade Publishing, New York, 1981

The sun had gone down but the snow in the wind gave off its own light. It came in thick tufts like new wool—washed before the weaver spins it. Ayah reached out for it like her own babies had, and she smiled when she remembered how she had laughed at them. She was an old woman now, and her life had become memories. She sat down with her back against the wide cottonwood tree, feeling the rough bark on her back bones; she faced east and listened to the wind and snow sing a high-pitched Yeibechei song. Out of the wind she felt warmer, and she could watch the wide fluffy snow fill in her tracks, steadily, until the direction she had come from was gone. By the light of the snow she could see the dark outline of the big arroyo a few feet away. She was sitting on the edge of Cebolleta Creek, where in the springtime the thin cows would graze on grass already chewed flat to the ground. In the wide deep creek bed where only a trickle of water flowed in the summer, the skinny cows would wander, looking for new grass along winding paths splashed with manure.

Ayah pulled the old Army blanket over her head like a shawl. Jimmie's blanket—the one he had sent to her. That was a long time ago and the green wool was faded, and it was unraveling on the edges. She did not want to think about Jimmie. So she thought about the weaving and the way her mother had done it. On the tall wooden loom set into the sand under a tamarack tree for shade. She could see it clearly. She had been only a little girl when her grandma gave her the wooden combs to pull the twigs and burrs from the raw, freshly washed wool. And while she combed the wool, her grandma sat beside her, spinning a silvery strand of yarn around the smooth cedar spindle. Her mother worked at the loom with yarns dyed bright yellow and red and gold. She watched them dye the yarn in boiling black pots full of beeweed petals, juniper berries, and sage. The blankets her mother made were soft and woven so tight that rain rolled off them like birds' feathers. Ayah remembered sleeping warm on cold windy nights, wrapped in her mother's blankets on the hogan's sandy floor.

The snow drifted now, with the northwest wind hurling it in gusts. It drifted up around her black overshoes—old ones with little metal buckles. She smiled at the snow which was trying to cover her little by little. She could remember when they had no black rubber overshoes; only the high buckskin leggings that they wrapped over their elkhide moccasins. If the snow was dry or frozen, a person could walk all day and not get wet; and in the evenings the beams of the ceiling would hang with lengths of pale buckskin leggings, drying out slowly.

She felt peaceful remembering. She didn't feel cold any more. Jimmie's blanket seemed warmer than it had ever been. And she could remember the morning he was born. She could remember whispering to her mother, who was sleeping on the other side of the hogan, to tell her it was time now. She did not want to wake the others. The second time she called to her, her mother stood up and pulled on her shoes; she knew. They walked to the old stone hogan together, Ayah walking a step behind her mother. She waited alone, learning the rhythms of the pains while her mother went to call the old woman to help them. The morning was already warm even before dawn and Ayah smelled the bee flowers blooming and the young willow growing at the springs. She could remember that so clearly, but his birth merged into the births of the other children and to her it became all the same birth. They named him for the summer morning and in English they called him Jimmie.

It wasn't like Jimmie died. He just never came back, and one day a dark blue sedan with white writing on its doors pulled up in front of the boxcar shack where the rancher let the Indians live. A man in a khaki uniform trimmed in gold gave them a yellow piece of paper and told them that Jimmie was dead. He said the Army would try to get the body back and then it would be shipped to them; but it wasn't likely because the helicopter had burned after it crashed. All of this was told to Chato because he could understand English. She stood inside the doorway holding the baby while Chato listened. Chato spoke English like a white man and he spoke Spanish too. He was taller than the white man and he stood straighter too. Chato didn't explain why; he just told the military man they could keep the body if they found it. The white man looked bewildered; he nodded his head and he left. Then Chato looked at her and shook his head, and then he told her, "Jimmie isn't coming home anymore," and when he spoke, he used the words to speak of the dead. She didn't cry then, but she hurt inside with anger. And she mourned him as the years passed, when a horse fell with Chato and broke his leg, and the white rancher told them he wouldn't pay Chato until he could work again. She mourned Jimmie because he would have worked for his father then; he would have saddled the big bay horse and ridden the fence lines each day, with wire cutters and heavy gloves, fixing the breaks in the barbed wire and putting the stray cattle back inside again.

She mourned him after the white doctors came to take Danny and Ella away. She was at the shack alone that day they came. It was back in the days before they hired Navajo women to go with them as interpreters. She recognized one of the doctors. She had seen him at the children's clinic at Cañoncito about a month ago. They were wearing khaki uniforms and they waved papers at her and a black ball-point pen, trying to make her understand their English words. She was frightened by the way they looked at the children, like the lizard watches the fly. Danny was swinging on the tire swing on the elm tree behind the rancher's house, and Ella was toddling around the front door, dragging the broomstick horse Chato made for her. Ayah could see they wanted her to sign the papers, and Chato had taught her to sign her name. It was something she was proud of. She only wanted them to go, and to take their eyes away from her children.

She took the pen from the man without looking at his face and she signed the papers in three different places he pointed to. She stared at the ground by their feet and waited for them to leave. But they stood there and began to point and gesture at the children. Danny stopped swinging. Ayah could see his fear. She moved suddenly and grabbed Ella into her arms; the child squirmed, trying to get back to her toys. Ayah ran with the baby toward Danny; she screamed for him to run and then she grabbed him around his chest and carried him too. She ran south into the foothills of juniper trees and black lava rock. Behind her she heard the doctors running, but they had been taken by surprise, and as the hills became steeper and the cholla cactus were thicker, they stopped. When she reached the top of the hill, she stopped to listen in case they were circling around her. But in a few minutes she heard a car engine start and they drove away. The children had been too surprised to cry while she ran with them. Danny was shaking and Ella's little fingers were gripping Ayah's blouse.

She stayed up in the hills for the rest of the day, sitting on a black lava boulder in the sunshine where she could see for miles all around her. The sky was light blue and cloudless, and it was warm for late April. The sun warmth relaxed her and took the fear and anger away. She lay back on the rock and watched the sky. It seemed to her that she could walk into the sky, stepping through clouds endlessly. Danny played with little pebbles and stones, pretending they were birds eggs and then little rabbits. Ella sat at her feet and dropped fistfuls of dirt into the breeze, watching the dust and particles of sand intently. Ayah watched a hawk soar high above them, dark wings gliding; hunting or only watching, she did not know. The hawk was patient and he circled all afternoon before he disappeared around the high volcanic peak the Mexicans called Guadalupe.

Late in the afternoon, Ayah looked down at the gray boxcar shack with the paint all peeled from the wood; the stovepipe on the roof was rusted and crooked. The fire she had built that morning in the oil drum stove had burned out. Ella was asleep in her lap now and Danny sat close to her, complaining that he was hungry; he asked when they would go to the house. "We will stay up here until your father comes," she told him, "because those white men were chasing us." The boy remembered then and he nodded at her silently.

If Jimmie had been there he could have read those papers and explained to her what they said. Ayah would have known then, never to sign them. The doctors came back the next day and they brought a BIA policeman with them. They told Chato they had her signature and that was all they needed. Except for the kids. She listened to Chato sullenly; she hated him when he told her it was the old woman who died in the winter, spitting blood; it was her old grandma who had given the children this disease. "They don't spit blood," she said coldly. "The whites lie." She held Ella and Danny close to her, ready to run to the hills again. "I want a medicine man first," she said to Chato, not looking at him. He shook his head. "It's too late now. The policeman is with them. You signed the paper." His voice was gentle.

It was worse than if they had died: to lose the children and to know that somewhere, in a place called Colorado, in a place full of sick and dying strangers, her children were without her. There had been babies that died soon after they were born, and one that died before he could walk. She had carried them herself, up to the boulders and great pieces of the cliff that long ago crashed down from Long Mesa; she laid them in the crevices of sandstone and buried them in fine brown sand with round quartz pebbles that washed down the hills in the rain. She had endured it because they had been with her. But she could not bear this pain. She did not sleep for a long time after they took her children. She stayed on the hill where they had fled the first time, and she slept rolled up in the blanket Jimmie had sent her. She carried the pain in her belly and it was fed by everything she saw: the blue sky of their last day together and the dust and pebbles they played with; the swing in the elm tree and broomstick horse choked life from her. The pain filled her stomach and there was no room for food or for her lungs to fill with air. The air and the food would have been theirs.

She hated Chato, not because he let the policeman and doctors put the screaming children in the government car, but because he had taught her to sign her name. Because it was like the old ones always told her about learning their language or any of their ways: it endangered you. She slept alone on the hill until the middle of November when the first snows came. Then she made a bed for herself where the children had slept. She did not lie down beside Chato again until many years later, when he was sick and shivering and only her body could keep him warm. The illness came after the white rancher told Chato he was too old to work for him anymore, and Chato and his old woman should be out of the shack by the next afternoon because the rancher had hired new people to work there. That had satisfied her. To see how the white man repaid Chato's years of loyalty and work. All of Chato's fine-sounding English talk didn't change things.

It snowed steadily and the luminous light from the snow gradually diminished into the darkness. Somewhere in Cebolleta a dog barked and other village dogs joined with it. Ayah looked in the direction she had come, from the bar where Chato was buying the wine. Sometimes he told her to go on ahead and wait; and then he never came. And when she finally went back looking for him, she would find him passed out at the bottom of the wooden steps to Azzie's Bar. All the wine would be gone and most of the money too, from the pale blue check that came to them once a month in a government envelope. It was then that she would look at his face and his hands, scarred by ropes and the barbed wire of all those years, and she would think, this man is a stranger; for forty years she had smiled at him and cooked his food, but he remained a stranger. She stood up again, with the snow almost to her knees, and she walked back to find Chato.

It was hard to walk in the deep snow and she felt the air burn in her lungs. She stopped a short distance from the bar to rest and readjust the blanket. But this time he wasn't waiting for her on the bottom step with his old Stetson hat pulled down and his shoulders hunched up in his long wool overcoat.

She was careful not to slip on the wooden steps. When she pushed the door open, warm air and cigarette smoke hit her face. She looked around slowly and deliberately, in every corner, in every dark place that the old man might find to sleep. The bar owner didn't like Indians in there, especially Navajos, but he let Chato come in because he could talk Spanish like he was one of them. The men at the bar stared at her, and the bartender saw that she left the door open wide. Snowflakes were flying inside like moths and melting into a puddle on the oiled wood floor. He motioned to her to close the door, but she did not see him. She held herself straight and walked across the room slowly, searching the room with every step. The snow in her hair melted and she could feel it on her forehead. At the far corner of the room, she saw red flames at the mica window of the old stove door; she looked behind the stove just to make sure. The bar got quiet except for the Spanish polka music playing on the jukebox. She stood by the stove and shook the snow from her blanket and held it near the stove to dry. The wet wool smell reminded her of newborn goats in early March, brought inside to warm near the fire. She felt calm.

In past years they would have told her to get out. But her hair was white now and her face was wrinkled. They looked at her like she was a spider crawling slowly across the room. They were afraid; she could feel the fear. She looked at their faces steadily. They reminded her of the first time the white people brought her children back to her that winter. Danny had been shy and hid behind the thin white woman who brought them. And the baby had not known her until Ayah took her into her arms, and then Ella had nuzzled close to her as she had when she was nursing. The blonde woman was nervous and kept looking at a dainty gold watch on her wrist. She sat on the bench near the small window and watched the dark snow clouds gather around the mountains; she was worrying about the unpaved road. She was frightened by what she saw inside too: the strips of venison drying on a rope across the ceiling and the children jabbering excitedly in a language she did not know. So they stayed for only a few hours. Ayah watched the government car disappear down the road and she knew they were already being weaned from these lava hills and from this sky. The last time they came was in early June, and Ella stared at her the way the men in the bar were now staring. Ayah did not try to pick her up; she smiled at her instead and spoke cheerfully to Danny. When he tried to answer her, he could not seem to remember and he spoke English words with the Navajo. But he gave her a scrap of paper that he had found somewhere and carried in his pocket; it was folded in half, and he shyly looked up at her and said it was a bird. She asked Chato if they were home for good this time. He spoke to the white woman and she shook her head. "How much longer?" he asked, and she said she didn't know; but Chato saw how she stared at the boxcar shack. Ayah turned away then. She did not say good-bye.

She felt satisfied that the men in the bar feared her. Maybe it was her face and the way she held her mouth with teeth clenched tight, like there was nothing anyone could do to her now. She walked north down the road, searching for the old man. She did this because she had the blanket, and there would be no place for him except with her and the blanket in the old adobe barn near the arroyo. They always slept there when they came to Cebolleta. If the money and the wine were gone, she would be relieved because then they could go home again; back to the old hogan with a dirt roof and rock walls where she herself had been born. And the next day the old man could go back to the few sheep they still had, to follow along behind them, guiding them, into dry sandy arroyos where sparse grass grew. She knew he did not like walking behind old ewes when for so many years he rode big quarter horses and worked with cattle. But she wasn't sorry for him; he should have known all along what would happen.

There had not been enough rain for their garden in five years; and that was when Chato finally hitched a ride into the town and brought back brown boxes of rice and sugar and big tin cans of welfare peaches. After that, at the first of the month they went to Cebolleta to ask the postmaster for the check; and then Chato would go to the bar and cash it. They did this as they planted the garden every May, not because anything would survive the summer dust, but because it was time to do this. The journey passed the days that smelled silent and dry like the caves above the canyon with yellow painted buffaloes on their walls.

* * *

He was walking along the pavement when she found him. He did not stop or turn around when he heard her behind him. She walked beside him and she noticed how slowly he moved now. He smelled strong of woodsmoke and urine. Lately he had been forgetting. Sometimes he called her by his sister's name and she had been gone for a long time. Once she had found him wandering on the road to the white man's ranch, and she asked him why he was going that way; he laughed at her and said, "You know they can't run that ranch without me," and he walked on determined, limping on the leg that had been crushed many years before. Now he looked at her curiously, as if for the first time, but he kept shuffling along, moving slowly along the side of the highway. His gray hair had grown long and spread out on the shoulders of the long overcoat. He wore the old felt hat pulled down over his ears. His boots were worn out at the toes and he had stuffed pieces of an old red shirt in the holes. The rags made his feet look like little animals up to their ears in snow. She laughed at his feet; the snow muffled the sound of her laugh. He stopped and looked at her again. The wind had quit blowing and the snow was falling straight down; the southeast sky was beginning to clear and Ayah could see a star.

"Let's rest awhile," she said to him. They walked away from the road and up the slope to the giant boulders that had tumbled down from the red sandrock mesa throughout the centuries of rainstorms and earth tremors. In a place where the boulders shut out the wind, they sat down with their backs against the rock. She offered half of the blanket to him and they sat wrapped together.

The storm passed swiftly. The clouds moved east. They were massive and full, crowding together across the sky. She watched them with the feeling of horses—steely blue-gray horses startled across the sky. The powerful haunches pushed into the distances and the tail hairs streamed white mist behind them. The sky cleared. Ayah saw that there was nothing between her and the stars. The light was crystalline. There was no shimmer, no distortion through earth haze. She breathed the clarity of the night sky; she smelled the purity of the half moon and the stars. He was lying on his side with his knees pulled up near his belly for warmth. His eyes were closed now, and in the light from the stars and the moon, he looked young again.

She could see it descend out of the night sky: an icy stillness from the edge of the thin moon. She recognized the freezing. It came gradually, sinking snowflake by snowflake until the crust was heavy and deep. It had the strength of the stars in Orion, and its journey was endless. Ayah knew that with the wine he would sleep. He would not feel it. She tucked the blanket around him, remembering how it was when Ella had been with her; and she felt the rush so big inside her heart for the babies. And she sang the only song she knew to sing for babies. She could not remember if she had ever sung it to her children, but she knew that her grandmother had sung it and her mother had sung it:

The earth is your mother,
    she holds you.
The sky is your father,
    he protects you.
Sleep,
sleep.
Rainbow is your sister,
    she loves you.
The winds are your brothers,
    they sing to you.
Sleep,
sleep.
We are together always
We are together always
There never was a time
when this
was not so.

THE
PEDERSEN KID

WILLIAM H. GASS

From In the Heart of the Heart of the Country,
Harper and Row, New York, 1968

PART ONE
1

Big Hans yelled, so I came out. The barn was dark, but the sun
burned on the snow. Hans was carrying something from the crib.
I yelled, but Big Hans didn't hear. He was in the house with what
he had before I reached the steps.

It was the Pedersen kid. Hans had put the kid on the kitchen
table like you would a ham and started the kettle. He wasn't saying anything. I guess he figured one yell from the crib was
enough noise. Ma was fumbling with the kid's clothes which were
stiff with ice. She made a sound like whew from every breath.
The kettle filled and Hans said,

Get some snow and call your pa.

Why?

Get some snow.

I took the big pail from under the sink and the shovel by the
stove. I tried not to hurry and nobody said anything. There was a

drift over the edge of the porch, so I spaded some out of that. When I brought the pail in, Hans said,

There's coal dust in that. Get more.

A little coal won't hurt.

Get more.

Coal's warming.

It's not enough. Shut your mouth and get your pa.

Ma had rolled out some dough on the table where Hans had dropped the Pedersen kid like a filling. Most of the kid's clothes were on the floor where they were going to make a puddle. Hans began rubbing snow on the kid's face. Ma stopped trying to pull his things off and simply stood by the table with her hands held away from her as if they were wet, staring first at Big Hans and then at the kid.

Get.

Why?

I told you.

It's Pa I mean—

I know what you mean. Get.

I found a cardboard box that condensed milk had come in and I shoveled it full of snow. It was too small as I figured it would be. I found another with rags and an old sponge I threw out. Campbell's soup. I filled it too, using the rest of the drift. Snow would melt through the bottom of the boxes but that was all right with me. By now the kid was naked. I was satisfied mine was bigger.

Looks like a sick shoat.

Shut up and get your pa.

He's asleep.

Yeah.

He don't like to get waked.

I know that. Don't I know that as good as you? Get him.

What good'll he be?

We're going to need his whiskey.

He can fix that need all right. He's good for fixing the crack in his face. If it ain't all gone.

The kettle was whistling.

What are we going to do with these? ma said.

Wait, Hed. Now I want you to get. I'm tired of talking. Get, you hear?

What are we going to do with them? They're all wet, she said.

I went to wake the old man. He didn't like being roused. It was too hard and far to come, the sleep he was in. He didn't give a damn about the Pedersen kid, any more than I did. Pedersen's kid was just a kid. He didn't carry any weight. Not like I did. And the old man would be mad, unable to see, coming that way from where he was asleep. I decided I hated Big Hans, though this was hardly something new for me. I hated Big Hans just then because I was thinking how Pa's eyes would blink at me—as if I were the sun off the snow and burning to blind him. His eyes were old and they'd never seen well, but shone on by whiskey they'd glare at my noise, growing red and raising up his rage. I decided I hated the Pedersen kid too, dying in our kitchen while I was away where I couldn't watch, dying just to pleasure Hans and making me go up snapping steps and down a drafty hall, Pa lumped under the covers at the end like dung covered with snow, snoring and whistling. Oh he'd not care about the Pedersen kid. He'd not care about getting waked so he could give up some of his liquor to a slit of a kid and maybe lose one of his hiding places in the bargain. That would make him mad enough if he was sober. I tried not to hurry though it was cold and the Pedersen kid was in the kitchen.

He was all shoveled up like I thought he'd be. I shoved at his shoulder, calling his name. I think he heard his name. His name stopped the snoring, but he didn't move except to roll a little when I shoved him. The covers slid down his skinny neck so I saw his head, fuzzed like a dandelion gone to seed, but his face was turned to the wall—there was the pale shadow of his nose on the plaster—and I thought: well you don't look much like a pig-drunk bully now. I couldn't be sure he was still asleep. He was a cagey sonofabitch. He'd heard his name. I shook him a little harder and made some noise. Pap-pap-pap-hey, I said.

I was leaning too far over. I knew better. He always slept close to the wall so you had to lean to reach him. Oh he was smart. It put you off. I knew better but I was thinking of the Pedersen kid mother-naked in all that dough. When his arm came up I ducked away but it caught me on the side of the neck, watering my eyes, and I backed off to cough. Pa was on his side, looking at me, his eyes winking, the hand that had hit me a fist in the pillow.

Get the hell out of here.

I didn't say anything—my throat wasn't clear—but I watched him. He was like a mean horse to come at from the rear. It was better, though, he'd hit me. He was bitter when he missed.

Get the hell out of here.

Big Hans sent me. He told me to wake you.

A fat turd to Big Hans. Get out of here.

He found the Pedersen kid by the crib.

Get the hell out.

Pa pulled at the covers. He was tasting his mouth.

The kid's froze like a pump. Hans is rubbing him with snow. He's got him in the kitchen.

Pedersen?

No, Pa. It's the Pedersen kid. The kid.

Nothing to steal from the crib.

Not stealing, Pa. He was just lying there. Hans found him froze. That's where he was when Hans found him.

Pa laughed.

I ain't hid nothing in the crib.

You don't understand, Pa. The Pedersen kid. The kid—

I shittin well understand.

Pa had his head up, glaring, his teeth gnawing at the place where he'd grown a mustache once.

I shittin well understand. You know I don't want to see Pedersen. That cock. Why should I? That fairy farmer. What did he come for, hey? God dammit, get. And don't come back. Find out some shittin something. You're a fool. Both you and Hans. Pedersen. That cock. That fairy farmer. Don't come back. Out. Shit. Out. Out out.

He was shouting and breathing hard and closing his fist on the pillow. He had long black hairs on his wrist. They curled around the cuff of his nightshirt.

Big Hans made me come. Big Hans said—

A fat turd to Big Hans. He's an even bigger turd than you. Fat, too, fool, hey? I taught him, dammit, and I'll teach you. Out. You want me to drop my pot?

He was about to get up so I got out, slamming the door. He was beginning to see he was too mad to sleep. Then he threw things. Once he went after Hans and dumped his pot over the banister. Pa'd been shit-sick in that pot. Hans got an ax. He didn't even bother to wipe himself off and he chopped part of Pa's door down before he stopped. He might not have gone that far if Pa hadn't been locked in laughing fit to shake the house. That pot put Pa in an awful good humor—whenever he thought of it. I always felt the thought was present in both of them, stirring in their chests like a laugh or a growl, as eager as an animal to be out. I heard Pa cursing all the way downstairs.

Hans had laid steaming towels over the kid's chest and stomach. He was rubbing snow on the kid's legs and feet. Water from the snow and water from the towels had run off the kid to the table where the dough was, and the dough was turning pasty, sticking to the kid's back and behind.

Ain't he going to wake up?

What about your pa?

He was awake when I left.

What'd he say? Did you get the whiskey?

He said a fat turd to Big Hans.

Don't be smart. Did you ask him about the whiskey?

Yeah.

Well?

He said a fat turd to Big Hans.

Don't be smart. What's he going to do?

Go back to sleep most likely.

You'd best get that whiskey.

You go. Take the ax. Pa's scared to hell of axes.

Listen to me, Jorge, I've had enough of your sassing. This kid's froze bad. If I don't get some whiskey down him he might die. You want the kid to die? Do you? Well, get your pa and get that whiskey.

Pa don't care about the kid.

Jorge.

Well he don't. He don't care at all, and I don't care to get my head busted neither. He don't care, and I don't care to have his shit flung on me. He don't care about anybody. All he cares about is his whiskey and that dry crack in his face. Get pig-drunk— that's what he wants. He don't care about nothing else at all. Nothing. Not Pedersen's kid neither. That cock. Not the kid neither.

I'll get the spirits, ma said.

I'd wound Big Hans up tight. I was ready to jump but when ma said she'd get the whiskey it surprised him like it surprised me, and he ran down. Ma never went near the old man when he was sleeping it off. Not any more. Not for years. The first thing every morning when she washed her face she could see the scar on her chin where he'd cut her with a boot cleat, and maybe she saw him heaving it again, the dirty sock popping out as it flew. It should have been nearly as easy for her to remember that as it was for Big Hans to remember going after the ax while he was still spattered with Pa's sour yellow sick insides.

No you won't, Big Hans said.

Yes, Hans, if they're needed, ma said.

Hans shook his head but neither of us tried to stop her. If we had, then one of us would have had to go instead. Hans rubbed the kid with more snow . . . rubbed . . . rubbed.

I'll get more snow, I said.

I took the pail and shovel and went out on the porch. I don't know where ma went. I thought she'd gone upstairs and expected to hear she had. She had surprised Hans like she had surprised me when she said she'd go, and then she surprised him again when she came back so quick like she must have, because when I came in with the snow she was there with a bottle with three white feathers on its label and Hans was holding it angrily by the throat. Oh he was being queer and careful, pawing about in the drawer and holding the bottle like a snake at the length of his arm. He was awful angry because he'd thought ma was going to do something big, something heroic even, especially for her—I know him . . . I know him . . . we felt the same sometimes—while ma wasn't thinking about that at all, not anything like that. There was no way of getting even. It wasn't like getting cheated at the fair. They were always trying, so you got to expect it. Now Hans had given ma something of his—we both had when we thought she was going straight to Pa—something valuable, a piece of better feeling; but since she didn't know we'd given it to her, there was no easy way of getting it back.

Hans cut the foil off finally and unscrewed the cap. He was put out too because there was only one way of understanding what she'd done. Ma had found one of Pa's hiding places. She'd found one and she hadn't said a word while Big Hans and I had hunted and hunted as we always did all winter, every winter since the spring that Hans had come and I had looked in the privy and found the first one. Pa had a knack for hiding. He knew we were looking and he enjoyed it. But now ma. She'd found it by luck most likely but she hadn't said anything and we didn't know how long ago it'd been or how many other ones she'd found, saying nothing. Pa was sure to find out. Sometimes he didn't seem to because he hid them so well he couldn't find them himself or be-

cause he looked and didn't find anything and figured he hadn't
hid one after all or had drunk it up. But he'd find out about this
one because we were using it. A fool could see what was going on.
If he found out ma found it—that'd be bad. He took pride in his
hiding. It was all the pride he had. I guess fooling Hans and me
took doing. But he didn't figure ma for much. He didn't figure
her at all. And if he found out—a woman had—then it'd be bad.

Hans poured some in a tumbler.

You going to put more towels on him?

No.

Why not? That's what he needs, something warm to his skin,
don't he?

Not where he's froze good. Heat's bad for frostbite. That's why
I only put towels on his chest and belly. He's got to thaw slow.
You ought to know that.

Colors on the towels had run.

Ma poked her toe in the kid's clothes.

What are we going to do with these?

Big Hans began pouring whiskey in the kid's mouth but the
mouth filled without any getting down his throat and in a second
it was dripping from his chin.

Here, help me prop him up. I got to hold his mouth open.

I didn't want to touch him and I hoped ma would do it but she
kept looking at the kid's clothes piled on the floor and the pool of
water by them and didn't make any move to.

Come on, Jorge.

All right.

Lift, don't shove . . . lift.

Okay, I'm lifting.

I took him by the shoulders. His head flopped back. His
mouth fell open. The skin on his neck was tight. He was cold all
right.

Hold his head up. He'll choke.

His mouth is open.

His throat's shut. He'll choke.

He'll choke anyway.

Hold his head up.

I can't.

Don't hold him like that. Put your arms around him.

Well jesus.

He was cold all right. I put my arm carefully around him. Hans had his fingers in the kid's mouth.

Now he'll choke for sure.

Shut up. Just hold him like I told you.

He was cold all right, and wet. I had my arm behind his back. He sure felt dead.

Tilt his head back a bit . . . not too much.

He felt cold and slimy. He sure was dead. We had a dead body in our kitchen. All the time he'd been dead. When Hans had brought him in, he'd been dead. I couldn't see him breathing. He was awful skinny, sunk between the ribs. We were getting him ready to bake. Hans was basting him. I had my arm around him, holding him up. He was dead and I had hold of him. I could feel my muscles jumping.

Well jesus christ.

He *is* dead. He *is*.

You dropped him.

Dead? ma said.

He's dead. I could feel. He's dead.

Dead?

Ain't you got any sense? You let his head hit the table.

Is he dead? Is he dead? ma said.

Well christ no, not yet, not yet he's not dead. Look what you done, Jorge, there's whiskey all over.

He *is* dead. He *is*.

Right now he ain't. Not yet he ain't. Now stop yelling and hold him up.

He ain't breathing.

Yes he is, he *is* breathing. Hold him up.

I ain't. I ain't holding any dead body. You can hold it if you want. You dribble whiskey on it all you want. You can do anything you want to. I ain't. I ain't holding any dead body.

If he's dead, ma said, what are we going to do with these?

Jorge, god damn you, come back here—

I went down to the crib where Big Hans had found him. There was still a hollow in the snow and some prints the wind hadn't sifted snow over. The kid must have been out on his feet, they wobbled so. I could see where he had walked smack into a drift and then backed off and lurched up beside the crib, maybe bumping into it before he fell, then lying quiet so the snow had time to curl around him, piling up until in no time it would have covered him completely. Who knows, I thought, the way it's been snowing, we mightn't have found him till spring. Even if he was dead in our kitchen, I was glad Big Hans had found him. I could see myself coming out of the house some morning with the sun high up and strong and the eaves dripping, the snow speckled with drops and the ice on the creek slushing up; coming out and walking down by the crib on the crusts of the drift . . . coming out to play my game with the drifts . . . and I could see myself losing, breaking through the big drift that was always sleeping up against the crib and running a foot right into him, right into the Pedersen kid curled up, getting soft.

That would have been worse than holding to his body in the kitchen. The feeling would have come on quicker, and it would have been worse, happening in the middle of a game. There wouldn't have been any warning, any way of getting ready for it to happen, to know what I'd struck before I bent down, even though Old Man Pedersen would have come over between snows looking for the kid most likely and everybody would have figured that the kid was lying buried somewhere under the snow; that maybe after a high wind someday somebody would find him lying like a black stone uncovered in a field; but probably in the spring somebody would find him in some back pasture thawing out with the mud and have to bring him in and take him over to the Pedersen place and present him to Missus Pedersen. Even so, even with everyone knowing that, and hoping one of the Pedersens would find him first so they wouldn't have to pry him up out of the mud or fetch him out from a thicket and bring him in and give him to Missus Pedersen in soggy season-old clothes—even then, who would expect to stick a foot all of a sudden through the crust losing at the drift game and step on Pedersen's kid lying all crouched together right beside your own crib? It was a good thing Hans had come down this morning and found him, even if he was dead in our kitchen and I had held him up.

When Pedersen came over asking for his kid, maybe hoping that the kid had got to our place all right and stayed, waiting for the blizzard to quit before going home, Pa would meet him and bring him in for a drink and tell him it was his own fault for putting up all those snow fences. If I knew Pa, he'd tell Pedersen to look under the drifts his snow fences had made, and Pedersen would get so mad he'd go for Pa and stomp out calling for the vengeance of God like he was fond of doing. Now though, since Big Hans had found him, and he was dead in our kitchen, Pa might not say much when Pedersen came. He might just offer Pedersen a drink and keep his mouth shut about those snow fences. Pedersen might come yet this morning. That would be best because Pa would be still asleep. If Pa was asleep when Pedersen came he wouldn't have a chance to talk about those snow fences, or offer Pedersen a drink, or call Pedersen a bent prick or a turd machine or a fairy farmer. Pedersen wouldn't have to refuse the drink then, spit his chaw in the snow or call on God, and could take his kid and go home. I hoped Pedersen would certainly come soon. I hoped he would come and take that cold damp body out of our kitchen. The way I felt I didn't think that today I'd be able to eat. I knew every bite I'd see the Pedersen kid in the kitchen being fixed for the table.

The wind had dropped. The sun lay burning on the snow. I got cold just the same. I didn't want to go in but I could feel the cold crawling over me like it must have crawled over him while he was coming. It had slipped over him like a sheet, icy at first, especially around the feet, and he'd likely wiggled his toes in his boots and wanted to wrap his legs around each other like you do when you first come to bed. But then things would begin to warm up some, the sheet feeling warmer all the time until it felt real cozy and you went to sleep. Only when the kid went to sleep by our crib it wasn't like going to sleep in bed because the sheet never really got warm and he never really got warm either. Now he was just as cold in our kitchen with the kettle whistling and ma getting ready to bake as I was out by the crib jigging my feet in our snow. I had to go in. I looked but I couldn't see anyone trying to come down where the road was. All I could see was a set of half-filled prints jiggling crazily away into the snow until they sank under a drift. There wasn't anything around. There wasn't anything: a tree or a stick or a rock whipped bare or a bush hugged by snow sticking up to mark the place where those prints came up out of the drift like somebody had come up from underground.

I decided to go around by the front though I wasn't supposed to track through the parlor. The snow came to my thighs, but I was thinking of where the kid lay on the kitchen table in all that dough, pasty with whiskey and water, like spring had come all at once to our kitchen, and our all the time not knowing he was there, had thawed the top of his grave off and left him for us to find, stretched out cold and stiff and bare; and who was it that was going to have to take him to the Pedersen place and give him to Missus Pedersen, naked, and flour on his bare behind?

2

Just his back. The green mackinaw. The black stocking cap. The yellow gloves. The gun.

Big Hans kept repeating it. He was letting the meaning have a chance to change. He'd look at me and shake his head and say it over.

"He put them down the cellar so I ran."

Hans filled the tumbler. It was spotted with whiskey and flecks of flour.

"He didn't say nothing the whole time."

He put the bottle on the table and the bottom sank unevenly in the paste, tilting heavily and queerly to one side—acting crazy, like everything else.

That's all he says he saw, Hans said, staring at the mark of the kid's behind in the dough. Just his back. The green mackinaw. The black stocking cap. The yellow gloves. The gun.

That's all?

He waited and waited.

That's all.

He tossed the whiskey off and peered at the bottom of the glass.

Now why should he remember all them colors?

He leaned over, his legs apart, his elbows on his knees, and held the glass between them with both hands, tilting it to watch the liquor that was left roll back and forth across the bottom.

How does he know? I mean, for sure.

He thinks he knows, Hans said in a tired voice. He thinks he knows.

He picked up the bottle and a hunk of dough was stuck to it.

Christ. That's all. It's how he feels. It's enough, ain't it? Hans said.

What a mess, ma said.

He was raving, Hans said. He couldn't think of anything else. He had to talk. He had to get it out. You should have heard him grunt.

Poor poor Stevie, ma said.

He was raving?

All right, is it something you dream? Hans said.

He must have been dreaming. Look—how could he have got there? Where'd he come from? Fall from the sky?

He came through the storm.

That's just it, Hans, he'd have had to. It was blizzarding all day. It didn't let up—did it?—till late afternoon. He'd have had to. Now what chance is there of that? What?

Enough a chance it happened, Hans said.

But listen. Jesus. He's a stranger. If he's a stranger he's come a ways. He'd never make it in a blizzard, not even knowing the country.

He came through the storm. He came out of the ground like a grub. Hans shrugged. He came.

Hans poured himself a drink, not me.

He came through the storm, he said. He came through just like the kid came through. The kid had no chance neither, but he came. He's here, ain't he? He's right upstairs, right now. You got to believe that.

It wasn't blizzarding when the kid came.

It was starting.

That ain't the same.

All right. The kid had forty-five minutes, maybe an hour before it started to come on good. That isn't enough. You need the whole time, not a start. In a blizzard you got to be where you're going if you're going to get there.

That's what I mean. See, Hans? See? The kid had a chance. He knew the way. He had a head start. Besides, he was scared. He ain't going to be lazying. And he's lucky. He had a chance to be lucky. Now yellow gloves ain't got that chance. He has to come farther. He has to come through the storm all the way. But he don't know the way, and he ain't scared proper, except maybe by the storm. He hasn't got a chance to be lucky.

The kid was scared, you said. Right. Now why? You tell me that.

Hans kept his eyes on the whiskey that was shining in his glass. He was holding on hard.

And yellow gloves—he ain't scared? he said. How do you know he ain't scared, by something else besides wind and snow and cold and howling, I mean?

All right, I don't know, but it's likely, ain't it? Anyway, the kid, well maybe he ain't scared at all, starting out. Maybe his pa was just looking to tan him and he lit out. Then first thing he knows it's blizzarding again and he's lost, and when he gets to our crib he don't know where he is.

Hans slowly shook his head.

Yes yes, hell Hans, the kid's scared of having run away. He don't want to say he done a fool stunt like that. So he makes the whole thing up. He's just a little kid. He made the whole thing up.

Hans didn't like that. He didn't want to believe the kid any more than I did, but if he didn't then the kid had fooled him sure. He didn't want to believe that either.

No, he said. Is it something you make up? Is it something you come to—raving with frostbite and fever and not knowing who's there or where you are or anything—and make up?

Yeah.

No it ain't. Green, black, yellow: you don't make up them colors neither. You don't make up putting your folks down cellar where they'll freeze. You don't make up his not saying anything the whole time or only seeing his back or exactly what he was wearing. It's more than a make-up; it's more than a dream. It's like something you see once and it hits you so hard you never forget it even if you want to; lies, dreams, pass—this *has* you; it's like something that sticks to you like burrs, burrs you try to brush off while you're doing something else, but they never brush off, they just roll a little, and the first thing you know you ain't doing what you set out to, you're just trying to get them burrs off. I know. I got things stuck to me like that. Everybody has. Pretty soon you get tired trying to pick them off. If they was just burrs, it wouldn't matter, but they ain't. They never is. The kid saw something that hit him hard like that; hit him so hard that probably all the time he was running over here he didn't see anything else but what hit him. Not really. It hit him so hard he couldn't do anything but spit it out raving when he come to. It hit him. You don't make things like that up, Jorge. No. He came through the storm, just like the kid. He had no business coming, but he came. I don't know how or why or when exactly, except it must have been during the blizzard yesterday. He got to the Pedersen place just before or just after it stopped snowing. He got there and he shoved them all in the fruit cellar to freeze and I'll bet he had his reasons.

You got dough stuck to the bottom of Pa's bottle.

I couldn't think of anything else to say. What Hans said sounded right. It sounded right but it couldn't be right. It just couldn't be. Whatever was right, the Pedersen kid had run off from his pa's place probably late yesterday afternoon when the storm let up, and had turned up at our crib this morning. I knew he was here. I knew that much. I'd held him. I'd felt him dead in my hands, only I guess he wasn't dead now. Hans had put him to bed upstairs but I could still see him in the kitchen, so skinny naked, two towels steaming on him, whiskey drooling from the corners of his mouth, lines of dirt between his toes, squeezing ma's dough in the shape of his behind.

I reached for the bottle. Hans held it away.

He didn't see him do it though, I said.

Hans shrugged.

Then he ain't sure.

He's sure, I told you. Do you run out in a blizzard unless you're sure?

It wasn't blizzarding.

It was starting.

I don't run out in blizzards.

Crap.

Hans pointed the doughy end of the bottle at me.

Crap.

He shook it.

You come in from the barn—like this morning. As far as you

know there ain't a gun in yellow gloves in a thousand miles. You come in from the barn not thinking anything special. You just get inside—you just get inside when you see a guy you never saw before, the guy that wasn't in a thousand miles, that wasn't in your mind even, he was so far away, and he's wearing them yellow gloves and that green mackinaw, and he's got me and your ma and pa lined up with our hands back of our necks like this—

Hans hung the bottle and the glass behind his head.

He's got me and your ma and your pa lined up with our hands here back of our necks, and he's got a rifle in between them yellow gloves and he's waving the point of it up and down in front of your ma's face real slow and quiet.

Hans got up and waved the bottle violently in ma's face. She shivered and shooed it away. Hans stopped to come to me. He stood over me, his black eyes buttons on his big face, and I tried to look like I wasn't hunching down any in my chair.

What do you do? Hans roared. You drop a little kid's cold head on the table.

Like hell—

Hans had the bottle in front of him again, smack in my face.

Hans Esbyorn, ma said, don't pester the boy.

Like hell—

Jorge.

I wouldn't run, ma.

Ma sighed. I don't know. But don't yell.

Well christ almighty, ma.

Don't swear neither. Please. You been swearing too much— you and Hans both.

But I wouldn't run.

Yes, Jorge, yes. I'm sure you wouldn't run, she said.

Hans went back and sat down and finished his drink and poured another. He could relax now he'd got me all strung up. He was a fancy bastard.

You'd run all right, he said, running his tongue across his lips.

Maybe you'd be right to run. Maybe anybody would. With no gun, with nothing to stop him.

Poor child. Wheweee. And what are we going to do with these?

Hang them up, Hed, for christ's sake.

Where?

Well, where do you, mostly?

Oh no, she said, I wouldn't feel right doing that.

Then jesus, Hed, I don't know. Jesus.

Please Hans, please. Those words are hard for me to bear.

She stared at the ceiling.

Dear. The kitchen's such a mess. I can't bear to see it. And the baking's not done.

That's all she could think of. That's all she had to say. She didn't care about me. I didn't count. Not like her kitchen. I wouldn't have run.

Stick the baking, I said.

Shut your face.

He could look as mean as he liked, I didn't care. What was his meanness to me? A blister on my heel, another discomfort, a cold bed. Yet when he took his eyes off me to drink, I felt better. I was going to twist his balls.

All right, I said. All right. All right.

He was lost in his glass, thinking it out.

They're awful cold in that cellar, I said.

There was a little liquor burning in the bottom. I was going to twist his balls like the neck of a sack.

What are you going to do about it?

He was putting his mean look back but it lacked enthusiasm. He was seeing things in his glass.

I saved the kid, didn't I? he finally said.

Maybe you did.

You didn't.

No. I didn't.

It's time you did something then, ain't it?

Why should I? I don't think they're freezing. You're the one who thinks that. You're the one who thinks he ran for help. You're the one. You saved him. All right. You didn't let his head hit the table. I did that. You didn't. No. It was you who rubbed him. All right. You saved him. That wasn't the kid's idea though. He came for help. According to you, that is. He didn't come to be saved. You saved him, but what are you going to do now to help him? You've been feeling mighty, ain't you? thinking how you did it. Still feel like a savior, Hans? How's it feel?

You little bastard.

All right. Little or big. Never mind. You did it all. You found him. You raised the rumpus, ordering everybody around. He was as good as dead. I held him and I felt him. Maybe in your way he was alive, but it was a way that don't count. No—but you couldn't leave him alone. Rubbing. Well I felt him . . . cold . . . christ! Ain't you proud? He was dead, right here, dead. And there weren't no yellow gloves. Now, though, there is. That's what comes of rubbing. Rubbing . . . ain't you proud? You can't believe the kid was lying good enough to fool you. So he was dead. But now he ain't. Not for you. He ain't for you.

He's alive for you too. You're crazy. He's alive for everybody.

No he ain't. He ain't alive for me. He never was. I never seen him except he was dead. Cold . . . I felt him . . . christ! Ain't you proud? He's in your bed. All right. You took him up there. It's your bed he's in, Hans. It was you he babbled to. You believe him too, so he's alive for you then. Not for me. Not for me he ain't.

You can't say that.

I am saying it though. Hear me saying? Rubbing . . . You didn't know what you was bringing to, did you? Something besides the kid came through the storm, Hans. I ain't saying yellow gloves did neither. He didn't. He couldn't. But something else did. While you was rubbing you didn't think of that.

You little bastard.

Hans, Hans, please, ma said.

Never mind that. Little or big, like I said. I'm asking what you're going to do. You believe it. You made it. What are you going to do about it? It'd be funny if right now while we're sitting here the kid's dying upstairs.

Jorge, ma said, what an awful thing—in Hans's bed.

All right. But suppose. Suppose you didn't rub enough—not long and hard enough, Hans. And suppose he dies up there in your bed. He might. He was cold, I know. That'd be funny because that yellow gloves—he won't die. It ain't going to be so easy, killing him.

Hans didn't move or say anything.

I ain't no judge. I ain't no hand at saving, like you said. It don't make no difference to me. But why'd you start rubbing if you was going to stop? Seems like it'd be terrible if the Pedersen kid was to have come all that way through the storm, scared and freezing, and you was to have done all that rubbing and saving so he could come to and tell you his fancy tale and have you believe it, if you ain't going to do nothing now but sit and hold hands with that bottle. That ain't a burr so easy picked off.

Still he didn't say anything.

Fruit cellars get mighty cold. Of course they ain't supposed to freeze.

I leaned back easy in my chair. Hans just sat.

They ain't supposed to freeze so it's all right.

The top of the kitchen table looked muddy where it showed. Patches of dough and pools of water were scattered all over it. There were rusty streaks through the paste and the towels had run. Everywhere there were little sandy puddles of whiskey and water. Something, it looked like whiskey, dripped slowly to the floor and with the water trickled to the puddle by the pile of clothes. The boxes sagged. There were thick black tracks around the table and the stove. I thought it was funny the boxes had gone so fast. The bottle and the glass were posts around which Big Hans had his hands.

Ma began picking up the kid's clothes. She picked them up one at a time, delicately, by their ends and corners, lifting a sleeve like you would the flat, burned, crooked leg of a frog dead of summer to toss it from the road. They didn't seem human things, the way her hands pinched together on them, but animal—dead and rotting things out of the ground. She took them away and when she came back I wanted to tell her to bury them—to hide them somehow quick under the snow—but she scared me, the way she came with her arms out, trembling, fingers coming open and closed, moving like a combine between rows.

I heard the dripping clearly, and I heard Hans swallow. I heard the water and the whiskey fall. I heard the frost on the window melt to the sill and drop into the sink. Hans poured whiskey in his glass. I looked past Hans and Pa was watching from the doorway. His nose and eyes were red, his feet in red slippers.

What's this about the Pedersen kid? he said.

Ma stood behind him with a mop.

3

Ever think of a horse? Pa said.

A horse? Where'd he get a horse?

Anywhere—on the way—anyplace.

Could he make it on a horse?

He made it on something.

Not on a horse though.

Not on his feet.

I ain't saying he made it on anything.

Horses can't get lost.

Yes they can.

They got a sense.

That's a lot of manure about horses.

In a blizzard a horse'll go home.

That's so.

You let them go and they go home.

That's so.

If you steal a horse, and let him go, he'll take you to the barn
you stole him from.

Couldn't give him his head then.

Must have really rode him then.

And known where he was going.

Yeah, and gone there.

If he had a horse.

Yeah, if he had a horse.

If he stole a horse before the storm and rode it a ways, then
when the snow came, the horse would be too far off and wouldn't
know how to head for home.

They got an awful good sense.

Manure.

What difference does it make? He made it. What difference
does it make how? Hans said.

I'm considering if he could have, Pa said.

And I'm telling you he did, Hans said.

And I've been telling you he didn't. The kid made the whole
thing up, I said.

The horse'd stop. He'd put his head into the wind and stop.

I've seen them put their rears in.

They always put their heads in.

He could jockey him.

If he was gentle and not too scared.

A plower is gentle.

Some are.

Some don't like to be rid.

Some don't like strangers neither.

Some.

What the hell, Hans said.

Pa laughed. I'm just considering, he said. Just considering,
Hans, that's all.

Pa'd seen the bottle. Right away. He'd been blinking. But he
hadn't missed it. He'd seen it and the glass in Hans's hand. I'd ex-

pected him to say something. So had Hans. He'd held on to the glass long enough so no one would get the idea he was afraid to, then he'd set it down casual, like he hadn't any reason to hold it or any reason to put it down, but was putting it down anyway, without thinking. I'd grinned but he hadn't seen me, or else he made out he hadn't. Pa'd kept his mouth shut about the bottle though he'd seen it right away. I guess we had the Pedersen kid to thank for that, though we had him to thank for the bottle too.

It's his own fault for putting out all them snow fences, Pa said. You'd think, being here the time he has, he'd know the forces better.

Pedersen just likes to be ready, Pa, that's all.

Hell he does. He likes to *get* ready, that cock. Get, get, get, get. He's always getting ready, but he ain't never *got* ready. Not yet, he ain't. Last summer, instead of minding his crops, he got ready for hoppers. Christ. Who wants hoppers? Well that's the way to get hoppers—that's the sure way—get ready for hoppers.

Bull.

Bull? You say bull, Hans, hey?

I say bull, yeah.

You're one to get ready, ain't you? Like Pedersen, ain't you? Oh what a wrinkled scrotum you got, with all that thinking. You'd put out poison for a million, hey? You know what you'd get? Two million. Wise, oh these wise men, yeah. Pedersen *asked* for hoppers. He *begged* for hoppers. He went on his knees for hoppers. So me? I got hoppers too. Now he's gone and asked for snow, gone on his knees for snow, wrung his fingers off for snow. Is he ready, tell me? Hey? Snow? For real snow? Anybody ever ready for real snow? Oh jesus, that fool. He should have kept his kid behind them fences. What business—what—what business— to send him here. By god, a man's got to keep his stock up. Look—Pa pointed out the window. See—see—what did I tell you—snowing . . . always snowing.

You seen a winter it didn't snow?

You were ready, I guess.

It always snows.

You were ready for the Pedersen kid too, I guess. You was just out there waiting for him, cooling your cod.

Pa laughed and Hans got red.

Pedersen's a fool. Wise men can't be taught. Oh no, not old holy Pete. He never learned all the things that can fall out the sky and happen to wheat. His neck's bent all the time too, studying clouds—hah, that shit. He don't even keep an eye on his kid in a blizzard. A man by god's got to keep his stock up. But you'll keep an eye out for him, hey, Hans? You're a bigger fool because you're fatter.

Hans's face was red and swollen like the skin around a splinter. He reached out and picked up the glass. Pa was sitting on a corner of the kitchen table, swinging a leg. The glass was near his knee. Hans reached by Pa and took it. Pa watched and swung his leg, laughing. The bottle was on the counter and Pa watched closely while Hans took it.

Ah, you plan to drink some of my whiskey, Hans?

Yeah.

It'd be polite to ask.

I ain't asking, Hans said, tilting the bottle.

I suppose I'd better make some biscuits, ma said.

Hans looked up at her, keeping the bottle tilted. He didn't pour.

Biscuits, ma? I said.

I ought to have something for Mr. Pedersen and I haven't a thing.

Hans straightened the bottle.

There's a thing to consider, he said, beginning to smile. Why ain't Pedersen here looking for his kid?

Why should he be?

Hans winked at me through his glass. No wink would make me a friend of his.

Why not? We're nearest. If the kid ain't here he can ask us to help him hunt.

Fat chance.

He ain't come through. How do you consider that?

I ain't considering it, Pa said.

Why ain't you? Seems to me like something worth real long and fancy considering.

No it ain't.

Ain't it?

Pedersen's a fool.

So you like to say. I've heard you often enough. All right, maybe he is. How long do you expect he'll wander around looking before he comes over this way?

A long time. A long time maybe.

The kid's been gone a long time.

Pa arranged his nightshirt over his knee. He had on the striped one.

How long's a long time? Hans said.

The kid's been gone.

Oh Pedersen'll be here before too long now, Pa said.

And if he don't?

What do you mean, if he don't? Then he don't. By god, he don't. It ain't no skin off my ass. If he don't he don't. I don't care what he does.

Yeah, Big Hans said. Yeah.

Pa folded his arms, looking like a judge. He swung his leg. Where'd you find the bottle?

Hans jiggled it.

You're pretty good at hiding, ain't you?

I'm asking the questions. Where'd you find it?

Hans was enjoying himself too much.

I didn't.

Jorge, hey. Pa chewed his lip. So you're the nosy bastard.

He didn't look at me and it didn't seem like he was talking to me at all. He said it like I wasn't there and he was thinking out loud. Awake, asleep—it didn't fool me.

It wasn't me, Pa, I said.

I tried to get Hans's attention so he'd shut up but he was enjoying himself.

Little Hans ain't no fool, Big Hans said.

No.

Now Pa wasn't paying attention.

He ain't no kin to you, Pa said.

Why ain't he here then? He'd be looking too. Why ain't he here?

Gracious, I'd forgot all about Little Hans, ma said, quickly taking a bowl from the cupboard.

Hed, what are you up to? Pa said.

Oh, biscuits.

Biscuits? What in hell for? Biscuits. I don't want any biscuits. Make some coffee. All this time you been just standing around.

For Pedersen and little Hans. They'll be coming and they'll want some biscuits and coffee, and I'll put out some elderberry jelly. The coffee needed reminding, Magnus, thank you.

Who found the bottle?

She scooped some flour from the bin.

Pa'd been sitting, swinging. Now he stopped and stood up.

Who found it? Who found it? God dammit, who found it? Which one of them was it?

Ma was trying to measure the flour but her hands shook. The flour ran off the scoop and fell across the rim of the cup, and I thought, Yeah, You'd have run, Yeah, Your hands shake.

Why don't you ask Jorge? Big Hans said.

How I hated him, putting it on me, the coward. And he had thick arms.

That snivel, Pa said.

Hans laughed so his chest shook.

He couldn't find nothing I hid.

You're right there, Hans said.

I could, I said. I have.

A liar, Hans, hey? You found it.

Pa was somehow pleased and sat on the corner of the table again. Was it Hans he hated most, or me?

I never said Jorge found it.

I've got a liar working for me. A thief and a liar. Why should I keep a liar? I'm just soft on him, I guess, and he's got such a sweet face. But why should I keep a thief . . . little movey eyes like traveling specks . . . why?

I ain't like you. I don't spend every day drinking just to sleep the night and then sleep half the day too, fouling your bed and your room and half the house.

You been doing your share of lying down. Little Hans is half your size and worth twice. You—you got a small dick.

Pa's words didn't come out clear.

How about Little Hans? Little Hans ain't showed up. Folks must be getting pretty worried at the Pedersens'. They'd like some news maybe. But Pedersen don't come. Little Hans don't come. There's a thousand drifts out there. The kid might be under any one. If anybody's seen him, we have, and if we haven't, nobody's going to till spring, or maybe if the wind shifts, which ain't likely. But nobody comes to ask. That's pretty funny, I'd say.

You're an awful full-up bastard, Pa said.

I'm just considering, that's all.

Where'd you find it?

I forgot. It needed reminding. I was going to have a drink.

Where?

You're pretty good at hiding, Hans said.

I'm asking. Where?

I didn't, I told you, I didn't find it. Jorge didn't find it neither.

You bastard, Hans, I said.

It hatched, Hans said. Like the fellow, you know, who blew in. He hatched. Or maybe the kid found it—had it hid under his coat.

Who? Pa roared, standing up quick.

Oh Hed found it. You don't hide worth a damn and Hed found it easy. She knew right away where to look.

Shut up, Hans, I said.

Hans tilted the bottle.

She must have known where it was a long time now. Maybe she knows where they're all hid. You ain't very smart. Or maybe she's took it up herself, eh? And it ain't yours at all, maybe that.

Big Hans poured himself a drink. Then Pa kicked the glass out of Hans's hand. Pa's slipper flew off and sailed by Hans's head and bounced off the wall. The glass didn't break. It fell by the sink and rolled slow by ma's feet, leaving a thin line. The scoop flew a light white cloud. There was whiskey on Hans's shirt and on the wall and cupboards, and a splash on the floor where the glass had hit.

Ma had her arms wrapped around her chest. She looked faint and she was whewing and moaning.

Okay, Pa said, we'll go. We'll go right now, Hans. I hope to god you get a bullet in your belly. Jorge, go upstairs and see if the little sonofabitch is still alive.

Hans was rubbing the spots on his shirt and licking his lips when I hunched past Pa and went out.

PART TWO

1

There wasn't any wind. The harness creaked, the wood creaked, the runners made a sound like a saw working easy, and everything was white about Horse Simon's feet. Pa had the reins between his knees and he and Hans and I kept ourselves close together. We bent our heads and clenched our feet and wished we could huddle both hands in one pocket. Only Hans was breathing through his nose. We didn't speak. I wished my lips could warm my teeth. The blanket we had wasn't worth a damn. It was just as cold underneath and Pa drank from a bottle by him on the seat.

I tried to hold the feeling I'd had starting out when we'd hitched up Horse Simon when I was warm and decided to risk the North Corn Road to the Pedersen place. It catty-cornered and came up near the grove behind his barn. We figured we could look at things from there. I tried to hold the feeling but it was warm as new bath water and just as hard to hold. It was like I was setting out to do something special and big—like a knight setting out—worth remembering. I dreamed coming in from the barn and finding his back to me in the kitchen and wrestling with him and pulling him down and beating the stocking cap off his head with the barrel of the gun. I dreamed coming in from the barn still blinking with the light and seeing him there and picking the shovel up and taking him on. That had been then, when I was warm, when I was doing something big, heroic even, and well worth remembering. I couldn't put the feeling down in Pedersen's back yard or Pedersen's porch or barn. I couldn't see myself, or him, there. I could only see him back where I wasn't any more—standing quiet in our kitchen with his gun going slowly up and down in ma's face and ma shooing it away and at the same time trying not to move an inch for getting shot.

When I got good and cold the feeling slipped away. I couldn't imagine him with his gun or cap or yellow gloves. I couldn't imagine me coming on to him. We weren't anyplace and I didn't care. Pa drove by staring down the sloping white road and drank from his bottle. Hans rattled his heels on the back of the seat. I just tried to keep my mouth shut and breathe and not think why in the name of the good jesus christ I had to.

It wasn't like a sleigh ride on an early winter evening when the air is still, the earth is warm, and the stars are flakes being born that will not fall. The air was still all right, the sun straight up and cold. Behind us on the trough that marked the road I saw our runners and the holes that Simon tore. Ahead of us it melted into drifts. Pa squinted like he saw where he knew it really went. Horse Simon steamed. Ice hung from his harness. Snow caked his belly. I was afraid the crust might cut his knees and I wanted a drink out of Pa's bottle. Big Hans seemed asleep and shivered in his dreams. My rear was god almighty sore.

We reached a drift across the road and Pa eased Simon round her where he knew there wasn't any fence. Pa figured to go back to the road but after we got round the bank I could see there wasn't any point in that. There were rows of high drifts across it.

They ain't got no reason to do that, Pa said.

It was the first thing Pa'd said since he told me to go upstairs and see if the Pedersen kid was still alive. He hadn't looked alive to me but I'd said I guessed he was. Pa'd gone and got his gun first, without dressing, one foot still bare so he favored it, and took the gun upstairs cradled in his arm, broke, and pointing down. He had a dark speckled spot on the rump of his nightshirt where he'd sat on the table. Hans had his shotgun and the forty-five he'd stolen from the Navy. He made me load it and when I'd stuck it in my belt he'd said it'd likely go off and keep me from ever getting out to stud. The gun felt like a chunk of ice against my belly and the barrel dug.

Ma'd put some sandwiches and a Thermos of coffee in a sack. The coffee'd be cold. My hands would be cold when I ate mine even if I kept my gloves on. Chewing would be painful. The lip of the Thermos would be cold if I drank out of that, and I'd spill some on my chin which would dry to ice; or if I used the cup, the tin would stick to my lip like lousy liquor you didn't want to taste by licking off, and it would burn and then tear my skin coming away.

Simon went into a hole. He couldn't pull out so he panicked and the sleigh skidded. We'd had crust but now the front right runner broke through and we braked in the soft snow under-neath. Pa made quiet impatient noises and calmed Simon down.

That was damn fool, Hans said.

He lost his footing. Jesus, I ain't the horse.

I don't know. Simon's a turd binder, Hans said.

Pa took a careful drink.

Go round and lead him out.

Jorge is on the outside.

Go round and lead him out.

You. You go round. You led him in.

Go round and lead him out.

Sometimes the snow seemed as blue as the sky. I don't know which seemed colder.

Oh god I'll go, I said. I'm on the outside.

Your old man's on the outside, Hans said.

I guess I know where I am, Pa said. I guess I know where I'm staying.

Can't you let up, for christ's sake? I'm going, I said.

I threw off the blanket and stood up but I was awful stiff. The snow dazzle struck me and the pain of the space around us. Getting out I rammed my ankle against the sideboard's iron brace. The pain shot up my leg and shook me like an ax handle will when you strike wrong. I cursed, taking my time jumping off. The snow looked as stiff and hard as cement and I could only think of the jar.

You've known where that brace was for ten years, Pa said.

The snow went to my crotch. The gun bit. I waded round the hole trying to keep on tiptoe and the snow away from my crotch but it wasn't any use.

You practicing to be a bird? Hans said.

I got hold of Horse Simon and tried to coax him out. Pa swore at me from his seat. Simon kicked and thrashed and lunged ahead. The front right runner dug in. The sleigh swung around on it and the left side hit Simon's back legs hard behind the knees. Simon reared and kicked a piece out of the side of the sleigh and then pulled straight ahead tangling the reins. The sleigh swung back again and the right runner pulled loose with a jerk. Pa's bottle rolled. From where I sat in the snow I saw him grab for it. Simon went on ahead. The sleigh slid sideways into Simon's hole and the left runner went clear of the snow. Simon pulled up short though Pa had lost the reins and was holding on and yelling about his bottle. I had snow in my eyes and down my neck.

Simon didn't have no call to do that, Hans said, mimicking Pa.

Where's my bottle? Pa said, looking over the side of the sleigh at the torn snow. Jorge, go find my bottle. It fell in the snow here somewheres.

I tried to brush the snow off without getting more in my pockets and up my sleeves and down my neck.

You get out and find it. It's your bottle.

Pa leaned way over.

If you hadn't been so god damn dumb it wouldn't have fell out. Where'd you learn to lead a horse? You never learned that dumb trick from me. Of all the god damn dumb tricks I never seen any dumber.

Pa waved his arm in a circle.

That bottle fell out about here. It couldn't have got far. It was corked, thank god. I won't lose none.

Snow was slipping down the hollow of my back. The forty-five had slipped through my belt. I was afraid it would go off like Big Hans said. I kept my right forearm pressed against it. I didn't want it slipping off down my pants. I didn't like it. Pa shouted directions.

You hid it, I said. You're such a hand at hiding. You find it then. I ain't good at finding. You said so yourself.

Jorge, you know I got to have that bottle.

Then get off your ass and find it.

You know I got to have it.

Then get off.

If I get down off here, it ain't the bottle I'm coming after. I'll hold you under till you drown, you little smart-talking snot.

I started kicking around in the snow.

Hans giggled.

There's a trace broke, he said.

What's so damn funny?

I told you that trace was worn.

I kicked about. Pa followed my feet.

Hell. Not that way. He pointed. You know about everything there is, Hans, I guess, he said, still watching me. First little thing you figure out you tell somebody about. Then somebody else knows. So then they can do what needs to be done, and you don't have to—jesus, not there, *there*. Don't it, Hans? don't it always let you out? You ain't going deep enough. I never figured that out. How come somebody else's knowing always lets you out? You're just a pimp for jobs, I guess. You ain't going deep enough, I said.

It ain't my job to fix traces.

Hey, get your hands in it, *your hands*. It's clean. You always was that way about manure. Why ain't it your job? Too busy screwing sheep? Try over there. You ought to have hit it. No, *there*, not there.

I never fixed traces.

Christ, they never needed fixing while you been here hardly. Jorge, will you stop nursing that fool gun with your cock and use both hands.

I'm cold, Pa.

So'm I. That's why you got to find that bottle.

If I find it do I get a drink?

Ain't you growed up—a man—since yesterday!

I've had a few, Pa.

Ha. Of what, hey? Hear that, Hans? He's had a few. For medicine maybe, like your ma says. The spirits, the spirits, Jorgen Segren . . . ha. He's had a few he says. He's had a few.

Pa.

He's had a few. He's had a few. He's had a few.

Pa. I'm cold, Pa.

Maybe. Only look, for god's sake, don't just thrash about like a fool chicken.

Well, we're finished anyway, Hans said.

We're finished if we don't find that bottle.

You're finished, maybe. You're the only one who needs that bottle. Jorge and I don't need it, but there you are, old man, eh? Lost in the snow.

My gloves were wet. Snow had jammed under my sleeves. It was working down into my boots. I stopped to pick some out with a finger if I could.

Maybe some of ma's coffee is still hot, I said.

Say. Yeah. Maybe. But that's *my* coffee, boy. I never got none. I ain't even had breakfast. What are you stopping for? Come on. Hell, Jorge, it's cold.

I know that better than you. You're sitting there all nice and dry, bossing; but I'm doing all the work and getting the snow inside me.

Say. Yeah. That's right.

Pa leaned back and grinned. He clutched the blanket to him and Hans pulled it back.

It's easier to keep warm moving around, anybody knows that. Ain't that right, Hans? It's easier to keep warm moving, ain't it?

Yeah, Hans said. If you ain't got a blanket.

See there, Jorge, hey? You just keep good and warm . . . stirring. It'd be a pity if your pee should freeze. And moving around good prevents calluses on the bottom. Don't it, Hans?

Yeah.

Hans here knows. He's nothing but calluses.

You'll wear out your mouth.

I can't find it, Pa. Maybe some of ma's coffee is still warm.

You damn snivel—you ain't looking. Get tramping proper like I told you and find it. Find it fast, you hear. You ain't getting back up on this sleigh until you do.

I started jumping up and down, not too fast, and Pa blew his nose with his fingers.

Cold makes the snot run, he says, real wise.

If I found the bottle I'd kick it deep under the snow. I'd kick it and keep kicking it until it sank under a drift. Pa wouldn't know where it was. I wouldn't come back to the sleigh either. They weren't going anywhere anyway. I'd go home though it was a long walk. Looking back I could see our tracks in the trough of the road. They came together before I lost them. It would be warm at home and worth the walk. It was frightening—the endless white space. I'd have to keep my head down. Winded slopes and rises all around me. I'd never wanted to go to Pedersen's. That was Hans's fight, and Pa's. I was just cold . . . cold . . . and scared and sick of snow. That's what I'd do if I found it—kick it under a drift. Then later, a lot later in the spring one day I'd come out here and find the old bottle sticking out of the rotting snow and stuck in the mud like dough, and I'd hide it back of the barn and have a drink whenever I wanted. I'd get some real cigarettes, maybe a carton, and hide them too. Then someday I'd come in and Pa'd smell whiskey on me and think I'd found one of his hiding places. He'd be mad as hell and not know what to say. It'd be spring and he'd think he'd taken them all in like he always did, harvesting the crop like he said.

I looked to see if there was something to mark the place by but it was all gone under snow. There was only the drifts and the deep holes of snow and the long runnered trough of the road. It might be a mudhole we was stuck in. In the spring cattails might grow up in it and the blackbirds come. Or it might be low and slimy at first and then caked dry and cracked. Pa'd never find out how I came by the bottle. Someday he'd act too big and I'd stick his head under the pump or slap his skinny rump with the backside of a fork full of manure. Hans would act smart and then someday—

Jee-suss, will you move?

I'm cold, Pa.

You're going to be a pig's size colder.

Well, we're finished anyway, Hans said. We ain't going nowhere. The trace is broke.

Pa stopped watching me thrash the snow. He frowned at

Horse Simon. Simon was standing quiet with his head down.

Simon's shivering, he said. I should have remembered he'd be heated up. It's so cold I forgot.

Pa yanked the blanket off of Hans like Hans was a bed he was stripping, and jumped down. Hans yelled but Pa didn't pay attention. He threw the blanket over Simon.

We got to get Simon moving. He'll stiffen up.

Pa ran his hand tenderly down Simon's legs.

The sleigh don't seem to have hurt him none.

The trace is broke.

Then Hans stood up. He beat his arms against his body and jigged.

We'll have to walk him home, he said.

Home, hey, Pa said, giving Hans a funny sidewise look. It's a long walk.

You can ride him then, Hans said.

Pa looked real surprised and even funnier. It wasn't like Hans to say that. It was too cold. It made Hans generous. There was some good in cold.

Why?

Pa waded, patting Simon, but he kept his eye on Hans like it was Hans might kick.

Hans let out a long impatient streamer.

Jesus—the trace.

Hans was being real cautious. Hans was awful cold. His nose was red. Pa's was white but it didn't look froze. It just looked white like it usually did—like it was part of him had died long ago. I wondered what color my nose was. Mine was bigger and sharper at the end. It was ma's nose, ma said. I was bigger all over than Pa. I was taller than Hans too. I pinched my nose but my gloves were wet so I couldn't feel anything except how my nose hurt when I pinched it. It couldn't be too cold. Hans was pointing at the ends of the trace which were trailing in the snow.

Tie a knot in it, Pa was saying.

It won't hold, Hans said, shaking his head.

Tie a good one, it will.

It's too cold to get a good knot. Leather's too stiff.

Hell no, it ain't too stiff.

Well, it's too thick. Can't knot something like that.

You can do it.

She'll pull crooked.

Let her pull crooked.

Simon won't work well pulling her crooked.

He'll have to do the best he can. I ain't going to leave this sleigh out here. Hell, it might snow again before I got back with a new trace. Or you got back, hey?

When I get home I'm going to stay there and I'm going to eat my breakfast if it's suppertime. I ain't coming back out here trying to beat another blizzard and wind up like the Pedersen kid.

Yeah, Hans said, nodding. Let's get this damn thing out of here and get Simon home before he stiffens. I'll tie the trace.

Hans got down and I stopped kicking. Pa watched Hans real careful from his side of Horse Simon and I could see him smiling like he'd thought of something dirty. I started to get on the sleigh but Pa shouted and made me hunt some more.

Maybe we'll find it when we move the sleigh, I said.

Pa laughed but not at what I said. He opened his mouth wide, looking at Hans, and laughed hard, though his laugh was quiet.

Yeah, maybe we will, he said, and gave Simon an extra hard pat. Maybe we will, hey, at that.

I didn't find the bottle and Big Hans tied the trace. He had to take his gloves off to do it but he did it quick and I had to admire him for it. Pa coaxed Simon while Hans, boosting, heaved. She got clear and suddenly was going—skidding out. I heard a noise like a light bulb busting. A brown stain spread over the sleigh track. Pa peered over his shoulder at the stain, his hands on the halter, his legs wide in the snow.

Oh no, he said. Oh no.

But Big Hans broke up. He lifted a leg clear of the snow. He hit himself. His shoulders shook. He hugged his belly. He rocked back and forth. Oh—oh—oh, he screamed, and he held his sides. Tears streamed down his cheeks. You—you—you, he howled. Hans's cheeks, his nose, his head was red. Found—found—found, he choked.

Everything about Pa was frozen. The white hair that stuck out from his hat looked hard and sharp and seemed to shine like snow. Big Hans went on laughing. I never saw him so humored. He staggered, weakening—Pa as still as a stake. Hans began to heave and gasp, running down. In a minute he'd be cold again, worn out, and then he'd wish he could drink out of that bottle. Its breaking had made him drunk. The stain had stopped spreading and was fading, the snow bubbling and sagging. We could melt and drink the snow, I thought. I wanted that bottle back bad. I hated Hans. I'd hate Hans forever—as long as there was snow.

Hans was puffing quietly when Pa told me to get in the sleigh. Then Hans climbed awkwardly on. Pa took the blanket off Horse Simon and threw it in the sleigh. Then he got Simon started. I pulled the blanket over me and tried to stop shivering. Our stove, I thought, was black . . . god . . . black . . . lovely sooty black . . . and glowed rich as cherry through its holes. I thought of the kettle steaming on it, the steam alive, hissing white and warm, not like my breath coming slow and cloudy and hanging heavy and dead in the still air.

Hans jumped.

Where we going? he said. Where we going?

Pa didn't say nothing.

This ain't the way, Hans said. Where we going?

The gun was an ache in my stomach. Pa squinted at the snow.

For christ's sake, Hans said. I'm sorry about the bottle.

But Pa drove.

2

Barberry had got in the grove and lay about the bottom of the trees and hid in snow. The mossycups went high, their branches put straight out, the trunk bark black and wrinkled. There were spots where I could see the frosted curls of dead grass frozen to the ground and high hard-driven piles of snow the barberry stuck its black barbs from. The wind had thrown some branches in the drifts. The sun made shadows of more branches on their sides and bent them over ridges. The ground rose up behind the grove. The snow rose. Pa and Hans had their shotguns. We followed along the drifts and kept down low. I could hear us breathing and the snow, earth, and our boots squeaking. We went slow and all of us was cold.

Above the snow, through the branches, I could see the peak of Pedersen's house, and nearer by, the roof of Pedersen's barn. We were making for the barn. Once in a while Pa would stop and watch for smoke but there was nothing in the sky. Big Hans bumped into a bush and got a barb through his woolen glove. Pa motioned Hans to hush. I could feel my gun through my glove— heavy and cold. Where we went the ground was driven nearly bare. Mostly I kept my eyes on Big Hans's heels because it hurt my neck so to look up. When I did, for smoke, the faint breeze caught my cheek and drew the skin across the bone. I didn't think of much except how to follow Hans's heels and how, even underneath my cap, my ears burned, and how my lips hurt and how just moving made me ache. Pa followed where a crazy wind had got in among the oaks and blown the snow bare from the ground in flat patches against their trunks. Sometimes we had to break through a small drift or we'd have gone in circles. The roof of Pedersen's house grew above the banks as we went until finally we passed across one corner of it and I saw the chimney very black in the sun stick up from the steep bright pitch like a dead cigar rough-ashed with snow.

I thought: the fire's dead, they must be froze.

Pa stopped and nodded at the chimney.

You see, Hans said unhappily.

Just then I saw a cloud of snow float from the crest of a drift and felt my eyes smart. Pa looked quick at the sky but it was clear. Hans stomped his feet, hung his head, swore in a whisper.

Well, Pa said, it looks like we made this trip for nothing. Nobody's to home.

The Pedersens are all dead, Hans said, still looking down.

Shut up. I saw Pa's lips were chapped . . . a dry dry hole now. A muscle jumped along his jaw. Shut up, he said.

A faint ribbon of snow suddenly shot from the top of the chimney and disappeared. I stood as still as I could in the tubes of my clothes, the snow shifting strangely in my eyes, alone, frightened by the space that was bowling up inside me, a white blank glittering waste like the waste outside, coldly burning, roughed with waves, and I wanted to curl up, face to my thighs, but I knew my tears would freeze my lashes together. My stomach began to growl.

What's the matter with you, Jorge? Pa said.

Nothing. I giggled. I'm cold, Pa, I guess, I said. I belched.

Jesus, Hans said loudly.

Shut up.

I poked at the snow with the toe of my boot. I wanted to sit down and if there'd been anything to sit on I would have. All I wanted was to go home or sit down. Hans had stopped stomping and was staring back through the trees toward the way we'd come.

Anybody in that house, Pa said, would have a fire.

He sniffed and rubbed his sleeve across his nose.

Anybody—see? He began raising his voice. Anybody who was in that house now would have a fire. The Pedersens is all most likely out hunting that fool kid. They probably tore ass off without minding the furnace. Now it's out. His voice got braver. Anybody who might have come along while they was gone, and gone in, would have started a fire someplace first thing, and we'd see the smoke. It's too damn cold not to.

Pa took the shotgun he'd carried broken over his left arm and turned the barrel over, slow and deliberate. Two shells fell out and he stuffed them in his coat pocket.

That means there ain't anybody to home. There ain't no smoke, he said with emphasis, and that means there ain't *no*body.

Big Hans sighed. Okay, he muttered from a way off. Let's go home.

I wanted to sit down. Here was the sofa, here the bed—mine—white and billowy. And the stairs, cold and snapping. And I had the dry cold toothaching mouth I always had at home, and the cold storm in my belly, and my pinched eyes. There was the print of the kid's rear in the dough. I wanted to sit down. I wanted to go back where we'd tied up Horse Simon and sit numb in the sleigh.

Yes yes yes, let's, I said.

Pa smiled—oh the bastard—the *bastard*—and he didn't know half what I knew now, numb in the heart the way I felt, and with my burned-off ears.

We could at least leave a note saying Big Hans saved their kid. Seems to me like the only neighborly thing to do. And after all the way we come. Don't it you?

What the hell do you know about what's neighborly? Hans shouted.

With a jerk he dumped his shotgun shells into the snow and kicked at them until one skidded into a drift and only the brass showed. The other sank in the snow before it broke. Black powder spilled out under his feet.

Pa laughed.

Come on, Pa, I'm cold, I said. Look, I ain't brave. I ain't. I don't care. All I am is cold.

Quit whimpering, we're all cold. Big Hans here is awful cold.

Sure, ain't you?

Hans was grinding the black grains under.

Yeah, Pa said, grinning. Some. I'm some. He turned around. Think you can find your way back, Jorge?

I got going and he laughed again, loud and ugly, damn his soul. I hated him. Jesus, how I did. But no more like a father. Like the burning space.

I never did like that bastard Pedersen anyway, he said as we started. Pedersen's one of them that's always asking for trouble. On his knees for it all the time. Let him find out about his kid himself. He knows where we live. It ain't neighborly but I never said I wanted him a neighbor.

Yeah, Hans said. Let the old bastard find out himself.

He should have kept his kid behind them fences. What business did he have, sending his kid to us to take care of? He went and asked for snow. He went on his knees for snow. Was he ready? Hey? Was he? For *snow*? Nobody's ever ready for *snow*.

The old bastard wouldn't have come to tell you if it'd been me who'd been lost, I said, but I wasn't minding my words at all, I was just talking. Neighbor all over him, I said, he has it coming. I was feeling the sleigh moving under me.

Can't tell about holy Pete, Hans said.

I was going fast. I didn't care about keeping low. I had my eyes on the spaces between trees. I was looking for the place where we'd left Simon and the sleigh. I thought I'd see Simon first, maybe his breath above a bank or beside the trunk of a tree. I slipped on a little snow the wind hadn't blown from the path we'd took. I still had the gun in my right hand so I lost my balance. When I put out my left for support, it went into a drift to my elbow and into the barberry thorns. I jerked back and fell hard. Hans and Pa found it funny. But the legs that lay in front of me weren't mine. I'd gone out in the blazing air. It was queer. Out of the snow I'd kicked away with my foot stuck a horse's hoof and I didn't feel the least terror or surprise.

Looks like a hoof, I said.

Hans and Pa were silent. I looked up at them, far away. Nothing now. Three men in the snow. A red scarf and some mittens . . . somebody's ice and coal . . . the picture for January. But behind them on the blank hills? Then it rushed over me and I thought: this is as far as he rid him. I looked at the hoof and the shoe which didn't belong in the picture. No dead horses for January. And on the snowhills there would be wild sled tracks and green trees and falling toboggans. This is as far. Or a glazed lake and rowdy skaters. Three men. On his ass: one. Dead horse and gun. And the question came to me very clearly, as if out of the calendar a girl had shouted: are you going to get up and walk on? Maybe it was the Christmas picture. The big log and the warm orange wood I was sprawled on in my flannel pajamas. I'd just been given a pistol that shot BBs. And the question was: was I going to get up and walk on? Hans's shoes, and Pa's, were as steady as the horse's. Were they hammered on? Their bodies stolen? Who'd left them standing here? And Christmas cookies cut in the shape of the kid's dead wet behind . . . with maybe a cherry to liven the pale dough . . . a coal from the stove. But I couldn't just say that looks like a hoof or that looks like a shoe and go right on because Hans and Pa were waiting behind me in their wool hats and pounding mittens . . . like a picture for January. Smiling. I was learning to skate.

Looks like this is as far as he rid him.

Finally Pa said in a flat voice: what are you talking about?

You said he had a horse, Pa.

What are you talking about?

This here horse.

Ain't you never seen a shoe before?

It's just a horse's hoof, Hans said. Let's get on.

What are you talking about? Pa said again.

The man who scared the Pedersen kid. The man he saw.

Manure, Pa said. It's one of Pedersen's horses. I recognize the shoe.

That's right, Big Hans said.

Pedersen only has one horse.

This here's it, Big Hans said.

This horse's brown, ain't it?

Pedersen's horse has got two brown hind feet. I remember, Big Hans said.

His is black.

It's got two brown hind feet.

I started to brush away some snow. I knew Pedersen's horse was black.

What the hell, Hans said. Come on. It's too cold to stand here and argue about the color of Pedersen's goddamn horse.

Pedersen's horse is black, Pa said. He don't have any brown on him at all.

Big Hans turned angrily on Pa. You said you recognized his shoe.

I thought I did. It ain't.

I kept scraping snow away. Hans leaned down and pushed me. The horse was white where frozen snow clung to his hide.

He's brown, Hans. Pedersen's horse is black. This one's brown.

Hans kept pushing at me. God damn you, he was saying over and over in a funny high voice.

You knew all along it wasn't Pedersen's horse.

It went on like singing. I got up carefully, taking the safety off. Later in the winter maybe somebody would stumble on his shoes sticking out of the snow. Shooting Hans seemed like something I'd done already. I knew where he kept his gun—under those magazines in his drawer—and though I'd really never thought of it before, the whole thing moved before me now so naturally it must have happened that way. Of course I shot them all—Pa in his bed, ma in her kitchen, Hans when he came in from his rounds. They wouldn't look much different dead than alive only they wouldn't be so loud.

Jorge, now—look out with that thing, Jorge. Jorge.

His shotgun had fallen in the snow. He was holding both hands in front of him. Afterwards I stood alone in every room.

You're yellow, Hans.

He was backing slowly, fending me off—fending—fending— Jorge . . . Jorge . . . hey now . . . Jorge . . . Like singing.

Afterwards I looked through his magazines, my hand on my pecker, hot from head to foot.

I've shot you, yellow Hans. You can't shout or push no more or goose me in the barn.

Hey now wait, Jorge—listen— What? Jorge . . . wait . . . Like singing.

Afterwards only the wind and the warm stove. Shivering I rose on my toes. Pa came up and I moved the gun to take him in. I kept it moving back and forth . . . Hans and Pa . . . Pa and Hans. Gone. Snow piling in the window corners. In the spring I'd shit with the door open, watching the blackbirds.

Don't be a damn fool, Jorge, Pa said. I know you're cold. We'll be going home.

. . . yellow yellow yellow yellow . . . Like singing.

Now Jorge, I ain't yellow, Pa said, smiling pleasantly.

I've shot you both with bullets.

Don't be a fool.

The whole house with bullets. You too.

Funny I don't feel it.

They never does, do they? Do rabbits?

He's crazy, jesus, Mag, he's crazy—

I never did want to. I never hid it like you did, I said. I never believed him. I ain't the yellow one but you you made me made me come but you're the yellow yellow ones, you were all along the yellow ones.

You're cold is all.

Cold or crazy—jesus—it's the same.

He's cold is all.

Then Pa took the gun away, putting it in his pocket. He had

his shotgun hanging easy over his left arm but he slapped me and
I bit my tongue. Pa was spitting. I turned and ran down the path
we'd come, putting one arm over my face to ease the stinging.

You little shit, Big Hans called after me.

3

Pa came back to the sleigh where I was sitting hunched up under
the blanket and got a shovel out of the back.

Feeling better?

Some.

Why don't you drink some of that coffee?

It's cold by now. I don't want to anyhow.

How about them sandwiches?

I ain't hungry. I don't want anything.

Pa started back with the shovel.

What are you going to do with that? I said.

Dig a tunnel, he said, and he went around a drift out of sight,
the sun flashing from the blade.

I almost called him back but I remembered the grin in his face
so I didn't. Simon stamped. I pulled the blanket closer. I didn't
believe him. Just for a second, when he said it, I had. It was a joke.
Well I was too cold for jokes. What did he want a shovel for?
There'd be no point in digging for the horse. They could see it
wasn't Pedersen's.

Poor Simon. He was better than they were. They'd left us in
the cold.

Pa'd forgot about the shovel in the sleigh. I could have used it
hunting for his bottle. That had been a joke too. Pa'd sat there
thinking how funny Jorge is out there beating away at the snow,
I'll just wait and see if he remembers about that shovel. It'd be
funny if Jorge forgot, he'd thought, sitting there in the blanket
and bobbing his head here and there like a chicken. I'd hear about
it when we got home till I was sick. I put my head down and
closed my eyes. All right. I didn't care. I'd put up with it to be

warm. But that couldn't be right. Pa must have forgot the same as me. He wanted that bottle too bad. Now it was all gone. It was colder with my eyes closed. I tried to think about all that under-wear and the girls in the pictures. I had a crick in my neck.

Whose horse was it then?

I decided to keep my eyes closed a while longer, to see if I could do it. Then I decided not to. There was a stream of light in my eyes. It was brighter than snow, and as white. I opened them and straightened up. Keeping my head down made me dizzy. Everything was blurry. There were a lot of blue lines that moved.

Did they know the horse even so? Maybe it was Carlson's horse, or even Schmidt's. Maybe he was Carlson in yellow gloves, or Schmidt, and the kid, because he came in sudden from the barn and didn't know Carlson had come, saw him in the kitchen holding a gun like he might of if it'd been Schmidt, and the kid got scared and run, because he didn't understand and it'd been snowing lots, and how did Schmidt get there, or Carlson get there, if it was one of them, so the kid got scared and run and came to our crib where the snow grew around him and then in the morning Hans found him.

And we'd been god damn fools. Especially Hans. I shivered. The cold had settled in my belly. The sun had bent around to the west. Near it the sky was hazy. The troughs of some of the drifts were turning blue.

He wouldn't have been that scared. Why'd Carlson or Schmidt be out in a storm like that? If somebody was sick, they were closer to town than either the Pedersens or us. It was a long way for them in this weather. They wouldn't get caught out. But if the horse was stole, who was there but Carlson and Schmidt or maybe Hansen to steal it from?

He goes to the barn before the snow, most likely in the night, and knows horses. Oats or hay lead it out. He's running away. The blizzard sets down. He drives himself and the horse hard, bending in the wind, leaning over far to see fences, any marks, a road. He makes the grove. He might not know it. The horse runs into the barberry, rears, goes to its knees; or a low branch of a mossycup he doesn't see knocks him into a drift; or he slides off when the horse rears as the barbs go in. The horse wanders a little way, not far. Then it stops—finished. And he—he's stunned, windburned, worn like a stone in a stream. He's frozen and tired, for snow's cold water. The wind's howling. He's blind. He's hungry, frozen, and scared. The snow is stinging his face, wearing him smooth. Standing still, all alone, it blows by him. Then the snow hides him. The wind blows a crust over him. Only a shovel poking in the drifts or a warm rain will find him lying by the horse.

I threw off the blanket and jumped down and ran up the path we'd made between the drifts and trees, slipping, cutting sharply back and forth, working against my stiffness, but all the time keeping my head up, looking out carefully ahead.

They weren't by the horse. A hoof and part of the leg I'd uncovered lay by the path like nothing more went with them. Seeing them like that, like they might have blown down from one of the trees in a good wind, gave me a fright. Now there was a slight breeze and I discovered my tongue was sore. Hans's and Pa's tracks went farther on—toward Pedersen's barn. I wasn't excited any more. I remembered I'd left the blanket on the seat instead of putting it on Simon. I thought about going back. Pa'd said a tunnel. That had to be a joke. But what were they doing with the shovel? Maybe they'd found him by the barn. What if it really was Schmidt or Carlson? I thought about which I wanted it to be. I went more slowly in Pa's tracks. Now I kept down. The roof of Pedersen's barn got bigger; the sky was hazier; here and there little clouds of snow leaped up from the top of a drift like they'd been pinched off, and sailed swiftly away.

They *were* digging a tunnel. They didn't hear me come up. They were really digging a tunnel.

Hans was digging in the great drift. It ran from the grove in a

WILLIAM H. GASS / THE PEDERSEN KID 393

high curve against the barn. It met the roof where it went lowest and flowed onto it like there wasn't a barn underneath. It seemed like the whole snow of winter was gathered there. If the drift hadn't ended in the grove it would have been swell for sledding. You could put a ladder on the edge of the roof and go off from there. The crust looked hard enough.

Hans and Pa had put about a ten-foot hole in the bank. Hans dug and Pa put what Hans dug in small piles behind him. I figured it was near a hundred feet to the barn. If we'd been home and not so cold, it would have been fun. But it would take all day. They were great damn fools.

I been thinking, I started out, and Hans stopped in the tunnel with a shovel of snow in the air.

Pa didn't turn around or stop.

You can help dig, he said.

I been thinking, I said, and Hans dropped the shovel, spilling the snow, and came out. I been thinking, I said, that you're digging in the wrong place.

Hans pointed to the shovel. Get digging.

We need something to carry snow with, Pa said. It's getting too damn far.

Pa kicked at the snow and flailed with his arms. He was sweating and so was Hans. It was terrible foolish.

I said you was digging in the wrong place.

Tell Hans. It's his idea. He's the hot digger.

You thought it was a good idea, Hans said.

I never did.

Well, I said, it ain't likely you'll find him clear in there.

Pa chuckled. He ain't going to find us neither.

He ain't going to find anybody if he's where I think.

Oh yeah—*think*. Hans moved nearer. Where?

As far as he got. It really didn't make much difference to me what Hans did. He could come as close as he liked. In the snow near that horse.

Hans started but Pa chewed on his lip and shook his head.

Probably Schmidt or Carlson, I said.

Probably Schmidt or Carlson, shit, Pa said.

Of course, Hans shouted.

Hans scooped up the shovel, furious, and carried it by me like an ax.

Hans has been working like a thrasher, Pa said.

You'll never finish it.

No.

It's higher than it needs to be.

Sure.

Why are you digging it then?

Hans. Hans wants to.

Why, for christ's sake?

So we can get to the barn without being seen.

Why not cross behind the drift?

Hans. Hans says no. Hans says that from an upstairs window he could see over the bank.

What the hell.

He's got a rifle.

But who knows he's upstairs?

Nobody. We don't know he's even there. But that horse is.

He's back where I said.

No he ain't. You only wish he was. So does Hans, hey? But he ain't. What did the kid see if he is—his ghost?

I walked into the tunnel to the end. Everything seemed blue. The air was dead and wet. It could have been fun, snow over me, hard and grainy, the excitement of a tunnel, the games. The face of a mine, everything muffled, the marks of the blade in the snow. Well I knew how Hans felt. It would have been wonderful to burrow down, disappear under the snow, sleep out of the wind in soft sheets, safe. I backed out. We went to get Hans and go home. Pa gave me the gun with a smile.

We heard the shovel cutting the crust and Hans puffing. He was using the shovel like a fork. He'd cut up the snow in clods around the horse. He grunted when he drove the shovel in. Next he began to beat the shovel against the snow, packing it down, then ripping the crust with the side of the blade.

Hans. It ain't no use, Pa said.

But Hans went right on pounding with the shovel, spearing and pounding, striking out here and there like he was trying to kill a snake.

You're just wasting your time. It ain't no use, Hans. Jorge was wrong. He ain't by the horse.

But Hans went right on, faster and faster.

Hans. Pa had to make his voice hard and loud.

The shovel speared through the snow. It struck a stone and rang. Hans went to his knees and pawed at the snow with his hands. When he saw the stone he stopped. On his knees in the snow he simply stared at it.

Hans.

The bastard. I'd have killed him.

He ain't here, Hans. How could he be? The kid didn't see him here, he saw him in the kitchen.

Hans didn't seem to be listening.

Jorge was wrong. He ain't here at all. He sure ain't here. He couldn't be.

Hans grabbed up the shovel like he was going to swing it and jumped up. He looked at me so awful I forgot how indifferent I was.

We got to think of what to do, Pa said. The tunnel won't work.

Hans didn't look at Pa. He would only look at me.

We can go home, Pa said. We can go home or we can chance crossing behind the bank.

Hans slowly put the shovel down. He started dragging up the narrow track to the barn.

Let's go home, Hans, I said. Come on, let's go home.

I can't go home, he said in a low flat voice as he passed us.

Pa sighed and I felt like I was dead.

PART THREE

1

Pedersen's horse was in the barn. Pa kept her quiet. He rubbed his hand along her flank. He laid his head upon her neck and whispered in her ear. She shook herself and nickered. Big Hans opened the door a crack and peeked out. He motioned to Pa to hush the horse but Pa was in the stall. I asked Hans if he saw anything and Hans shook his head. I warned Pa about the bucket. He had the horse settled down. There was something that looked like sponges in the bucket. If they was sponges, they was hard. Hans turned from the door to rub his eyes. He leaned back against the wall.

Then Pa came and looked out the crack.

Don't look like anybody's to home.

Big Hans had the hiccups. Under his breath he swore and hiccuped.

Pa grunted.

Now the horse was quiet and we were breathing careful and if the wind had picked up we couldn't hear it or any snow it drove. It was warmer in the barn and the little light there was was soft on hay and wood. We were safe from the sun and it felt good to use the eyes on quiet tools and leather. I leaned like Hans against the wall and put my gun in my belt. It felt good to have emptied that hand. My face burned and I was very drowsy. I could dig a hole in the hay. Even if there were rats, I would sleep with them in it. Everything was still in the barn. Tools and harness hung from the walls, and pails and bags and burlap rested on the floor. Nothing shifted in the straw or moved in hay. The horse stood easy. And Hans and I rested up against the wall, Hans sucking in his breath and holding it, and we waited for Pa, who didn't make a sound. Only the line of sun that snuck under him and lay along the floor and came up white and dangerous to the pail seemed a living thing.

Don't look like it, Pa said finally. Never can tell.

Now who will go, I thought. It isn't far. Then it'll be over. It's just across the yard. It isn't any farther than the walk behind the drift. There's only windows watching. If he's been, he's gone, and nothing's there to hurt.

He's gone.

Maybe, Jorge. But if he came on that brown horse you stumbled on, why didn't he take this mare of Pedersen's when he left?

Jesus, Hans whispered. He's here.

Could be in the barn, we'd never see him.

Hans hiccuped. Pa laughed softly.

Damn you, said Big Hans.

Thought I'd rid you of them hics.

Let me look, I said.

He must be gone, I thought. It's such a little way. He must be gone. He never came. It isn't far but who will go across? I saw the house by squinting hard. The nearer part, the dining room, came toward us. The porch was on the left and farther off. You could cross to the nearer wall and under the windows edge around. He might see you from the porch window. But he'd gone. Yet I didn't want to go across that little winded space of snow to find it out.

I wished Big Hans would stop. I was counting the spaces. It was comfortable behind my back except for that. There was a long silence while he held his breath and afterwards we waited.

The wind was rising by the snowman. There were long blue shadows by the snowman now. The eastern sky was clear. Snow sifted slowly to the porch past the snowman. An icicle hung from the nose of the pump. There were no tracks anywhere. I asked did they see the snowman and I heard Pa grunt. Snow went waist-high to the snowman. The wind had blown from his face his eyes. A silent chimney was an empty house.

There ain't nobody there, I said.

Hans had hiccups again so I ran out.

I ran to the dining room wall and put my back flat against it,

pushing hard. Now I saw clouds in the western sky. The wind was
rising. It was okay for Hans and Pa to come. I would walk around
the corner. I would walk around the wall. The porch was there.
The snowman was alone beside it.

All clear, I shouted, walking easily away.

Pa came carefully from the barn with his arms around his gun.
He walked slow to be brave but I was standing in the open and I
smiled.

Pa sat hugging his knees as I heard the gun, and Hans
screamed. Pa's gun stood up. I backed against the house. My god,
I thought, he's real.

I want a drink.

I held the house. The snow'd been driven up against it.

I want a drink. He motioned with his hand to me.

Shut up. Shut up. I shook my head. Shut up. Shut up and die, I
thought.

I want a drink, I'm dry, Pa said.

Pa bumped when I heard the gun again. He seemed to point
his hand at me. My fingers slipped along the boards. I tried to dig
them in but my back slipped down. Hopelessly I closed my eyes. I
knew I'd hear the gun again though rabbits don't. Silently he'd
come. My back slipped. Rabbits, though, are hard to hit the way
they jump around. But prairie dogs, like Pa, they sit. I felt
snowflakes against my face, crumbling as they struck. He'd shoot
me, by god. Was pa's head tipped? Don't look. I felt snowflakes
falling softly against my face, breaking. The glare was painful,
closing the slit in my eyes. That crack in pa's face must be awful
dry. Don't look. Yes . . . the wind was rising . . . faster flakes.

2

When I was so cold I didn't care I crawled to the south side of the
house and broke a casement window with the gun I had forgot I
had and climbed down into the basement ripping my jacket on
the glass. My ankles hurt so I huddled there in the dark corner

places and in the cold moldy places by boxes. Immediately I went to sleep.

I thought it was right away I woke though the light through the window was red. He put them down the cellar, I remembered. But I stayed where I was, so cold I seemed apart from myself, and wondered if everything had been working to get me in this cellar as a trade for the kid he'd missed. Well, he was sudden. The Pedersen kid—maybe he'd been a message of some sort. No, I liked better the idea that we'd been prisoners exchanged. I was back in my own country. No, it was more like I'd been given a country. A new blank land. More and more, while we'd been coming, I'd been slipping out of myself, pushed out by the cold maybe. Anyway I had a queer head, sear-eyed and bleary, everywhere ribboned. Well, he was quick and quiet. The rabbit simply stumbled. Tomatoes were unfeeling when they froze. I thought of the softness of the tunnel, the mark of the blade in the snow. Suppose the snow was a hundred feet deep. Down and down. A blue-white cave, the blue darkening. Then tunnels off of it like the branches of trees. And fine rooms. Was it February by now? I remembered a movie where the months had blown from the calendar like leaves. Girls in red peek-a-boo BVDs were skiing out of sight. Silence of the tunnel. In and in. Stairs. Wide tall stairs. And balconies. Windows of ice and sweet green light. Ah. There would still be snow in February. Here I go off of the barn, the runners hissing. I am tilting dangerously but I coast on anyway. Now to the trough, the swift snow trough, and the Pedersen kid floating chest down. They were all drowned in the snow now, weren't they? Well more or less, weren't they? The kid for killing his family. But what about me? Must freeze. But I would leave ahead of that, that was the nice thing, I was already going. Yes. Funny. I was something to run my hands over, feeling for its hurts, like there were worn places in leather, rust and rot in screws and boards I had to find, and the places were hard to reach and the fingers in my gloves were stiff and their ends were sore.

My nose was running. Mostly interesting. Funny. There was a cramp in my leg that must have made me wake. Distantly I felt the soft points of my shoulders in my jacket, the heavy line of my cap around my forehead, and on the hard floor my harder feet, and to my chest my hugged-tight knees. I felt them but I felt them differently . . . like the pressure of a bolt through steel or the cinch of leather harnessor the squeeze of wood by wood in floors . . . like the twist and pinch, the painful yield of tender tight together wheels, and swollen bars, and in deep winter springs.

I couldn't see the furnace but it was dead. Its coals were cold, I knew. The broken window held a rainbow and put a colored pattern on the floor. Once the wind ran through it and a snowflake turned. The stairs went into darkness. If a crack of light came down the steps, I guessed I had to shoot. I fumbled for my gun. Then I noticed the fruit cellar and the closed door where the Pedersens were.

Would they be dead already? Sure they'd be. Everybody was but me. More or less. Big Hans, of course, wasn't really, unless the fellow had caught up with him, howling and running. But Big Hans had gone away a coward. I knew that. It was almost better he was alive and the snow had him. I didn't have his magazines but I remembered how they looked, puffed in their bras.

The door was wood with a wooden bar. I slipped the bar off easily but the door itself was stuck. It shouldn't have stuck but it *was* stuck—stuck at the top. I tried to see the top by standing on tiptoe, but I couldn't bend my toes well and kept toppling to the side. Got no business sticking, I thought. There's no reason for that. I pulled again, very hard. A chip fell as it shuddered open. Wedged. Why? It had a bar. It was even darker in the fruit cellar and the air had a musty earthen smell.

Maybe they were curled up like the kid was when he dropped. Maybe they had frost on their clothes, and stiff hair. What color would their noses be? Would I dare to tweak them? Say. If the old lady was dead I'd peek at her crotch. I wasn't any Hans to rub them. Big Hans had run. The snow had him. There wasn't any kettle, any stove, down here. Before you did a thing like that, you'd want to be sure. I thought of how the sponges in the bucket had got hard.

I went back behind the boxes and hid and watched the stairs. The chip was orange in the pattern of light. He'd heard me when I broke the glass or when the door shook free or when the wedge fell down. He was waiting behind the door at the top of the stairs. All I had to do was come up. He was waiting. All this time. He waited while we stood in the barn. He waited for Pa with his arms full of gun to come out. He took no chances and he waited.

I knew I couldn't wait. I knew I'd have to try to get back out. There he'd be waiting too. I'd sit slowly in the snow like Pa. That'd be a shame, a special shame after all I'd gone through, because I was on the edge of something wonderful, I felt it trembling in me strangely, in the part of me that flew high and calmly looked down on my stiff heap of clothing. Oh what Pa'd forgot. We could have used the shovel. I'd have found the bottle with it. With it we'd have gone on home. By the stove I'd come to myself again. By it I'd be warm again. But as I thought about it, it didn't appeal to me anymore. I didn't want to come to myself that way again. No. I was glad he'd forgot the shovel. But he was . . . he was waiting. Pa always said that he could wait; that Pedersen never could. But Pa and me, we couldn't—only Hans stayed back while we came out, while all the time the real waiter waited. He knew I couldn't wait. He knew I'd freeze.

Maybe the Pedersens were just asleep. Have to be sure the old man wasn't watching. What a thing. Pa pretended sleep. Could he pretend death too? She wasn't much. Fat. Gray. But a crotch is a crotch. The light in the window paled. The sky I could see was smoky. The bits of broken glass had glimmered out. I heard the wind. Snow by the window rose. From a beam a cobweb swung stiffly like a net of wire. Flakes followed one another in and disappeared. I counted desperately three, eleven, twenty-five. One lit beside me. Maybe the Pedersens *were* just asleep. I went to the door again and looked in. Little rows of lights lay on the glasses and the jars. I felt the floor with my foot. I thought suddenly of snakes. I pushed my feet along. I got to every corner but the floor was empty. Really it was a relief. I went back and hid behind the boxes. The wind was coming now, with snow, the glass glinting in unexpected places. The dead tops of roofing nails in an open keg glowed white. Oh for the love of god. Above me in the house I heard a door slam sharply. He was finished with waiting.

The kid for killing his family must freeze.

The stair was railless and steep. It seemed to stagger in the air. Thank god the treads were tight, and didn't creak. Darkness swept under me. Terror of height. But I was only climbing with my sled under my arm. In a minute I'd shoot from the roof edge and rush down the steep drift, snow smoke behind me. I clung to the stair, stretched out. Fallen into space I'd float around a dark star. Not the calendar for March. Maybe they would find me in the spring, hanging from this stairway like a wintering cocoon.

I crawled up slowly and pushed the door open. The kitchen wallpaper had flowerpots on it, green and very big. Out of every one a great red flower grew. I began laughing. I liked the wallpaper. I loved it; it was mine; I felt the green pots and traced the huge flower that stuck out of it, laughing. To the left of the door at the head of the stair was a window that looked out on the back porch. I saw the wind hurrying snow off toward the snowman. Down the length of it the sky and all its light was lead and all the snow was ashy. Across the porch were footprints, deep and precise.

I was on the edge of celebration but I remembered in time and scooted in a closet, hunkering down between brooms, throwing my arms across my eyes. Down a long green hill there was a line of sheep. It had been my favorite picture in a book I'd had when I was eight. There were no people in it.

I'd been mad and Pa had laughed. I'd had it since my birthday in the spring. Then he'd hid it. It was when we had the privy in the back. God, it was cold in there, dark beneath. I found it in the privy torn apart and on the freezing soggy floor in leaves. And down the hole I saw floating curly sheep. There was even ice. I'd been seized, and was rolling and kicking. Pa had struck himself and laughed. I only saved a red-cheeked fat-faced boy in blue I didn't like. The cow was torn. Ma'd said I'd get another one someday. For a while, every day, even though the snow was piled and the sky dead and the winter wind was blowing, I watched for my aunt to come again and bring me a book like my ma'd said she would. She never came.

And I almost had Hans's magazines.

But he might come again. Yet he'd not chase me home, not now, no. By god, the calendar was clean, the lines sharp and clear, the colors bright and gay, and there were eights on the ice and red mouths singing and the snow belonged to me and the high sky too, burningly handsome, fiercely blue. But he might. He was quick.

If it was warmer I couldn't tell but it wasn't as damp as by the boxes and I could smell soap. There was light in the kitchen. It came through the crack I'd left in the closet door to comfort me. But the light was fading. Through the crack I could see the sink, now milky. Flakes began to slide out of the sky and rub their corners off on the pane before they were caught by the wind again and blown away. In the gray I couldn't see them. Then they would come—suddenly—from it, like chaff from grain, and brush the window while the wind eddied. Something black was bobbing. It was deep in the gray where the snow was. It bounced queerly and then it went. The black stocking cap, I thought.

I kicked a pail coming out and when I ran to the window my left leg gave way, banging me against the sink. The light was going. The snow was coming. It was coming almost even with the ground, my snow. Puffs were rising. Then, in a lull when the snow sank and it was light enough to see the snowbank shadows growing, I saw his back upon a horse. I saw the tail flick. And the snow came back. Great sheets flapped. He was gone.

3

Once, when dust rolled up from the road and the fields were high with heavy-handled wheat and the leaves of every tree were gray and curled up and hung head down, I went in the meadow with an old broom like a gun, where the dandelions had begun to seed and the low ground was cracked, and I flushed grasshoppers from the goldenrod in whirring clouds like quail and shot them down. I smelled wheat in the warm wind and every weed. I tasted dust in my mouth, and the house and barn and all the pails burned my eyes to look at. I rode the broom over the brown rocks. I hunted Horse Simon in the shade of a tree. I rode the broom over the brown meadow grass and with a fist like pistol butt and trigger shot the Indian on Horse Simon down. I rode across the dry plain. I rode into the dry creek. Dust rose up behind me. I went fast and shouted. The tractor was bright orange. It shimmered. Dust rolled behind it. I hid in the creek and followed as it came. I waited as its path curved toward me. I watched and waited. My eyes were tiny. I sprang out with a whoop and rode across the dry plain. My horse had a golden tail. Dust rolled up behind me. Pa was on the tractor in a broad-brimmed hat. With a fist like a pistol butt and trigger, going fast, I shot him down.

Pa would stop the tractor and get off and we'd walk across the creek to the little tree Simon stood his bowed head under. We'd sit by the tree and Pa would pull a water bottle out from between its roots and drink. He'd swish it around in his mouth good before he swallowed. He'd wipe off the top and offer it to me. I'd take a pull like it was fiery and hand it back. Pa'd take another drink and sigh and get on up. Then he'd say: you feed the chickens like I told you? and I'd say I had, and then he'd say: how's the hunting? and I'd say pretty good. He'd nod like he agreed and clap Simon on the behind and go on off, but he'd always say I'd best not play in the sun too long. I'd watch him go over the creek, waving his hat before his face before he put it on. Then I'd take a secret drink out of the bottle and wipe my lips and the lip of it. After that I'd go and let the ragweed brush against my knees, and then, sometimes, go home.

The fire had begun to feel warm. I rubbed my hands. I ate a stale biscuit.

Pa had taken the wagon to town. The sun was shining. Pa had gone to meet Big Hans at the station. There was snow around but mud was flowing and the fields had green in them again. Mud rode up on the wagon wheels. There was sweet air sometimes and the creek had water with the winter going. Through a crack in the privy door I saw him take the wagon to the train. I'd a habit, when I was twelve, of looking down. Something sparkled on the water. It was then I found the first one. The sun was shining. Mud was climbing the wagon wheels and Pa was going to the train and down the tight creek snow was flowing. He had a ledge beneath the seat. You could reach right down. Already he had a knack for hiding. So I found it and poured it out in the hole. That was the last year we had the privy because when Big Hans came we tore it down.

I ate an apple I'd found. The skin was shriveled but the meat was sweet.

Big Hans was stronger than Simon, I thought. He let me help him with his chores, and we talked, and later he showed me some of the pictures in his magazines. See anything like that around here? he'd say, shaking his head. Only teats like that round here is on a cow. And he would tease, laughing while he spun the pages, giving me only a glimpse. Or he would come up and spank me on the rump. We tore the privy down together. Big Hans hated it. He said it was a dirty job fit only for soldiers. But I helped him a lot, he said. He told me that Jap girls had their slice on sideways and no hair. He promised to show me a picture of one of them and though I badgered him, he never did. We burned the boards in a big pile back of the barn and the flames were a deep orange like the sun going down and the smoke rolled darkly. It's piss wet, Hans said. We stood by the fire and talked until it sank down and the stars were out and the coals glowed and he told me about the war in whispers and the firing of big guns.

Pa liked the summer. He wished it was summer all year long. He said once whiskey made it summer for him. But Hans liked the spring like me, though I liked summer too. Hans talked and showed me this and that. He measured his pecker once when he had a hard one. We watched how the larks ran across the weeds and winked with their tails taking off. We watched the brown spring water foam by the rocks in the creek, and heard Horse Simon blow and the pump squeak.

Then Pa took a dislike to Hans and said I shouldn't go with Hans so much. And then in the winter Hans took a dislike to Pa as he almost had to, and Hans said fierce things to ma aboutPa's drinking, and one day Pa heard him. Pa was furious and terrible to Ma all day. It was a night like this one. The wind was blowing hard and the snow was coming hard and I'd built a fire and was sitting by it, dreaming. Ma came and sat near me, and then Pa came, burning inside himself, while Hans stayed in the kitchen. All I heard was the fire, and in the fire I saw Ma's sad quiet face the whole evening without turning, and I heard Pa drinking, and nobody not even me said anything the whole long long evening. The next morning Hans went to wake Pa and Pa threw the pot and Hans got the ax and Pa laughed fit to shake the house. It wasn't long before Hans and I took to hating one another and hunting Pa's bottles alone.

The fire was burning down. There was some blue but mostly it was orange. For all Pedersen's preparing like Pa said he always did, he hadn't got much wood in the house. It was good to be warm but I didn't feel so set against the weather as I had been. I thought I'd like winter pretty well from now on. I sat as close as I could and stretched and yawned. Even if his cock was thicker . . . I was here and he was in the snow. I was satisfied.

He was in the wind now and in the cold now and sleepy now like me. His head was bent down low like the horse's head must be and he was rocking in the saddle very tired of holding on and only rocking sleepy with his eyes shut and with snow on his heavy lids and on his lashes and snow in his hair and up his sleeves and down inside his collar and his boots. It was good I was glad he was there it wasn't me was there sticking up bare in the wind on a horse like a stick with the horse most likely stopped by this time with his bowed head bent into the storm, and I wouldn't like lying all by myself out there in the cold white dark, dying all alone out there, being buried out there while I was still trying to breathe, knowing I'd only come slowly to the surface in the spring and would soon be soft in the new sun and worried by curious dogs.

The horse must have stopped though he made the other one go on. Maybe he'd manage to drive this one too until it dropped, or he fell off, or something broke. He might make the next place. He just might. Carlson's or Schmidt's. He had once before though he never had a right or any chance to. Still he had. He was in the thick snow now. More was coming. More was blowing down. He was in it now and he could go on and he could come through it because he had before. Maybe he belonged in the snow. Maybe he lived there, like a fish does in a lake. Spring didn't have anything like him. I surprised myself when I laughed the house was so empty and the wind so steady it didn't count for noise.

I saw him coming up beside our crib, the horse going down to its knees in the drift there. I saw him going to the kitchen and coming in unheard because of all the wind. I saw Hans sitting in the kitchen. He was drinking like Pa drank—lifting the bottle. Ma was there, her hands like a trap on the table. The Pedersen kid was there too, naked in the flour, towels lapping his middle, whiskey and water steadily dripping. Hans was watching, watching the kid's dirty toes, watching him like he watched me with his pin-black eyes and his tongue sliding in his mouth. Then he'd see the

cap, the mackinaw, the gloves wrapped thick around the gun, and
it would be the same as when Pa kicked the glass from Big Hans's
hand, only the bottle this time would roll on the floor, squirting.
Ma would worry about her kitchen getting tracked and get up and
mix biscuits with a shaky spoon and put the coffee on.

They'd disappear like the Pedersens had. He'd put them away
somewhere out of sight for at least as long as the winter. But he'd
leave the kid, for we'd been exchanged, and we were both in our
own new lands. Then why did he stand there so pale I could see
through? Shoot. Go on. Hurry up. Shoot.

The horse had circled round in it. He hadn't known the way.
He hadn't known the horse had circled round. His hands were
loose upon the reins and so the horse had circled round. Everything was black and white and everything the same. There wasn't
any road to go. There wasn't any track. The horse had circled
round in it. He hadn't known the way. There was only snow to the
horse's thighs. There was only cold to the bone and driving snow
in his eyes. He hadn't known. How could he know the horse had
circled round in it? How could he really ride and urge the horse
with his heels when there wasn't anyplace to go and everything
was black and white and all the same? Of course the horse had circled round, of course he'd come around in it. Horses have a sense.
That's all manure about horses. No it ain't, Pa, no it ain't. They
do. Hans said. They do. Hans knows. He's right. He was right
about the wheat that time. He said the rust was in it and it was. He
was right about the rats, they do eat shoes, they eat anything, so
the horse has circled round in it. That was a long time ago. Yes, Pa,
but Hans was right even though that was a long time ago, and how
would you know anyway, you was always drinking . . . not in summer . . . no, Pa . . . not in spring or fall either . . . no, Pa, but in
the winter, and it's winter now and you're in bed where you belong—don't speak to me, be quiet. The bottle made it spring for
me just like that fellow's made it warm for you. Shut up. Shut up. I
wanted a cat or a dog awful bad since I was a little kid. You know

those pictures of Hans's, the girls with big brown nipples like bottle ends . . . Shut up. Shut up. I'm not going to grieve. You're no man now. Your bottle's broken in the snow. The sled rode over it, remember? I'm not going to grieve. You were always after killing me, yourself, Pa, oh yes you were. I was cold in your house always, Pa. Jorge—so was I. No. I was. I was the one wrapped in the snow. Even in the summer I'd shiver sometimes in the shade of a tree. And Pa—I didn't touch you, remember—there's no point in haunting me. *He* did. He's even come round maybe. Oh no jesus please. Round. He wakes. He sees the horse has stopped. He sits and rocks and thinks the horse is going on and then he sees it's not. He tries his heels but the horse has finally stopped. He gets off and leads him on smack into the barn, and there it is, the barn, the barn he took the horse from. Then in the barn he begins to see better and he makes out something solid in the yard where he knows the house is and there are certain to be little letups in the storm and through one of them he sees a flicker of something almost orange, a flicker of the fire and a sign of me by it all stretched out my head on my arm and near asleep. If they'd given me a dog, I'd have called him Shep.

I jumped up and ran to the kitchen only stopping and going back for the gun and then running to the closet for the pail which I dropped with a terrible clatter. The tap gasped. The dipper in the pail beneath the sink rattled. So I ran to the fire and began to poke at it, the logs tumbling, and then I beat the logs with the poker so that sparks flew in my hair.

I crouched down behind a big chair in a corner away from the fire. Then I remembered I'd left the gun in the kitchen. My feet were sore and bare. The room was full of orange light and blackened shadows, moving. The wind whooped and the house creaked like steps do. I was alone with all that could happen. I began to wonder if the Pedersens had a dog, if the Pedersen kid had a dog or cat maybe and where it was if they did and if I'd known its name and whether it'd come if I called. I tried to think of its name as if it was something I'd forgot. I knew I was all muddled up and scared and crazy and I tried to think god damn over and over or what the hell or jesus christ, instead, but it didn't work. All that could happen was alone with me and I was alone with it.

The wagon had a great big wheel. Papa had a paper sack. Mama held my hand. High horse waved his tail. Papa had a paper sack. We both ran to hide. Mama held my hand. The wagon had a great big wheel. High horse waved his tail. We both ran to hide.

Papa had a paper sack. The wagon had a great big wheel. Mama held my hand. Papa had a paper sack. High horse waved his tail. The wagon had a great big wheel. We both ran to hide. High horse waved his tail. Mama held my hand. We both ran to hide. The wagon had a great big wheel. Papa had a paper sack. Mama held my hand. High horse waved his tail. Papa had a paper sack. We both ran to hide. Papa had a paper sack. We both ran to hide.

The wind was still. The snow was still. The sun burned on the snow. The fireplace was cold and all the logs were ashy. I lay stiffly on the floor, my legs drawn up, my arms around me. The fire had gone steadily into gray while I slept, and the night away, and I saw the dust float and glitter and settle down. The walls, the rug, the furniture, all that I could see from my elbow looked pale and tired and drawn up tight and cramped with cold. I felt I'd never seen these things before. I'd never seen a wasted morning, the sick drawn look of a winter dawn or how things were in a room where things were stored away and no one ever came, and how the dust came gently down.

I put my socks on. I didn't remember at all coming from behind the chair, but I must have. I got some matches from the kitchen and some paper twists out of a box beside the fireplace and I put them down, raking the ashes aside. Then I put some light kindling on top. Pieces of orange crate I think they were. And then a log. I lit the paper and it flared up and flakes of the kindling curled and got red and black and dropped off and finally

the kindling caught when I blew on it. It didn't warm my hands
any, though I kept them close, so I rubbed my arms and legs and
jigged, but my feet still hurt. Then the fire growled. Another log.
I found I couldn't whistle. I warmed my back some. Outside
snow. Steep. There were long hard shadows in the hollows of the
drifts but the eastern crests were bright. After I'd warmed up a little I walked about the house in my stocking feet, and snagged my
socks on the stairs. I looked under all the beds and in all the closets and behind most of the furniture. I remembered the pipes
were froze. I got the pail from under the sink and opened the
door to the back porch against a drift and scooped snow in the
pail with a dipper. Snow had risen to the shoulders of the snowman. The pump was banked. There were no tracks anywhere.

I started the stove and put snow in a kettle. It always took so
much snow to make a little water. The stove was black as char. I
went back to the fireplace and put more logs on. It was beginning
to roar and the room was turning cheerful, but it always took so
much fire. I wriggled into my boots. Somehow I had a hunch I'd
see a horse.

The front door was unlocked. All the doors were, likely. He
could have walked right in. I'd forgot about that. But now I knew
he wasn't meant to. I laughed to see how a laugh would sound.
Again. Good.

The road was gone. Fences, bushes, old machinery: what there
might be in any yard was all gone under snow. All I could see was
the steep snow and the long shadow lines and the hard bright
crest about to break but not quite breaking and the hazy sun rising, throwing down slats of orange like a snow fence had fallen
down. He'd gone off this way yet there was nothing now to show
he'd gone; nothing like a bump of black in a trough or an arm or
leg sticking out of the side of a bank like a branch had blown
down or a horse's head uncovered like a rock; nowhere Pedersen's
fences had kept bare he might be lying huddled with the horse on
its haunches by him; nothing even in the shadows shrinking while

I watched to take for something hard and not of snow and once alive.

I saw the window I'd broke. The door of the barn hung ajar, banked steeply with snow. The house threw a narrow shadow clear to one end of the barn where it ran into the high drift that Hans had tunneled in. Higher now. Later I'd cut a path out to it. Make the tunnel deeper maybe. Hollow the whole bank like a hollow tree. There was time. I saw the oaks too, blown clean, their twigs about their branches stiff as quills. The path I'd taken from the barn to the house was filled and the sun was burning brightly on it. The wind had curled in and driven a steep slope of snow against the house where I'd stood. As I turned my head the sun flashed from the barrel of pa's gun. The snow had risen steeply around him. Only the top of the barrel was clear to take the sun and it flashed squarely in my eye when I turned my head just right. There was nothing to do about that till spring. Another snowman, he'd melt. I picked my way back to the front of the house, a dark spot dancing in the snow ahead of me. Today there was a fine large sky.

It was pleasant not to have to stamp the snow off my boots, and the fire was speaking pleasantly and the kettle was sounding softly. There was no need for me to grieve. I had been the brave one and now I was free. The snow would keep me. I would bury pa and the Pedersens and Hans and even ma if I wanted to bother. I hadn't wanted to come but now I didn't mind. The kid and me, we'd done brave things well worth remembering. The way that fellow had come so mysteriously through the snow and done us such a glorious turn—well it made me think how I was told to feel in church. The winter time had finally got them all, and I really did hope that the kid was as warm as I was now, warm inside and out, burning up, inside and out, with joy.

414